Dear Reader,

I have four great S̶... to get you in the holiday mood this month! To start with, Judy Jackson's Canadian heroine suddenly finds her life whirling *Out of Control*. Then Stella Whitelaw takes *her* heroine to Barbados where nothing (and no one) is quite as it seems! In Kay Gregory's novel, Iain and Phaedra play out their involving story against a dramatic Cornish backdrop. And, last (but by no means least!) *will* Jocasta be *Betrayed* in Angela Drake's latest *Scarlet* romance?

You will notice that each of these authors has been published in *Scarlet* before and we are delighted to see their names back on our list. One of the things that makes *Scarlet* so special, I believe, is the very individual style each of our authors brings to her writing. And, of course, they also offer us a wonderful variety of settings for their books. It's lovely, isn't it, to be able to enjoy visiting a different country without having to leave home?

So, whether you're reading this book on a train, a bus or a plane, sitting at home or having a well earned vacation – I hope you'll enjoy *all* the *Scarlet* titles I have chosen for you this month.

Till next month,

Sally Cooper

SALLY COOPER,
Editor-in-Chief – *Scarlet*

ANGELA DRAKE

BETRAYED

Enquiries to:
Robinson Publishing Ltd
7 Kensington Church Court
London W8 4SP

First published in the UK by Scarlet, 1997

A copy of the British Library Cataloguing in
Publication data is available from the British Library

ISBN 1–85487–962–6

Printed and bound in the EC

10 9 8 7 6 5 4 3 2 1

PROLOGUE

A smoke-filled room. Men in grey suits. Naked and ruthless ambition stalking the atmosphere.

It was spring in Westminster, London. Dawn light was seeping into the sky, throwing a pearly-white gleam onto the drained faces of the eight men around the table. They had been locked into plans and discussions since nine-thirty the previous evening and their patience and tempers were wearing thin.

One by one weary eyes looked towards their leader, an inscrutable and powerful figure sitting at the head of the table. He showed no sign of strain, giving every appearance of being able to carry on working indefinitely.

The man sitting on his right, the only other member of the group who still appeared fully alert, leaned towards him and spoke into his ear with soft urgency.

The leader listened. He narrowed his eyes in consideration and then gave a brief nod, indicating agreement with the suggestion of his colleague. Spreading his hands in an abrupt and dismissive gesture, he permitted his exhausted cohorts to gather up their papers and ties and jackets and retire to some quiet place where they could catch up on a few hours' sleep before the schedule of the next punishing working day claimed their energies.

The leader watched them leave, an air of faint disdain in his cold eyes. He turned to the man on his right, the only one who was not making a bid for instant escape. A faint smile curved the leader's lips. He touched his companion's arm. There was one more matter which required discussion. Something rather private, just between the two of them.

CHAPTER 1

'Oh, won't you look at that? Heavenly! Utterly gorgeous!' The speaker tugged at the arm of the woman beside her, demanding immediate attention.

Jocasta Shand glanced at her companion with a wry and affectionate smile. The two of them were standing in the Old Town Square in Prague, part of a growing assembly gathering beneath the ancient Town Hall Clock, waiting for it to strike and enact its fascinating hourly pantomine.

Jocasta, however, was well aware that Minette, blonde, chocolate-box pretty and utterly irrepressible, had little interest in the antics of the historical clock. She saw that Minette's huge blue eyes were firmly fixed on the two very compelling men standing a little apart from the crowd, an expression of faintly detached irony on their faces.

Making a rapid assessment, Jocasta noted that one of the men was very dark, wiry and slender, whilst the other was fair and of a much more substantial and muscular build.

With idle curiosity she wondered which one had taken Minette's fancy.

'Never mind the local talent,' she told Minette with mock sternness. 'You're supposed to be spending your time absorbing culture.'

Minette chuckled. 'Who says I can't do both?'

'Past experience,' retorted Jocasta with brisk affection.

'Oh, stop looking at me like a beady old aunt,' said Minette, unable to tear her gaze away from the two objects of her growing interest.

'I *am* your aunt,' Jocasta said mildly.

Minette looked up at her. 'But not old – even if a little beady,' she said fondly.

'Thanks! But don't forget I'm supposed to be acting as your chaperon on this trip. If I fail in my duties of exerting a little aunt-like control I'll be in serious trouble with your parents!'

Minette did not consider this jokey observation worth replying to and simply laughed. In fact, for Minette, the whole issue of Jocasta's being her aunt was a bit of a joke, even though technically it was the truth.

Jocasta's brother, Miles, was fourteen years her senior, and his daughter, Minette, had been born when he was a very young man. Thus there was a gap of only nine years between Minette and her aunt Jocasta.

But, at eighteen, the wayward Minette gave the impression of still being quite a child, whereas Jocasta, at twenty-seven, with her own thriving textile business and a cool, level-headed personality, seemed perfectly equipped to provide the adult and steadying influence Minette required.

'Keep your eyes on the clock. It's just about to strike,' Jocasta warned, squeezing Mintette's arm in an attempt to regain her attention.

4

Minette gave a fleeting glance towards the ornate fifteenth-century astronomical clock. All around, in an expectant wave, expensive camera equipment was raised between almost every pair of hands that could be seen. No one had any intention of missing the brief exciting performance about to begin.

No one, that was, except Minette. Jerking her arm free from Jocasta's light restraint, she turned again towards the two focal points of her main interest.

Jocasta sighed. Did Miles really expect her to work miracles with the exuberant Minette and return her to England and his fatherly arms as a reformed girl? A girl who no longer regarded virtually all handsome creatures in trousers as infinitely fascinating?

A murmur of anticipation ran through the little crowd eagerly observing the clock. The carefully crafted miniature skeleton, which stood just beneath the clock's face in a macabre representation of Death, gave a sudden clicking pull on the rope that it held in its right hand and at the same time raised and inverted the hourglass held in its left. Instantly a small pantomime was set in motion. Two windows opened above the clock and a procession of Christ's apostles moved slowly round, displaying themselves to the onlookers in the curious jerking way of all clockwork figures.

Tinkling metallic chimes sounded the hour. Voices in the crowd sighed with delight.

Finally the little doors shut behind the last apostle and all was still and quiet again. The crowd looked on for a second or two and then lowered their cameras and began to move away in search of fresh entertainment.

Jocasta gave Minette a heavy nudge. 'I hope you saw at least something of that interesting performance.'

'Yes, sure,' said Minette, still far more interested in the two men, who had well and truly captured her imagination and were now sauntering away down the square.

Jocasta consulted her guidebook. 'So, what shall we look at next?'

'Mmm?' said Minette vaguely.

'We're in a beautiful ancient city, packed with the treasures of the past,' Jocasta observed with gentle irony. 'We're supposed to be seeing the sights, Minette. There are people back home working away in dusty little offices who'd give anything to be here . . .'

'What? Oh, yes,' agreed Minette, eager to appease her companion but more concerned at losing sight of two very desirable potential admirers.

'So what would you like to look at next?' Jocasta enquired patiently.

Minette's eyes rapidly scanned the Old Town Square, a place crammed with some of the most superb examples of European architecture, both Romanesque and Gothic. 'That church with the green domes,' she said with sudden decisiveness, arousing Jocasta's instant suspicions.

And, sure enough, once they'd reached the steps leading up to the great doors of the St Nicholas Church, with its startling white façade and crown-like cupolas, there were the two prime targets of Minette's sightseeing ambitions of the day. Very much flesh and blood, very male – and absolutely nothing to do with centuries of history or marble statues.

Jocasta felt a flash of sharp annoyance. She eyed the two men with a weary kind of curiosity, and was reluctant to admit that they were certainly very striking in physique. As she watched they both raised cameras, preparing themselves to record the church on film for posterity.

'It's amazing how some people spend all their time behind the lens of a camera,' Jocasta commented caustically. 'I sometimes wonder if they have any interest at all in looking at the buildings in real life.'

'Now you *do* sound like a crabby old aunt,' Minette laughed, fluffing out her hair and smoothing her eyebrows with a finger wetted on her dainty pink tongue. She was like a huntress carefully preparing to snare her prey.

Following Minette's gaze, Jocasta saw that she was staring with especial interest at the fair-haired man. But all that could be seen was the back of his head, a shapely neck and very broad shoulders covered in a thick cowboy-style blue denim shirt. His face was almost completely turned away from them as he looked upwards, scrutinizing the complexities of the church's elegant pillars and life-like statues.

'There's been a church on this site since the twelfth century,' Jocasta recited from the guidebook, knowing that she was speaking to deaf ears but refusing to admit final defeat. 'The dome has frescoes depicting the lives of St Nicholas and St Benedict.'

'Fascinating!' said Minette obligingly.

The fair-haired man moved slightly, revealing more of his chiselled profile. Minette drew in a sharp breath. 'I was right. It's him. It really is him.'

7

'Who?' Jocasta enquired, doggedly studying the guidebook for further details of the church's history and architecture.

'Maxwell Swift.'

Jocasta looked up from her book and raised her eyebrows. 'So? I'm afraid that means nothing to me.'

Minette shook her head in mock despair. 'Jocasta, Jocasta! Get real. Maxwell Swift is a household name.'

'Not in my house, he isn't.'

'Yes, *yes*. Even you must know about him. He plays Dr Snow in *The Long Road*.'

'Is that a TV soap?' Jocasta enquired.

'Of course it is. Don't tell me you've never heard of it?'

'Well, to tell the truth I have,' Jocasta admitted with a smile. 'Although I've never watched it.'

'You're a culture snob, Jo.'

'Maybe. But I don't get a lot of time for TV.'

'No,' Minette agreed crisply. 'That business eats up all your time. You're getting to be a positive workaholic. You want to watch it. All work and no play will make Jocasta a dull girl.'

Minette's laugh was merry and lyrical, tilting the corners of her sweet full mouth and lighting her eyes with the youthful sparkle of life.

Observing all this zest and vivacity, Jocasta felt suddenly ancient. She sighed. 'Yes,' she said slowly, 'maybe you're right.

Minette shot her an anxious glance. 'Oh, heavens, I didn't mean to hurt your feelings. Darling Jo, I'm really sorry. Don't look so sad. That was a crass thing to say – and I was only being flip.'

8

Jocasta laughed. 'You're forgiven. And maybe I should take due notice – even of flipness.'

Minette pressed her small white teeth into the soft fullness of her lower lip. For months she had longed to ask Jocasta exactly what had happened between her and Alexander Rivers in order to cast all those shadows of sadness around her marvellous amber eyes and drive her to throw herself into her work like a woman pursued by demons.

It was common knowledge in the family that Jo and the handsome, power-crazy Rivers, who had been her lover for over two years, had mysteriously decided to split up – just at a time when everyone had expected them to announce a date for the wedding. But Jocasta had never been willing to offer any details as to the reasons. In fact her calm determination to keep her problems to herself had driven Minette mad with curiosity. She had also been deeply admiring of Jocasta's will-power and strength. Minette's own secrets slipped from her pretty lips like wriggling fish through buttery fingers.

Jocasta sensed the sympathy flowing from Minette and felt a huge surge of affection for her. 'For goodness' sake, put yourself out of your misery and go and ask the great man for his autograph,' she told her with a wry smile. 'Go on! I won't interfere. I'll wait here unobtrusively and improve my mind even further in the contemplation of culture!'

Minette chuckled. 'Ask for his autograph? Mark myself out as just one more docile and predictable fan? Not likely. I shall go and introduce myself. Even better – I'll give him the name of our hotel!'

Jocasta gasped. 'Minette! Minette . . .'

But she was gone, worming her way through the little crowd of sightseers.

Jocasta watched, cringing, from half-closed eyelids as Minette walked boldly up to the TV superstar and planted herself firmly in front of him in order to claim his attention.

And she got it. Instantly and in full. Soon his head was inclined towards hers, a lazy grin spreading over his undeniably attractive features as he listened to her volley of provocative chatter. His companion looked on with similar amused interest, and it was clear that both men were intrigued with the lively, curvy blonde.

Oh, Minette! moaned Jocasta inwardly. How could I have been stupid enough to think I might be able to take your mind off the opposite sex for a while by bringing you along with me on a combined business trip and sightseeing tour of Europe?

Feeling her cheeks become warm with colour, she turned away from the smiling threesome and looked across to the east side of the square, busying herself in contemplation of the huge stone bell hanging on the corner of a building which had once formed part of a Gothic town palace.

But even the most stubborn and careful perusal of a historic site was no protection against Minette's social ambitions. She came breezing up to tap Jocasta's shoulder, all vivacity and sparkle, and still prattling. And bringing along her two new acquaintances in her wake.

'Jo, darling, meet Maxwell Swift and Greg Shields. Max is a shining superstar and Greg's a film director who'll soon be fantastically famous. They're here in Prague for the next few days, just like us. Isn't that super?'

Maxwell Swift raised his finely defined eyebrows. 'Shining superstar indeed? I'm flattered,' he said, grinning.

Minette looked up at him. 'And a national hero too. Rough, tough East End boy made good.'

'You shouldn't believe everything you read in the gossip columns,' Maxwell said, amused.

'Oh, I can tell fact from fiction. You're the rags to riches story of the decade, Max,' she countered merrily, as though and he and she had been pals for years.

Jocasta felt her spine stiffen as though a rod had been thrust against her skin. Minette's unashamed brashness still had the capacity to astound her. And to make her inwardly shamed and angry.

Calling up massive reserves of self-control, she forced herself to conceal any sign of negative feeling as she raised her head to smile at Minette's all-too-willing captives.

The dark-haired Greg extended a hand of greeting and murmured, 'Nice to meet you.' The words were said in a politely detached way that almost neutralized the squirming embarrassment Jocasta felt on both her own and Minette's behalf. She took the hand that was offered, smiling in relieved response.

Turning to Maxwell Swift, she found him equally socially adroit. But as his hand reached out for hers there was something in the steadiness of his deep blue gaze which temporarily unnerved her. The look from

11

his eyes was strangely intense, an unwavering and naked stare: assessing, knowing and powerful. Within the span of a brief second he seemed to be stripping her bare, not only in body but in soul.

Staring into Maxwell Swift's sharply defined features, Jocasta experienced a swift flash of something akin to panic. For a moment she froze, completely at a loss to understand why this should be.

Withdrawing her hand, and struggling to keep up a façade of social politeness, she blurted out the first question that came to mind. 'Whereabouts are you staying? Somewhere central?' she suggested hopefully, recalling that their own hotel was quite a way from the centre of Prague, several stops out on the underground.

'We're right out of town,' Greg said, smiling. 'At the Consul. Super place. Away from all the crowds.'

Minette's eyes opened wide. She was almost jumping up and down with excitement. 'That's where we're staying! How fantastic! And how amazing that we haven't bumped into you before now.'

'We only flew in this morning. Checked into the hotel less than an hour ago,' Maxwell explained, his heart-breaking smile seemingly permanently in place.

Jocasta was aware of her own face setting into harsh, stern lines. She made a rapid review of the possibilities of moving to another of the town's hotels. But the reservations for this trip had all been made weeks ago. Besides which, the facilities at their hotel were excellent.

'I'm throwing a party in my suite tonight,' Maxwell said, looking down at Jocasta, his long, beautifully

12

sculpted mouth easing itself into an expression of sympathetic understanding and warm hospitality. She began to understand why Maxwell Swift had gained huge popularity as a TV hero. He had the sort of smile that could melt slabs of granite.

Something within her stiffened with dislike. Or was it self-defence? 'Tonight? Ah, well I had thought of booking for the opera . . .' Jocasta was painfully aware that her wild casting about for excuses was clear for everyone to see.

'God! You didn't honestly think you'd get me to an opera, did you?' Minette protested, throwing back her head and laughing in disbelief.

Jocasta had a sudden urge to smack her. Instead, giving Minette a ferociously warning look, she launched into a patient explanation of how Mozart had premiered his masterpiece *Don Giovanni* at the Estates Theatre in Prague, how that historic theatre was the only one left in Europe where he had conducted in person, how a visit there was essential.

'Fine,' said Minette. 'We'll go and be Mozarty tomorrow night or the night after. What's the hurry?'

'Look,' Maxwell Swift interposed with smooth courtesy, in the manner of one practised and skilled at pouring oil on troubled waters, 'either one of you or both of you are most welcome to come along to the party tonight. There's no need to decide now. I shan't be at all offended whatever your preferences.' He smiled down at Jocasta, clearly amused at her discomfiture.

You patronizing bastard, she thought furiously, narrowing her eyes. Men! she growled to herself

13

grimly. Screw the whole blasted pack of them – figuratively, of course, not literally! Especially the ones who fancied they could charm the birds from the trees with a mere lift of their elegant eyebrows.

'Greg and I are just off for quick lunch at the Hogo Fogo round the corner,' Maxwell continued with casual friendliness. 'Why don't you join us?'

Jocasta had read about the Hogo Fogo in her comprehensive tour guide. It was one of the trendy places where the beautiful young professionals of Prague liked to hang out. Minette would love it. She would drink several glasses of wine and become even more animated and reckless than she was normally.

Jocasta found herself both troubled and cornered. But she hesitated to make any more cautionary remarks and had to content herself with staring hard at Minette, her big, eloquent eyes full of warning.

But Minette simply stared back, issuing silent warnings of her own. *I'm eighteen. I'm grown up. I'll choose my own friends and my own entertainments. I love you, Jo, but don't you dare try to run my life for me.*

She's right, thought Jocasta. I can do my best to keep her on the rails, but she isn't a child and I'm not her keeper.

'I've got a couple of business appointments this afternoon,' Jocasta announced with cheerful politeness to the three pairs of watching eyes. 'So I'll give lunch a miss, if you'll excuse me.' She smiled around at her small audience, her outward air of confidence perfectly restored. She touched Minette's arm affec-

14

tionately. 'Enjoy yourself. I'll see you back at the hotel for dinner.'

Swinging her bag over her shoulder, she turned and walked away, melting into the crowds of tourists, bitterly regretting having been forced to play the role of killjoy.

CHAPTER 2

Anton Zanek's consulting rooms were situated on the fourth floor of a late-nineteenth-century building in the New Town quarter of Prague.

Jocasta stood in the impressively spacious cage lift, admiring its criss-cross mesh iron doors as it cranked its way slowly upwards.

Flicking open a small case of pressed face-powder, she swiftly checked her reflection in the tiny mirror. She was struck by how pale she looked, her skin luminous and porcelain-white, forming a startling contrast to the scattering of cinammon-coloured freckles.

She dabbed a little powder on her nose and whisked a thin film of amber gloss over her lips. She looked again in the mirror. 'You'll do,' she told herself with a wry smile, putting up a hand to her hair and tucking some stray strands behind her ears.

Dr Anton Zanek rose from behind his vast desk and moved across the room to take both her hands in his. 'Jocasta! It is so good to see you.'

They smiled at each other with the warm regard which two people feel when they have shared past difficulties and striven together to conquer seemingly unsurmountable obstacles.

Dr Zanek was small and thin, with dark hair, sallow skin and a wrinkled yet compelling monkey-face from which two prominent grey eyes shone with life and vigour. It had often struck Jocasta that he could be summed up as a conspicuously ugly man who had devoted his awesome intelligence and energies to making others beautiful.

He pressed her hands within his for a few moments and then, gently releasing them, raised his fingers to her chin, tilting her face towards the light from the window. In silence he regarded her with the intent and shrewdly assessing eye of an experienced cosmetic surgeon.

Jocasta held herself perfectly still, giving him time to make his appraisal. 'Well?' she demanded. 'What do you think?

'I'm pleased,' he said with slow satisfaction. He turned her face once again, in order for the light to fall on different contours. 'Yes, I must confess that I'm not at all ashamed of that little piece of work.'

'It's brilliant,' Jocasta said, smiling. 'A work of art.'

'Thank you.'

'You didn't ever believe it would turn out so well, did you?' she said, settling herself into the chair he waved her towards.

'I had occasional doubts.'

'You certainly did. And no wonder! My face was the most terrible mess when I first came to you.'

'Your nose was badly damaged from your accident,' he countered with gentle firmness. 'The rest was simply a tidying up job.'

Jocasta shook her head in the face of his modesty. The work which Dr Zanek had done to repair her shattered nose and her scarred face seemed nothing less than a miracle.

'Remind me, how long is it now since your fall? Since you first came to me?' he said, flicking through her case notes on his desk as he spoke.

'Just less than a year.' The day of the accident had been the most traumatic of her life. She remembered the events of its first fateful few hours vividly, and yet her memories were curiously off balance, as though she were viewing them from behind a distorting lens.

It had been a beautiful early autumn morning. Jocasta had been staying with Alexander at his beautiful house in the Worcestershire countryside. Energized and vigorous after a night's breathless lovemaking, Alexander had wakened her at seven, kissed her back into life and then dragged her off to the stables, where he had wickedly tossed her the challenge of getting up on his newly acquired mare – a seventeen-hand ex-steeple-chaser.

Jocasta, a reasonably experienced rider, had understood immediately on leaving the stable yard that the animal was as highly strung as a priceless violin. She had felt the power in the horse's great quarters, seen the nervous twitch of veins under the skin of the deep, muscular neck.

As the mare broke into a gallop, straining to get her neck ahead of Alexander's dark bay stallion, Jocasta had had a sense of utter helplessness. She felt that she was astride a juggernaut, a powerhouse of unbridled energy. She recalled telling herself with grim irony that this horse was a five-litre engine with no brakes.

They were at full gallop when a pheasant flew out, clacking and squawking, from a bush at the edge of the field. The mare had shied and swerved into the adjacent ditch, throwing Jocasta off instantly, then smashing into her face with both panicking hind feet as she struggled from the squelching floor of the gully and fled away.

For Joanna, trapped and dazed, there had been sharp grinding pain, the taste of warm fresh blood. And then a merciful blankness.

She recalled waking in an expensive private clinic. She had looked round desperately for Alexander, longing for the comfort of his presence. But he wasn't there. The doctor caring for her had explained that Alexander had been called urgently to Westminster. There was a crucial bill going through parliament. Every member of the party was needed to vote if the government were not to be defeated and brought down.

The doctor had gone on to tell her she had taken a terrible and bloody battering. However, she was not to despair, he had referred her to a highly skilled Czech surgeon who was already on his way from Prague to see her. He felt sure that Anton Zanek would be able to salvage something from the wreckage of her face.

She had spent long hours, lying staring at the ceiling, touching her face with trembling, tentative fingers. When she asked the nursing staff for a mirror, they had merely given her soothing words and a sedative and said she should wait until morning. But in the morning the pain and shock had all come back, breaking through her drugged semi-consciousness, demanding to be heeded afresh. And when they at last brought a mirror she almost passed out again with the shock of what she saw.

Now, almost a year later, as she recalled the beginning of that first day after the accident – all the confusion and loneliness, all the horror and despair – Jocasta gave a little sigh.

Anton Zanek looked up from his scanning of her notes and raised his dark eyebrows enquiringly.

'When you arrived to see me that first morning, you seemed like a saviour!' she said to him with a slow, droll smile. 'I felt as though I was all washed up and shattered. But you gave me the hope that I could be put back together again. And that is exactly what you proceeded to do! You performed miracles, Dr Zanek!'

'I did my job,' he said simply.

There was a short pause. He looked at her with a small frown of curiosity. 'So, did you book an appointment with me simply to give me the pleasure of seeing the long-term results of my handiwork?' he wondered politely.

Jocasta said nothing. She felt herself filled with uncertainties.

'Are you here in Prague on business?' he asked, easing the awkward silence.

'Yes. I'm making a tour of the main European cities, setting up a network of outlets for my yarns.'

He nodded. 'Good, good. So, your vision of expansion for the marketing of your beautiful materials is becoming a reality?'

'Yes, indeed. Things are going extremely well. In fact far and away outstripping anything I'd ever dared hope,' she reflected, and then smiled. The continuing success of her blossoming business, which had grown from such small beginnings, was perhaps the most vital and positive factor in her life at present. It was the business that kept her motivated, that gave her a sense of self-worth and kept her confidence buoyant. Without the business she shuddered to think what would have happened to her.

The telephone on Dr Zanek's desk gave two sharp trills. 'Excuse me,' he said, picking up the receiver and speaking into it softly.

Jocasta caught his eye, silently asking if she should wait outside whilst he continued to speak. He smiled and shook his head, indicating that she might like to look at the small pile of leaflets and magazines on the table behind her.

Jocasta got up and gave a cursory glance through them, eventually selecting Dr Zanek's current brochure, which set out the startling range of face and body improvements available at his clinics in Prague, Paris and London.

Besides offering a comprehensive service to repair the damage to the human face and body caused by accidents, Anton Zanek's clinics also offered a full range of cosmetic services previously unattainable in the countries behind the old Iron Curtain.

Eyelids could be tightened, lips made fuller, noses shortened, lengthened or straightened. Stomachs and thighs could be totally reshaped through the removal of excessive fat. Breasts could be expanded and uplifted, or reduced, if so wished.

As Jocasta studied the diagrams and details of the page in front of her she felt her heart begin to speed up at the prospect of openly voicing the request she had been considering for months.

Dr Zanek dropped the receiver back onto its cradle. He had been watching her as he talked, observing her keen interest in certain sections of his comprehensive booklet. 'Well?' he prompted gently.

She looked up. Her face was suddenly warm with colour. 'I've been thinking about further surgery,' she said.

'I see.' His face was stripped of emotion or judgement. He was the professional who revealed as little as possible of his own private opinions.

She looked away from him. 'Breast surgery,' she said eventually, her voice no more than a low whisper.

He nodded. 'Go on.'

'Breast reduction,' she said flatly.

'Ah.' He drew in a long breath, tapping his fingers against the desktop, saying nothing.

'Could you do it for me?' she asked defensively.

He spread his hands in a gesture of assent. 'Oh, yes, it would be a perfectly straightforward procedure.' He smiled, then formed his fingers into an inverted V and pressed them against his small squat nose, watching her with interest.

Jocasta was suspicious. She had expected him to make objections. She had expected him to reassure her that her breasts were perfectly acceptable as they were. Damn it, she had expected him to take away all the hurt of Alexander's slow, devastating rejection of her in the months following the accident.

'Will you do it, then?' she asked, her voice cold and businesslike.

He continued to watch her, his face coolly clinical and unreadable. He raised his shoulders. 'Probably. If you insist. Rich clients may instruct doctors like me to do whatever they wish.'

'That's not a proper answer,' she said.

He made a small noise in his throat.

'Will you let me make an appointment now, fix a definite date? I can come to any of your European clinics at a date to suit you.' She heard her tone becoming strident and insistent.

'I'm afraid you'll have to wait. I believe I'm fully booked for the next six months. For *non-urgent* surgery, that is,' he said evenly.

Her face froze. Very slowly she got to her feet. 'I understand perfectly,' she informed him stiffly. 'You're telling me no. I get the impression I've made rather a fool of myself.'

She walked quickly to the door, a flush of dark heat crawling up the back of her neck. Anton Zanek followed her. He put a gently restraining hand on her shoulder. 'Jocasta, stop. Listen to me.'

She stood quite still, sensing that he was going to trespass on territory formerly regarded as a total no-go area. She stiffened.

He spoke very softly. 'We both know that the hurt you suffered from losing Alexander was even greater than the pain you suffered from the crushed bones in your face . . .'

She opened her eyes wide, staring at him in dismay.

Silencing the protest that was growing in her throat, he continued with his theme. 'You must not go on deceiving yourself, trying to invent flesh and blood reasons why he abandoned you. You have to stop telling yourself that if only your body were in some way more "perfect" then he would love you again.'

Her eyes flared in disbelief. No one had ever been this frank with her. Telling her things which were so deeply buried that she had not truly recognized them herself.

He went on. 'My advice is that you should give yourself more time to – '

She swung around, her eyes glowing with amber fire. 'Don't! Don't even mention Alexander's name to me. No one's allowed to do that, not even you!'

Hearing that beloved name on someone else's lips brought the memory of her former lover hurtling back into the forefront of her memory. She saw his face as clearly as though he were there in the room beside her. That cool, piercing smile, the look that told her she was all that he could ever want in a woman. The look that told her she was completely in his power.

Sweat broke out on her skin.

Dr Zanek's hand pressed into her shoulder, but she shook it off. Suddenly, without warning, she had a sudden recollection of the encounter in the Old Town Square earlier on. She saw the smooth, lazily assured features of Maxwell Swift. She recalled the panic that had risen up when he'd turned his penetrating gaze on her. That deep, long look. The look with which Alexander had enslaved her.

'Jocasta,' Dr Zanek said with soft urgency, 'you have suffered a great deal in this past year, and not only from the accident and the loss of your lover. You have to understand that it can take a good deal of time before the particular trauma you suffered can fully heal.'

Her eyes flared again with wild feeling. 'No! Not *that*. Please, no. Never mention that to me again. Never!'

She ran out onto the landing, her heels echoing on the stone-flagged floor. Violently she banged on the button to summon the lift.

24

Chiding himself for having gone beyond his brief, Anton Zanek walked slowly back into his consulting room. Looking down from the window, he saw Jocasta emerge into the street and walk rapidly away. An elegant, talented woman. And beautiful too. That statuesque body, the full, curved breasts and hips, the long, moulded thighs. Maybe such attributes were at odds with the sexless, emaciated look favoured by high fashion, but he happened to know that they were what most men coveted and admired in real flesh and blood women.

And yet Jocasta was dissatisfied with herself. She had asked to have the flesh of her splendid full breasts slashed with a knife, mutilated and diminished. In that she was not unusual; many women worried about their breasts, which were after all the ultimate outward symbol of femininity. But Anton Zanek knew from experience that Jocasta might just as easily have made a plea to have her stomach made flat as a board, or to remove soft, voluptuous flesh from the insides of her thighs.

Like hundreds of the women he had treated, she was driven to punish herself for the wrongs done to her by the man she had adored. She was constantly asking herself why he had abandoned her, what she had done wrong. And, not coming up with any reasonable answers, she had decided that she must change herself, make herself conform to some crazy ideal of female perfection.

Anton Zanek watched Jocasta round the corner and vanish into the street beyond. He knew perfectly well that she had no need of surgery. What she needed was simply the love of one special man who would make her feel once again beautiful and precious.

CHAPTER 3

Jocasta made her way into Prague's Mustek underground system and stood on the platform, glancing into the darkness of the tunnel. A growing growling rumble gave warning of a train's imminent arrival.

Always alert and curious, Jocasta looked around with interest at her waiting companions. She guessed that they were, in the main, natives of the city, people dressed in the crisp, formal clothes suitable for office and shop work.

It struck her that there was an air of pride and quietly increasing affluence about the Pravians. She sensed their keen appreciation of the new freedom that had come with the tearing down of the Iron Curtain at the close of the 1980s, a feeling almost tangible in the atmosphere.

Young women with beautifully cut hair and impeccable make-up showed off their trim bodies in snappy little suits, their long legs elegant in shiny bronze tights. The men were dark-suited, with immaculate cream shirts and tastefully coloured ties.

There were older women too, not dressed in the forefront of fashion but nevertheless very careful in the matter of their appearance. Jocasta guessed that they were women who earned a living from domestic jobs in restaurants and hotels whilst also carrying the responsibility of caring for a family at home. She noticed that one or two of them carried carefully polished zip-top shopping bags, from the corner of which a small dog's head poked out, staring around with the nonchalant interest of a seasoned traveller.

Dogs in bags, thought Jocasta, smiling to herself. That was certainly a novelty she hadn't come across before in her many international journeys.

The train slid into the station, its doors opening smoothly to the accompaniment of a recorded voice urging caution in leaving and boarding. Stepping inside, Jocasta found the interior of the train bare and functional compared with those in Paris or London, but it was meticulously clean. No dropped cigarette ends on the floor here, no crumpled and abandoned newspapers. Even the dogs were impeccably behaved, sitting still and quiet in the confines of their bags, their soulful eyes gazing up into their owners' faces.

Jocasta liked to make use of the public transport system in the various cities she visited, welcoming the opportunity to discover something of the ambience of each place, its individual mood and flavour.

It was six in the evening now, the peak of the rush hour. After leaving Zanek, Jocasta had spent around two hours in negotiation with a potential new customer in one of Prague's recently opened and most elegant knitwear boutiques. The owner, who still liked to do all the buying himself, had been prickly and hesitant at first, a feature she had found characteristic of many of the eastern European cities, where newly fledged entrepreneurs were still feeling their way around the hazards of the cut and thrust of the free market.

It had only been after some very hard talking that she had pulled off a pleasingly large order for one of the ranges of her luxury mohair yarns. She had been tired and drained, but exhilarated too. Netting a new customer and opening a promising new account had demanded her total concentration and energy. And by the time she had concluded her transactions her feelings of fulfilment and satisfaction had been given a huge boost and her mood was once again light and buoyant.

The sudden dark anger she had felt in Zanek's office had mainly evaporated, and memories of Alexander had been relegated once more to a safe place in the background of her memories.

She liked to tell herself that she had forgiven Alexander for the callous and cruel treatment he had meted out to her. It was comforting to believe that the whole episode of their love affair was now closed and that Alexander was stripped of his power to hurt her any more.

But she was not fool enough to pretend that there were no longer any moments of danger, fleeting seconds when she could be caught off guard and her vulnerability exposed afresh. You didn't love a man with all your heart and body and mind for two years without some permanent scars remaining.

Walking energetically through the tall gilt and glass doors of the hotel's main entrance, she scanned across the vast lobby, with its tables and sofas, and the gleaming cocktail bar which ran the length of the far wall.

Instantly her eyes were drawn to the laughing trio sitting around a table under the nodding fronds of a potted palm. Minette and her two hunky companions of the morning.

That young protégée of mine, thought Jocasta with good-natured exasperation. Hasn't she had her fill of male admiration yet?

She had brief thoughts of slipping unobtrusively to the lifts, going up to her room, throwing off all her clothes and and then running a deep hot bath in which she would soak for however long it suited her.

But Maxwell Swift had already seen her. In fact, it was tempting to suspect that he had, for some unimaginable reason, been watching out for her.

He rose from his low chair with a graceful, serpent-like movement and walked swiftly towards her. His long stride meant that he had no difficulty in intercepting her before she had even got within striking distance of the lifts.

'Hello,' he said, smiling down at her in that easy, lazy way of his. There was a certain good-natured detachment about him, thought Jocasta, as though the march of humanity passing before his gently ironic gaze was an endless source of private amusement, with her, Jocasta, being just one more contributor to the entertainment.

Self-satisfied, she thought to herself, looking up at him. Smug and superior, with an ego over-inflated by fawning producers and sighing fans.

His deep blue eyes glowed with amusement, as though her thoughts were written in blazing letters on her forehead for him to read. 'Have you had a good afternoon?' he enquired with pleasant courtesy.

29

'Very much so,' she returned coolly, declining to make the polite and obvious response of enquiring about the quality of his own enjoyment.

'Minette has been a highly entertaining companion – ' he remarked. He was clearly on the point of elaborating on this comment, but Jocasta cut in to silence him.

'Minette's like a young sailor,' she said drily. 'She's at an age when it seems like fun to have a man in every port.' Her eyes glinted up at him. 'But she's a heartless little head-hunter, I'm afraid, so I'd watch out if I were you.'

He gave a low laugh in his throat, and it grieved Jocasta to note that it was a pretty attractive, sexy sort of laugh. 'Greg's a tough country boy from Texas. I'm sure he's well up to coping,' he commented, his eyes staring down into hers.

Jocasta was not slow to note the implied suggestion behind the words. The message was surely clear. Greg and Minette were already an item, which must conveniently leave the field free for Maxwell to come on to Jocasta.

One had to admire such breathtaking confidence and presumption, she thought, with a grim internal smile.

'I wondered if you'd had a change of heart and decided to join us at the party in my suite later on,' Maxwell continued. 'I do hope so.' His smile was enough to crush boulders to a pile of sand.

'That's very kind. But I've had quite a tough afternoon,' she informed him, cool but impeccably polite. 'I think I'll probably have dinner and then get an early night. So perhaps you'll excuse me.' She gave him her most frank and stunning smile, staring straight up into his eyes, her gaze never flinching.

*You may have a face to launch a million housewives'
hearts into an ocean of swooning bliss,* she was telling him,
but you won't cut any ice with me, dreamboat.

'That's a pity,' he said regetfully. He shrugged.
Smiled his heartbreaker smile again. 'But if you should
change your mind, you know you'll be more than
welcome.'

She nodded. 'Thank you.'

'Well,' he said, raising his eyebrows, 'maybe some
other time . . .'

'Maybe.' Gliding gracefully past him, she slipped
into the waiting lift and watched him shrink to no more
than a thin line as the doors rolled together.

'What's the score, then?' Minette queried brightly as
Maxwell rejoined her and Greg under the nodding
palm.

'Nil,' said Maxwell ruefully. 'No luck at all.'

'I'll have a go at her,' said Minette, stirring her
cocktail with the stick of the paper umbrella which
had been perched precariously on the rim of the
glass. 'Once she's wound down from her business
appointments and had a chance to check through all
that wretched paperwork she can't bear to be parted
from, she'll be much more relaxed.'

'She's a pretty stubborn lady,' Maxwell observed
quietly, looking thoughtful. 'I think her mind's well
and truly made up.'

'Hah! I'm going to unmake it for her. She needs to
have a bit of fun for a change,' said Minette warmly.
'Besides which, I'm fed up of watching European TV in
my room every night, going to bed early and living the

31

life of a nun.' She winked broadly at Greg, who winked back.

'I hadn't quite thought of you in the role of nun,' he said mockingly.

'Neither had I until I came on this trip with Jo,' said Minette. 'We're like two vestal virgins.'

Greg glanced at her, pulling a wry face. 'You're certainly an odd couple. Two worthy spinsters, aunt and niece, taking a chaste and sedate little trip through Europe.' He rolled his eyes in disbelief at the very thought of Minette's being involved in such an unlikely scenario. She leaned over and tapped him smartly on the knee.

They burst into laughter together. They had got on famously from the word go.

Maxwell, meanwhile, was uncharacteristically solemn and quiet. He got up and went to the bar. Instead of requesting a further whisky, Minette and Greg were surprised to hear him order an espresso coffee.

Greg found himself watching his friend and colleague with increasing interest. It was a while since he had seen Max so caught up with the idea of one particular woman. Since his split-up from Juliet Soul, his co-star in *The Long Road,* Max had become a field-player as far as women were concerned. 'Love 'em and leave 'em' had become his style. Here today and gone tomorrow – nothing heavy, nothing serious.

No, that wasn't quite fair, Greg decided, correcting himself. Max couldn't be accused of a 'love 'em and leave 'em' approach because he never seemed to get as far as really loving any of them in the first place. Many had been called but no single one chosen, as it were.

Maybe it was Jocasta Shand's steady refusal to be available which had caught Max's interest. Wherever Max went women fell over themselves to attract his attention. They left notes in the lobbies of hotels, asking him to take supper in their private suites. They hung about at the bar, hoping he might buy them a drink. The less subtle simply sidled up to him, slipping into his pocket the plastic entry cards which gave access to their rooms. The shamelessness of some of these women, and the lengths to which they were prepared to go, never ceased to amaze Greg.

It struck him that it must be a hell of a facer for a man like Max when an undeniably desirable and able woman failed so much as to register the famous Swift charm. Maybe it was her very coolness that had inflamed in him what seemed like a strong and steadily escalating attraction.

Minette turned to Greg, noting his silence. She had been temporarily engrossed in watching the arrival of some spectacularly glamorous new guests. Two rivetingly eye-catching women, tall, slender and very blonde, were checking in at the desk. And not only were they gorgeous, they were swathed in swirling floor-length ranch mink – a sight you no longer saw in London. The anti-fur league would have lynched the pair of them before they'd even got to the door of their car.

Minette felt faintly revolted and at the same time intrigued. But now that they had moved away to supervise the loading of their designer luggage into the lifts her attention returned to Greg. 'You're very quiet all of a sudden, pal,' she said, giving him a little nudge.

33

'Pondering deeply,' responded Greg. 'Don't worry, I don't do it very often.'

Max came back from the bar and placed his coffee cup on the table.

'Cheers!' said Greg.

Max smiled. 'Did you notice Sophia and Carla at the desk?' he said casually.

Minette jerked upright in her chair. 'The Lolotti sisters? Those two gazelles dripping with mink?'

'The very ones.'

'Oh, cool. Fantastic!' Minette leaned back in her chair with a sigh. 'Are all the rich and beautiful people here in Prague tonight?' she asked Max mischievously.

'Looks like there's a good proportion,' he agreed.

'Are you going to ask the Lolottis to your party? Oh! Say you are.'

'I faxed them at their hotel in Rome yesterday,' replied Max evenly, taking a sip of his coffee.

Minette leaned forward. 'And?'

He laughed. 'I'd guess they're already preparing themselves for battle.'

Minette breathed in hard. Her lips formed a determined pout and her bright eyes glinted. Curling one of her small fists into a ball, she brought it down on the table with a thump. 'Right!' she said, getting up and waving her companions a temporary farewell. 'Right!'

Lying in the bath, Jocasta thought about her brief interchange with Maxwell Swift and wondered if she had overreacted. Where was the harm in going to a party? She could always circulate a little, have a glass of wine or two, then make her polite farewells and still get an early night.

There was just something about Maxwell Swift that unnerved her, sent alarm bells sounding in some far distant corner of her mind.

As she stepped out of the bath and wrapped herself in a huge white bathsheet she heard the mechanism of the main entrance door give a small click. 'Minette?' she called out questioningly.

'No. It's Maxwell Swift come to make wild passionate love with you.' Minette's face loomed round the door.

'I should be so lucky,' Jocasta murmured acidly. Turning to the mirror, she grasped the rope of her hair within her right hand and then swept it onto the top of her head and secured it with an ebony clip in one fluid movement.

'I can never work out how you do that,' said Minette. 'It's a really clever trick. Neat. Perhaps I'll grow my hair, just to learn the secret.' She sat down on the edge of the bath and watched Jocasta stroke cleanser onto her face and then begin to wipe it off with a thick ball of tissue.

'Come on, then,' said Jocasta. 'What is it you wanted to say to me? Or should I say demand of me? Or maybe you're going to have a go at bullying me to go to your hero Maxwell Swift's penthouse suite bash?'

'He should be your hero. He's more your age than mine,' Minette said naughtily. 'And he *could* be your hero, you know, if you would just condescend to get down from your high horse for a minute or two.'

'I like being up on my high horse. It's safer there. No one can reach me,' Jocasta retorted. She unscrewed the cap from a tube of pale beige foundation, squeezed a marble-sized ball onto the palm of one hand and began to smooth it onto her nose and cheeks with the other.

'Why are you putting on make-up if you're planning to spend all evening in your room working?' Minette enquired with seeming innocence.

'Because I'm intending to go to the dining room and enjoy a nice quiet dinner. It's a rather elegant place, the dining room in this hotel. And you know me, Minette. I'm the sort of uptight, old-fashioned female who never ventures out in public without her stockings on and her make-up in place. I shall probably wear a tiara as well.' She stepped back from the mirror and observed herself critically.

'That's fine by me,' said Minette. 'I like my old aunt to look glamorous. It means all I need do is bask in the reflected glory.'

Jocasta smiled. 'I've always thought it was the other way round. Since you got past the grubby knees and Doc Martens stage at any rate.' She opened up a palette-shaped tray of russet-toned eyeshadow. Raising the loaded brush-tip to her left eyelid, she began to apply the colour with the deft swiftness of an expert.

Minette paused and reconsidered her tactics. 'I don't want to miss Maxwell Swift's party,' she said softly. 'And I'd much rather you came along too. I'd rather not go by myself.'

Jocasta finished the decoration of her right eyelid in silence. And then she said, 'Minette, do you honestly believe you're being subtle? Do you think I haven't spotted that you're gently leading me up a garden path that will end up at the door to Maxwell Swift's suite?'

'Subtlety was never my strong point,' Minette responded smartly, although she looked a little offended. 'I was simply trying not to charge around through your feelings like a bull in a china shop.'

'My feelings?' Jocasta queried, turning to look at Minette in the flesh rather than in the mirror.

'Yes. You're really touchy today.'

'Am I?'

'Yes.'

'I'm sorry.'

'I know it was a bit tacky of me to nip off with Greg and Max for lunch. But honestly, Jo, it was all perfectly innocent. And you could have come too – and still got to your appointments.'

'Yes,' Jocasta said with a sigh. 'I know. I just hate being steamrollered.' She unwrapped the towel and laid it over the bathside. She had already put out her bra, pants and suspender belt on the chair in the corner of the room, and now she began to step into them.

Minette watched her, admiring the statuesque proportions of her aunt's slender but shapely body. Jocasta's skin was as white as marble and had an exquisite soft gleam to it. Minette knew that Jocasta never sunbathed, having ultra-sensitive freckly skin which easily burned. And so her skin was as white and unblemished as that of a child.

She continued to watch as Jo leaned forward slightly to ease her breasts into the cups of her lacy bra. There was nothing childish about those breasts, Minette said to herself. Just look at them – simply fabulous. Jo could have made a fortune as a Page Three model. In fact she could make the *Playboy* centrefold, with her long legs and that ridiculously tiny waist swelling out into those magnificent rounded hips. She was quite simply stunning.

All that feminine gorgeousness going down the plughole, thought Minette, with a mingling of regret and irritation. No lover to appreciate it all.

Jocasta was rolling on shiny bronze stockings. 'I'm sorry if I'm being a drag,' she said suddenly. 'I can see this trip must have turned out pretty boring for you.'

'No!' Minette chewed on her lip. 'It's just that you seem to be so . . .'

Jocasta looked up. 'Go on.'

'Well . . . so anti-men.'

Minette saw a nerve twitch in Jocasta's temple. 'That's hardly surprising,' Jocasta snapped acerbically, 'since you're always attracting them in droves like the Pied Piper.'

'He attracted children,' said Minette, half smiling. 'And rats.'

'Exactly,' Jocasta replied, walking away into the bedroom and rifling through the clothes in her wardrobe with a noisy and ferocious clashing of hangers.

'I'd like to know why my playing the role of the Pied Piper means you have to carry on like Lucrezia Borgia,' Minette protested.

'Do you know the history of Lucrezia Borgia?' Jocasta enquired, swinging round to face her.

'No. I just have something at the back of my mind about her poisoning a load of guys who got on her nerves. Stop quizzing me, Jo. You're not one of my A level tutors.'

Jocasta threw a black dress onto the bed. 'Thank God for that!'

The unspoken issue of Minette's disastrous A level results suddenly loomed up between them.

'Oh, for Christ's sake!' Minette exclaimed, sparking into anger. 'Leave it out, Jo. People are more than the grand sum of their exam results.' Grimacing, she struggled to retrieve her self-control. She didn't trust herself not to get into a full-scale row, knowing that Jocasta, like her brother, Minette's father, hated ugly scenes.

'Yes, of course they are. Minette, I'm sorry. I'm truly sorry if I've offended you,' Jocasta said in a low voice. 'And I know I'm not the best of company at the moment. I just . . .' She stopped.

'Yes?' Minette urged.

'I just feel this great need to protect you. I suppose it's utterly stupid, and inappropriate too. You're not a kid any more, as you quite rightly keep reminding me.'

'So what do you want to protect me from?' Minette's lips flickered with amusement. 'Men? Is that it?'

'Yes, men.'

Minette walked swiftly to the door. She put her hand on the brass knob and then she turned back. 'It's not me you're really wanting to protect, Jo. It's yourself. You're scared out of your wits about getting involved with a guy again.'

The two women stared at each other, amazed at the frank turn the conversation had taken.

'You've been like that ever since that bastard Alexander Rivers ditched you,' Minette said flatly, daring at last to say what she had long suspected, turning the knife in the wound she had opened up.

39

Jocasta gasped. 'Stop it!'

'No, I won't stop it. It's time you came to terms with it, Jo. It's time you stopped being so saintly and in control of your feelings. All that phoney business of pretending that it was a mutual decision to go your separate ways, that he had his life to lead and you had yours. He dropped you like a hot brick!'

Jocasta's eyes flared with emotion, and for a shimmering, blood-red moment, Minette was almost afraid. There was something strong and deep and primitive about Jocasta. Let loose from the confines of her impeccable manners and self-restraint, who could say what she might do?

'Covering things up, burying your real feelings,' said Minette explosively, ploughing on, brave and relentless. 'That's just the way Dad handles all the bad news, isn't it? It's a family trait. The Shands are good old English stock, all stiff upper lip and iron rod backbone. Except me, of course. I'm the naughty little black sheep.'

Jo stared at her, amazed and admiring. 'A sheep? You're looking more like a positive vixen!'

'Fine. Excellent. And this vixen says that all that gritting your teeth and never showing any real blood-and-guts feeling is a load of tripe!'

'She does?' Jo's voice was cool and even.

Minette's keen intuition told her that Jocasta's fury had lasted no more than a few seconds, that now she had stamped on it and knocked it unconscious. She was well in charge of herself once more, burying all the nasty memories in a nice safe place.

'The vixen says it's time things changed,' Minette observed, opening the door. 'And now she's going to her own little lair, or wherever it is vixens hang out, to put on some spectacular mate-hunting gear.'

Aunt and niece confronted each other, eyes glinting with purpose and feeling.

'OK, fine,' said Jocasta quietly.

'I'll meet you in the dining room in half an hour,' Minette said breathlessly, slipping around the door and shutting it softly behind her.

Running down the wide, thickly carpeted corridor she almost collided with four girls all dressed in black.

'*Sorree*,' one of them said with heavy sarcasm as Minette, in full flight, brushed against her hip.

Minette wasn't in the slightest bit bothered about confrontations in corridors. What she was concerned about was Jo. How to prise her from the invisible carapace she had so skilfully constructed around herself. How to persuade her to come to Maxwell Swift's party and get to know him a little better.

CHAPTER 4

Jocasta zipped up the back of her stunningly simple black dress, clipped on a pair of stunningly classical gold ear-studs, then picked up the phone and booked a call through to England.

She sat on the bed, trying not to be tense, staring at the phone and waiting for it to make some kind of response.

When it eventually let out a quavery warble, her nerves gave a little jerk.

Miles's voice came over the line, crisp and intense.

'Jocasta! Hello. How are things going? I hope nothing's wrong.'

Jocasta heard the note of concern and faint accusation in his voice, as though she should not be bothering him unless there was some sort of crisis. Miles was the sort of man who gave you the sense of being almost permanently too busy to attend to any but the most weighty and urgent matters. Miles was a brilliant research scientist, a highly respected figure in his field. He was a man who disliked small talk and trivia – the wasting of time.

'Not at all,' she said, trying to sound reassuring. 'I simply wanted to let you know that we'd arrived safely here in Prague yesterday.' And after all, she thought, with a spark of unusual hostility towards her brother, he was the one who had specifically requested that she keep him informed of her and Minette's progress on their travels.

There was a slight pause. 'Good, good. I'll tell Ginny. She'll be glad to hear it.' He made a little sound, a soft exhalation, a faint sigh of irritation. 'Well, I suppose you've already done some interesting sightseeing.'

'Yes. We have.'

'I'd have thought you'd be going to the opera tonight. They're doing Mozart's *Clemenza di Tito*. I'm sure I gave you the relevant leaflets before you set off.'

'I'm sure you did.'

'You need to capitalize on any opportunity to get Minette to expand her cultural horizons. God knows, they couldn't be much narrower. I doubt if she knows the difference between an aria and a concerto.'

'Maybe she's not too keen to find out,' Jocasta ventured, her heart speeding up a little. Challenging Miles, on however small an issue, was a little like arguing with God.

'That's not the point.' He stopped for a moment and then his voice took on a new urgency. 'You're not to go soft on her, Jocasta. Don't forget she's having this trip at my expense. I wouldn't have minded so much if I'd been giving her the holiday as a reward for good exam results. In the circumstances . . .' His voice faltered for a split second, as though his regret on this score had robbed him of speech. 'Well, I certainly don't want it all to turn out a colossal waste of time and money.'

'So I've to book seats for the opera and drag her there if necessary. Is that it?' Jocasta asked, trying to keep the edge from her voice.

'Well, basically yes.' He sounded amazed that anyone could even consider the notion of letting Minette – or any young person – off the hook of constant exposure to high art and culture.

Jocasta had always known that her brother was a man of very firm views, and that he had no problems with imposing them on others. But because he had been a supremely supportive father-figure to her when their father had died, and because his views had always seemed so well-considered and high--minded, she had never questioned his right to bring others round to his own way of thinking.

But now, having been with Minette on her own for a few days, having the chance to get to know her as a person rather than a young relative, it was beginning to dawn on her what a burden Miles's determination and forcefulness must have been for Minette as a child. And still was, even now she was virtually an adult.

'Jocasta?' His voice was staccato and impatient. 'Are you still there?'

'Yes. Look, I'll find out about booking seats for the opera tomorrow. And you've no need to worry about us, Miles,' she added swiftly, realizing as she spoke that this was probably as far from the truth as she could have got. At least on Minette's account.

'Good. Fine.' She could hear a new edge to his voice. 'I can't talk any longer. Ginny and I are just about to set off to the Berwicks' for dinner. It's a celebration to mark their daughter Rebecca's going up to Oxford next week.'

The pointed and deeply regretful way in which he mentioned Rebecca's success made Jocasta feel almost personally responsible for Minette's spectacular failure. Suddenly she felt desperately protective on Minette's behalf, ready to rush warmly to her defence should there be any more parently attacks.

But the opportunity did not present itself. Miles had already made clipped farewells and hung up.

Jocasta sat motionless for a few moments, thinking about her niece. It was undeniably true that Minette was proving to be pretty wayward and altogether something of a handful on this trip. And in the past she had been a source of such dreadful anxiety to Ginny, her mother, that the poor woman had been placed on heavy medication as a result. Jocasta recalled the little cabinet in Ginny's pretty bathroom, the tidy rows of bottles stacked with Valium and sleeping pills.

But Minette was no empty-headed bimbo. As a child she had always been advanced in her development, alert and questioning. What was more, the distressingly personal remarks she had made earlier on to Jocasta had been remarkably perceptive. In fact they had been bulls'-eyes every one, hitting the raw target of Jocasta's jagged nerves.

Jocasta tapped thoughtfully on her teeth with her finger, considering, reviewing options. Suddenly she rose to her feet, a decision made.

She slipped on black suede high heels. She sprayed scent on her arms and throat. Glancing in the mirror, she judged that she was adequately decked out to grace even the most glitzy party. The fashion editors' unified chorus of simple black taking one anywhere was not to be ignored.

Grasping her slim bag, she slipped out into the corridor.

As the dining room was only one floor down she decided not to bother to take the lift, and instead turned into the well of the staircase.

Four girls dressed like her, entirely in black, lounged against the wall next to the lift. She felt their eyes on her, observing and assessing in that predatory, wolfish manner that some women are able to project with an almost alarming power.

Smiling, she ran gracefully down the steps. Minette was waiting for her outside the dining room. Inevitably Greg and Maxwell were in tow. Dogs sniffing round a bitch on heat, thought Jocasta wearily. *Damn,* she went on to herself. *They'll suggest making up a foursome for dinner and I'll look like a sour old cow if I refuse.*

'Do join us for dinner,' Greg said predictably, smiling with boyish and mischievous appeal.

She hesitated.

'If you'd rather be on your own . . .' Maxwell said softly, his eyes holding hers with that unnerving penetrating stare.

She laughed. 'I can't think of a more foolproof way of persuading me to be sociable.'

Once they were settled, Max smiled at her across the table. It was an intimate smile. A smile that roused a small thrill even though she still fancied she had him

46

marked down as a smoothie, charm-the-birds-from-the-trees man.

Greg and Minette, meanwhile, were sparking off each other like dry twigs rubbing together. Wisecracks tumbled from their lips and they shook with constant mirth at each other's jokes. There was something about them that reminded Jocasta of giggling schoolkids.

She sighed inwardly, feeling patient and rather old.

With Minette and Greg fully involved in a combat of wit, Jocasta found herself forced into a tête-à-tête with Max.

And she was forced to admit that he was faultlessly charming as a companion. Contrary to her previous guess, that he would be the kind of man whose only interest was to talk of himself, he patiently set about teasing information from her; wanting to know about her growing business, the customers she had gained in Prague, her general aspirations for the future.

She found herself becoming slowly disarmed, her brittle feelings gradually softening. As she spoke, and his eyes held hers, she fancied she saw in them a profoundness of approval, a depth of respect for her achievements and her style. But, even so, an undercurrent of defensivenes still ticked away inside her.

It was the sheer unswerving intensity of his stare that worried her. That blue gaze of his locked into hers with such total concentration that she could have been persuaded to believe that she was the only woman on earth who currently interested him. She began to feel a faint stirring of excitement, the tingling thrill that comes from sensing the hungry admiration of a magnetic and charismatic male.

47

And yet she was increasingly disturbed, feeling somehow *fixed on*, targeted.

It was Minette who eventually broke the spell. Leaning across to Jocasta, she tapped her arm. 'Hey, Jo, take a look at those two just coming in!'

Jocasta glanced up towards the imposing entrance which separated the dining room from the marble-floored gallery beyond. Beneath the gleaming gilded arch stood two tall, serpentine women. They both had silver-blonde hair, glittering and worn loose in a cascade which fell down their backs to reach the globes of their buttocks.

They stood quite still, framed within the arch, poised as though waiting for an army of cameras to click and flash.

'The Lolotti sisters,' Minette explained helpfully. 'They're a duo singing act.'

Jocasta smiled. 'I have heard of them,' she remonstrated mildly. 'Even ancient, crusty old me.' She watched the two women as they surveyed the huge dining room with a mingling of disdain and vulnerability on their beautiful faces.

'How to make an entrance!' Jocasta murmured with an amused smile. Turning to catch Max's eye, she noted that he was showing no interest whatsoever in the new arrivals. He was still staring at her.

Warmth lapped up into Jocasta's neck. She turned swiftly away from Max, fixing her full attention on the two provocative women in the doorway. They were dressed identically in clinging silver lurex, their gowns slit at the front up to mid-thigh, the fabric cut to fan out at the back into the swoop of a fish's tail.

Several waiters glided up, guiding and coaxing the two sinuous creatures to a table in the centre of the room. The men walked protectively beside them in the manner of outflanking riders guarding precious cargo under danger of attack.

Once settled, and napkins having been unfurled with a flourish and placed reverently on their laps, the Lolotti sisters looked slowly around them.

'Checking out the audience appreciation,' Minette giggled to Greg.

'Are they getting enough, do you think?' he wondered, his eyebrows arching expressively.

'I doubt if "enough" is a word that comes into Sophia's and Carla's vocabulary,' Max commented with velvet irony.

Jocasta shot him a sharp glance. He's no fool, she thought. In fact he's a pretty shrewd observer.

'You said they were coming to your party. Will they be giving us a floorshow?' Minette asked Max, leaning over the table and smiling at him, the neckline of her dress sagging so that her pert apple-breasts nearly spilled out.

'I shouldn't think we'll be able to stop them,' Max said, smiling back into her face and ignoring the eyeful being presented to him almost literally on a plate.

A slow grin crept over Minette's features as she contemplated the fun ahead at Max's fabulous bash, beginning soon and going on far into the night. 'Are they really as wild as people say when they get going?'

'We can but hope,' said Greg. His rubbery, mobile features pulled themselves into a succession of meaningful grimaces. 'They're reputed to be pretty hot stuff.'

49

'Do they actually get their kit off when they perform?' Minette wondered with languid curiosity, sliding a wicked look at Jocasta.

'Ah,' said Greg, 'now there's an interesting question. From the rumours I've heard, they behave like a kind of social catalyst – bringing about change in everyone else but remaining unchanged themselves.' He gave another display of facial gymnastics.

'I get it,' Minette said smugly. 'They stay dressed and everyone else strips off.'

Jocasta forced herself to smile and tried valiantly not to experience any of the disapproving feelings she associated with the peppery elderly ladies who had taught her in primary school. She had visions of some sort of glamorous and expensive orgy taking place in Maxwell Swift's suite and felt herself wince internally.

As if to echo her thoughts, Minette announced, 'Cool, cool, cool! We're going to have one hell of an evening.' She lay back in her chair, beaming with fresh anticipation. 'Absolutely grade-A fantastic.' She nudged Jocasta mischievously. 'Hear that, Jo? The first grade A I've had in years!'

Warning bells were now ringing like screaming fire alarms throughout Jocasta's head. And beneath them was the low, steady undertone of Miles's cautioning words. 'You're not to go soft on her, Jocasta . . .'

With an inbreath of resignation Jocasta acknowledged that there was no question of her not turning up at Max's party.

There was probably no question of her getting any rest at all until the dawn arrived.

CHAPTER 5

Max looked around the large reception room of his suite. The hotel staff had set up a long table against one wall. Bottles of very expensive wines stood on the top in military rows, and in front of them were similarly precise lines of gleaming glasses. The tiny morsels of edible refreshment were elegantly presented but very simple: bowls piled with glossy caviar and fish-shaped plates stacked with criss-crossed slivers of smoked salmon. He gave a wry smile, struck by the thought that the outward manifestations of extravagance were often deceptively simple.

Surveying the hospitality he was about to offer his guests – the surroundings, the refreshments, the ambience – he had a sharp sense of unreality. From time to time this happened to him. Suddenly he was no longer the superstar, fawned over by constantly smiling agents and producers, the man whose friends and party guests were as famous and wealthy as himself. Instead he was the tough, scruffy kid from the East End, surviving in a human jungle where everyone else was grimly fighting for survival.

The people he had lived amongst in those times would not have recognized caviar if their noses had been rubbed in it. His own parents had often not known where the money for the next meal was coming from, and their bitter quarrels had frequently been sparked off by a disagreement as to which of their kids most needed a pair of new shoes. It was perhaps the shoes he remembered most: the soles that had actually worn through to let in the damp from the pavements, the tips which had been too small for his growing bones, the pairs which had been bought at jumble sales and worn by previous feet quite differently shaped from his own.

And just look at you now, Max Swift, he told himself with a grin of irony, fingering the cuffs of his Calvin Klein denim shirt and the Rolex watch on his wrist.

Sometimes it all seemed so odd he wanted to throw back his head and roar with laughter.

He thought ahead to the gathering tonight. Most of the guests would be media people. The newly liberated Prague was a hot focus of attention for TV producers and script-writers on the look-out for a good story and evocative locations. He guessed Greg was by no means the only film director interested in charting the city's recent turbulent history.

And members of the acting profession seemed to crawl out from unexpected corners anywhere in the world if they got a sniff of a free bash and some celebrity socializing.

And as for the Lolotti sisters! They were an item all on their own. They had both had a recent shot at seducing him – without any success. He was doubtful that they would try again, but then he couldn't be sure; that aspect of his life had gone completely crazy since he'd become famous. Women literally threw himselves at him, and he had rapidly had to learn the skills of fighting them off in the least wounding way possible.

He sometimes saw himself living in a world of glittering brightness and dark shadows. A curious world of dramatic contrasts – bright fantasy and clouded reality.

The thought led him to Jocasta Shand. He stood very still. She was reality: beautiful, warm, transparently genuine.

It was approaching ten o'clock by the time Jocasta and Minette left the dining room and made their way to their rooms. Max and Greg had excused themselves some minutes earlier, Max murmuring about the need to check on the last-minute arrangements for his party. He had urged Jocasta once again to accept his invitation to join them, and Minette had noticed that this time she had not been so firm in refusing.

'So you are going to come after all, Jo, aren't you?' Minette said with satisfaction, looking absurdly pleased, like a child given an unexpected gift. She squeezed Jocasta's arm affectionately.

'I truly don't believe I could stay away,' Jocasta responded drily.

Minette linked her arm within Jocasta's and pulled her along towards the lifts.

'No,' said Jocasta disentangling herself. 'You go on up, I think I should go up to my room and make myself a little more . . . festive-looking.'

'You look absolutely gorgeous.' Minette squinted up at her suspiciously. 'Hey, you're not planning on ducking out at the last minute, are you?'

53

'Thanks for your confidence in me, sweetheart! No, I'm not going to creep secretly off to bed. I truly do think I look a little severe. I'll go and put on a suitably sparkly necklace or something.'

Minette's glance became sly. 'I'm beginning to think you're succumbing to the Maxwell Swift super-special line in charm . . .'

Jocasta laughed. 'If you must know, I don't want to come along to a party looking like someone's severe and disapproving old aunt.'

Minette looked up at her questioningly.

'What I'm saying is I don't want to be a drag, Minette,' she said softly.

'You aren't. You're a terrific travelmate. I really like being with you.'

The two stared at each other for a moment, a new and warm contact springing up between them.

'Go on, then,' said Minette. 'But don't be too long. Goodness knows what I'll get up to without my chaperon to keep a beady eye on me.'

Jocasta went up the stairs. In the corridor leading to her room there was that strange complete silence that settles in the softly carpeted enclosed spaces of exclusive hotels.

She slipped her card into the slot of the steel lock and waited for the little red light to wink and the mechanism to give the brisk click signalling the release of the security system.

Pushing the door open and then closing it behind her, she went into the bathroom and splashed cold water on her face. She looked critically at her reflection in the large mirror.

What she had said to Minette was perfectly true. She had no wish to be a dampener on anyone's fun. And she had come round to the feeling that the overall impression she projected was rather too severe.

She looked at her mirror image, starkly clear under the bright spotlights set into the frame of the glass. Flawless white skin. Huge eyes so delicately made-up no one would know there was any artificial colour there. Hair classically twisted, secured and immaculate. Dress classically cut and in impeccably restrained taste. Yes, the whole picture was altogether a touch uptight.

'Mmm,' she said to herself, pulling off her dainty stud earrings and abandoning them on the edge of the washbasin. She had thoughts of pulling the clip from her hair and letting it fall loose down her back. Then she remembered the two snake-like Lolotti sisters and their cascading mermaid tresses, and thought better of it.

Going back into the main room, she took her jewellery case from the neat, unobtrusive safe provided beside the door and examined its sparse contents – none of which could be called gaudy.

Suddenly she laughed at herself for this absurd concern over the image she was trying to create. What was wrong with simply being herself?

Still smiling, she lifted out some pearl and diamond drop earrings that Alexander had given her in the early days of their relationship. They were large and important-looking, and she guessed they had cost a great deal of money. Since the break with Alexander she had hardly been able to bring herself to look at them let alone wear them.

Now, with a twinge of defiance, she put them on. She went back to the mirror. She turned her head, admiring the soft gleam of the fat pear-shaped pearls, the unrelenting twinkle of the forty-four diamonds encrusting the studs that supported them. The earrings were quality items, yet there was just a dash of ostentation about them. Even a touch of brash tartiness.

'Oh, yes, Jocasta, you'll do fine,' she told her newly decked reflection. Smiling to herself, she slipped out of the door and back into the corridor.

She pressed the signalling buttons on both lifts and tapped her foot as she waited, wondering which one would make it first.

There was a smooth whirr and a click as one arrived almost instantly. The doors rolled silently open, as though slicing through butter, and she stepped through them into the empty mirror-lined box beyond.

As the doors made the click preparatory to their rolling shut again there was a sudden rushing explosion of black-stockinged legs, of flying black hair and clanking heavy steel jewellery.

The four black-clad girls she had seen earlier erupted into the lift, seemingly emerging from nowhere.

Their presence was like an intrusion. They seemed curiously out of place in the hushed box of the lift. Through the mirror-clad walls their reflections stetched out into an infinity of black figures representing an army.

Startled, Jocasta found it necessary to press herself against the far wall of the lift as the girls crowded in. They appeared to have no awareness of her presence. She felt as though she were suddenly invisible.

56

The doors began to close. Jocasta watched their gliding motion – and as the gleaming panels moved towards each other all the things in her vision seemed to shift, to go into slow motion.

With a gesture of involuntary self-protection she pressed herself further against the wall. Although as yet she was aware of no tangible reason for alarm, already some primitive alerting mechanism had awakened inside her.

The girls' presence filled and invaded the whole area of the lift: their darkness and animal power, their sharp musky scent, the jangling brutality of the arsenal of their weighty jewellery.

Whilst each one in turn slid a cursory glance at Jocasta, they made no open acknowledgement of her presence. Moreover, they were silent, volunteering no conversation to each other, communicating only by snatched glances, narrowed eyes and foxy smiles.

Jocasta felt her breathing slow and deepen. She slid a tongue around her dry lips. She was aware that her face had frozen into an expression of bland impartiality, a desire to project an air of disinterested pleasantness.

There was a strong, dark sexiness, a fearless and troublesome anarchy about these girls. They sprawled against the walls of the lift, stretching out long lithesome arms covered in glinting steel bands encrusted with heavy black stones. They raised and flexed fingers girdled with fat and menacing rings that looked more like weapons than seductive adornments.

Jocasta began to experience creeping and naked fear.

And then, without warning, they all turned to stare at her, fastening their eyes on her face, on her shoulders and breasts, on her hips and her long legs.

Their stares were frank, protracted and insolent. As if at a signal they all looked away from her again, raising their heads like wolves about to howl. But no sound came from them. Instead they just smiled. Holding each other's gaze, they widened their eyes in some kind of communal evil anticipation and went on smiling. On and on.

Jocasta could feel a warm stickiness between the flesh of her back and the wall of the lift where the two connected. She was aware of pressing herself closer and closer to the smooth glass of the wall, as though she would like to melt into it.

At a nod from one of them, the girl opposite her slammed both of her palms against the control panel beside the door of the lift. Each and every command button was activated simultaneously.

The lift responded with an instant soft shudder and then stopped, suspended.

Joanna felt a wing of pure panic open inside her. Her heart speeded up as she realized how vulnerable she was here in this sealed, featureless lift, powerless to escape, unable to do or say anything to attract help from the outside.

Positioning themselves to lounge once more against the walls of the lift, the girls turned to face her. They fixed their eyes on a point around the base of her throat, and Jocasta had a swift understanding of how a fox must feel, surrounded by hounds.

Through the dryness of her mouth she managed to croak, 'What do you want?'

They were silent and still, making no response, utterly impassive. After what seemed an age one of the girls stepped forward. 'Rich bitch,' she whispered with slow deliberation. Her voice was low and savage, the words spat out with horrible disdain and hatred.

Surprising Jocasta by making a sudden lunging spring, the girl reached out and tore one of the pearl earrings from her ear.

Jocasta's mind raced. They want money, she thought, they want to rob me. And curiously with that thought came a slight sense of relief.

But the next few seconds were anything but reassuring. Flinging the earring to the floor, the girl raised her hand and slapped Jocasta so hard across her cheek that she was unable to stop herself crying out. A second blow on the other cheek followed immediately, knocking the breath from her body with the shock of the impact.

Jocasta flung up her arms to protect her face. As she did so she felt herself seized by what seemed like a hundred rough and punishing hands. She felt herself turned round, the zip of her dress wrenched down. In a moment her dress was torn from her; she was aware of its slow slide to the floor to end up as a crumpled black puddle of fabric around her ankles. From there it was roughly kicked away into a far corner of the lift.

'No,' she moaned, 'no.' At last she was beginning to understand the full horror of what was happening to her.

But already her suspender belt had been torn off, her bra roughly snapped at the fastener and then pulled away from her. Now her panties too were seized, and together with her stockings were rolled down her legs with brutal and aggressive hands.

Jocasta found herself naked. Utterly stripped. Vulnerable and humiliated.

And all the time this horrifying, unbelievable assault was going on the girls were completely silent.

They turned her to face them once more. Jocasta could not look at them. She bowed her head, miserably numb and passive, waiting for whatever they had in store for her next. Through her confusion she was aware of the trembling in her body and limbs, a feverish shivering born of fear and astounded incomprehension.

They stepped back from her, still surveying the results of their work. Low noises sounded in their throats. It appeared that they were satisfied.

The girl who had been the one to bring the lift to a standstill now made a swift, knowing press on the control buttons in order to bring it to life again. The smooth gliding resumed. They were going up – up through floors three and four and on towards the penthouse.

Swiftly the girls gathered together Jocasta's discarded pieces of clothing and stuffed them into the waistbands of their black jeans.

The lift arrived at the penthouse, and stopped.

The girl who seemed to play the role of main protagonist, assisted by one of the others, grasped Jocasta by the arms and dragged her towards the doors of the lift, which were now opening.

Jocasta felt herself pushed through the opening, staggering and then falling onto the carpeted floor beyond. An earring was flung out to fall beside her elbow, swiftly followed by her slim black envelope bag.

Through her shock she registered the closing of the lift's doors and the soft whirring sound of the motor as it began its journey downwards.

Reality seemed to her like a small dot in some far distance. For a few fragmented seconds time had no meaning as her mind moved swiftly back and forth through the raw sensations of what had just happened to her.

And then suddenly she came to her senses, realized her responsibility to extract herself from this humiliating experience with as much speed and dignity as possible.

Cautiously she raised her head and looked around her. Like all of the hotel's landings and corridors above ground-floor level, there was no sign of life. The muffled silence was unbroken.

A thick pale green carpet stretched away into the furthest corners of the huge area comprising the hotel's luxurious penthouse. At one end were huge glass doors, beyond which she could see the the turquoise glitter of an indoor pool. Looking in the opposite direction, she saw a discreet polished steel sign with the words 'Penthouse Suite' etched on it in dark red.

Getting slowly to her feet, picking up her bag and mechanically placing the flung earring inside it, she turned her back on the sign leading to Maxwell Swift's suite and tentatively approached the lifts once more. But pressing the summoning buttons had no effect on either of the control panels. Both lifts were registering their presence on the second floor – the floor on which her own suite was situated – and both appeared to be stubbornly stuck there.

With a sinking heart she came to realize that the lifts had been deliberately immobilized. She imagined the four girls commandeering the control systems, smiling to themselves at their devious ingenuity.

Wearily she understood that there was no question of returning unobtrusively to her own suite.

She wondered if there would be a possibility of gaining entry to the swimming pool area – more importantly of gaining the marvellous comforting protection of a towelling gown to cover her nakedness.

Like a wounded animal, she slid her way furtively along the wall as she made her way to the glass doors. Slithering in that clandestine manner, concealing her back from view, seemed somehow less shocking than strolling free across the carpet, boldly proclaiming her nakedness.

But the swimming pool area was closed, the notice on the door politely announcing that its opening times were from seven a.m. until nine-thirty p.m.

Her head was beginning to ache unbearably now, and her cheeks burned from the heavy blows she had received. Her legs still trembled.

She knew there was only one option open to her, and her spirits sank at the thought of it.

Hunching herself once more against the wall, she made her way back to the lift area and then onwards towards the Penthouse Suite.

The entry door was large, solid and very impressive. Through the thick wood she could hear little more than a few faint scufflings.

She breathed in deeply and then placed her finger on the entry button and pressed it.

She waited, stroking violently shaking fingers over her bruised cheeks.

The door swung open. Jocasta was aware of brightness and noise and activity in the huge room beyond. But it was the person of Maxwell Swift who filled her immediate vision. And the relief at seeing him was enormous.

'Sweet Jesus,' he whispered. And as his arms reached out she felt her legs crumple and her body sag against him.

With one swift movement he released himself from the lightweight cream linen jacket he was wearing and wrapped it around her shoulders.

She felt the dignity that had been so brutally stripped from her begin to make a slow return.

Maxwell put an arm around her and steered her quickly into the suite and through into the large bathroom, which mercifully was situated just inside the main door.

He pushed her down gently onto one of the wide wicker chairs which were placed around the edge of the oval-shaped sunken bath and knelt down beside her.

She took deep breaths. His presence was hugely comforting. She reached out her hand and touched his shoulder, feeling the strength of his flesh and his bones through the thin fabric of his shirt. 'I need to break the spell,' she said. 'I need to feel reality again.'

'I'm real.' He smiled. He took her hand, guided it down his arm, over the warmth of his chest. 'There – feel.'

She stared at him. And then she closed her eyes, letting the breaths come into her body and tumble out again, one after the other.

Still kneeling, still keeping close to her, he switched on one of the bath taps and held a towel beneath it, letting it soak in the cold stream of water.

He placed the wet towel over her burning, stinging cheeks. His movements were sure and strong, yet very tender.

'They didn't rob me,' Jocasta told him suddenly, creasing her face in bewilderment. 'They could have taken my jewellery and the money in my bag. But they just – threw them back at me.'

She stared at him, her eyes wide with speculation and an uneasy new fear.

He let the towel drop to the floor and stroked his hand over her flaming cheeks. 'Who did this, Jocasta?' he asked slowly.

She shook her head, raised her shoulders in a gesture of bewildered ignorance. Her bones felt stiff and sore, no doubt from the impact of being flung from the lift.

'And what exactly did they do to you?' Maxwell persisted softly.

She frowned, her brain not yet ready to make immediate connections, form responses. They had a sudden flash of understanding of what lay behind his quietly meaningful question. She gave a sharp gasp. 'Oh, no. It wasn't that,' she exclaimed, a warm wave of fresh horror sweeping through her. 'Not rape. No!'

Maxwell sighed. 'Thank Christ for that.'

For a fleeting second she had the curious sense that he had been expecting her to answer differently, almost as if he knew something she did not.

He turned his head slightly away from her and she slipped a glance at him from beneath her long lashes.

For the first time she had a full appreciation of the firm sculpted line of his jaw, the long classical sweep of his nose. And those long sensitive lips . . .

Old, buried sensations uncoiled and stirred somewhere deep inside her, startling her. She had thought there was no room in her feelings at present for anything except the aftermath of revulsion and fear.

'I need to get some clothes,' she told him. He turned back to face her and she gave a faint smile at the absurdity of this whole incredible situation in which she found herself. She, Jocasta Shand, always impeccably turned out, always so in charge of herself, always so 'together'.

He frowned, concerned. 'I don't want you to expose yourself to any more danger.'

Jocasta got to her feet, attempting to gather up every last shred of her courage and resolve. 'I rather think that little episode was a one-off. Those girls were no more than kids. They were just having a few kicks.'

'The people who attacked you were all *girls*?'

'Yes.'

'My God!'

'Creepy, isn't it?'

He grimaced. 'Look, I won't hear of your taking the risk of going back to your suite on your own. And, in any case, you're not wearing a stitch except my jacket.'

She glanced around, spotting the dark towelling robe thrown over one of the chairs. Perfectly acceptable for a quick dash down the corridors. 'I shall be all right, Maxwell,' she said firmly. 'Truly I will.'

Even as the brave words of resolve came from her lips she found herself confronted with a sharp new recollection of what had happened to her in the confines of the lift, at the mercy of strangers who had seemed to have no regard whatsoever for her feelings of distress.

She recalled the touch of their hands on the intimate parts of her body. Brutal hands, their hard fingers probing without mercy. Panic-stricken, she felt tears pressing in her throat as she relived the humiliation of standing naked before the four girls as their hard, disinterested eyes roamed over her in disdainful assessment.

She began to tremble again, her body shaking like a tree tossed in a night storm.

Max's eyes filled with fresh concern.

'Why should they have been so interested in me?' she cried out. 'There must have been some reason. It must have been more than just getting themselves a cheap thrill . . .' Her eyes opened wide as she stared at him.

Again she tried to get a grip on her fragmented emotions. She took a deep breath. She straightened her shoulders. 'There's no point going over and over it. After all, in the run of awful things that happen to people it was pretty mild. Think of what you read in the papers every day – people being knifed, battered, murdered.'

Suddenly she found herself sobbing uncontrollably. His arms moved swiftly around her and she put her face against the smooth skin of his neck. He held her very firmly, as a father might hold a child. His caring was strong and real and very physical.

In time she regained control of herself. 'I'm sorry,' she said, rubbing her hand over her wet cheeks.

'No. There's no need. You've been through one hell of a time tonight.' He seemed about to say something further and then stopped, looking down at her.

She realized that she did not want him to leave her on her own, and she had a certain feeling that his own reluctance to be separated from her was equally strong.

'I'll come with you down to your suite,' he said. 'You can either get some fresh clothes or just crawl into bed. Whatever you decide – I won't leave you.'

She smiled at the sudden intensity in his voice. Every trace of his usual easy, lazy style had vanished.

'No. You've got guests to think about and keep happy. Anyway, I've got the feeling that coming to your party would be far better "treatment" for me than crawling off to bed.'

His lips curved into a smile. 'Good, good.'

'But I *shall* need some fresh clothes,' she agreed, smiling up at him.

'No problem. I'll go get some things for you. Just tell me what to bring,' he said crisply.

Jocasta laughed, imagining him riffling through her drawers, puzzling over how to match up undergarments, stockings and shoes. Men were completely hopeless at that kind of thing. Especially the charismatic sexy sort of men; they seemed to be the very worst.

Alexander had been totally useless. Adept at pulling off diplomatic coups all over the world, he hadn't even been able to pack his own suitcase. If his personal assistant hadn't been around to do the job then, she, his lover, had had to take pity on him and do it on his behalf. Jocasta remembered it only too well.

'Minette can go and get some things for me,' she said, beginning to feel much less shaky now, far more like her normal self. It dawned on her that for the past hour or so she had completely forgotten about Minette. There had been too much to worry about on her own account. Her terrifying ordeal had quite driven away all her petty anxieties about her flighty niece. 'Yes, of course. Minette! She's the obvious one to help.'

Max made a little sound in his throat. He looked vaguely uneasy.

'Look, if you'll get Minette to come in here, I'll explain to her what's happened and then she can go down with me to my suite, make sure I'm sure OK – '

'Jocasta . . .' Max interrupted, but she was in that state of excitement that comes with the rediscovery of one's ability to take charge of one's life again after, for a time, there had been only despair and helplessness.

'And with Minette to look after me you'll have no need to neglect your guests, Max. Perfect!' she exclaimed, her eyes glittering with nervous energy.

'Jocasta,' he repeated softly, 'Minette isn't here.'

Jocasta froze. 'Not here?'

'No.'

The look in her eyes made his heart give a painful twist. He was beginning to feel like one hell of rotten bastard. 'You see,' he explained evenly, 'my parties aren't as wild as people like to make out. I think Minette was getting a little bored.' He paused. 'She's gone out to sample the Prague nightlife. With Greg.'

CHAPTER 6

Minette drew in a large gulp of the night air and felt a surge of wonderful liberation.

Greg, walking along beside her, his long rubbery face registering faint amusement, enquired what kind of nightlife she had in mind to while away the next few hours.

'Anything,' she laughed gaily. 'Everything.'

He looked down at her glistening blonde head with mocking but tolerant affection. He was beginning to wonder what kind of a life this young woman had had in the past. He was asking himself what she had been deprived of to make her so hungry for the harmless pleasures most kids of her age took for granted.

'Let's get ourselves a drink in a wine bar and make a few plans,' he suggested, grabbing onto her hand and holding her tight as she swung dizzily from one side of the pavement to the other, gazing up at the lights beaming from the castle on the hill, swerving to take in the details of the dress and style of the passing crowds.

Greg was almost having to run to keep up with her, she was moving so swiftly, It seemed to him that she was desperate to drink in all the different sounds and sights, wanting ever more.

'Calm down. This isn't Paris or London,' he laughed. 'You'll get yourself arrested on suspicion of being on drugs.'

'I did once try speed,' she admitted. 'At a party. It made me feel absolutely vile. I was sick all over the hall carpet.'

'Then it probably wasn't speed.'

'No, I wondered about that myself once I stopped throwing up.'

'Popping pills at parties must be one of the most dangerous occupations of the 1990s,' Greg smiled. 'People really shouldn't do it.'

'You sound worryingly knowledgeable. You're not in the business, are you?' Minette asked.

'No. But I've been around a bit. I'm no wet-behind-the-ears innocent.'

Minette nodded. 'I know. I could tell that the minute I laid eyes on you.'

'So that's why you made a bee-line, then? Jeeze! Max and I sure felt targeted when you homed in.'

She gave a low chuckle in her throat. 'You certainly didn't turn too many hairs. And you two must get pounced on all the time. Max is as much a household name as Marmite. And don't think that up-and-coming film directors like you will be able to hide in obscurity for much longer.'

Increasingly intrigued with his young companion, Greg eventually settled on a basement wine bar at the bottom of a flight of ancient stone steps. Steps with deep, foot-shaped grooves in their centres.

'Thousands of feet must have trod this path before us,' observed Minette.

'Not for the same purpose as us,' Greg told her. 'One or two of these below-ground places have grim connections with the rather darker side of political revenge and brutality in the past.'

'Don't tell me,' said Minette. 'I was never keen on history. All those battles and torture chambers and killings.'

'Mmm, well, I hate to alarm you but I have a vague idea this particular bar is one of those where the city executioners used to gather for a jar after a good day's work. Around four hundred years ago, I think.'

Minette grimaced. 'Grim, grim, grim.'

In fact the bar turned out to be a subdued and elegant basement, stunningly decorated with carefully restored murals. The atmosphere was intimate, the service attentive. After their second glass of wine Greg looked across at Minette and grinned.

'You're looking vaguely disappointed,' he observed. 'This is clearly far too staid for would-be ravers. Time to move on, I think.'

After more trekking around the streets, with Minette gazing fascinated at the passing night populace, they ended up in a rock café, where the noise level was such that conversation was impossible.

The group performing was a wild-looking threesome. Twenty-somethings, English with cropped hair, sleeveless leather waistcoats and a heavy glistening of pure animal sweat.

Greg judged them to be passably good, but no better than any local group he might have chanced on in a bar

71

on the outskirts of any small-time town, either in the UK or the USA.

'Dance?' Minette mouthed at him.

Breathing in dutifully, Greg got to his feet. Together they gyrated on a space the size of a thumb-nail between the crowded tables.

For an hour or so they let the wine and the primitive animal power of the music take them away to another world.

Greg was interested to find himself growing bored. The band was turning out to be mediocre and banal: the dancing was of the unstimulating 'hands-off' variety.

He found himself wanting simply to talk to Minette, not to vibrate around her like some sex-crazed animal performing a ritual dance.

'Let's move on, babe!' he yelled, leaning forward and hurling the words directly into her ear.

Her face broke into a smile. 'Yes, fine!' she said. At least that was what he gathered from his lip-reading efforts.

They wandered back up the crazily hollowed-out stone steps, at ease with each other, companionable, as though they had been mates for years.

'So where now?' she asked, and he could tell that her racing, restless energy longed for more and new stimulation.

'I'm not the world's great expert on Prague nightlife,' Greg told her, smiling. 'I've only been to the place a couple of times before.'

'That's a couple more times than I have,' she said crisply.

72

'You make it sound as though you've never been out of sweet little England,' he teased.

'Wrong. I've been pretty well all around the world. My parents took me everywhere as a kid,' she said.

'I'm glad to hear it. Maybe I'll stop feeling sorry for you, then.'

'Huh!' she snorted. 'You haven't heard the whole story yet. I've been a whole lot of places, seen a whole lot of things, but the idea wasn't to enjoy myself. My father thinks of travel as something noble and worthy that you do to improve your mind – a bit like reading poetry or listening to classical music. "Travel extends your intellectual horizons." Get it?'

'So you've seen the world's museums and churches and art collections but you've never dipped a toe into the dark, seething chasm of international nightlife?'

Minette chuckled. She put her arm through his and squeezed it. 'Got it in one. Not so much as a seedy little basement where you can drink until dawn.'

'What can I say? Let's waste no more time and go in search of seediness,' said Greg.

They eventually found a tiny crowded beerhouse room at the back of a little café. Bodies seemed to be almost piled on top of each other, although it was hard to tell where one body started and another began through the thick fog of cigarette smoke.

There was no music here, just the fierce, drumming roar of constant talk and laughter.

A waiter brought them chilled beer in steel tankards. It was remarkably good. Minette began to drink deeply; the wine she had drunk earlier had made her thirsty.

'This all right for you?' Greg asked, gesturing into the haze of throbbing humanity.

'Perfect,' she responded.

Greg found himself fascinated at being with a companion at once so inexperienced and yet somehow so . . . knowing.

'So what's on your mind, Minette?' he said eventually.

She looked at him, her eyes bright and glittery with the alcohol she had consumed. She was by no means drunk, though, he noticed.

She leaned forward so that her head almost touched his. 'Me,' she said. 'And my whole life. And how I've made a mess of it.' Suddenly her lively face became still and reflective. 'Sometimes I think my father hates me for what I've done.'

'Isn't that what a lot of kids think their parents think?' he said calmly, playing for time.

'Maybe.' She glanced at him slyly. 'You don't know what I've done yet. Or rather what I *haven't* done!'

'Uh-oh, I smell a confessional session coming on.'

'Yes. You'll think I'm a real little cow for talking like this about my dad.'

'I'm not taking you terribly seriously,' he responded evenly. 'You've had a skinful. And drink has a way of talking all of its own.'

'They say drink loosens the tongue, don't they?'

'That's right.'

'My tongue doesn't need any loosening; it's always on the go,' she said, giving him a hard stare.

He stopped smiling. He looked at her and felt faintly puzzled and concerned. 'OK. Go on, Minette. Shoot. Get it off your chest, whatever it is that's bugging you.'

She ran a finger around the rim of her tankard. 'I can say things to you, Greg. You're non-shockable. And you're grown-up too. Not many people are that.'

Greg took a drink of his beer. He waited.

'I sometimes think my dad's a tiny bit crazy,' she said reflectively. 'Anyone who knows him would say I was a wicked girl if they heard me. Plenty of them think I'm a wicked girl anyway. In my parents' eyes failing your A levels comes somewhere between being a street tart and a serial-granny killer on the great scale of human wickedness.'

She paused, and a twist of pain and distaste momentarily distorted her features. She bit on her lip so hard the print of her teeth was still there when she opened her mouth to drink more beer.

'I'm still listening,' said Greg.

'My father is one of the cleverest and most respected research scientists in Britain,' she told him. 'He's positively loaded with whatever it takes to give you a high I.Q. In fact his Q isn't just high, it's way up in outer space.'

Greg laughed. He loved this girl's warmth and wit. What the hell had happened to her to mix in such bitterness with the rest of the fizzing cocktail?

'He's a geneticist,' she went on, stroking her finger down the side of the tankard and making stripes through the mist of cold droplets. 'It's one of the most complicated areas of all the research sciences. You have to be seriously bright even to be a lab technician, never mind professor of the department – which is what Dad is, as you'll have guessed. He's had loads of offers from the States, of course. Mega-money, mega-status. Of course he wouldn't go. His loyalty lies in the field of British science.'

'Nothing wrong with that,' Greg said.

'No. That's true. It just gives a clue to the kind of attitude of mind he has. Narrow. His mind is like polished steel, glinting and pointed and infinite – like a needle stretching from here to the moon.' She stopped, staring into her beer. 'But with him it's all depth. The breadth is a bit on the short side.' In a jerky gesture of anxiety she threw her hands up to cover her face. 'God! I shouldn't be saying stuff like this!' she burst out. Greg gave her time to calm down. He was trying to work things out. 'So he wanted you to follow in his footsteps? Right?'

She looked up. '"Wanted"' isn't really the word. More like decreed, ordered, commanded. I'm the only child, you see. My mum had three miscarriages before me. She went to clinics and saw every doctor under the sun. And then suddenly everything went like clockwork and I turned up. A miracle. A flesh and blood creation – genetics in motion, if you get the point.'

'You were a kind of living embodiment of his life's work?'

'Yes. God, how stupid this must all sound!'

He shook his head. 'No. So, let's get this straight, babe. Your daddy's obsessive about his work – so your future as a geneticist was all mapped out from the moment of birth?'

'From the moment of conception, I should think. And I went along with it until I was around fifteen, when I finally admitted to myself that I'd had enough of someone else drawing the map on my behalf.'

76

'Hardly surprising,' Greg said with a wry smile.

'I hated working all the time, being a little Einstein and running away with all the top marks so that the other kids loathed my guts. But most of all I began to hate anything to do with science. I told my parents I wanted to do Art and English Literature at A level. You'd have thought I'd suggested going to work as a stripper in the local club on Friday nights. Dad went ballistic. He went charging up to school and got me registered for Physics, Chemistry and Biology. And Mum just agreed with him – well, what else can you do when you're married to a towering genius?'

Greg held up a finger, indicating to the waiter that they needed more beer. He had the feeling they were only at the beginning of a rather long session. It struck him that he was sitting opposite a bottle of seething chemicals – from which the cork had just popped.

'I felt as though I'd been fastened into a cage,' said Minette. 'I felt crazy with rage and I had this awful panic that I'd never be set free from the bars imprisoning me. Then it dawned on me that I could fight back and escape.' A luminous smile broke through her anger and frustration. 'The method was so wonderfully simple, I couldn't believe I hadn't thought of it before.'

Two fresh tankards of frothing beer arrived on the table in front of them. Minette reached out and took one, drank thirstily. 'This is good,' she said. She looked around her. 'I like this place.'

It's a dump, thought Greg, amused. But it's not a cage. Far from it.

'God, you must be bored out of your wits with me rattling on like this,' she exclaimed.

'The very opposite,' he said. 'We aspiring film directors must seize on tales of life in the raw wherever we find them.' He reached out and touched the back of her hand lightly with his fingers. His mocking tone concealed a depth of sincere curiosity. 'So don't stop. Tell me the secret of your great escape.'

She laughed. 'For years I'd worked like a fiend on my school assignments, on my homework and my exam preparation. My father had trained me up to it so that it seemed as inevitable and vital as breathing. But I suddenly realized that it wasn't – that there were other ways of living your life and surviving.' Her eyes lit up. 'Do you know, Greg, when I thought about my new plan I used to fizz with excitement?'

'So what *did* you do? Just shut down?'

'Oh, no. If you do that you get the teachers on your back and your parents hauled up to school to "discuss your progress" and drag you back onto the straight and narrow work treadmill. And then if that doesn't work they send you off to the educational shrink to have your brain analyzed, which must be a fate worse than death.'

'Lots of sympathy and understanding, but basically it would all be aimed at getting you back on the treadmill?'

'Exactly. I had friends newly back from the shrink to the treadmill to prove it. No, what I did was truly brilliant. I simply started to turn in the very minimum for my class assignments and my homework – just enough to keep the teachers from alerting the parents. And then, at exam times, I spent hours in my room with my books open, and I'd stagger out around midnight with eyes red from exhaustion, but in fact I'd been reading blockbuster novels. And when I sat the exams I wrote reams, but I made bloody sure it was just rubbishy enough to have no chance of making the pass grade.'

'Hey! A really neat plan. Detailed too. And cunning as hell!' mocked Greg, who found himself astonished to think that intelligent parents could have managed to mishandle things with such clumsiness.

'You see, when you fail exams no one can really do anything,' Minette mused. 'They just all wring their hands and talk about the need to make a bigger effort. Your parents moan and rage, and phone up the school complaining. And then the teachers get the wind up in case it's their fault, and it looks bad on the national league tables – '

'Let me guess what comes next,' Greg interrupted. 'The headteacher sends for your parents and tells them you're going through an adolescent crisis and it'll all turn out right in the end once your hormones settle down? They just have to sit tight and have lots of patience.'

'Correct on all counts. You'll do all right as a film director,' Minette told him. 'You've got a knack for understanding things about life.'

'And what happens now?' Greg asked. 'Which road do you travel down next?'

'I don't know. I haven't found it yet.' She drank more beer and stared at him, her eyes hard.

'How long will it take to find?'

'I've no idea. Don't crowd me, Greg,' she warned. 'I've had enough of all that.'

Greg was silent for a while, giving time for her turbulent thoughts to settle.

'What's your little game, then, Minette?' he demanded with quiet intensity.

'She jerked her head around. 'What?'

'I'm talking about tonight. I'm talking about the way you worked on getting yourself out of the hotel. Getting *me* out of the hotel. Why?'

'To have a good time, of course. Rave a little.' She narrowed her eyes, loving the sport of teasing him.

'No, there was more to it than that.'

'Really?' She opened her eyes wide in mock innocence, leading him on.

'I'm going to make a guess – and I might be way out of line . . .'

'Feel free! Shoot!'

'I'm going to make a guess that your little ploy was to quit the scene so as to leave the field free for Max to get it together with Jocasta.'

'Get it together?' Minette arched her eyebrows.

'OK. I'll be brutal. Seduce her.'

Minette raised her hands in a gesture of applause. 'That's a pretty good theory.' She glanced at him, narrowing her eyes. 'Or she could seduce him. I'm a big believer in equal opportunities.'

Greg smiled. 'I'll certainly buy that.'

'You see,' she explained with deadly seriousness, 'Jo's had a tough time over the last year. She got involved with a seriously grotty ratbag bastard who had the arrogance to walk all over her as though she were nothing more than a rug on the floor. And now I think it's time she got herself a really scruptious man who'll truly appreciate her. And Max is just the one, isn't he? He's gorgeous, and he's sensitive but tough.

80

He's the just the man she needs to bring her back into the world of love and lust and make her feel good about herself again.'

Greg felt his mouth drop open. 'Listen to me, babe,' he warned. 'Max isn't a sexy toy – some kind of throbbing robot to be manipulated like a puppet. He's a man. And a pretty damn high-quality one at that!'

Minette smiled. 'Terrific. A1 excellent. He's even more suitable than I thought!'

CHAPTER 7

Max sat in Jocasta's suite, attempting to be neutral and unobtrusive whilst she moved agitatedly to and fro, riffling through her wardrobe, rummaging in drawers.

Clearly she was still in a state of shock. In fact she seemed to him quite unlike the woman he had observed before the evening's ugly events had taken place, rattling her confidence and disturbing her air of quiet yet strong self-possession.

She was unable to settle on any one task, flitting about the room picking things up, then putting them down again. Sighing, she would go into the bathroom, and he would hear the taps turned on, then turned off again as she returned to pace through the suite's large sitting room area.

He had no intention of leaving her on her own. He was prepared to wait until she had got herself dressed again and gathered her scattered feelings together, even if that took an eternity.

In the meantime he was becoming increasingly interested in looking through her business promotion leaflets, which lay in bright profusion on the huge leather-topped desk which had been thoughtfully provided by the hotel for the use of its business clients.

'SHAND WOOLS' was the bold, simple heading on the various glossy pamphlets which outlined the range of products available, giving illustrated details of the process of manufacture leading from the gathering of the raw material to the finished article.

And beside the promotion materials was a stack of thick white cards on which were mounted a bewildering variety of richly coloured woollen yarns.

Max handled the strands of yarns curiously. Homecrafts such as knitting were virtually unknown to him. None of the women he had known had been interested in such activities. The only one he could remember who had had such skills was some ancient aunt who he could vaguely picture clicking away making tiny pink or blue coats for the expected babies of family and friends.

He could tell that these yarns were of a highly superior quality. The textures felt substantial and firm within his fingers, yet these were not hairy chunky yarns, these were threads of finesse and elegance. And the colour tones were marvellously rich and vivid.

He glanced up and saw that Jocasta was dressed again. But now, instead of being svelte and smart in black, she was wearing a softly drifting and very feminine gown in a shade of muted sea-green which formed a beautiful background to the glow of her deep auburn hair.

He felt his breath catch in his throat as he registered the strong female sexiness beneath her elegant and ladylike façade. A stirring of straightforward animal desire thrust between his thighs, sending a glow of heat up his backbone and into the flesh covering his shoulderblades and the base of his neck.

Steady! he warned himself. He was not a man who allowed his feelings and impulses to rule him. From an early age he had found it advantageous to be in control of his emotions. And he would like things to stay that way.

Jocasta looked across and met his eyes. A smile of warm connection flashed between them.

She is simply exquisite, he thought, at the same time noticing her intense paleness and experiencing a twinge of fresh concern. He wondered whether the livid red marks caused by the blows to her cheeks earlier had faded, or if she had applied masking make-up. Whatever the reason, her face was now as white as fine bone china. There was only a tiny spattering of bronze freckles and a touch of pinkish-brown lipgloss to provide any colour.

His heart contracted with sympathy for her. And once again he gave himself a firm warning.

'Feeling better?' he asked, aiming for cheerful, dispassionate tones. He had her marked down as a woman who most definitely would not welcome feeling hounded.

She shrugged, gave a tight and rueful smile. She glanced towards the cards in his hands.

'The yarns for my next autumn and winter range,' she commented crisply. 'What do you think? Do you like them?'

'Very much. They seem to be of an exceptional quality and beauty. But I have to say that my judgement is little better than instinct. I know more or less nothing about these kind of materials – or what you're supposed to do with them.'

She smiled, then crossed the room to sit beside him. She picked up a card from the desk, taking a strand of one of the displayed yarns between her thumb and forefinger and rubbing it with thoughtful assessment. 'Maybe instinct is no bad way to judge,' she commented slowly. And somehow he didn't think she was talking about judging the quality of her business's main product.

'So, Shand Wools is based on the production and sale of these fantastic-looking yarns?' he prompted gently, noting that she had drifted off into her thoughts again, her face pensive and wistful.

She turned back to the card, took up another strand and worked it between her fingers. 'These yarns are produced exclusively from the fleeces of the hardy breeds of sheep that graze the moors and fells of northern England,' she told him. 'They have to be hardy, you see, because those hillsides are bleak and windswept – some of the grazing is little more than spiky scrub grass.'

'I see,' he said slowly. He glanced across to her, an eyebrow raised in question.

'That's the kind of grass growing beside the boggy ditches which water the hillsides,' she added helpfully.

'Thanks for putting me in the picture. I could easily get out of my depth in this sort of conversation.' He was impressed by the detail of her knowledge, her enthusiasm for her business.

'So, you're a north-country girl?' he asked.

'I was born in County Durham – that's pretty far up in the north. Have you heard of it?' she asked, smiling mischievously before adding, 'I'll bet you're a real south-country boy. Never been further than fifty miles north of London!'

'Wrong! When I was a struggling young actor I toured all the provinces – most of them up in the north. What I don't know about the backstreets of Sheffield and Barnsley isn't worth knowing,' he assured her in a brilliant parody of a Yorkshire accent.

She smiled. 'Well, I left Durham after my father died and moved a little further south. Now I live in a converted coach-house on the edge of the North Yorkshire moors.'

'Ah, so you've chosen to stay in the heart of the land from which your product originates?' he commented.

She smiled. 'Yes, that's right – living on the land in true farming tradition. My father was farmer, you see. He had a couple of hundred acres and a huge herd of prime dairy cows. He worked very, very hard, and I suppose that's what killed him in the end. But he had a great pride in his business, and he made a great success of it.'

Max found himself staring at her in growing fascination. There was such depth about her, such determination. And he guessed that when she had talked of her father's liking for hard work she had also been describing herself.

For a number of years Max had lived in a world populated by the glittering and brittle creatures who decorated the TV and film screens. Many of them worked with far more energy at promoting their images and their fame than at the actual craft of their profession.

But this woman, Jocasta, was utterly absorbed in her work, far more concerned about the quality and genuineness of her merchandise than the effect she was creating as a person. For Jocasta the yarns were the promotable, saleable commodities, not herself.

'You shouldn't be spending time talking to me about my business,' she said quietly, placing the cards back on the desk. 'You're neglecting your guests.'

'I left Sophia and Carla holding the fort. I doubt if anyone will miss me. Basically, as long as the booze supplies hold up everyone will be happy. And, as nearly all the guests are TV and film people, they'll have absolutely no difficulty entertaining themselves. You see, Jocasta, we media folk are always endlessly fascinated by our own glittering egos!' His long lips arched into a slow smile of self-mockery.

She made a small grimace. 'I'll guess that's your considered opinion of what *I* was thinking about *you* this morning. Big star, big ego! And now you're getting back at me for my standoffishness!'

He laughed. 'Not at all. But I must confess I didn't see a whole lot of approval in your eyes when we first met.'

'I'm sorry,' she said stiffly. 'Sometimes I can give this impression of being prickly and disapproving.' She looked at him with mute appeal.

She went on to murmur something very softly. It sounded like, 'But I'm not really,' although he couldn't be quite sure.

Max found himself becoming increasingly drawn to her. She seemed to be such a fascinating mixture of self-confidence and startling vulnerability. 'Shall we go join the throng, then?' he suggested evenly. 'Are you sure you're up to it?'

She threw her head up in a small gesture of determination. 'Try me!'

She walked purposefully ahead of him, through the door of the suite and out into the hallway beyond. But as they stood waiting for the lift he saw her face cloud once more with the darkness of anxiety.

'Don't look so worried,' he said gently. 'It will be all right this time. You're safe. You're with me now. And I swear, I'd half kill anyone who tried to lay a finger on you. Male or female.'

The lift arrived with a barely perceptible shudder and its doors yawned open. Max placed his hand reassuringly under Jocasta's elbow and they stepped inside.

As Max pressed the button for the Penthouse Suite she said abruptly, 'It wasn't myself I was worrying about. It was Minette who was on my mind. Still is.'

'Minette will be fine.'

She looked grave, frowning at her hands. 'I just wish she hadn't taken off like that.'

'Taken off! She's simply gone out to have a look at the Prague nightlife.'

'I feel as though she's run away and vanished.'

'Good heavens, Jocasta, run away from what? From who? You?'

'Yes, probably.'

'Why should she do that?'

'I feel as if I've been coming on too heavy and serious with her. I do try not to. But somehow I always seem to manage to mess things up.'

'Minette can look after herself, Jocasta. And you should stop blaming yourself for what she chooses to do.'

Jocasta sighed.

'You're not responsible for her, Jocasta,' he insisted. 'She's eighteen, fully responsible for herself. It isn't even as though you're her parent.'

'No. You're right.'

He looked down at her bowed head. 'You don't sound too convinced.'

'I simply can't help being worried about her, that's all. Suppose anything should happen . . .' Jocasta imagined Minette wandering the streets, being set upon by the same vicious quartet who had attacked her. Only this time they would do the job more thoroughly . . .

The lift stopped. There was complete stillness and silence. As the doors began to open Max pressed the 'close' button, and in instant obedience they slid together again.

Jocasta looked up at him, her eyes wide and questioning.

Max raised his arm and placed it on the wall against which she was leaning. Effectively she was trapped. She gave a little start of alarm. And then, as she looked into his face, she felt a huge surge of reassurance, knowing that he would never hurt her.

'Listen to me,' he said. 'As far as I can tell, Minette truly adores you. There is nothing to worry about on any score regarding the way you're getting along with Minette. So will you please give some more time to thinking of yourself for a change? You're the one who's

89

been attacked, the one who's been hurt. You're the one we should all be worrying about.' His glance sharpened and his voice became firm to the point of harshness. 'And you're the one who needs all the tender loving care.'

Their eyes locked suddenly together. For a breathless moment they both felt a keen stab of desire as his last words echoed in the air.

Jocasta flushed slightly. There was a sensation of slow heat creeping along her shoulders and neck, a sensation that was long forgotten – and most pleasantly arousing.

For a moment his lips seemed to move towards hers, and her breathing slowed and deepened.

Straightening up with a sudden decisive movement, Max broke the spell that had woven itself into the growing communicatin between them. Removing his imprisoning arm, he smiled his slow, lazy smile of pure charm.

'You really must stop getting yourself so wound up,' he told her in soft, chiding tones. 'Minette will come to no harm whatsoever with Greg. He's one hundred per cent solid gold dependable.'

The words clanged in her mind, arousing harsh and bitter memories. Jocasta looked up and her eyes hardened as she sought his. She shook her head. 'No one is one hundred per cent dependable,' she said coldly, pressing her finger on the button to reopen the lift doors.

Max's suite seethed with the noise of excited conversation and laughter. The hectic gaiety met the two of them like a wall of sound as they walked through the door.

Propelling her forward with firm authority, his arm wound protectively around her, Max set about introducing her to the groups of people who milled about like restless flocks of birds, juggling with glasses and cigarettes.

Jocasta noticed the hard stares of curiosity as she was looked over and sized up. She could almost hear these sharp and glittering men and women asking themselves who was this stranger, this intruder from outside their charmed circle, who had presumed to capture Max Swift's eye.

She smiled back at them, trying to look pleasant, trying very hard indeed not to give any hint of a proprietorial attitude towards Max. But the mingling of fascination and faint hostility was almost menacing, and it didn't take her long to realize that, for them, Max Swift was as awe-inspiring and unobtainable as royalty – a man for whose interest and favours both men and women would fight.

From the corner of her vision she saw the two Lolotti sisters slinking their way across the room, making a bee-line for Max. Although still clad in the shimmery, clingy mermaid-style dresses which had made such an impact in the hotel dining room earlier on, the two women still struck Jocasta as more serpentine than anything else. She could imagine that their mouths were filled with long silvery tongues which would flick out with deadly intent if one was unfortunate enough to cross them.

They pushed their way through the chattering throng, which parted in a falling wave of obedience as they swept forward.

Slithery serpents with the relentless crushing power of bulldozers, Jocasta thought, smiling to herself.

'Da-ar-ling,' they crooned to Max. 'Where have you been all this time?'

Their eyes slid warily over Jocasta, and she had a feeling that they were wishing she would melt away and leave the field clear for them.

Standing on either side of Max, and taking an arm each, they led him away to the six-foot grand piano which stood importantly in the far corner of the suite.

As he allowed himself to be gently steered onto the stool facing the keyboard Jocasta saw the lazy, amused grin which curved his lips, and she understood instantly that he was in no way impressed by his captors' blatant and seductive sexuality, that in fact he viewed the two sultry and exotic sisters as something of a joke.

He raised his hands to the keys and played the introduction to *Embraceable You*.

Sophia began to sing, her voice low, gravelly and husky, reminiscent of Marlene Dietrich in her fabulous interpretation of *Where Have All the Flowers Gone?*

As Sophia sang, her long body curving itself around Max, Carla swarmed onto the top of the piano and began a sinuous dance on the gleaming wood. It was a snake-like dance performed lying down, with the maximum of twisting, gyrating hips and a tantalizing display of long legs and taut breasts.

Jocasta watched, fascinated. She heard the man standing beside her mutter to his companion, 'Christ, I hope she's going to strip. Can't wait!'

Sophia went on singing, her dark-chocolate voice curling into the corners of the room, hypnotic like opium. And now Carla slithered down from the piano and began to squirm her way into the breathless audience.

Grasping a willing male around the waist, she unbuttoned his shirt and slid her hand inside. Her eyes narrowed to glittering slits as she moved her fingers over his naked flesh. The man gave a sharp gasp of pleasure. He reached out and made a grab at Carla's cleavage, but she was too quick for him. Whipping off his shirt with one spectacular flourish, she then appeared to lose interest in him.

Spinning around, she advanced with the speedy stealth of a predatory cat on the nearest woman available. She ran her hands lingeringly over the woman's breasts, over the fabric of her filmy blouse, her eyes glinting with wicked anticipatory pleasure.

Sophia crooned on as Carla, moving in perfect rhythm to the tempo of the song, deprived the woman of her blouse, then snapped open the front fastening of her bra. The woman's breasts were startlingly bared, in full view of the mesmerized, highly appreciative audience. She stood quite still, unabashed, proud to display the twin badges of her femininity. As the onlookers watched her nipples hardened and swelled into two erect pink domes.

A murmur of ripe eroticism rippled through the room as Carla cupped a hand around the lower curve of the woman's left breast, held it there for a brief moment, and then, seeking fresh distraction, moved away in search of her next victim.

By the time the song had finished a significant number of the audience had no more than half their clothes on. Couples had sunk down onto sofas, openly fondling one another.

Carla the catalyst, thought Jocasta, recalling Greg's remarks earlier on, during their conversation at dinner.

She smiled to herself with wry amusement. She was not in any way shocked by the developments taking place, rather finding herself in the position of an interested yet detached observer.

Flicking a glance towards the piano, she tried to gauge Max's reaction to the scene, which showed every sign of developing into a full-blown orgy. But, as she might have guessed, he was merely smiling his slow, inscrutable smile, looking down at the piano keys as he played the accompaniment for Sophia, only occasionally glancing up.

Then, for a moment, his glance sharpened and linked suddenly with hers, as though he were beckoning to her. Her heart gave a jabbing leap of pleasure so sweet and sharp her hand flew up to her breastbone as though in self-defence.

From the side of her vision she became aware of the predatory Carla advancing in her direction. Her earlier feelings of calm detachment instantly began to change and darken. Carla's eyes seemed to glow yellow, like those of a she-wolf, as she moved steadily forward. She looked menacingly purposeful, and totally devoid of any shred of normal human sympathy or scruples.

Jocasta caught the arm that stretched out to grasp at her and deflected it with some force. 'Oh, no, you don't!' she exclaimed with a knowing smile. 'I've been subjected to outrage already this evening. Once is enough.'

As she turned her back on the party, preparing to exit with dignity and swiftness, she was aware of Max getting up from the piano, attempting to force a way through the press of guests.

CHAPTER 8

Jocasta registered the painful pounding of her heart as she ran down the four flights of steps from the penthouse to the floor containing her own suite.

Recalling Carla Lolotti's yellowish lupine eyes, and the earlier spectacle of eight equally merciless black orbs, she felt that she had had quite enough of ruthless and aggressive females for one evening.

At the approach to each corner she experienced an extra dart of fear. At any moment she expected some unknown new assailant to materialize.

Reaching her door, operating the lock, then sliding through into the safety of the suite beyond brought a feeling of huge relief. She leaned against the door's inner side for a moment, taking in deep breaths.

Tossing her bag onto a chair, she went into the bathroom and confronted her mirror reflection with a hard, unflinching stare.

With tentative, exploratory fingers she dabbed at the bruised areas of her cheeks. They were certainly tender, but no longer stinging and throbbing. And when she looked at her face she could find no evidence of any deeper, psychological type of damage. In some curious way it seemed that the ordeal she had endured and survived had empowered her with a feeling of new strength.

Max Swift had helped there, of course. She had sensed his admiration for her calmness about the whole episode. And he, too, had been calm, finding ways to enable her to resolve her feelings of disbelief and confusion rather than charging about bullishly, calling the police and demanding the instant instigation of aggressive investigations.

Which was exactly what Alexander would have insisted on. He would have called up everyone he could think of, making decrees about what should be done, pulling all the influential strings he knew in order to get things moving.

'Alexander,' she murmured aloud. And again, 'Alexander.' She watched herself whilst she spoke the precious name to the woman in the mirror. And she noticed that the reflection showed not so much as a flicker of a wince. She noticed too that the real flesh and blood woman was able to speak that once almost hallowed name out loud with not a flicker of regret. 'Maybe you're cured at last, Jocasta,' she said to her image, applying some fresh lipstick and pouting herself a kiss.

She smiled at the crazy jumble of feelings swirling inside her. A sense of tingling expectancy hovered in the surrounding atmosphere. She knew that before very long Max Swift was sure to come and check up on her. She was also keenly aware that her abrupt exit from the party – whilst motivated by entirely genuine emotions – would have tantalized and disturbed him.

But what was far more important, and utterly incredible, was her sure knowledge that he wanted her – not as a casual one-night stand, but in order to plant the seeds of a relationship that would grow and blossom into something deep and very special.

The mirror had misted now in the heat from the lights and the steam from the basin. She rubbed her hand over the glass, clearing a space in which she could look at herself again.

She smiled a slow, whimsical smile, realizing that it was a long time since she had looked in a mirror and been pretty well contented with what she saw.

Kicking off her shoes, yet still fully dressed, she went through into the bedroom and stretched out on the bed.

She glanced at the clock. Two a.m. She wondered if Minette was back in the hotel yet. She recalled Max's words, sternly reminding her that Minette was a responsible adult, that she, Jocasta, should stop blaming herself for the impetuous exploits Minette chose to get herself into.

And it was not as if Minette was out and about all on her own. Minette was with Greg, who seemed a level-headed, coping kind of guy. She really should stop wasting energy worrying.

A gentle but urgent knocking sounded on the outer door to the suite. Although Jocasta had been expecting it, and whilst she was pretty certain whose hand was doing the knocking, her heart nevertheless gave a huge bound.

She heard his voice as she swung her legs off the bed and went through into the main room to open the door. 'Jocasta! Please don't be alarmed. It's Max.'

She released the lock mechanism and he walked straight in. He looked down at her, running a hand impatiently through his thick hair. 'Are you all right?'

'Of course I'm all right.'

Looking up at him, at the mingling of concern and questioning in his deep blue eyes, she knew now for certain that something vital was going to happen between them. The anticipation sent tingles of pure excitement running through her veins. And yet at the same time she felt marvellously composed, almost serenely calm.

'Come and have a nightcap,' she told him. 'What shall it be? Red wine, white wine, champagne?'

She opened the refrigerator, running her fingers over the chilled bottles of wine and mixers, checking on the supply of ice.

'Whisky,' he said crisply. 'Ice – no water.'

She clinked fat cubes of ice into two tumblers and poured whisky over them. Handing him one of the glasses, she picked up the other and raised it to her lips. 'Cheers!'

They sank into low chairs, opposite each other.

'Cheers!' he echoed. He took a long sip. 'Were you revolted?' he asked her suddenly. 'By what was going on up in my suite? Shocked, perhaps?'

'No.' She stared at him, frowning a little. 'Did you think I would be?'

His eyes registered some brief emotion she could not quite identify. For a moment she could have sworn that the suave, socially poised Max was experiencing an unpleasant stab of unease.

'Surely you didn't think I was such a prude and a prig that I'd be scandalized by some harmless fooling around?'

'I'm sorry,' he said. 'I just thought when you took off so suddenly . . .'

'Well, I'll have to admit I thought Carla's antics were a touch on the provocative side, but the people involved were all over the age of consent, I'd guess . . .' She smiled at him with a mischievous light in her eye. 'As for me – I simply wasn't in the mood for that sort of game-playing.'

He stared into his whisky. 'I wish to God you hadn't had to put up with seeing all that tackiness.'

'Why?'

He did not answer for a few moments. 'I felt it put me in a bad light,' he admitted, and she could see this sort of thing was not easy for him. Apologizing for himself.

'You mean,' she said slowly, 'that I might think badly of you because of the way in which two ultra-sophisticated women tried to manipulate your party?'

'Yes, something like that.' He paused. 'Do you think badly of me?' he asked, in a low voice husky with uncertainty. And an urgency which made Jocasta's breath halt in her throat.

She looked across at him and felt heat wash up into her temples in a red tide. There had been only one man in her life before who had had anything approaching this power of magnetism for her. Alexander had been her sun and moon and stars for a time, yet, now, sitting here with Max, she suddenly felt Alexander's power finally sliding away from her, leaving her free.

A tremor ran through her body. *I am no longer in thrall to Alexander*, she thought in amazement. She had the feeling that an essential organ had been removed from her body, an organ that had been diseased and hurting for far too long and in desperate need of being cut out, of being replaced by a new and healthy one.

'Jocasta,' Max prompted harshly. 'Answer my question. Do you think badly of me?'

She stared at him, her eyes roaming over his smooth golden skin and the gliding shift of muscles in his neck and his jaw. There was the insistent beat of a vein in his temple beneath the thick shining hair. She felt herself become faint with uncontainable longing. 'No, Max,' she breathed. 'No. Quite the reverse.'

A tiny voice of panic cried out inside her. *This is dangerous. It's all too sudden, too soon.* She allowed her eyes to drink Max in and told herself that in no way was it too soon. It was, in fact, almost too late. She had been in serious danger of becoming turned off love and its fullest expression for ever.

She put her whisky down on the table, then moved to stand beside Max's chair. He looked up. He ran a hand through his hair.

She knelt down, leaning against him, her breasts pressed to the hard bones of his long legs.

He took in a long sighing breath. 'Jocasta!' he breathed. He started to frame some further words, but she placed a silencing finger over his lips. Pushing his knees apart, she moved herself closer to him. Her arms lifted themselves to circle his neck. Her face moved towards his and they held each other in stillness and silence for a long, exquisite moment.

Jocasta began to murmur endearments into the warmth of his neck. Her hands tenderly framed his face like two soft white wings. Although their lips had not touched yet, she knew that when it happened she would feel pure ecstasy. The knowledge sent a spurt of joy zinging into her heart and veins.

Slowly she tilted her head back, exposing the marble-whiteness of her throat. She opened her lips in a gesture of the fullest acceptance. There was a moment of shivering suspense as they stared into each other's eyes with the marvellous anticipation of all the rapture that they both knew was going to be theirs.

Max slid his arms around her, his hands tracing a line from her neck across her shoulders, then back to cross at her waist in a firm and protective circle.

'Darling Max,' she breathed, feeling herself wonderfully and securely held.

In a swift moment all doubts left her as desire asserted itself over every other emotion.

He stood up and pulled her to her feet, crushing her hard against the length of his body.

She put up her hand and laid it against his collarbone, turned her face up to his and stared hard into his eyes. It was a frank, luxurious and voluptuous gaze. Not co-quettish, not even seductive – certainly not seductive in a cunning or manipulative way. This was the naked appeal of a warm, pulsing, needy woman for the closeness, the reassurance and the racing excitement of mating with a man she wanted and trusted.

He took her face in his hands, cupping her cheeks, stroking her temples with the pads of his long, sensitive fingers. His eyes held hers and she felt no fear at the spring that had been activated between them. A sense of utter trust rolled through her like a warm and hungry tide.

'Jocasta,' he breathed, 'you are so wantable, so beautiful. I had never imagined . . .' His voice sank to a whisper and died away as his lips touched hers.

The brief brushing of the flesh of his mouth against hers unleashed a stab of pure and urgent desire. It was a sensation Jocasta had not experienced for more than a year. There had been long lonely months when her feelings had been cold and numb. Her body had seemed leaden and apathetic and her natural appetites so shrunken and depressed that she had believed the keen longing for the touch of a man would never happen for her again.

Nibbling at Max's lips, smiling with delight at the taste of him, she considered the compliment he had paid her. For all that he was famous, a sex icon, a star sighed for by millions of women, she had an instinct that he was no idle flatterer. 'You called me beautiful,' she murmured, teasing his tongue with hers as she spoke, 'but that's far too serious a word for someone like me.'

'No.' He grasped her more firmly, pulling her body closer to the firm, hard length of his own. 'You have great beauty, Jocasta. True loveliness. And such courage, such strength.'

He stared down at her with longing, as though he would like to devour her. Jocasta parted her lips, her breathing accelerating as she felt herself opening up, body and soul, ready to give herself fully.

His eyes were moving over her hair, taking in its deep and heavy auburn lustre. The texture of it aroused a primitive animal excitement which stirred in his chest and his loins.

Jocasta tilted her head slightly. Her eyes held his, inviting him to do whatever his desires dictated.

Slowly his hand moved to the clip which held the heavy twist of her hair at the back of her head. Slowly he exerted pressure on it, easing it upwards through the thick strands of coiled hair until it rested between his fingers. There was a moment of stillness and suspense, and then the knot uncurled itself in one swift movement, sinking downwards and unfurling itself in a great silky russet swathe which reached the small of her back.

Max looked at it in wonder. His hands moved to the crown of her head and then travelled down the length of the shining fall of hair.

Jocasta gave a low chuckle. 'You're a hair freak.'

He turned her around and buried his face in the strands. 'I'm beginning to think I'm a Jocasta freak,' he murmured.

She twisted in his arms so that their faces and lips were together again. 'You say I'm beautiful,' she said teasingly. 'You take down my hair. Well, now I think it's time to find out what *you're* made of,' she whispered mischievously, easing the top button of his shirt from its tight little slit, then starting on the next one.

She slipped just one exploring finger inside the gap she had opened up. She began to move it to and fro, rotating it in a gently caressing rhythm, at the same time staring into his eyes and smiling with a glint of wickedness.

'It's been a very long time since I saw a man without his clothes on,' she breathed. 'A very, very long time since I *touched* a man . . .' Her finger made contact with a hard male nipple and Max let out a sharp groan of pleasure.

'I can't compete on that score,' he said drily, recovering himself enough to practise his inexhaustible irony. 'It's no more than hours since I laid eyes on the most fabulously sexy woman who simply turned up on my doorstep – stark naked!'

Jocasta narrowed her eyes to glinting threads. She put her free hand in the V opening of his shirt, gave a quick tug and released the remaining buttons, parting the fabric and exposing his muscled naked chest. She gave a secret smile, recalling the rampant and seductive Carla Lolotti and judging herself to be well up to Carla's standard – at least where Max was concerned. In one lightning-urgent movement she bent her head, swooping on the nipple that had not received the caress of her fingers. Gently, slowly, tantalizingly she began to nibble.

She could hear his breathing accelerate, could almost feel the rivulets of blood begin to race in his veins.

'You teasing vixen!' he exclaimed. 'Dear God, I'll bet you've driven men crazy in your time.'

Jocasta raised herself up and kissed his mouth with a fierceness which had him gasping. She then drew back a little, resisting his attempts to capture her mouth again. 'No. Not *men*. There was just one man.'

Her eyes widened, the pupils seemed to swell and darken. She was unable to speak and there was a sudden still silence. 'I'll tell you one day,' she said very softly, reaching for his lips again and silencing any further conversation.

Their kissing became deeper, more urgent. At first there had been light brushing, brief touching, a sweep of the length of one lip over another. Those first kisses had been like some gently erotic dance, with the participants circling around each other, advancing and retreating, one moment teasing, the next moving towards some kind of fulfilment. Now the mood had darkened. And desire was rising up in a hot red flood.

Jocasta sucked in the juices from Maxwell's mouth, revelling in the clean masculine flavour of him. He tasted of green woods and midnight rain. She began to feel desperate for more of him, as though she could not drink enough of him.

She felt her nipples become erect and painfully swollen within the thin gauzy fabric of her bra. She felt suddenly wild and abandoned, a hot volcano of desire.

She pulled off his shirt and flung it onto the floor. Her hand moved to the crotch of his jeans and she could feel the hard insistent bulge there. She cried aloud with wanting, not a wanting for her own immediate pleasure, but an overwhelming desire to please him. To give him a taste of the ecstasy that a throbbing, experienced woman can give to a man.

His hands were in her hair again, and he was massaging her scalp with his strong fingers. She looked up at him and then sank slowly to her knees. She felt the rhythm of his fingers falter against her scalp as she deftly unfastened his belt and then pulled at the zip of his jeans.

Once again she looked up at him, smiling her long, deep smile straight into his eyes.

He sighed. 'You angel,' he murmured. His hands moved slowly over her breasts, still enclosed within the fabric of her dress. She sighed with pleasure to be touched by a man with such exquisite sensitivity.

She was greedy for all the sensation he was giving her, and yet at the same time she wanted to be able to savour each exquisite feeling as a separate source of bliss. And just at this moment all she wanted was to roam over his masculinity, feeling him, rubbing him, kissing and sucking him. She felt exultant, as though she had the power to take them both on a brief journey to heaven.

Sensing her need, Maxwell stood quite still. She pushed the thick denim fabric down over his hard, firm haunches, bringing the thinner fabric of his cotton shorts with it so that his hips and upper thighs were bared. As her hands reached behind him to stroke the full tightness of his buttocks his manhood sprang out free, delighting her with its silky tensile smoothness.

She trailed her hands down over his bare buttocks, slipping her fingers teasingly into the crack, then upturning her palms and stroking them over him. Slowly she steepled the fingers of both her hands and placed them tenderly around him. She stared up at him again. His face was twisted with a strange, dream-like rapture, and through the raging heat of her desire she felt a sudden huge surge of pure and loving affection for him. 'I have you in the palm of my hand,' she whispered.

He took in a sharp breath and held himself tense. His self-control was awesome. Very slowly, Jocasta stroked him, squeezing very gently, then rubbing with increasing authority.

She formed her lips into an O and took him into her mouth. The taste of him was wonderful. She sucked at him hungrily, her own desire mounting to explosion point, love juices soaking the waiting flesh between her thighs.

Max pressed his hands down on her shoulders. He lifted her head and bent to kiss her lips, pressing his tongue into her mouth as though it were a weapon. 'You marvel . . . you miracle,' he whispered to her. 'But now I take charge.'

He raised her back onto her feet. Then he lifted her into his arms – lifted her so high that his hands were beneath her buttocks. Jocasta wriggled within his grasp, trying to persuade him to raise his head to enable her to kiss his lips, trying to gain at least some freedom of movement. But he kept her a prisoner, at the same time kicking off his leather loafers and ridding himself of his jeans.

Now naked, but in no way disempowered, he slowly relaxed his grip. As she slid down across his naked body so her dress was raised, slithering up over her stockings and suspenders, revealing her brief panties and the swell of her partially bared buttocks.

He gathered her into his arms and carried her into the bedroom, where he dropped her gently onto the bed, watching her squirm with anticipation as he advanced on her.

He pulled the dress over her shoulders and head and tossed it to one side. Then he turned her bodily so that she was lying on her stomach. Unclipping the fastening of her bra, he pulled that off too, and then, astounding her, he swiftly placed his arms around her waist and raised her into a kneeling position so that her breasts, unsupported, swung down like two beautiful globes.

Cupping his hands around them, he began to groan with pleasure as he stroked and caressed the firm, silk-like flesh. 'You are so very beautiful,' he murmured over and over, so that there was no possibility of her doubting the depth of his sincerity.

Jocasta felt herself drifting in a warm ocean of bliss. Suddenly her body felt ultimately desirable, her full breasts – which in the past had been so subtly mocked and derided by Alexander – no longer a part of her to hide in shame but the most wonderful symbol of her feminity.

'Ahh,' she exclaimed, writhing with pleasure beneath his touch. And then his hands had moved to knead the mounds of her buttocks; he had drawn off the soaked panties and his lips were moving along the path his fingers had just taken. His tongue flicked and darted, awakening showers of incandescent sparks of pleasure. She heard herself crying out, moaning with ecstasy.

And then he turned her again. 'Now,' he growled softly. 'Now!'

With a swift thrust he plunged deep inside her, and she drew in her breath in shivering gasp of new pleasure. Ah – he felt so good, filling her up, driving away every sensation except that of the most intense rapture.

She opened up for him, her insides seeming to uncurl like the petals of a flower, softly enfolding him.

His thrusts were deep and merciless, thrilling her to a pitch of excitation that was almost unbearable. She felt herself to be a tumbling mountain stream, cascading relentlessly onwards in a shimmering, sparkling torrent of dizzy pleasure.

He groaned as he exploded inside her. She looked up at him and saw the spasms of ecstasy twitching the muscles of his face. She felt her own climax swirling deep in her hips and thighs, reverberating on and on so that she thought the bliss would never stop.

'Dear God,' she breathed, hardly able to bear yet another spasm of joy.

She lay against him, feeling the thundering of both of their hearts, beating in synchronization.

Eventually the newly fledged lovers quietened, lying relaxed in each other's arms. She put out her hand and stroked his face very tenderly. 'Max,' she breathed. 'Max, my darling one.'

She glanced at the digital clock glowing on the television set beside the bed. It was nearly 4.30. Their lovemaking must have lasted for an age, and yet it had seemed like no more than a few shining golden seconds.

And she had not thought of Minette once.

'What are you smiling at?' he wondered, stroking his finger over her silky eyebrows.

'Pure and perfect happiness,' she said, nuzzling her head into the skin of his neck and gently dropping into a sweet, untroubled sleep.

Max cradled her body within the curve of his arms. His own body was spent and drugged with the bitter-sweet pleasure of making love to a woman to whom he was so passionately drawn that he felt he could adore her for an eternity. His happiness was as intense as hers, but painfully marred by the dark and troubling considerations that surged restlessly through his active brain.

The past twenty-four hours had not been at all what he had expected. More importantly, Jocasta Shand had not been at all what he had expected – nor what he had been subtly led to believe. The scheme that had been cobbled together in London had seemed harmless and pretty straightforward. He had never for a moment considered the possibility of his feelings getting involved.

The plan of campaign had been perfectly simple and mainly innocent – until he had met the target.

But now . . . He gave a small groan. Now his loyalties had entirely changed.

Watching the sleeping Jocasta lying curled so trustingly against him, he wondered what escape route he could find to free himself from the cage of betrayal into which he had so freely and casually placed himself.

Had things gone too far? Was it already too late?

This time he had to press his hand against his lips to stifle the groan of guilt and distress.

Greg and Minette made their way through the dawn quietness of Prague's deserted streets.

They held hands, swinging their arms in easy companionship.

'Sober yet?' he asked.

'As a judge. I never get drunk – just more and more daring and reckless.' Minette squinted up at him, her eyes full of glinting cat-like challenge.

'God help me,' murmured Greg.

'He won't need to. You're the sort of guy that doesn't need any help.'

'You think so?'

'A boy from Texas with a millionaire daddy and a budding career in film directing! With assets like that who needs a helping hand? Even a divine one?'

'I never said Daddy was a millionaire.'

'You didn't need to. I could see the dollar signs flashing up when you talked about his being "in oil".'

Greg grinned. 'OK, then. You win. Yeah, he's a millionaire all right.' He wriggled his face into a series of rubbery grimaces.

'Dollars or pounds?'

'Both.' Greg looked down at her, smiling quizzically, intensely curious. 'Does it matter?'

Minette shrugged. 'No. I'm not a green-eyed little gold-digger, if that was what was bothering you. I just like to know things about people. It's sort of my hobby. People investigation.'

'Your daddy likes strands of DNA, but you like real life flesh and blood?' He smiled.

'Mmm. You make it sound a bit physical. I was talking more about minds. You know, what makes people tick.'

'Ah!'

'Don't look so downcast. I like the physical bits and pieces as well.' Taking him completely by surprise, she sprang up onto her toes and rammed a fierce kiss onto his lips.

'Jeez!' Greg staggered backwards.

Minette had twisted away from him and was now running down the path ahead, her slender legs flashing like those of an Olympic sprinter.

He set off after her, having the advantage of legs which were around half as long again as hers. Spinning her round to him, he bent her backwards and returned the kiss.

Minette threw her arms around his neck and swarmed up his beanstalky body like a baby monkey.

'Oh, God, you sure take all the prizes in the kissing department, Greggie boy.'

After some hot, breathless moments, he placed her gently on the ground again. She smiled up at him. She took his hand and they walked along together again, the moment of passion having in no way spoiled their easy camaraderie.

'I'll tell you something I bet you don't know,' he said. 'There are just seven paths in this park – and they all lead to a huge statue of the great Russian revolutionary leader Lenin. Would you like to see him?'

'Not a lot,' said Minette. 'But I'll go along for the hell of it – just to please you!'

In time they arrived at a point where the path widened out into a circle whose perimeter gathered up all the other six paths like the spokes of a great wheel.

At the central point of the space was a huge stone plinth. It had a curiously empty and abandoned look about it.

Minette glanced up at Greg, who had arranged his features so as to give nothing away.

'Is that where he was – old Lenin?' she asked, nodding towards the plinth.

'Yep.'

'So where's he gone?'

'Who knows? To a stone-crusher's grave, I'd guess. They tore him down in the "Velvet Revolution" of 1989, when eastern Europe freed itself from Communist rule.'

'Oh,' said Minette.

'Sorry – history lesson. Culture. Boring, boring.'

'No. It was interesting. It must be the way you tell it, Greg.'

They laughed into each other's eyes.

Minette eyed the huge flat plinth with speculation. 'It's like a great big circular bed,' she said.

'A touch on the hard side,' he said, grinning.

There was a short silence. Minette slanted her eyes at up at him, then slowly and meaningfully moved them downwards to view his lower regions with wicked speculation. 'Like you,' she said with husky suggestion, reaching out and touching the bulge in his jeans.

'Minette!' he gasped. 'Christ,' he murmured, his desire bulging obviously.

'Are you cross?' She had not taken her hand away, was rubbing him with a rhythmic affection which made him feel on the point of exploding.

'No. But my eyes are watering.'

'Oh, come on!' She narrowed her eyes into slits, her fingers working on him with slow, relentless intent. 'Make a poor, exiled girl happy . . .' Suddenly her eyes were wide and round, full of genuine pleading; she wanted him really badly.

'Minette!' he protested, but once they had kissed some more he was helpless to resist her.

He laid his jacket on the cool stone of the plinth and then he laid Minette very gently on top of it.

Whilst they clung together, kissing ravenously, he managed to reach down and pull off her little panties, before unzipping his jeans and lying down against her.

He placed his hand between her legs, stroking with long arousing sweeps. She was as wet and throbbing and slippery as a shoal of wriggling fish.

'Mmm, nice, nice, nice,' she said contentedly. She stared up deep into his eyes. 'Greg,' she whispered, 'I like you most enormously.' She smiled dreamily. 'And you're about to go where no man has ever been before.'

Greg's eyes bulged. Nerves twitched in unison all over his body like a string orchestra playing a little symphony.

'Christ, Minette, you certainly know how to put the wind up a guy.' He stared down at her, his eyes tender. 'Look, is this OK? Are you sure, sweetheart?'

'Oh, very, very OK,' she murmured, gasping with the tiny shock of pain and pleasure as he entered her with wonderfully gentle authority. 'Absolutely A1 plus.'

CHAPTER 9

Jocasta woke, stretching luxuriously. Her body was filled with a deep, soft glow of rapture, and her mind leapt with anticipation at the prospect of all the new delights she would be discovering with Max in the days and weeks ahead.

Turning lazily, she saw that the bedcovers were thrown back. She was alone. Max had gone.

For a moment she felt a spark of panic. She had been brutally deserted and rejected before. Was it possible it could happen to her again? She felt her throat dry, her heart begin to pump painfully.

She sat up, deftly twisting the long rope of her hair into a knot and reaching for a clip to secure it. She forced herself to smile, instructed herself to remain calm. Swiftly shrugging into her white satin robe, she left the bedroom and went through into the living area of the suite, firmly telling herself that, whatever the reason for Max's absence, there was bound to be a simple explanation.

She saw him instantly, and her heart gave a huge leap. He was sitting in one of the low armchairs, his body totally still, his eyes staring ahead of him.

Touching his shoulder lightly, she smiled down at him. 'Darling,' she whispered.

He turned his head very slowly and looked up at her. She saw that his eyes were filled with deep tenderness, with all kinds of recollections of what had happened between them just a few hours before.

Remembering the uninhibited intimacies, the roaring torrent of passion that had been unleashed once the damned-up floodgates had opened, Jocasta felt a flash of hot, naked desire strike between her thighs.

She longed for him to touch her again, to roam over every inch and crevice of her skin. She wanted to feel his hands on her flesh, his lips and his tongue bringing her to a peak of breathless wanting. She ached to feel his lean hips moving to cover her, to feel him thrusting deep, deep inside her.

But there was something in his face and his manner that sounded a note of faint warning. It was in all her instincts to fling herself into his arms, but her sensitivity to the faint darkness in his mood held her back.

'What is it?' she whispered gently. 'Couldn't you sleep?' she wondered with a smile, silently chiding him for leaving her alone in her bed whilst she had been in the warm pit of unconsciousness, sleeping with the blissful oblivion of a woman who has been thoroughly and marvellously loved, and has only been seeking the comfort of rest so that she can wake up ready for more.

He sighed, feeling that her dark amber eyes were burning into him. 'No,' he replied tersely.

'That sounded rather un-lover-like,' she teased.

'I'm sorry.'

She looked at him with growing concern. Feeling an overwhelming need to be physically close to him, she slid down onto his knee and placed her arms loosely around his neck. 'What's the matter?' she asked tenderly.

He pushed his hand through his hair with the faintly distracted gesture she was coming to know so well. Just watching him made her heart contract. 'Are you regretting it?' She tilted his face to hers with gentle but insistent fingers. 'Are you sorry we made love?'

He shook his head. He looked somehow – sad.

Jocasta had a sharp, tingling memory of the feel of him deep inside her, of how he had awakened an exquisite sensation almost akin to pain in the secret darkness of her body.

Still he said nothing.

'I don't regret one little thing that we did together,' she burst out, her face alight. 'You made me feel wanted and hungry and female. This morning I feel glowing, sparkling. And it's all because of you.'

He gave a small groan. His arms went around her and he pulled her head to his. The deep, endless kiss made her dizzy with renewed joy. As his tongue wound with hers she touched his face with her fingers. When they had made love in the night she had been delighted to find that the touch of her fingers had aroused him, bringing a pleasure as delicious as the one he had kindled in her. He had been utterly hers, just as she had been completely his.

She drew back from him. She wanted to share everything with him. All her most secret thoughts, even the darkness that had swirled in her mind for the past year.

'I feel as though you've pulled me out of a black pit,' she said to him. 'I'd begun to think I couldn't love again – that my female needs and desires had crawled away to some secret place to die like a spent, sick animal.'

He made a low noise in his throat.

'No,' she said, placing her fingers over his mouth, 'let me go on. I've been uptight and buttoned up for far too long.'

Suddenly he smiled. 'God!' he groaned. 'I think I'm going crazy with love with for you.' His arms were like steel bonds around her, pinning her so close to his ribs she felt the breath squeezed from her chest.

'I want you to help me relearn,' she said slowly. 'About loving, about long, lingering sex and that pure, deep pleasure which comes from mating with the one man you want above all others in the world. Will you help me? Will you?' Her eyes shone watery-bright with feeling.

'Oh, Jocasta. Oh, my lovely sweet Jocasta.' His hands glided over her shoulders, sweeping down to her waist.

She sensed that love over the months and years with Max would be like a growing source of light, like the wintry dawn that softly colours the darkened hillsides and rivers in a rosy gleam of light. It would be a swelling glow that would suddenly burst into brilliance, blinding and dazzling – drenching her with a radiance that would almost blind her.

I'm getting carried away, she thought, smiling and hugging her thoughts to her with secret delight.

She nestled her head into Max's neck, and then cupped his face with her hands and stroked him with infinite tenderness.

She felt him stiffen slightly. Yet she knew that he wanted her again. She could almost hear the tension of expectation and reawakened desire roaring in his veins. Beneath her ear, his heart drummed and thundered.

And yet . . . there was some insurmountable barrier holding him back. She drew away from him. 'There *is* something wrong. Tell me, Max. Whatever it is, tell me.' She stared at him, frowning.

'My love . . .' he murmured.

'Are you worrying on my behalf?' she asked, with a swift flash of insight. 'About making love to me when we've only known each other for a few hours? Is that it?' He drew in a long breath. 'That's part of it,' he said. 'You see . . .'

'I wanted it,' she insisted. 'I was just as much an initiator as you. And I don't give a damn!'

He smiled. 'You're a miracle,' he whispered. 'And you were a positive lioness when you were making love.'

'Mmm,' she commented with irony, 'I bet you'd have been hard-pressed to believe that of me this time yesterday.'

He nodded.

'So would I,' she told him.

She saw a fresh frown darkening his face, further words beginning to form in his mind. Careful words, words she suddenly knew she didn't want to hear. Leaning back into his embrace, she put her lips against his, pressing into him until the sensation was such that there was no going back.

A warm red tide of passion washed over them.

'Max! Max!' she breathed.

His hands were already at work on her breasts, teasing her nipples into tautness, his head was moving down . . .

This is the cold light of morning, Jocasta thought. There is no concealing darkness to act as a cloak, no mellow soft lights to throw fantastic shadows, no residue of wine to create desire through mere physical sensation. What they were about to do now would be born solely of their powerful need to be fused together once again.

Max's narrow and supremely sensitive fingers continued on their dizzily pleasurable journey. Tingles of longing pierced Jocasta's nerves, and she arched her back, giving herself up fully to his deepest explorations. Her white satin gown gaped open, exposing her beautiful, voluptuous white nakedness.

His fingers moved across the curve of her hips and the softness of her thighs, seeking out the most delicate and tender folds of flesh that lay between then. Jocasta's spirit soared upwards.

Then, into their idyll, came a brisk tap on the door, a little scratching of fingernails. 'Jo! Jo! Come on, get out of bed. I'm starving!'

'Minette!' breathed Jocasta.

'Christ Almighty,' groaned Max, closing his eyes in despairing disbelief.

'Caught *in flagrante*,' whispered Jocasta in his ear, sliding off his knee and pulling the edges of her wrap together, knotting the long satin tie.

'Well, at least you don't have to worry any more about whether she's still alive and kicking,' Max said with grim humour. They looked at each other, sharing a smile of affectionate connection at the absurdity of the situation.

But, having enjoyed even a brief taste of Max's loving, Jocasta felt herself fully reassured again. Not even this crazy interruption could upset her. She was able to see the funny side of things because she knew there would be hours and hours of freedom in the very near future, when she and Max would finish what they had just started.

Minette erupted through the door, her eyes shining, her skin glowing. She gave no indication whatsoever of having spent a night without sleep, let alone of any of the other activities which had followed.

'Well, hello there!' she said with deep meaning on spotting Max.

He had risen to his feet. He was a truly skilled actor, appearing completely relaxed and his usual laid-back self as he looked Minette over with lazy shrewdness.

'And what time do you call this, young lady?' he enquired, perfectly parodying the heavy fatherly tones of a man around twenty years his senior. 'Your aunt has been worried sick about you. Have you no considera-tion? No respect for your elders?'

'Absolutely none. And what about you? What have you to say for yourself? Alone with my aunt in her private suite, with her wearing only a scrap of clothing. Her good name could be forever compromised. Have you no shame, sir?'

Max threw back his head and laughed. 'Are we doing Dickens, here? Or Jane Austen? Have you ever thought of being an actress, Minette?'

Minette looked across to Jocasta, who was observing this brief interchange with amusement. Minette smiled her cat-like smile. Turning back to Max, she said, 'I sometimes think I already am.'

'I hope you brought Greg back safely,' he remarked drily. 'Whole and unscathed.'

'In the main,' she confirmed, eyes glinting.

Max moved to Jocasta and placed a light kiss on the top of her head. Flashing her a deep look, he made his way swiftly to the door, vanishing with a brief salute.

'Well!' said Minette, rolling the word around her tongue. 'Well, well, well!'

Jocasta sank down into a chair. She smiled a slow, languid smile. 'I really don't know what to say,' she ventured after a time.

'You don't need to *say* anything,' Minette informed her, squatting down cross-legged on the floor. 'It's stamped out on your forehead in blazing letters.'

Jocasta looked up. 'Oh, heavens! What is?'

'Something about the cat having got the cream and feeling very pleased with itself.' Minette said, staring at her with the fixation of a predator marking its prey.

Jocasta grimaced, gave a twisted little smile.

'I see I'll have to spell it out for you,' taunted Minette. 'I'm talking about plain, straightforward sexual gratification.'

Now Jocasta flinched. 'You're so direct, Minette. So fearless . . .'

'Go on.'

'And, well – so coarse.'

'I'm real,' said Minette. 'Crude and basic. So tell me, put me out of my misery – did you really have sex with him?'

'Oh, please!'

122

'Did you?'

'Yes. If that's the same thing as making love.'

Minette heaved a huge sigh. 'Good. Great. Fantastic!' She sat down at Jocasta's feet. 'Gosh, Jo. I'm really proud of you.'

'Are you?'

'Yes. But I'm amazed too.'

'So am I,' said Jocasta, looking decidedly sheepish. She touched Minette's arm tentatively. 'It just felt . . . right,' she finished apologetically.

I know the feeling, thought Minette ruefully. *Only too well*. 'We're living in the 1990s,' she told Jocasta in cheery tones. 'There's no need for the wringing of hands and useless weeping and wailing just because you've made love with the right guy for you.'

Jocasta sometimes worried that Minette seemed too knowing. So sophisticated in the ways of the world. At eighteen, she, Jocasta, had been something of an innocent, with virtually nothing of the jokey cynicism of her niece.

She saw that Minette was staring hard at her. 'Max must be one hell of a tiger in the sack. Your cheeks are all bruised, Jo. Does he have a thing about munching faces – like that mad psycho in *Silence of the Lambs*?

Jocasta put a hand up to her cheek. Very quickly, trying to be as matter-of-fact as possible, she sketched out for Minette what had happened to her in the lift the previous evening on the way up to Max's suite.

'But that's simply horrendous!' Minette exclaimed, her eyes ferocious with outrage. 'Didn't you call the police?'

'No.' Jocasta paused, feeling the need to make some excuse for her passive acceptance of what had happened. 'I was terribly shocked, you see. I didn't think – '

'What about Max?' Minette snapped back. 'Didn't he think? Why didn't *he* call them?'

Jocasta was silent. Last night she had been glad that Max had not made that kind of gesture, that he had simply focused on *her*. But looking at it now, from Minette's point of view, she began to ask herself questions. A small worm of unease crawled inside her. *Why* hadn't he taken some action?

She thought for a while, then said with relief, 'What would have been the point? The girls had already vanished. It would just have been a waste of police time.'

'You can't know that. They might be a known gang operating in luxury hotels. The police need information like that. And anyway, it's good for victims of violent crimes to know that someone's bothered enough to make a fuss. To put on record what's been done to them, not just have it shoved under the carpet.'

'Very well, I take your point,' Jocasta responded heatedly. 'But it's not fair to blame Max. It was my responsibility to do any reporting necessary. And, in any case, no one could possibly have taken such good care of me after it happened than he did. He was so considerate, so understanding. Oh, you've no idea,' she concluded, her face rosy with the energy of rushing to Max's defence. 'He was absolutely wonderful . . .'

'OK, OK. Let it drop. You're probably right. Ringing the police wouldn't have produced any worthwhile result,' said Minette.

'And what did you get up to?' Jocasta enquired, swerving to a new topic and fixing Minette with a stern eye.

'Plenty. Nothing you need worry about.' Minette sprang to her feet, all energy and restlessness. 'Can we get breakfast now?'

'Give me a few minutes to dress.' Jocasta went through to the bathroom and took a quick shower. She pulled on simple jeans and a shirt. Looking in the mirror, she quickly stroked fresh make-up over her bruised cheeks. Just before turning away, she caught the expression in her eyes, staring out at her from the glass. The soft glow of newly fledged rapture seemed as plain as the sign Minette had jokingly talked about being written on her forehead.

A picture of Max came into her head; the curve of his jaw, the twist of his long, kissable lips, the sweep of his thick hair over his forehead. Her veins and sinews and muscles twitched with longing at the thought of seeing him again, touching him, making love.

A long sigh escaped her.

'Are you OK?' Minette called out.

'Fine. Just coming.'

'So what happens now?' Minette enquired as they shut the door of the suite behind them and walked towards the lifts.

Jocasta guessed Minette was referring to her new relationship, her startling acquisition of a lover. Angling for more juicy morsels of information. 'Breakfast,' she announced crisply. 'And then I'd thought about a trip out to the Mozart museum.' She held her breath, bracing herself for the inevitable protest.

'All right,' said Minette obligingly. 'Not meeting the amorous Max, then?'

'We don't have to live in each other's pockets,' Jocasta responded brightly. Privately she was already in that state of horrible agitation suffered by new lovers, the exquisite yet awful suspense of wondering when the next chance would come for her to be with her one precious man. Feverishly wondering if that much desired man still wanted to be with her.

Desperately she tried to ignore the evil little voices that echoed and taunted in her head. *Maybe it was just a one-night stand. Maybe he's already off the boil. Maybe he's already on a flight out of Prague.*

Jocasta took in a long breath. Those kinds of hysterical fears were behind her now. They were the sorts of things she had used to feel with Alexander. Dark imaginings which had eventually come to be the truth.

She focused her mind on Max. As she remembered looking deep into Max's frank blue eyes she knew that with him things would be different.

Nevertheless, she couldn't help taking a quick, scanning sweep around the dining room to check if he were there. But it was almost eleven by now, and she and Minette were virtually the only diners left.

'Greg and Max are going to do a bit of exploring up at the castle today,' Minette announced casually as she ploughed her way through a huge multinational breakfast of cold continental sausages, a pile of crispy bacon, two fried eggs sunny side up and a mountain of brioches.

Jocasta looked up from applying jam to her croissant. 'Oh?'

'Mmm. They're looking for some good filming sites. They're going to make a film about the history of Prague – all the wars and revolutions starting from the tenth century and ending up with the founding of the Czech Republic. It'll be a bang up-to-date epic with attitude.'

Jocasta laid her knife down. 'Go on.'

'Greg's directing and Max has the lead role. He's playing the parts of all the major Prague heroes, starting with the most ancient and ending up with the current president.'

'Very ambitious,' Jocasta suggested drily.

'Oh, Greg's well up to it. He likes to do a lot of preliminary researching – looking around for good locations to use when filming starts. He's a very visual sort of director, apparently.' She waved her fork in a sweeping artistic gesture. 'You know, heavily into camera angles and all that kind of thing.'

'Really?' Jocasta prompted.

'And Max is dead keen on getting all the authentic background information too. That's why they're here.'

Jocasta felt a curious twist of nausea. 'I see,' she said eventually.

Minette peered at her. 'Didn't Max tell you all about it?'

'No.'

Minette shrugged, then grinned wickedly. 'I suppose there wasn't much time for talking – what with you getting set upon by those evil girls and then by him later on.'

Jocasta framed a sharp retort and then let it pass unsaid. She noticed that Minette hadn't allowed herself

127

to show a flicker of surprise at Max's lack of basic communication. But Jocasta wasn't fooled. She knew that Minette thought it was decidedly weird. Again a twist of disquiet probed within.

'We spent quite a bit of time talking about the business,' Jocasta said evenly. 'He was very interested. In all the various yarns and the manufacturing and so on.'

'Keen on knitting, is he?' Minette wondered naughtily, pulling a face.

Jocasta laughed. 'Stop it! He's one of those men who are actually interested in what other people are doing, not forever talking about themselves.'

And I thought you'd got him down as an ego on legs, thought Minette, smiling to herself.

'And in any case,' Jocasta added, striving for a businesslike manner, 'I'm thinking of diversifying into textiles in the near future. Cloth for suits and jackets.'

'He'll have to learn to sew, then,' said Minette, spreading enough butter onto a brioche to generate an instant heart attack.

'Oh, shut up and hurry up!' Jocasta told her, unable to prevent herself smiling.

When she had at last finished her massive refuelling project, Minette stifled a yawn and then declared her cheery enthusiasm for setting off to get clued up on Mozart.

As they sat on the rumbling tram that took them out to the outskirts of the city and the country house, Bertramka, where Mozart and his wife had stayed with friends during the preliminaries to the first staging of his opera *Don Giovanni*, Jocasta found herself eyeing Minette with faint suspicion.

128

There was something different about her today. For a start this easy acceptance of spending a few hours sightseeing – or culture-vulturing, as Minette would scornfully call it – didn't seem quite right. Throughout their stay in Rome, the week before, Minette had chafed constantly at anything that smacked of mind improvement.

Yet this morning she had even gone so far as to request a look at the guidebook, to prepare herself for what they were about to see.

It struck Jocasta how perverse life was, how you could get yourself all uptight and worried when things were going too well just as you did when they were going appallingly badly.

The thought brought her back to Max. A flame of desire leapt up, jostling for supremacy with a stab of fresh anxiety. *Stop it, stop it,* she told herself.

They got off the tram and walked along a wide road, then up a steep little cobbled path which seemed to be leading nowhere.

'Are you sure this is the way?' Jocasta asked, as Minette charged ahead, guidebook in hand.'

'Yep – come along. Where Minette leads, all others must follow.'

And, sure enough, she was right. Passing over the crest of the little hill, they found themselves in a delightful sloping garden, at the edge of which a surprisingly modern-looking low white villa nestled.

At the entrance was a smiling, white-haired matron of immense politeness who spoke immaculate English, quietly accepted their entrance fee and welcomed them in as though they were royalty.

129

'Did you notice the hushed tones?' Minette asked Jocasta. 'Obviously Mozart is next to God in her opinion. Maybe a notch higher.'

'Be quiet,' Jocasta told her, laughing. 'And behave yourself for once.'

They walked over gleaming polished wood floors through sun-soaked rooms, whose walls were covered with original handwritten fragments of Mozart's music encased in glass and framed in stern black wood.

'Wow!' said Minette, peering at the dense, starkly black musical writing. 'It looks like an army of starlings on a mesh of wires.' She stood back and looked around her. 'Pages and pages of it. This is really something. Now I know why Duchess What's-her-face at the ticket office was so reverential.' She grasped at Jocasta's arm. 'Look at this! He wrote all this himself – without the aid of computer technology. More than two hundred years ago. No wonder he died young!'

'Looking at originals is always fascinating,' Jocasta said evenly.

'Not with my dad breathing down my neck it wasn't. I can't tell you the seething hatred I used to feel for Reubens and Degas and Renoir and the whole bloody pack of them!'

'So what's different here?' Jocasta asked.

Minette shrugged. 'Who knows?'

'You do. But you're not telling,' Jocasta said, bending to examine the delicate little piano that Mozart himself had played on whilst composing tunes for his operas. 'Is it something to do with your night out with Greg?' she asked with cool casualness.

Minette's heart gave a frantic guilty buck. She really must come clean with Jo about what had happened between her and Greg. But how? When? 'Yes,' she said slowly, 'I suppose it is.'

Jocasta smiled. 'He kindled your imagination, did he? Talking about this forthcoming film?'

Minette cleared her throat. 'Mmm,' she muttered.

They moved through into the next room. There were more framed manuscripts, and original letters written by Mozart to his father on thick wrinkled paper. Dozens of them.

Minette squinted at them. 'Pity my German isn't good enough to understand this lot,' she said. 'Just imagine him finding the time to write all these letters as well as the music. Still, it's a good thing Mozart didn't have a phone. The bill would have been enormous.'

Jocasta took her arm. It was so good to see Minette showing a lively interest in something besides man-hunting.

'I'm beginning to think Greg was rather good for you last night,' she said with a wry smile.

Minette's heart gave another buck. *Oh, if only you knew how good*, she thought, her insides tingling with remembered heat.

'Greg's a lovely guy,' Minette said eventually, her face uncharacteristically serious.

'Well, I have to admit I had a few anxious moments about you going off with him last night. But all in all I think I ought to thank him for taking you in hand and giving you such a good time.' Jocasta gave a happy smile.

Minette looked down at the floor. There was an almost unbelievable innocence about Jo. She couldn't imagine any of her friends making the kind of remark that Jo had just made without intending some heavy innuendo. But Jo was simply being happy on her behalf. She had no suspicious thoughts. She always thought the best of people because she herself was so thoroughly decent and kind.

Jeez, I'm going to have to tell her – quick, thought Minette. *All this secrecy is making me feel about as sincere as Judas Iscariot.*

They wandered through the final display rooms of the charming villa and then walked a little way into the steeply sloping garden. It was mid-September, and already a horse chestnut tree at the far end of the lawn was sheathed in gold. As they walked along they could hear the odd fat conker thumping onto the grass.

'Jo,' said Minette, 'do you really think you've got something going with Max?'

Jocasta's face twitched with a spasm of pain. 'Well, yes. Yes! Of course I do. I wouldn't have – ' She stopped, her face flaming with feeling.

'You wouldn't have slept with him if you hadn't thought it was going to be serious?'

Jocasta turned to her, deep distress in her face. 'Oh dear, Minette, I've got the feeling that you think really badly of me for what happened. I've truly shocked you, haven't I?'

'No. No, no, no.'

'I wouldn't blame you for thinking I behaved stupidly,' she rushed on, 'that my morals are those of an alley cat. But it just wasn't like that. Please! Can you understand?' Jo looked at Minette with naked and heartbreaking pleading on her face.

And suddenly the way was opened for Minette. 'Yes. Truly, I do understand, Jo. Because . . .' She paused, looked down at her fingernails. 'Because in the early hours of this morning I did the same thing myself.'

CHAPTER 10

Jocasta looked at Minette as though she had physically struck her. Her heart gave a single lurch, a huge thump against her chest. 'Spell that out for me, Minette, please,' she said, hanging onto her calm.

'Greg and I had sex,' Minette said brutally, her heart sinking at Jocasta's reaction. 'In a park.' She had thought of adding, On a plinth which once had a statue of Lenin on it. She refrained.

'Dear God!' The hand that passed across Jocasta's forehead shook violently. 'How could you do that? With a man you'd only just met. How could you?' she blazed.

'You tell me, Jo.' Minette stared at Jocasta with hard warning. She lifted her eyebrows. 'How did you manage to bring yourself to do it? Screw a stranger?'

Jocasta gasped. 'It wasn't like *that*!'

'No?'

'No. It was different for me. It *is* different for me.'

'Rubbish,' said Minette. 'Don't you dare talk down to me and patronize me like that!'

'I'm twenty-seven. I'm – grown-up!' Jocasta protested. 'Making . . . sexual choices is different when you're older.'

'And I'm only eighteen. But I'll tell you, Jo, that doesn't mean I'm not grown-up too. And older doesn't always mean wiser,' she added dangerously.

Jocasta found herself flailing about like someone who had fallen into a fast-flowing river. 'What about the risk of pregnancy?'

'Oh, for goodness' sake. I had some condoms in my pocket.'

'What?'

'I was being responsible. Thinking ahead, just in case.' Minette gave her aunt a long, hard stare. 'What about you?' she challenged.

'That's none of your business!'

'Listen, Jo, you presume to enquire into my affairs and I'll return the compliment!'

Their voices were rising now, and full of anger. Tranquil tourists emerging from the Mozart museum looked around to locate the source of discord.

'I'm beginning to understand why your parents have been so worried about you,' Jocasta said shakily, a remark destined to act as a red rag to a bull.

'You understand nothing,' Minette flung at her. 'Although even then you're not nearly so far down the tunnel of blindness and self-will as they are.'

'That's a wicked thing to say about your parents. They love you terribly – care about you.'

'"Terribly" is the word. Oh, don't get me wrong. I love them both too. I just don't like them very much at the moment, for what they've done to me.'

Jocasta found herself baffled. And increasingly panic-stricken about what she was going to tell Miles. *We'll have to leave Prague right now*, she thought. *I have to get Minette out of Greg's clutches, I owe it to Miles to do that at the very least.*

But, having given birth to this thought, she understood immediately that she would never be able to put it into practice. Minette would do exactly as she wanted.

Minette stood up. 'That's it. That's all I've got to say. I'm sorry you're so upset.'

'No, wait!'

'I know exactly what you think. You think I'm a little tart. A slag. Why don't you just say it?'

'Please, Minette!'

Tears stood on Minette's lashes. 'I wanted to share things with you, not be devious and secretive. But obviously that would have been a better bet.' She began to stride over the sloping lawn, making her way down to the pathway which curved around the villa and led towards the exit gate.

Jocasta felt she had no choice but to follow. Things seemed to have run completely out of her control.

She caught up with Minette at the bottom of the steep cobbled hill which led into the broad main road.

'I'm going up to the castle to find Greg,' Minette said in a terse, choking voice, and Jocasta could see that she had upset her badly.

She cursed herself for the clumsy way she had handled the situation, jumping in with both feet in response to Minette's revelation. But then she had no experience of handling this kind of situation. She had no children of her own.

Swiftly she reminded herself that she must stop thinking of Minette as a child.

136

She put out a hand and touched Minette's arm, but it was shaken off.

'Just leave me to do my own thing, Jo. Don't dig yourself into a hole with me like Dad and Mum have done.'

Jocasta looked on helplessly as Minette miraculously spotted and stopped one of Prague's few taxis. As she disappeared into it, and the car began to move away, Jo found herself feebly waving, desperate to erase the last few awful minutes and make amends.

The taxi accelerated and drove through the green lights at the crossroads, disappearing into the distance.

Jocasta opted for the underground to get her back to the hotel, and arrived there around half an hour after Minette and she had parted, her feelings bruised and in disarray.

The row had upset her badly. Open hostility was not her style. She was always impeccably polite and courteous with her business colleagues, even when things went wrong. And as for her family relationships – well, she couldn't remember a single occasion when she had exchanged heated words with Miles. In fact the whole idea of it was unthinkable.

Thinking it over, she realized that even in the slow and painful process of her break-up with Alexander there had been no ugly scenes. It had all been conducted with icy formality. Like her brother, her former lover had not been a man of blazing, unbridled passions.

She walked through the huge glass entrance doors of the hotel, immersed in a daze of conflicting thoughts. So intense was her preoccupation that she did not instantly notice Max, who was sitting still and watchful in the lobby, placed in such a way that he was able to see all the many comings and goings of the guests.

Then, as though jerked on strings by the pull of his magnetism, she spun around to face in his direction as he sprang to his feet and came swiftly towards her.

The bitter interchange with Minette had temporarily driven away thoughts of Max. Now, as Jocasta saw him again in the flesh, saw him for the first time in the knowledge that he was her lover, she felt her heart soar upward on huge beating wings.

He came to stand close beside her. 'Jo,' he exclaimed in a low, deep voice. 'Thank God!'

She looked up at him, her former brittle uneasiness vanishing like April snow in a beam of sunlight. 'There was no need to worry,' she said, suddenly understanding that his thoughts must have been running on exactly the same lines as hers. He had been wondering if he had been no more than a convenient stud for her, a one-night stand called on to soothe her bruised feelings. He had feared he would never see her again, that she had already flown out of Prague to some far-flung corner of the world.

Her feelings were sweet and warm and melted. *Oh, Max,* she breathed silently.

He pushed a hand through his hair. His blue eyes glowed and darkened. 'I can't possibly tell you the things I've been thinking,' he said, smiling his slow smile. 'If I did you'd think I'd gone soft in the head.'

For a moment they stared deeply into each other's eyes and a current of longing and sympathy and trust flowed between them.

Max hooked his arm into hers. They walked across to the bar, where he ordered her a glass of chilled Chablis and himself a whisky. 'We have to do some serious talking,' he said, sitting down opposite her, his eyes fixed on her face.

'Do we?' she asked, smiling, because the feelings that had just been generated between them suggested to her that there was little need for talk. All that was needed was time: time to spend getting to know each other better in the most leisurely way possible. And a good deal of that time should surely be spent making love, she decided.

She was startled and surprised at herself at having such thoughts. Minette would have been astonished. And highly approving, no doubt. *Oh, Minette!* she whispered to herself, fresh distress and remorse gripping her.

He shook her arm. 'Jo! Are you listening to me?'

'Yes.' She turned to him. 'Yes, of course.'

'You seem . . . abstracted. Where have you been, darling? I was going crazy with the idea that I was never going to lay eyes on you again. You just took off. I got this awful feeling you didn't want to have anything more to do with me.'

She stared wide-eyed at him, trying to take in what he was saying. 'No! Oh, Max, of course not.'

He stared down into his drink. 'I'm not used to it,' he said in a low voice of grim irony. 'Women walking out on me. The problem's usually quite the opposite.'

She heard the slight catch in his voice. And there was a vulnerability in his tone that touched her heart. If they had been alone, in more intimate circumstances, she would have placed herself on his knee and drawn his head down to her breasts.

'I didn't walk out on you,' she protested softly.

'That's what it seemed like. After what we'd shared together last night.' He lifted an ironic eyebrow, but she could tell that his feelings were bruised.

'Minette and I always go out in the mornings to do a bit of exploring . . .' she began hesitantly.

He reached over and took both of her hands in his. 'It's OK, Jo, darling, you don't have to account to me for your every action. This isn't an inquisition. It's just that I was sick with the idea that you'd regretted what happened last night and simply decided to cut loose.'

'No, no!' Her frank gaze pleaded with him for understanding. And as she looked into his penetrating eyes she felt herself drowning in a warm lake of feeling. There was such sensitivity in those knowing eyes, such sensuality, such a mesh of deep emotions and human compassion.

She began to understand his huge popularity as a TV star and his magnetic pull for women solely through the image he projected on screen. There was some special, very desirable quality about him which drew one on to trust him and want to share things with him. She supposed that was what was meant by star quality: some undefinable charisma which was possessed by just a few very special people, making them hotly desirable public property.

He reached out and put his hand over hers. 'What's the matter? he asked softly. 'What's troubling you?'

Jocasta sighed. 'Minette. What else?'

She thought she saw a flash of pure surprise in his eyes, and then a strange kind of relief.

He shook his head in gentle chiding. 'So what's she been up to now?' he wondered with an indulgent smile. 'Aren't you ever going to stop playing the little mother?'

The muscles of her face jerked. 'We had a terrible row – in the garden at the Bertramka Mozart museum. People were looking at us as though we were a pair of mad dogs.'

His lips curled in lazy amusement. 'Hmm, it sounds as though you were providing some great entertainment.'

'Oh, I'm sure it had the makings of a wonderful drama,' she said bitterly. 'I'll have to tell Greg about it. He can use it as a scene for his next film.'

'That kind of thing's certainly grist to the mill of dramatic art,' Max agreed, his eyes alight with interest. 'Human anger, naked conflict, battles.'

'It was pure hell,' she said flatly. 'And incidentally I *am* intending to have a talk with Greg. And not about fictional dramatic possibilities either. This is a real-life matter. And no joke!'

He leaned forward, a small frown on his face. 'What's happened?'

'Minette and he . . . had sex together this morning. In a park,' she added with a shudder of fresh distaste. 'I suppose he's already told you?'

'No, he hasn't. He's not a bragger.'

'Well, that's a comfort at least.' She paused. Her thoughts raced on; she was still appalled at the prospect of having to explain to Miles why she had allowed his daughter be seduced like a common tart in a public park. Her face crumpled in renewed anxiety.

Max was leaning back now, surveying her through slightly narrowed eyes. 'Is what's happened between Greg and Minette so terrible?' he asked quietly.

She looked at him, shocked. 'Yes! Of course it is. You must see that.'

'Minette and Greg – getting things together.' He raised one eyebrow, a gesture of his which was remarkably eloquent and evocative. 'Terrible? Mmm?'

There was something in his expression which stopped her from repeating the string of lofty and moral protests she had made to Minette earlier.

Max looked down at his hands. 'We did the same thing, didn't we? Except not in a park.'

'Don't make fun of me,' she warned. 'This is really not something to be taken lightly. It's very serious.' She reached for her glass and then quickly withdrew her hand, humiliated to see it shaking so much.

'I certainly agree that what has happened between us is damn serious,' he told her, a low throb of feeling in his voice. 'But perhaps we shouldn't be in too much of a hurry to judge things between Minette and Greg. What they do is their own affair.' He looked hard at her and his eyes were full of steely challenge.

Jocasta sprang up, knocking over her wine glass in her agitation. It fell with a heavy crash on the table, miraculously still intact. A liquid tongue of wine seeped from it.

'Max, I'm sorry! You don't seem to understand. I can't talk to you about this. It's . . . Oh, heavens – I don't know!'

She swerved away from him, making for the lifts, almost running. But he pursued her, pushing back the closing doors and squeezing himself in beside her.

Reaching up to the control panel, he overrode her request for the lift to stop at her floor and they sailed on smoothly to the penthouse.

'We're going to have some time to ourselves,' he told her firmly, almost dragging her from the lift and along to his suite. 'Somewhere your little protégée won't come along and interrupt us.'

He drew her inside the door, then pulled her against him and began to kiss her with a fierceness that set her senses dancing, winging away into pure, clear air.

She laced her hands behind his head, crushing him ever closer, wanting to melt into him so that they were like one single person.

When he eventually pulled away from her she felt weak and drugged. She raised her hand and softly stroked her fingers over his thick silky hair. The sensation was exquisite. Softly her fingers moved over the lines of his face, down to the smooth skin of his throat.

'Just you and me,' he said, his voice so huskily intense she could barely hear the words. 'That's what matters.'

'Yes.' When she was with Max, close to him, she could believe that with utter conviction.

He had slipped his hand beneath her shirt, was caressing a nipple, teasing it into a hard bud of desire.

'I feel so – at one with you, Max,' she said on a rush of hot impulse. 'When you're close like this I feel I would trust my life to you.'

His hand faltered for a second in his caress.

She pressed on. There were things she had to say to him. To make him understand. To make *herself* understand. 'I think I feel that way because of what happened last night. That horrific assault – how I felt crushed and sullied. I was so humiliated, I felt so – *dirty*. And you seemed to see instantly into all the different shades of my feelings. You understood the pain I was feeling and

143

shared it with me, felt it with me. I think in those few minutes I learned more about you than I could have done in weeks and months in the ordinary run of things. Does that make sense?'

'Darling – ' he began, but she held up a hand, letting him know she still had more to tell him.

'I can't imagine that only forty-eight hours ago I knew nothing about you,' she told him, her lips brushing against his jaw. 'I have the feeling you've filled my life, that somehow you've always been there.' She looked up at him. 'And that you always *will* be there.'

He bent to kiss her throat, the pulse that was beating frantically at the cleft of her collarbone.

'And that's a truly terrifying confession to make,' she went on, 'to someone who other people might say was a perfect stranger.'

She felt rather than heard his responding sigh, registered the deep reverberations through his body. 'I hope to God I can prove to you I deserve it,' he told her.

Silencing any further attempts at verbal communication by pressing his lips on hers, he pushed her gently down onto the carpet. She felt him undo her jeans, pull aside her panties and, with no more preamble, plunge fiercely inside her.

All the jagged apprehensions of the morning evaporated.

For timeless, precious, gasping moments there was just Max. Only him. In her mind and her body. And in her heart.

CHAPTER 11

Minette walked the steep, narrow streets that led up to Prague's ancient castle. It was a long, hard climb, requiring a great deal of effort.

As she progressed upwards, her breathing deepening and accelerating, the hard, flame-red core of her anger began to soften, to be replaced by an aching drone of disquiet. She knew it was imperative that she see Greg and talk to him. But observing the huge crowds of camera-decked tourists who were making the same journey as she was made her realize the unlikelihood of simply bumping into him. Locating him would be as futile as trying to find a needle in a haystack.

The bitter exchange in the garden at the Mozart museum had rattled her just as much as it had Jo, and she hated the thought that she had made Jo unhappy. But Minette was a mistress of the art of concealment; her outer façade of bravado and snappy quips invariably concealed a fierce inner secrecy.

She had learned from an early age that that there was safety in hugging her most precious desires and longings to herself. In that way other people – most especially her father – didn't guess at the nature of those delicious, intensely private ambitions and then try to persuade her to give them up and think of something else instead.

But with Greg, early that morning, she felt she had yielded up just about every secret longing she could ever think of. And then she had yielded up the ultimate – herself.

And now she couldn't stop thinking about him. He had given her her first taste of sex, which had been delicious and, as far as she was concerned, no more than an appetizer for a whole lot more of the same, please.

But he had offered something else too. A glimpse of something she hadn't come across before. A glimpse of the possibility of love with no strings attached. Love just for herself, not for what she could deliver as a brilliantly achieving daughter or student.

Even Jo, who she loved quite fiercely, couldn't help thinking that she was 'wasting' herself by not trotting meekly along down the trail that the wonderful Miles had blazed.

Climbing doggedly on, peering into the fascinating dark interiors of the little shops selling pottery, carved wooden toys and perfect models of Prague's houses, Minette wished for the thousandth time that she had not been saddled with such an agile and restless brain. Being bright and sharp had many advantages, but plenty of drawbacks too. One of those being the difficulty of convincing your father that you had no intention whatsoever of following in his shining footsteps.

If I'd had the brains of a rice pudding he'd never have been able to even start thinking about it, she told herself grimly, fresh anger spurting up.

Puffing a little with exertion, she eventually reached the crown of the hill. The castle walls rose up in front of her, a huge, binding fortress enclosing a treasure trove of churches, towers and individual palaces. Passing through the gate into the first of the inner court-yards, she looked at the plan provided for the few tourists not carrying maps and guidebooks.

Oh, hell, she thought. This place is so huge and so complicated. I'll never find him here.

Disconsolately she wandered through into the second courtyard and then on into the third one, the heart of the complex. The walls and towering spires of a breath-taking cathedral stopped her in her tracks. Her face was drawn upwards, her eyes marvelling at the needle-sharp apexes of the two spires guarding the west front, the pale golden stone stark against a shimmering blue sky.

'Wow!' she whispered aloud. 'Positively awe-inspir-ing!' Wincing at her pun, she let her gaze drop a little lower, focusing on the gargoyles which leaned out from below the huge stained-glass rose window, their leering mouths wide open and spitting forth gutter spouts.

They were so ugly and so appealing they made her laugh out loud.

She gave a startled cry at feeling herself gently grasped from behind, hands reaching around her waist and lifting her briefly off her feet. 'Hi, there, little English tourist,' a voice drawled in her ear. 'What's the joke?'

A slow smile spread over her face. Greg! She felt her eyes glint shrewd and fox-like with mischief. 'Hi, there, Mr up-and-coming famous film director!' She twisted in his grasp, leapt up and landed him a ferocious lunging kiss, smack bang on his lips. She was so delighted to see him she thought her legs would melt and buckle beneath her. 'You were certainly up-and-coming this morning,' she whispered in his ear, giving his lobe a quick nibble.

'Don't remind me of my sins. I've been agonizing all morning.' He put his arm around her shoulders and they walked along the vast south wall of the cathedral, gazing up at its serene magnificence.

Minette wriggled her arm around his waist, pressing close to him 'Agonizing! You? No way!' She looked up into his quirky face, as mobile as a child's rubbery mask. She felt her insides wobble. *Making love makes you feel really affectionate* she thought, wanting to pull Greg's head down to hers and kiss him very thoroughly indeed.

As her eyes scanned the intricacies of the cathedral's architecture she grasped at this latest idea of hers, turning it over in her mind with curiosity. Her friends had always told her that sex was just horniness. Not usually much to do with any particular guy. It was all about technique, pressing the right buttons to get a great sensation. You got a nice thrill and then . . . well, that was probably that. Get on with the rest of your life.

'How do you like the bell tower?' Greg asked, indicating the cathedral's central tower, which stretched up seemingly to infinity. 'Cute, isn't it? With that neat little baroque helmet on top to keep it warm?'

'It's fantastic,' Minette exclaimed, suddenly hungry for all the history and culture contained in this ancient city which stood at the crossroads of Europe. She gave Greg's ribcage a violent squeeze of adoration.

'Prince Wenceslas was murdered in this cathedral,' Greg told her conversationally, shrugging his camera from his shoulder and squinting into it, lining up a shot.

'Wenceslas! The famous one in the Christmas carol – "Hither page and stand by me?" Didn't he drag his poor little pageboy out into the wind and snow so they could take firewood and wine to some starving beggar?'

'Not sure. You're way further on with your Christmas carols than me, babe. I had the upbringing of a philistine,' said Greg, grinning.

'Who murdered him?' Minette enquired, still keeping a close hold on Greg. She loved the feel of him, the hardness of his lean, beanstalky frame. The wonderful elastic pliability of the flesh stretched over it.

'His brother.'

'That makes sense. The ones you're closest to are the ones you'd sometimes most like to kill.' She flicked a wicked glance at Greg. 'So you'd better keep your distance if you want to stay alive.'

He lowered his camera. He looked very steadily into her face. Minette noticed that his eyes were a wonderful steely grey, like the mist over an alpine peak.

'Do I hear a message in those words?' he asked.

'Yep. I'm absolutely one hundred per cent sold on you, Greggie-boy. So – look out!'

He shook his head in smiling disbelief, seemingly quite unperturbed by her uninhibited enthusiasm.

'Tell me more about this agonizing you mentioned,' instructed Minette. 'I don't like the sound of it. And if you give me some spiel about the way you've been kicking yourself for deflowering a baby virgin, I might just be tempted to commit murder here and now.'

' "Deflowering". That's a good word,' he commented, running his arm around her shoulders again and propelling her on, his head tipping towards hers.

'Too delicate for you?' suggested Minette. 'What would be better? Seducing, abducting, despoiling? And then there's pillaging, pleasuring . . .?'

'You young Brits are so *earthy*,' he commented.

She laughed. 'Don't regard me as typical.'

'You really love words, don't you?' he commented, grinning down at her. 'I can almost see them rolling around your tongue like candy!'

'Hah!' She aimed a playful punch at his chest, but he bounded away, lithe and agile, evading her.

They wandered around the outer walls of the cathedral and then found themselves at the head of the endless rows of broad stone steps which led down from the old castle into the outskirts of the town centre.

Merchants peddling jewellery and various trinkets sat on the edge of the steps, smiling at them, tempting them with their various goods. An artist displaying a small gallery of meticulously sketched pencil portraits stopped Minette with a wave of his arm.

She smiled at him. 'Hello.'

'I do your portrait, miss,' he said. 'Very cheap. Only a few crowns.'

Minette dug into the pocket of her jeans. She had nothing more than small change. She smiled again at the artist, shrugging regretfully. 'I'm really sorry. I haven't enough to pay you.'

Behind her, she heard Greg saying, 'Go ahead, please.' She turned to him, curious and questioning.

'Go on,' he said, his eyes alight with warmth. 'Sit down there and pose. I'd like a memento of you – just as you are today.'

Minette sat on the edge of a step, fluffing out her hair and smoothing her eyebrows with the tips of her fingers. At the same time she watched the young artist adjust his easel, fix fresh paper to its smooth board.

Greg squatted beside her on the step below, positioned so he could see both artist and model.

The artist began his work, moving his thick pencil over the blank sheet in bold, swishing strokes.

Minette saw Greg's glance swivel sharply from the page to her face, his eyes tapered in assessment.

She looked at him, appealing for information, but he simply smiled, shaking his head and mouthing the message, 'Wait and see.'

Minutes went by. Minette found herself increasingly involved in observing the lines of Greg's uniquely individual, compellingly odd face. *Some people might call him ugly,* she judged. *But I think he's the most fascinating man I've ever laid eyes on.*

Slanting her eyes seductively, she blew him a pouting kiss. He raised his eyes heavenwards, making a show of pretending to ignore her proclamations of affection.

'There,' exclaimed the artist, in time. 'Is finished. What do you think? You like?'

He turned the easel to face Minette and she found herself confronted with a compelling mirror image of her face and shoulders, sketched out in dark grey pencil lines.

'Amazing!' she exclaimed. 'You've captured me on paper with nothing more than a pencil. Perfectly. In just a few minutes. How on earth do you do that?'

The young man smiled. The full meaning of her excited, rushing exclamations had quite eluded him. But he could tell that she was pleased.

'Yeah, really and truly amazing,' said Greg, digging into his pocket and dropping a number of coins into the young artist's palm.

'Is too much,' the artist said, looking up.

'No,' said Greg. 'It's far too little.'

They moved on down the steps. Greg rolled the stiff paper of the drawing into a fat tube which he slotted into the gaping pocket of his baggy jacket. He rested his arm once more on Minette's shoulders.

'Thanks,' said Minette. 'For the drawing, I mean.'

'You're welcome.' He dropped a light kiss on the top of her shiny blonde head.

Minette stopped in her tracks, waiting until he had progressed on to the next step and was then not so much taller than she. Pulling him back towards her, she pressed a brief but important kiss on his lips.

'Hey!' he exclaimed. 'Nice!'

'I'd like to kiss you until your lips fray at the edges,' Minette told him.

He laughed. 'But maybe not just here, babe. We wouldn't want to frighten the innocent tourists.'

Minette noted his tone: light and easy and casual. Just the sort of verbal style she herself often preferred to use in order to keep her true feelings strictly under wraps. Which was why now, listening to Greg, she found herself worried, wondering what *he* might be keeping to himself.

He clamped his arm firmly around her waist, holding her against him and propelling her gently forward.

'Greg,' she said, registering a little lump settling itself in her throat, 'it's OK, you know.'

'Yeah, of course it's OK. Everything's just fine!' he agreed, squinting down at her, his eyes amused and tenderly indulgent.

'No. Listen!' She rattled his arm. 'What I mean is – it's all right about this morning. In the park.' His grey eyes held hers steadily and a shiver of feeling zipped through her body. 'I don't want you to feel . . .'

'Feel what?'

'Oh, I don't know! That it was kind of serious and heavy. I mean,' she went on shakily, 'we're both grown-ups. And sometimes grown-up people just want to sleep with each other, and, well, it's no big deal.' The tears that had been gathering in a little pool behind her eyelids now spilled over into a running stream.

'You'd like me to think of it as a one-off happening?' he demanded. 'Wham, bam, thank you ma'am!'

'No!' she burst out. She groaned inwardly, realizing she had blown it, let him know that all her brave and permissive–sounding suggestions about people loving and leaving each other were a complete phoney.

Greg offered her a handkerchief. It was bright red and blue and it was warm from his body because it had been in his hip pocket. Worse, it smelled of him, which made her want to cry even harder. She dabbed at the rivulets sliding down her cheeks, coughing and sniffing and feeling enormously ashamed of herself.

They were approaching the end of the steps. The road led downwards, and at its curve was a beautiful church with baroque towers and domes and a wide half-circle staircase leading to its main door. Tourists sat relaxing there, an array of maps and cameras beside them.

Greg pushed her gently down onto the smooth stone stairway and sat beside her. He swivelled her towards him and wrapped his arms around her, putting his hand behind her head and pulling her to him so that her face was resting against his neck.

He had the feeling he had never before held anything so precious – or so needy.

He decided to say nothing for a while. Just give her time to release some of the emotions he guessed had been building up inside her for some time. He remembered the revelations that had poured out of her the night before when she had had a few drinks.

He held her very close, knowing that he was offering her some sort of safe place, a haven where she could just be herself for a while. His heart twisted with an almost painful tenderness which was something of a novelty for him. He put his fingers in her hair and gently massaged her scalp. He stroked the satiny skin of her slender neck.

'Greg, I'm in deep trouble with Jo,' she said after a while, snuffling into his handkerchief.

Jesus, he thought. These uptight middle-class English women. They were a pain in the ass. In fact there wasn't much to choose between them and the strung-up New England matrons back home in the States. He recalled holidays spent at his aunt's house in Boston, where the stiffest of upper lips had been the order of the day. His aunt had liked everything to be icy cool and correct on the surface, but he had sensed cauldrons of seething emotions boiling away underneath, ready to erupt at any moment.

Jocasta Shand struck him as a pleasant enough woman, and she was certainly stunningly attractive, with that fantastic auburn hair and those huge, speaking eyes. And what a figure! But the downside, at least in his opinion, was that she was as tense and taut as a finely tuned Stradivarius violin.

Little Minette was a darling sweet cuddly angel in comparison.

'She thinks I've been carrying on like a little tart,' Minette confessed, still sniffling.

'Christ! You didn't tell her about giving me your all on Lenin's plinth?'

Minette looked up, her eyes swimmy with a mingling of laughter and regret. 'Yes, I did. Oh, Greg, I'm sorry. I should have kept my mouth shut. But she's been so good to me . . . Are you very angry?'

'No. Not about that. Why should I be? Why the hell shouldn't she know? It's her making you feel guilty that makes me angry.'

'She just sees things in a different way from us. She's had a tough time. Don't think badly of her.'

Greg reckoned that it was time Minette made a bid for a taste of freedom – took a break from her controlling parents and her over-anxious travel companion. With leisurely curiosity he speculated on Jocasta Shand's possible plans for the immediate future.

'Come with me to Venice,' he demanded, gently pinching the skin beneath Minette's chin.

She looked up at him, her eyes pink and puffy, her brows frowning and puzzled. 'Venice! Gosh, how marvellous. What for?'

'So we can have all the time in the world to get to know each other a whole lot better. And because it's the place I happen to be going next,' he added, with a crinkly smile.

'What kind of knowing? The carnal sort?' Minette asked, looking suddenly mischievous and decidedly happier.

'Sure. And we might get round to deeper things as well.' He stroked her cheek very tenderly, brushing the skin with feather-light fingers as though he were smoothing fragments of earth from a long-buried Grecian urn. 'More cerebral,' he whispered seductively.

'I want to know every inch of you,' she sighed. 'Every centimetre of flesh and bone, every tiny nerve-cell in your lovely knobbly skull.' She put her fingers in his springy hair and massaged the skin covering the hard helmet of bone.

'Great,' said Greg. 'It's high time someone was able to confirm I'm in possession of a brain.'

'Venice,' Minette mused thoughtfully. 'You and me. Jo won't like that at all.'

'Jo's not your keeper, and you're not a pet monkey,' Greg observed coolly. It was gradually becoming clear to him what had prompted Minette to confess her supposed sins to Jo. It was obvious, really: Jo must have shared a similar sort of confession with her. In other words, Jo must have slept with Max, for God's sake! Oh, boy!

'You're a little diamond,' he told Minette softly, marvelling at her loyalty. He remembered Minette sprawled on the stone plinth that morning, the way

156

she had so softly yielded to his touch, her tiny split-second yelp of pain as he had driven himself deep inside.

And suddenly it was imperative to take on the job of making her happy.

CHAPTER 12

Max looked down at the drowsy Jocasta as she lay in his bed, her arms flung up above her head, her beautiful features serene, her breathing rhythmic and peaceful.

She looked like a woman deeply satisfied, and that gave him some shred of comfort, acted as some sort of antidote to his growing sense of uncertainty and conflict – neither of which were emotions he was familiar with.

He wandered across to the window and looked down into the street, idly observing the figures walking along the broad pavement. One of them stood out from all the others, capturing instant attention.

A girl of around eighteen, small and slender, her walk cat-like and delicate, full of spring and verve. She wore faded blue jeans which moulded to her narrow hips like a pair of suede gloves. Her blonde hair shone like satin, and as she raised a thin golden-brown arm to push aside a strand which had fallen across her eyes the silver of her bracelet flashed in the light.

Minette. She seemed to Max an icon of glowing youth; all laughter and jokiness, totally free from responsibilities, simply delighting in the world of the senses like any other young creature in the animal kingdom.

Minette reminded him of himself in former years, and the thought made him sigh. Today, looking at the slumbering Jocasta, and feeling his heart twist with a medley of complex emotions, youth suddenly seemed a long way away.

He went back to the bed and knelt down. Reaching forward, he placed his lips against the pulse of life which beat in the skin of Jocasta's white temple. 'Wake up, darling!' he murmured, shaking her shoulder tenderly. 'I think we might soon have a visitor.'

Jocasta's eyes snapped open. She came back instantly to full consciousness. 'Minette?'

'She's just arriving back at the hotel.'

Jocasta's features, which only moment before had been so blissfully relaxed, now tightened into an anxious frown. She pushed back the feather duvet and rose from the bed with one graceful movement, presenting Max with the magnificent spectacle of her naked body.

Looking at the full, firm globes of her buttocks, and the Junoesque curves of her marvellous breasts, he felt desire stir once again between his thighs.

He stepped in front of her, stopping her hurried progress towards her clothes, which lay in a tangled clump on the floor. He passed the open palm of one hand beneath the curve of each of her breasts, squeezing the nipples very gently with his long fingers so that she caught her breath.

'Don't leave me,' he said. It was a command not a request.

She stared at him, panic-stricken like a captured doe. 'I have to go and talk to Minette.'

'I know, I know. Minette! Oh, God!' he murmured. His blue eyes flashed with irritated frustration. 'I wasn't talking about leaving this minute. It was your more extended plans that were bothering me. I assume you're planning to pack up and whisk her out of Prague pronto? Away from Greg's evil clutches?'

She opened her eyes wide, and her lips too dropped open in amazement. 'How did you guess?'

'Oh, for heaven's sake, Jo, it hardly took the intellect of an Einstein to work that one out.' His eyes were crinkled in sardonic amusement, and his words were not spoken in anger, but Jocasta heard the tension behind them. Something steely that warned her not to play games with him.

She looked to the left and right of him, as though he were an immovable object. She tried to walk forward, but he held her back. 'Max!' With the protest came a sharp awareness of her nakedness and a flush rose into her face. 'Let me get past. Let me get dressed.' She stared up at him, pleading. 'Please, Max.'

'I'm sorry.' He stood aside, raking his hair with his fingers as he watched her swiftly slither into her clothes. He wanted to reach out and capture her. Keep her with him until Minette had found some salvation of her own and let Jocasta off the hook. Once Minette was out of the way he was sure that he and Jocasta could begin to build something together. Something very precious and permanent. And that he would find some way out of the hole he had dug for himself and seemed to be sinking into ever deeper.

If she were to go off with Minette now, not only would he be bereft, he would be wild with foreboding,

160

mad with anxiety. Because if she should stumble across any damning hints, hard evidence, even, without his being there to try to explain, he doubted that he would ever see her again.

But you couldn't hold people back against their will. It was neither right nor possible.

'I won't do anything hasty,' she promised, turning towards him as she fumblingly tried to button her shirt.

'Just as long as I know what's going on,' he told her, prising her fingers from the buttons and doing them up himself. 'Yes?'

She nodded, and then she wound her arms round him tightly. 'Max, darling, I know you think I've got a loose screw where Minette's concerned, but . . .'

'OK. I know, I know. You have this compulsion to take charge of her welfare. Christ! If I'd ever thought I'd be crazy about a woman who had a wayward niece shackled to her – ball and chain!'

Jo smiled. 'That's what it sometimes feels like.'

They held each other for a few moments, their breath mingling, warm and intimate.

'I won't leave Prague without letting you know where we're going,' she told him with deep tenderness. The words were meant to reassure him, but they simply made his heart sink further.

So she really meant to go. And not with him.

'She's my only brother's only child,' Jocasta added, her voice aching with her need to be listened to and understood. 'I really do love her very much. And him too. They're all I have.'

The words seemed to throb and reverberate in the silence that followed.

'No,' said Max. 'Now you have me.' He wanted to say: Trust me, but the words stuck in his throat.

She cupped her hands around his face and kissed his lips. Then, sliding herself from his arms, she walked quickly to the door.

Max listened to her footsteps in the corridor beyond. He sat down heavily on the edge of the bed and let his head drop down onto his clenched hands.

Minette had gone straight up to her own room. By the time Jocasta arrived she had already routed the wardrobe and all the drawers, thrown her stuff onto the bed and was now furiously flinging it into a variety of holdalls.

Jocasta watched her with growing apprehension.

Minette turned round. 'Hi,' she said with brittle politeness.

Jocasta felt utterly helpless, realizing that this frantic packing exercise had nothing to do with her own little scheme for spiriting Minette out of Prague and on to some unknown destination where Greg wouldn't be able to find her.

'Won't you talk to me?' she wondered hesitantly, having the intuitive feeling that Minette's mood was as dangerous as a bag of dry gunpowder.

'No.'

'Why not?'

'Because you'll try to persuade me to do something I don't want to do. And I'm sick of that.'

'You're afraid I'll succeed in persuading you?' A tiny spark of hope leapt up.

'No.' Minette swung round, eyes blazing. 'No, Jo. Don't flatter yourself. That's all in the past.'

A hand of ice clutched at Jocasta's innards. 'Where are you going?' She tried to sound calm.

'Venice.'

'Venice!'

'It's a city with canals in the north of Italy.'

Jocasta stared at her, wincing at the hurt of the sarcasm. 'You must be very, very angry with me,' she said at last.

'Damn right,' said Minette, tears springing up into her eyes. 'You made me feel like a little slag.'

'Oh, Minette.'

Minette clutched at her blonde fringe. 'Oh, for God's sake, Jo. Turn the heat down.'

'You're going to Venice with Greg?'

'That's right.'

'Oh, dear God!'

'Don't get upset. It could be worse. I could have sold myself into the white slave trade.'

Jocasta rubbed her hand over her eyes and down across her chin. 'Don't go, Minette,' she begged on a rush of desperate impulse. 'I'm only asking you that because I want to prevent you from making a terrible mistake.'

Minette's eyes glowed like burning coals. 'No, you're only asking me because you can't bear to think of displeasing your saintly brother, Miles. My father. The man with the platinum brain and the heart of ice. It's *him* you're always worrying about, not me.'

'That's not true!'

'Isn't it? Give yourself time to think, Jo. What's bothering you most? Protecting my virtue – which is lost already – or making the confessional phone call to Dad?'

163

Jocasta sank down onto the bed, which was now empty of most of the clothes and toiletries that had been scattered on it a few minutes before.

Minette started zipping up her luggage with swift, fierce movements. She delved into her shoulder bag, checking the whereabouts of her passport.

'You've got to be practical,' Jo gulped, suddenly reminded of the nuts and bolts of travelling. 'How will you manage for money? Miles won't send you any more. Not to Venice.' She paused. 'Look . . .' Biting her lip, she opened her bag, searching out her travellers' cheques.

Minette smiled. She pushed away Jocasta's hand and the offered cheques. She heaved her bags to the doorway.

'There's no need to bother about money,' she said, kicking open the door with her toe. 'Greg's loaded.'

Returning quickly to her own suite, Jocasta grabbed the phone and dialled the number of the Penthouse Suite.

'She's gone,' she exclaimed to Max, who'd answered instantly. 'Left for Venice. With Greg.'

'Yes, I've heard. Greg's just called me.' There was a short pause. 'Do you want to be on your own for a while?' he asked tactfully.

'No. That's the last thing I want.'

'I'll come down right now.'

She almost fell into his arms. 'Oh, God, Max,' she groaned. 'This is a nightmare.' She closed her eyes and breathed deeply. 'And now I'll have to call Miles and tell him what's happened.'

He watched her. A silent but compassionate presence.

'I'll do it now. I need to get it over with,' she decided. She grasped at Max's arm. 'And I want you to be here with me!'

'Are you sure?'

She nodded. 'Sit there,' she said, gesturing to a chair opposite the table on which the phone stood. 'Where I can see you and get some moral support.'

She activated the buttons to dial directly to England and sat waiting for the connection. Her innards twisted with nausea, but with a great effort of will she managed to keep her hands commendably steady.

Max was watching her. Connecting with his eyes, she smiled, made a wry grimace.

And then she heard Ginny answering the phone, her high-pitched girlish voice tinged with faint alarm. Ginny always sounded like that; she was a nervous, gazelle-like woman who you felt would be off at a bound if you did anything unexpected to startle or alarm her.

'Hello, Ginny,' Jocasta said, trying to sound buoyant and reassuring. 'It's Jo. How are you?'

'Jo! How lovely. Oh, I'm so pleased to hear from you. I got a sweet card from Minette this morning. She sounded to be having a wonderful time. You are *good* to her. I'm . . . we're so grateful.' Ginny's enthusiasm resounded in Jocasta's ears, making the task ahead seem even more horrendously difficult than she had already anticipated.

'Yes, well – we've had some good times.' She stopped, swallowed. 'Ginny, is Miles there?'

'No, he's giving a research paper in Oxford. He won't be back until tomorrow. Did you want to me to give him a message?' Ginny spoke with her habitual obliging politeness.

165

Jo's mind darted about in panic. It was a kind of unwritten law in the family that Ginny was never to be burdened with problems and difficulties. Ginny was somehow too delicate, in need of sheltering from the harsh realities of life because she could not deal with them. At least that was the message Miles had always conveyed.

But Ginny was Minette's mother, thought Jocasta. And she had every right to know about what had happened. Every right to know first, even before Miles did. Every right to make a decision as to what should happen next.

She realized, with a warm rush of shame, that in the past she had unquestioningly gone along with Miles's wish to protect Ginny and shield her, not only from the grittiness of life's ups and downs but from her own daughter.

'No, Ginny. It's all right. There's no need for me to leave a message for Miles. I can say what I have to say to you.' She breathed in deeply. She looked across to Max, and his steady gaze instantly calmed her.

'This is about Minette,' she continued carefully, 'but don't be alarmed. She's perfectly safe and well – that's the first thing I need to say to you.'

'Oh, dear,' Ginny said faintly, and Jocasta could picture her, alone in her and Miles's elegant country house, her face tense with foreboding, her thin hands clasping the phone so her knuckles shone white.

'She's met someone she's taken a liking to, and . . . they've gone off together to Venice for a few days.' Jocasta looked across to Max again. His lips curved into a slow smile of speculation and amusement. He raised his eyebrows, as though to say: Good start.

'A man?' asked Ginny, sounding ominously calm.

'Yes. His name's Greg Shields. He's a film director . . .'

'Oh, he'll have money, then. They won't be sleeping in fields and all that kind of thing?'

'Well, no.'

'Good. Things are so dangerous now if you're out on the road and living rough. When I was Minette's age I went all round southern France doing that. But things seemed to be different then.'

Jocasta found herself amazed at the way this conversation was turning out. 'I'm sure she'll be quite safe,' she agreed. 'He's a very pleasant and genuine person. He'll look after her.'

Ginny did not speak. There was just a faint crackle on the line. Jocasta wondered if they were still connected.

'I don't know if I ever told you,' Ginny said suddenly, her voice seeming to grow stronger by the minute, 'but when Minette was sixteen she used to swear that she wasn't going to sleep around at parties like her friends did.'

'Did she?' Jocasta murmured helplessly, silently appealing to Max and shaking her head in bewilderment.

'She said that she was going to keep her virginity until she was at least eighteen, and that when she lost it the man concerned would be really special.'

'I see. And how did you react to that, Ginny?'

'I thought it was pretty sensible, really. Providing she took all the right precautions. Of course I never breathed a word of it to Miles.'

'No. Of course not.' Unthinkable. 'Look, Ginny, I can't tell you how sorry I am about all this. I . . .'

167

'It's not your fault, Jo,' Ginny said softly, and Jocasta could hear a tremor of emotion creep into her voice. 'Ultimately it's Miles's and my fault. Because of all the things that happened in the past. I did warn him.'

'How will you tell him?'

'I'll simply tell him what you told me. I knew something like this would happen. I've known for years. But at least she's not in danger, and we know who she's with.'

'She still seems such a child,' Jocasta ventured worriedly, astounded at Ginny's apparent calm.

'In some ways. But she's eighteen. We have to give her some freedom now.'

'Do you want me to phone back tomorrow and speak to Miles?'

'Not unless you've any further news. I'll cope with Miles, Jo. I have done for years, you know!'

Jocasta paused. 'I'm sorry, Ginny,' she said finally. And she was not talking about Minette now.

She heard a faint responding murmur. And then there was a little click, and just the whine of the dialling tone.

'Well?' Max prompted gently.

'That was Ginny, my brother's wife. She said just about all the things I would never have expected and none of the things I would have.' She sighed, expressing a complex blend of bemusement and relief. 'How easy it is to misjudge people,' she added, musingly. 'To get things badly wrong.' She looked towards Max, her gaze troubled and penetrating. 'Does everyone do it? Or is it just me?'

'A universal trait,' he said crisply. 'So, how do you feel now?

168

'Free,' she said, suddenly realizing. 'Let off the hook.' A slow smile lit her face, like dawn sunshine creeping over a shaded hillside. 'And very hungry.'

'Ahh,' breathed Max. 'Dinner, then?'

'That will do for starters,' she told him, and her foxy smile sent his pulses sprinting like a hare sprung from a trap.

CHAPTER 13

On the flight from Prague to Paris, Jocasta promised herself that during the two precious days and nights she and Max were to spend alone together they would hold nothing back from each other about any of the darker things that had happened in their pasts, no matter how uncomfortable those would be to reveal. And after that they would be free to share their hopes for the future.

Because he had come so suddenly into her life, she sometimes felt – especially at those times when he was not there in the flesh – that he must be an invention of her imagination, not a real man at all.

But she knew that whatever faint doubts she had occasionally harboured about him he was gradually giving her back her belief that she could truly love again. He was showing her that love was a capacity, an energy, something you drew from within yourself and gave outwards.

She had felt, after the break with Alexander, that to love another man would be a betrayal of what she had felt for him. Any other love must surely be insincere, and false in some way. But as she tentatively allowed herself to trust Max she knew without a doubt that the pain about Alexander was steadily decreasing and fading. Love was not an exclusive club destined only for the charismatic Alexander, who had turned out to be a sham.

And, most important of all, she was keenly aware that sex with Max was of a kind she had never experienced before. It was not simply the sheer, stunning physicality of it – which made memories of Alexander's lovemaking pale into a memory as faded as an old black and white snapshot – it was the wonderful intimacy he shared with her when they were at their closest, their limbs entwined as they soared up to the heights of erotic passion. It was then that his wry remarks, the cool lift of his eyebrows, his teasing, mocking glances thrilled her beyond belief.

She glanced at him now, as he sat beside her in the aircraft, his head tilted back, his eyes half closed. Her heart contracted. He was a man of great finesse, a man of hidden depths cloaked under a veneer of easygoing charm. And she knew that she was falling desperately in love.

He took her to a hotel close to the Champs-Elysées. It was in the grand tradition, furnished and decorated in a style reminiscent of an eighteenth-century château.

Patiently, and in excellent French, Max eventually persuaded one of the equally grand and haughty reception staff to give him a suite on the first floor.

Their luggage was gathered up, sent on ahead of them on a gilded trolley pushed by a pageboy dressed in satin knee breeches. He seemed like an refugee from an aristocratic age of privilege long past.

Jocasta smiled, entertained. 'This really is pushing the boat out,' she commented, gazing around her.

'I want to,' said Max. 'You deserve the very best. And you see, Jo, there was a time when I could only afford to stand on the outer steps and look longingly into a place like this. I shall never forget what that felt like.'

Jocasta observed the hotel foyer's gilded opulence, spiced with dark red velvet and tasselled midnight-blue silk. 'And this feels much nicer? Being on the inside? One of lucky ones?'

He laughed. 'Most decidedly,' he said, his lips curving into a slow smile of self-mockery.

When they were at last alone, their luggage stacked neatly beside the vast Louis Quinze wardrobes, Max startled her by scooping her into his arms and crushing her fiercely against his chest. He kissed her with a violence that evinced a small yelp from her throat even as his tongue linked with hers, as his teeth nipped the soft flesh of her lower lip.

'Now!' he breathed. 'Now!'

Carrying her to the vast bedroom, he laid her gently on the bed and began to peel off her clothes as though they were on fire and about to burn her. Very soon she was wearing only her champagne lace bra and her flimsy panties. Desire was seething within her, filling up every vein in her body so that she was swollen and pulsing with sexual heat.

'You have such wonderful nipples,' he breathed, pushing aside her bra and bending to take one between his lips. He began to suck her, his movements very gentle now, slow and measured, as though he had placed some huge restraining device on himself and snapped the lock shut.

172

When he had thoroughly teased one nipple, awakening ripples of tiny flames which shot through her veins, he started on the other. Jocasta felt herself melting, powerless to do anything but lie back and let him arouse a storm of passion which she knew would shake her to her very bones.

She heard his low velvet growls of wanting as his lips moved downwards, blazing a trail of heat over her stomach and the crown of auburn hair between her legs.

Groaning, she spread herself wide for him. 'Max,' she gasped, clutching at him, hauling his shirt from his jeans and thrusting her hands around his back, grasping at him wildly and tearing his flesh with her nails.

She felt him thrust into her, filling her up, pushing aside every other sensation except him and his hard, punishing thrusts.

And then he had pulled out of her, and she had the sudden swooning sensation of his tongue flicking between the folds of her tender flesh, finding the hard, swollen bud. At the same time his long fingers began to explore the purple cave deep within.

Her body and mind felt on the point of explosion. He was there in every part of her. Max lying between her legs. Max licking her, flicking his tongue like a velvet lash. Max fingering her, taking possession of the most secret and intimate places which she now vowed would be kept only for him for evermore.

She heard herself let out a long, low, animal cry. And then he was inside her again, thrusting like a man crazed with desire. The shower of sensation that followed left her dazed and gasping and spent.

* * *

173

Later, dressed in their elegant, formal evening clothes, as they faced each other across a snowy white tablecloth laid out with an arsenal of gleaming cutlery, they smiled in conspiratorial memory of the primitive animal fury they had shared together earlier, the intense, hot pleasure of total abandonment which seemed to have bound them together for eternity.

Jocasta spread her white hands out on the table, considering how she would begin the story she had planned to tell him. Looking down, she noticed a tiny red speck under one of her white-rimmed nails.

'Oh, Max!' she exclaimed, her eyes wide with alarm. 'I didn't draw blood, did I?' She recalled the desperate grasping at him, the dark, pulsing hunger that could hardly wait to be satisfied.

He moved his shoulders within his shirt, his eyes glinting. 'I told you before you were a tigress!'

She grimaced.

'Don't waste any time worrying about it. I'm only too pleased to bear the scars of your regard for me,' he murmured drily.

'In days gone by you would have been a brave knight and true,' she observed.

His smile was ironic and sceptical. 'I suppose one can always dream!'

Jocasta pushed away her empty plate and took a long drink of wine. 'I used to be the lover of Alexander Rivers,' she told Max in a matter-of-fact voice. 'The controversial politician. He was shadow Foreign Secretary when I knew him. Now he's the party leader. And after the election he'll most probably be Prime Minister.'

She lowered the glass to the table and stroked its slender stem with two slow, rhythmic fingers.

She waited for a few reflective moments. When she looked up Max was watching her, his face calm, empty of any hasty or emotion-charged response. She was glad of that. She knew that she must tell Max about Alexander. All that was important to tell, that was. And she wanted the telling to be civilized. As cool and discriminating and detached as she now knew Alexander himself to be.

She spoke calmly at first. 'Of course I was aware that he had had a number of casual affairs before. He made no secret of it. I had the impression that he was trying to tell me that he had never been truly attached to anyone before. I was a fool, you see, Max. I was like all the others – deluding myself that I was different, that I was special, and this time he was serious. I truly believed he was in love, that he wanted commitment, permanence, marriage. I thought he wanted the same things I wanted. I thought I *understood* him! Oh, God, Max, I was so blind, so naïve. When it was all over, I felt so diminished and ashamed.'

Jocasta had never spoken with such openness to anyone before. She had kept her anguish to herself, walled it up in a distant part of her mind where it would be safe from curious speculators.

Max said nothing, and she felt encouraged to go further. She told him about the riding accident, those first few days in the clinic when she had been terrified and alone. She told him about Dr Zanek, the one person who had been there to give her hope for the future.

'At first I thought it was Alexander's shock about what had happened in the accident and the injuries I had suffered which marked the beginning of the end. I thought he was swamped with guilt because he had persuaded me to ride a horse which was obviously unreliable to the point of being dangerous. But when I look back I can see that the real end of his love for me came later.'

Now things became difficult. She looked across at Max and saw that his face was full of compassion. 'I got pregnant, you see. I wasn't expecting it, yet I was over the moon. But as soon as I told Alex I knew that he didn't share my joy. Oh, he said all the right things, and bought me flowers and champagne and so on – Alex is unsurpassed when it comes to creating the right image – but afterwards our lovemaking changed. I sensed that he no longer found me as desirable. Carrying a child seemed to have spoiled me for him in some way. He used to tease me about the way my figure would change. He'd make remarks about how I'd make a marvellous earth mother, with my superb child-bearing hips and my "Jersey cow tits".' Her eyelids fluttered with remembered pain.

She jerked her head up and stared hard at Max. 'Alex was a wicked, heartless bastard! Still is. And yet, funnily enough, he seems to be one of the most popular politicians around. Poor, foolish, driven man.'

Max gave a long sigh. As she had been speaking he had been painfully aware that he already knew this story. A story that had first been told to him as a brief and wicked fable – with the villainess painted in the blackest of colours. A story where certain facts coincided but the viewpoints of the tellers were as different as night from day.

'As far as Alex was concerned, the prospect of a child meant either marrying me – which was obviously not on his agenda – or my having an abortion. A mistress with an illegitimate baby is a dangerous loose cannon for an ambitious politician.' She gave a wry smile. 'Not that he had anything to fear from me on that score. I would have had my baby and gone away to live my own life with my child. But Alex could never believe that. He was as crass in his misjudgement of me as I was in mine of him.'

Max stood up abruptly. 'Jo, can we get out of here? It's oppressively hot. Let's take a walk along the river.'

She jumped up, concerned. He looked sick and drawn. Haggard. 'Are you ill, darling? Have you eaten something that's upset you?'

'No, no. Just let's get some fresh air.'

'I'll need a coat,' she said, touching her shoulders which were bare in a dark green silk shift dress.

'Yes. OK.'

'You go outside and get some air,' she told him. 'I won't be a minute.'

'No, I'll come up with you.'

'I'm sure I'll be perfectly safe in the lift here,' she smiled.

'I'm coming with you,' he said, and there was a sharpness in his tone which warned her not to argue.

Whilst Jocasta rummaged in her luggage to find a suitable coat Max went through into the bathroom. She heard water gushing from the taps.

She found a light apricot wool jacket and slung it over her shoulders. Idly, as she waited, she turned on the TV standing in the corner of the room, flicking casually through the channels as the picture swam into colourful life to fill the huge screen.

Eventually she came across a late-night current affairs programme from the UK. They were running a feature on the forthcoming election, starting with a profile of Alexander Rivers, the Leader of the Opposition.

Fascinated, Jocasta watched as an image of Alexander came onto the screen, entirely dominating it. He was on his election tour, visiting far-flung parts of the country and then various parts of London. He was smiling and relaxed, drinking in the public admiration, shrugging aside his security staff and reaching out to shake a sea of outstretched hands.

He radiated the confidence that comes from good breeding, good looks, a quick brain and an unswerving belief in one's own self-worth and importance. She noticed that he was heavier than he had been a year ago. The weight quite suited him, she decided, adding to his authority – a weight that was as much psychological as physical.

'Oh, yes, Alexander,' she murmured to herself, 'you're really forging ahead now.' But the magic that had previously drawn her to him was now a force which was almost repellent. She felt that she would recoil from him if she were to meet him again in the flesh.

He turned to face the camera and began to speak. His words flowed out in a stream of stylish eloquence. She recalled how his effortless fluency had once enchanted her.

Max came up behind her. He stood beside her, his arm brushing lightly against hers.

178

'Are you all right, darling?' she asked tenderly, turning towards him and lifting her hand to stroke his face.

'Yes, fine. Can we go out now?' he asked impatiently, his eyes narrowing as he glanced at the screen.

'Yes, of course. But just one moment! Look, they're doing a feature on Alexander. I'll be very interested to hear what novel angle he's going to put forward to dazzle his adoring public.'

Alexander went on speaking. His theme was one of opportunity for all, a society where each and every person could have the freedom to realize their most deeply held ambitions. It was stirring stuff.

Jocasta watched, more interested in her own reactions than Alexander's rousing words, the gist of which she had heard on many previous occasions.

She glanced at Max and saw that he was standing as still as carved marble. His eyes were fixed on the screen as though they had been dragged there by invisible wires.

Sensing a faint stab of vague alarm, she looked back at the screen. Alexander's face had disappeared now, to be replaced by a short film sequence which examined his background and experience. Then there was some footage of the people involved in working with him in the run-up to the election. Jocasta watched with fascinated curiosity, her hand seeking Max's, her fingers linking with his.

There were shots of Alexander outside one of London's big stockbroker firms, surrounded by admiring businessmen and also a few women, dressed soberly in grey and black, mirror images of the powerful men who were their colleagues. Idly, Jocasta wondered if Alex had slept with any of them. It was of no concern to her any more.

She felt her attention veer back to Max. It was hard to remain absorbed in the stiff, sober-suited men on the screen when a marvellous flesh-and-blood lover was standing so near to her, the flesh of their hands joined together, the warmth of his body warming hers.

Looking casually back at the screen, she registered a number of the serious-looking men moving away, preparing to disappear into sleek limousines. Her gaze was drawn to one of them in particular. A tall man with finely tooled features and a mane of glistening fair hair. He had not followed the others but had stayed behind and was talking earnestly with Alexander. His hand reached up to rake through the thick locks and push one back from his forehead.

That gesture! Already it was so familiar, locked into her brain, sealed into her emotions. That gesture belonged to one man and one alone.

Her hand recoiled from its link with Max as though his flesh were burning, or contaminated with some dreadful contagious disease.

She let out a low moan of horror and felt herself stagger dizzily as she sprang away from him. She caught her ankle on the leg of the low table beside her and almost fell to the floor. The pain of the impact was sharp, but nothing in comparison to the turmoil in her mind. Grasping the edge of the table, she steadied herself, her knuckles clenched and white.

'That's you!' she said, her voice a hoarse croak, barely more than a whisper. 'That's you. In London. With Alexander. You *know* him!'

It wasn't yet possible for her to appreciate all that meant. But she knew in her heart and in the very bones and soul of her that it was bad – more terrible than anything she had ever dreamed of.

CHAPTER 14

Everything in the room around Jocasta seemed to freeze.

She sensed Max moving towards her, reaching out to her. 'Jocasta!'

She flung out her arms in a gesture of fierce rejection and self-defence. 'No! Don't come near me,' she screamed at him, her exclamation fading to something between a cry and a moan.

She sank down onto her knees beside the table, wrapping her arms tightly around her breasts and rocking herself to and fro. Low animal sounds of pain sounded in her throat and she was powerless to curb them.

She felt Max's presence behind her, sensed his hesitation in approaching nearer, even though his arms were still held out towards her.

Her breath was coming heavily, pushing against the wall of her chest. Hating the idea that he would be able to hear each rasping breath and guess at all of her pain and confusion, she tried desperately to control her emotions.

She forced herself to think, willed her brain to make connections, to construct some logical explanation for what she had just seen. At first it was impossible, like trying to solve a mathematical equation after drinking too much champagne. She shook her head like a confused sleepwalker trying to jolt herself into waking. But gradually a pattern began to emerge, one which she knew was based on reason, not wild supposition.

'You *know* Alexander,' she repeated slowly. 'You're a friend of his. An associate.' She sat up, unwound her arms, and confronted Max with a challenging stare.

He closed his eyes, his forehead creased into lines of distress which matched hers.

'You're a member of Alexander's charmed circle,' she said through her bewilderment. 'You're one of the satellites that dances around his sun.'

He gave a low groan. 'Jo! Let me explain.'

She waved an angry hand, not wanting to hear. 'No, don't speak! You're a *friend* of Alexander. And yet all the time I was talking about him at dinner you never gave so much as a flicker of recognition.'

'I couldn't stop you, Jo,' he broke in harshly. 'You had a lot to get out of your system. You needed to do that. It would have been wrong for me to stop you . . .'

She gave a derisory laugh. 'Don't try to whitewash your actions with a pretence at consideration for my feelings.' She glared at him as he stood, silent and stricken, looking down at her. An idol with feet of clay. A Judas decked out as a handsome, shining god of love.

Fury and hate for Max welled up inside her. Juices poured into her mouth and for a moment she thought she would be physically sick.

'You never gave the faintest clue that you knew him,' she continued relentlessly, 'because you didn't ever want me to know.'

She had a feeling of being a fox cornered by baying hounds. Realization was beginning to seep into the active parts of her brain, growing and swelling into a full and terrible understanding of the way she had been hounded and pursued.

A moment before she had been weak and shaking, now she stiffened as though a steel rod had been thrust into her. The cloudy impressions which had been drifting in her imagination began to break up and clear, arranging themselves into photographic sharpness and brilliance. She tilted her head back and closed her eyes in grief. 'He sent you. It was a cold and calculating plan. Alexander sent you to me – didn't he?'

Max's lips were tight, and his voice was barely audible as he admitted, 'Yes.'

'You're not going to make some pathetic attempt to deny it?' Her eyes glittered.

'No.'

'Good. I think if you had I would have killed you.' She was panting as though she had just collapsed after running for miles. 'Although, on the other hand, I'm not sure that this frank confession doesn't make me even sicker. How can you stand there coolly admitting to such disgusting and wicked trickery?' Suddenly she sprang up, the unspeakable reality hitting her with new force. She moved towards him, her arms raised, blazing fury propelling her.

He caught her flailing arms in one hand, wrenched them behind her back and with his other arm pulled her firmly against him.

In disobedience to every ounce of her rational senses, Jocasta felt a shaft of desire pass through her body with a shimmering white heat. 'Dear God!' she moaned softly.

She felt his chest heave against hers. She heard his voice, pleading. 'Jocasta . . .'

'No!' she yelled. 'Don't! Don't say or do anything to try to make things better.' She struggled to free her hands, but he had her held so tightly she was powerless. She jerked her head up. 'Do you know what I want?' she whispered with venom. 'I want you to vanish from my life. I want you to stop existing in my head and in my heart. I want to erase every shred of you from the images in my brain, for you to disappear from my memory for ever. But you won't, will you? You'll stay there. On and on, torturing me. Oh, God, Max, I can't tell you how I'm going to hate you for that.'

He let go of her hands. He grasped her shoulders and shook them hard. 'Let me speak,' he demanded, his face hard. 'Let me explain. You don't know yet what sin I've committed.'

'There's nothing to explain Max. What you've admitted to so far is quite damning enough. Don't forget that you're facing the adoring and then discarded mistress of a man crazy for fame and money and power. I've been deceived and manipulated before. So give up any idea of trying to sweet-talk me into believing that anything even approaching that kind of treachery could ever be understandable or forgivable.'

The glance from her eyes was like a lash. She could feel a harsh twist of derisive contempt distorting her features, reflecting the cruel ugliness she felt internally.

Max looked down at the floor. A lock of hair fell over his eyes, but he made no move to push it back. His strong, broad shoulders drooped with despair.

A smile slowly curved the edges of Jocasta's tense mouth. She had the sudden understanding that there was a given amount of power in the atmosphere, just so much as could be distributed between them. And as the power ebbed from him so it seemed to flow into her. Minutes ago she had been weak and trembling, now she was newly energized. Power was pulsing inside her, bitter anger and hate – and a terrifying lust for retribution.

Sweet, sweet revenge, she told herself, knowing that was the only route she could take to escape from this snake-pit of hurting. She stepped back from him, facing him like an omnipotent and merciless queen about to bestow a reprimand on a pleading subject.

It just remained to discover the exact nature of the crime and the severity of the punishment.

'What did he send you to do?' she enquired with icy disdain. 'After you'd got me into bed, that is? What was the grand strategy, the clever supporting tactic? Alexander was always a lover of devious plans. Maybe this one had a code-name, like those fanciful operations in spy stories. Seduction Jocasta. Or maybe something more vulgar. Strip Jo Naked. That's a good one.' Her voice was like a tongue of flame, licking around his exposed flesh.

He flinched. But said nothing, which she found utterly damning.

'You must have thought I was such a fool to grab at the sweet, baited line of charm you threw out to me. And then you just reeled me in, didn't you?' she reflected. 'In fact you were so clever you engineered things so you didn't have to do much at all. I did it all for you. God, what a pathetic, gullible creature I must have been.' Her trust was rapidly deserting her. She felt like a dog whose trusted master had suddenly lost his senses and savagely beaten it.

'Jocasta, for Christ's sake, just listen. You must listen.' His eyes flared although his face was white and haggard.

His vulnerability acted as a spur to her new-found strength. She was the whipped dog who would turn. 'You moved so gently and quietly into my life,' she mused with dangerous calm. 'Suddenly you were just there. You even had the innocent help of Minette. What a gift! You were able to move in close to me with no problem at all. She spotted you and picked you out from the crowd at a glance. You're so damned charismatic, aren't you? Women just flow towards you like little iron filings drawn to a magnet.'

She moved close to him and touched the lapel of his jacket. 'A wolf in sheep's clothing,' she commented. 'A very polished, assured, gentle sort of wolf. So charming and elegant. So witty and laid-back. Oh, yes, you were perfect for gobbling up a silly sheep like me. But then you're an actor, aren't you, Max? You were simply doing your job – acting out a little drama for poor, susceptible Jocasta. And you did it superbly well because you're a very good actor. That's how you've earned the nice little fortune that lets you do your sleeping around in grand hotels like this.'

'I don't sleep around,' he growled, his head jerking up, suddenly on the attack again. 'And now you're going to listen to me for a change.'

She glared at him in defiance. She placed her hands over her ears and then slowly she removed them. She had the impression he would use force to silence her and make her listen if she put up any more resistance. 'Go on, then,' she said with icy disdain. 'Put your case. But I fear it's a pretty hopeless one.'

'You said that you were susceptible and a fool,' he said. 'But I've been far more guilty on both counts.'

'Ah, yes, I'll believe that.'

'I was completely taken in by Alexander. As a politician, as a natural leader, as a man. You see, Jo, I had a tough childhood and youth. I was in care for a while when my parents split up. Everyone gave me the impression that I'd never do anything in the world. I had good looks, a good physique, but no qualifications, none of the useful connections that get people on.

'There was no question of going on to higher education. The best I could hope for was a pedestrian job and marrying a rich woman if I got lucky. One of my advisory care workers actually said that to me. But I proved all the forecasters wrong.

'I had a lucky break on a talent show. And after that when I got offered TV and theatre work I went at it like a madman, and it paid off. I was the typical poor kid made good. I was the boy who'd pulled himself up by his boot straps, who had got on his bike and gone off to find fame and fortune.'

Jocasta listened with careful attention. But even as she took in the details of his story her eyes were wandering hungrily over his lean but strong body in the casual but exclusive clothes, the classically proportioned face with its fine, sensitive features, the thick mane of silky fair hair. She found herself still longing for him, for the touch of his lips and his hands, the taste of his tongue and the smell of his skin.

She was horrified at her own weakness. She forced her face to register blankness in response to what he was telling her.

'I've admired Alexander Rivers from afar for quite some time. But when I went to the party conference last year and heard him in person giving his famous "Riches for All" speech, I was hooked. I had the feeling he was talking just to me. But in fact he was connecting with everyone in the hall. He was so inspirational people all around were actually in tears.'

'Oh, yes,' Jocasta cut in. 'Alex is very good at that. But the high principles he peddles to others have no part in his own life. He's not into hard work and just reward. He wants mega-riches and complete power, and he wants them quick. And, what's more, he prefers others do the hard grind to get it for him.'

'Yes, I see that now. I told you – I was a complete fool.'

'You know that he's paranoid, don't you?' Jocasta flung at him. 'That he believes there are conspiracies on all sides to stop him getting what he wants?'

Max was silent.

'Oh, so you're not ready to go as far as that? You'll find I'm right in time. I just hope the rest of the country does, before he gets his hands on the ultimate power of being Prime Minister.' She paused, folded her arms. 'Well, come on, Max. So far you've told me a sob story about your childhood and given me a little spiel about the way you were sadly taken in by Alexander's magnetism. Now tell me the sordid details.'

He let out a long breath. 'I was introduced to him. We talked. He obviously saw me as a good publicity asset and he invited me to join the team on his election campaign. It seemed such a marvellous opportunity to do something worthwhile – '

'But instead you got landed with something rather tawdry,' she cut in bitterly. 'Don't bother to spell out the details, Max. I'll do it myself. He sent you on a mission with a brief to seduce me, get me hooked on a supply of endless fantastic sex, get me into such a state of infatuation with you that I couldn't think of anything else. Because, as we all know, no woman can resist you. Oh, yes, now I understand!' Her eyes blazed. 'Say something! Have I got it right? Was that the plan he sold you?'

'More or less.'

'God. How I'm going to hate you. I expect he told you I was going to make trouble for him, that I needed to be kept quiet. I could tell my story to the press, couldn't I? I could ruin things for him at such a crucial moment in his career. The headlines would have been terrific.' She paused, thinking. '"Power-hungry Alexander Rivers forced ex-mistress to abort their love-child." That would have been a good one, wouldn't it? His popularity ratings would have been axed at a stroke.'

Max pushed his hand through his hair in the individual gesture that been his downfall in her eyes. 'Jo, there's nothing I can say to make you forgive me. What I did was unforgivable. All I can say is that once I met you Alexander's plans went right out of the window. I could see straight away that what he had told me was a horrible distortion.'

'What *did* he tell you?' she asked curiously. 'Tell me, Max? You owe me that at least.'

'He thought that after your accident you became very . . . anxious.'

'Hardly surprising, since he virtually ditched me the minute it happened. Anxious,' she echoed. 'I suppose the words he actually used were more like "unbalanced, disturbed, crazy". I'll bet he made you think I was a kind of Semtex cocktail of neuroses about to explode.'

'He showed me a letter you wrote to him before you set off on your trip,' Max said wearily. 'It seemed to suggest that you were thinking of taking some action about what had happened earlier in the year.'

'About the abortion?'

'I assumed so.'

'Did you see the letter?'

'Yes. Well, I saw your signature. He showed me that to convince me the letter was genuine. He read parts out to me.'

'So you didn't actually see it?'

'No.'

'I'll tell you the real truth about that letter. I wrote it in the spirit of reassuring him, of trying to end our relationship on a note of adult reasonableness and forgiveness. Of course Alex is the kind of man who, if you tell him that the last thing you are thinking of is judging him harshly and making trouble, immediately concludes just the reverse. I can just imagine his reading out extracts of my pathetically genuine letter to you in such as way as to persuade you to share his own twisted view. It's not too difficult to be taken in by Alexander, Max. After all we've both been there, haven't we?'

His eyes flared with hope.

She put out her hand, as though to ward him off. 'We were both duped. But *I* didn't behave like a low rat and a cunning bastard.'

He rested his head in his hand. 'Jocasta, darling. Please believe me when I say that what happened between us was utterly stripped of any manipulation. As soon as I saw you, I realized my stupidity.'

'You simply omitted to tell me about it.'

'Christ! How could I tell you about it? You'd never have spoken to me again, let alone . . .'

The two of them stared at each other, recalling the nakedness of their passion. Its wild and primitive heat. Suddenly they looked away, the memory overwhelming them. Their eyes passed over chairs and tables and ornaments – anything but each other.

It occurred to Jocasta that even now, at this terrible moment, there was only one man in the world with whom she could contemplate sharing such animal passion. And that was the man standing close to her, the man she was about to put out of her life for ever. A rolling wave of hot fury swept over her as she contemplated this man, Maxwell Swift, who had made her crazy with desire and then shown himself to be a sham and a phoney – someone she must never allow herself to become enslaved by again.

'What now?' he said softly.

She heard the underlying tone of defeat and despair and found herself in danger of relenting in her harsh judgement of him. It wouldn't be difficult to persuade herself that there might be a way to forgive him, so that she could surrender to the dizzy, devilish temptation to feel him in her arms once more. But even as the idea flashed across the surface of her brain she rejected it violently. She must not be taken in again. Twice was surely enough.

'I shall leave,' she decided. 'Go back to England.'

'No. Darling, please, please don't. Please stay.'

Her heart jerked painfully against her ribs. She knew she must go quickly. He could so easily sway her. She mustn't let herself feel anything but contempt for him.

He looked so penitent and wild and desperate that her heart contracted with compassion. But he was nothing more than a cold-blooded trickster. He looked like everything she could ever desire: beautiful, sexy, tender, witty and oh, so warm – but that was just his façade, the actor's mask and cloak, exactly how he had planned to present himself so that she'd had no choice but to capitulate.

'God, Jo!' he exclaimed. 'If you knew how all this is hurting me. The last thing I want you to do is go and leave me. I don't think I can bear to be without you. I've never been in love like this.' His voice was husky with defeat, his wonderful blue eyes dulled with wretchedness.

I must go, she thought in panic. *I must go now before I fall into his charmed trap again.* 'You should have thought of that possibility when you cooked up your tawdry little deal with Alexander,' she told him. 'It's a rough old world, Max. And you seem to have got off lightly. All you've got is your just reward.' She looked at him with cold eyes. 'You know, there were a number of times back in Prague when I thought there was something . . . awry, something not quite fair and square about you.'

193

'What the hell do you mean?'

She searched her mind. And what came to the surface was Minette's puzzled anger about Max's failure to report the brutal attack on Jocasta to the police. Minette, who had been so enthusiastic about Max, had suddenly turned critical and suspicious. And for a time, she, Jocasta had shared her doubts.

Her mind clicked through possibilities, and it didn't take too long to land on what was surely obvious. 'Those girls. That assault. You set it up.' Her legs felt weak beneath her. 'You set it all up to make me vulnerable.' She clutched at her stomach, fearing she was going to be violently sick.

'No!'

'I don't believe you.'

He sprang at her, seizing her arm. 'Look at me, Jo.' He forced her chin up, compelled her eyes meet his. 'Tell me. Dare to tell me now that you don't believe me.'

Tears leapt into her eyes. His fingers were like iron rods. 'He did it,' she said wearily. 'Alex.'

'Yes.'

'You knew nothing about it?'

'Nothing, I swear.'

'I suppose he telephoned you that day and asked if we'd met up? He chatted to you about our plans for the evening?'

'Yes.' He sighed. 'I suppose I was implicated in a way. A kind of unknowing accessory. But he was just using me as a pawn in his game.'

'He must have contacts everywhere,' she said, thinking it over. 'Is he having me followed?'

'Good God, no.' He stared at her. 'Would he do that?'

'Oh, very likely.'

'Christ. I'm going to kill him.' His eyes were cold with fury.

Jocasta turned from him. She looked at her luggage, mainly still unpacked, ready to be moved. She picked up the phone and asked for a reservation to be made on the next flight for the UK. She asked for a taxi.

Max stared at her. She knew he was silently imploring her to give him another chance, to give *herself* a chance to get to know him properly – Max, the real man.

She closed her heart to him. She knew how easily she could be swayed, and her own defencelessness terrified her.

'Don't go!' he said.

She looked coldly at him. 'Don't follow me!'

She saw that his despair had been replaced by an angry and bitter sense of having been misjudged.

'I was wrong in what I did,' he admitted grimly. 'I deserve all your anger. I deserve to bear a heavy burden of guilt. But you have been wrong too, Jo. You've presumed to judge me without giving any real consideration to all the personal factors I've shared with you. Even common criminals get better treatment than that.'

His eyes glinted with dangerous ice-blue lights. He was not pleading now. Far from it.

Jocasta felt the power that streamed from him – the same kind of power that Alexander projected. She remembered the slight jarring sensation she had felt when she first saw Max and understood now that it had

195

been a spark of warning coming up from her unconscious mind. *Beware!* But she had taken no notice.

What draws me to these powerful men who live their lives in the public eye, on the centre stage? she wondered in bewilderment. How is it I've been so blind to their faults?

She heard him begin to speak again. She closed her eyes to try to shut him out. 'I'm leaving,' she said. 'And that will be that. It's finished, Max.'

She thought he might strike her, try to overpower her, take her by force and make her his own. There was a breathless moment of suspense and stillness.

And then there was a sharp knock on the door and the quaintly dressed pageboy came in with his trolley to collect her luggage.

Clasping her coat around her, she followed the rolling wheels of the trolley into the lift, then through the foyer and out into the road where a taxi waited with its engine running.

CHAPTER 15

Minette and Greg flew into Marco Polo Airport just as the setting sun was slanting across the lagoon. Its lingering brilliance tinted the water and the buildings beyond with a deep orange fluorescence.

The airport was packed. Crowds of shouting Italians and tourists of all nationalities flowed around the barriers, pushing and shoving.

'Keep hold of me!' Greg yelled at Minette through the din. He grasped her arm, pulling her close to him and holding on grimly.

'Where you go, I must go too,' she yelled back, grinning. 'Seems like I've no choice. Anyway you seem a good bet – the only sane person around.'

Once out of the concourse, Greg gave directions for their luggage to be loaded into a *motoscafo*, one of the fleet of Venice's motorized waterborne taxis. They settled themselves in the boat, shuffling up to make space for a seemingly endless stream of further passengers.

'I hope we don't sink,' said Minette, peering into the shimmering water, whose rocking waves were striped tangerine and black like a tiger. 'I wouldn't like to end my young days washed up and drowned, not even in the romantic Adriatic.'

As Greg linked his arm around her waist and dropped a kiss on the tip of her nose, the boat puttered off into the shifting waves. Seagulls followed them, screeching, weaving and dipping.

Minette had not seen Venice before. It was one of the places to which her father had never brought her. She had the impression that he thought the floating city had become over-popular, too commercialized and frivolous.

She looked around her transfixed as the boat chugged through the wide lagoon under a fiery bronze sky, passing the buoys and markers and causeways, and then finally – and magically – entering the glittering dark snake of the Grand Canal.

Ancient and elegant stone *palazzi* rose up on either side, their sea walls stained and crumbling from years of battering from the tides.

'Oh, just look in the water!' Minette exclaimed. 'There's a wobbly reflected palace for each real one.' She leaned further out of the boat to catch the full splendour of the eerie green images trembling in the waves.

Greg grabbed onto her more tightly. 'Sit back. You'll have us both overboard.'

'You'll have to be patient with me,' she said sweetly, opening her eyes wide and looking into his with mock innocence. 'This is my first time. Seeing Venice, I mean. I'm liable to get overexcited.'

'Yeah. You're clearly in the mood for a number of "first times",' he drawled, amused. 'I hardly dare think what's coming next.'

'A second time, I hope.' She let her hand dart briefly to his crotch and gave him an affectionate squeeze.

Greg blinked. 'Watch it!' he warned.

She wondered where they were going, if they would end up in a hotel similarly luxurious to the one in Prague, and all of the other places she had stayed with Jo on their brief tour together.

Thinking of Jo briefly darkened her carefree mood. But Minette had a strong sense that taking off with Greg had been the right thing to do. The *only* thing to do. She needed to be free of her family, to have a tiny stretch of time to be herself. And that was quite apart from the fact that she fancied Greg like crazy. She really didn't think she could have torn herself away from him.

In any case, Jo would be better off without her in the end. She, too, needed some freedom. Licence to get firmly to grips with Max. Oh, yes, it could all work out very nicely indeed.

As far as Minette was concerned Max was simply perfect for Jo. Because he was easygoing and ironic, because he was a star in the world of entertainment and the media, Max seemed to her the exact flipside of the coin from the tense, power-crazy Alexander Rivers. And handsome enough to launch a thousand *motoscafos* into the bargain.

She noticed that the boat was slowing, pulling in to a private landing. It stopped, its engine still puttering gently, the fumes furling along the darkening canal in a silvery white spindle.

'*Ola!*' shouted the boatman.

'Come on, babe.' Greg grasped the pile of luggage in one hand and Minette in the other. Stepping over the feet of their fellow passengers, they climbed over the side of the boat and, with their various bags, spilled out onto the tiny landing area in an unceremonious heap.

'What's this, then?' Minette asked, steadying herself and looking up at the impressive and ancient walls of a building which stretched up above them.'

'Palazzo Ambroni.' Greg squinted up at it. 'Neat, isn't it? What is it you Brits say? Desirable residence?'

'Des res.' She glanced at him. She couldn't believe what she had just begun to suspect. 'Whose is it?'

He raised his eyebrows.

'Not Daddy's?'

'Yep.'

'Jeez!' She tried not to gawp. 'Well, lucky for us. Is he in residence?'

'No. He only ever spends May and June here. And Christmas if he's in an evil mood.'

Greg dragged the luggage to a small door let into the sea wall of the building whose stone fabric, in common with those of all its neighbours, seemed to be in a state of steady disintegration. There was an even more decrepit and ancient-looking iron bell fixed into the stone beside it. Greg rattled the chain hanging down from its fat clapper and an agitated jangling rang out.

After some delay, during which Greg leaned against the wall, smiling conspiratorially at the intrigued Minette, scuffles sounded behind the door and it was slowly pushed open. A small, stooped man with a gnarled face and a cap of wiry grey hair peered out at them.

'Meester Greg,' he said eventually, his canny, suspicious features relaxing a little.

The two men shook hands warmly. Greg pulled Minette forward. 'Minette, meet Antonio Fiori. He guards the palace night and day. More "fiorious" than a pack of wolves.'

Antonio nodded, apparently quite unmoved to see a strange young woman turning up out of the blue. He bent stiffly to pick up the luggage, but Greg stopped him. 'No. I'll do it.'

'I am not too old,' Antonio protested.

'No, but you're well worth preserving. And not having to hump great bags up several flights of steps is something you've earned.' He handed Antonio the consolation prize of a single light bag.

Antonio moved the muscles of his face in something almost approximating a smile. He went ahead up the bare stone steps, muttering to himself.

Minette peered through the gloom of the stairway, which was lit from the top by one single weak bulb in a wrought-iron case.

She raised her head like a hare in the grass, scenting the wind. There was a pervading odour of earth and damp, of rotting wood and damp moss on cold stone. 'Mmm. It smells of centuries and centuries of life and death,' she said, breathing in deeply, instantly falling in love with the place. 'Are there ghosts?'

'Venice is packed with ghosts,' Greg said. 'I'll try to find you some.'

They had around forty steps to climb before they stepped out into an airy hallway with walls of golden stone and a floor of white marble veined with dull sienna. There was little furniture: just a huge carved table and two great chairs, their legs shaped like crossbows. The last fading rays of the sun shone through a line of arched windows, forming bronze bars of light which sliced through the gloom.

'Oh, my God! It's absolutely perfect,' breathed Minette.

'I thought you'd like it,' said Greg, dropping the luggage onto the floor and panting slightly. 'My only aim is to please you, ma'am,' he added, in an exaggerated Deep South drawl.

'No doubt you will later on,' she said, giggling, then immediately became serious as she spotted Antonio's stern eyes observing her.

Antonio brought them a cold supper of cured ham and a salad made with olives and tomatoes, drenched in an oily dressing filled with herbs.

Sitting like aristocrats, at opposite ends of a vast oak table, they ate hungrily, drinking the vintage local wine brought up from Greg's father's cellar. Antonio hovered in the background, gliding forward to fill the glasses as they neared empty.

'How has Antonio produced all this at the drop of a hat?' Minette asked softly.

'He lives here with his *amore*,' Greg explained. 'You never get to see her; she's a well-kept but well-known secret. We all pretend she doesn't exist. The two of them keep the place aired and immaculate, ready for any visitors. There's always food – just in case.'

'Fantastic. Is this the sort of thing daddys can do when they're millionaires?'

'Yeah. Sort of.' Greg looked vaguely uneasy. The idea of his father's huge wealth had always grated on him.

Multi-millionaire, more like, thought Minette. She glanced across at Greg. He was looking reflective, and ever so slightly sad, and she felt a huge surge of warmth for him. 'I'd like you to know,' she said to him in a clear, loud voice, 'that I'd be just as keen on you if you were as poor as a whole army of church mice. That doesn't mean that I don't think this is the most fabulous place I've ever seen, and that I don't hope I can come here thousands of times more. Just for the record, Greg.'

He stood up. As he walked down the length of the table towards her Minette felt her legs become as wobbly and watery as the reflections of the *palazzos* in the Grand Canal.

Oh, God, he's so gorgeous, she moaned to herself, looking at his long beanstalk legs, the furring of dark hair on his thin arms, at his wonderful grey eyes in that fantastically supple and knowing face.

He knelt down by her chair and their heads were on a level.

Minette ran her tongue over her lips. She looked at his mouth and wanted to eat him.

'Your eyes are full of life,' he said softly. 'Full of warmth and joy and loving. Did you know that?'

She shook her head, couldn't speak.

He put his hands around her face and kissed her very gently, his lips barely touching hers.

'I think I'm a bonfire that's about to light up,' she murmured.

He stood up and pulled her upright with him. 'Come with me, little girl,' he said, mimicking some evil Bluebeard.

They went up a further flight of stairs and onto the next floor. Through a number of open doors Minette saw huge airy rooms furnished with vast iron-framed beds. The covers were plump and pale-coloured, and mouthwateringly inviting.

'You choose,' he said.

'Anywhere,' she replied.

'You'd go anywhere with me?'

'Oh, yes.'

He led her into the nearest room and softly closed the door. Minette took his hand and drew him to the window. Looking down, she saw the canal far below, its waters inky-blue in the growing darkness.

Standing behind her, Greg slowly caressed her bottom through the fabric of her jeans. 'Beautiful!' she breathed.

She turned to him and reached up for a kiss. 'Don't stop,' she said as his hand faltered for a second in its rhythmic stroking whilst his lips worked magic on her.

'Now what shall I do to you?' he wondered, making a pretence at calm speculation.

'Anything you like,' said Minette, winding her arms around his neck. 'Are you very, very experienced?'

'I have had a little previous practice.'

'I don't want to know,' she said, opening his shirt and nibbling his nipples with hungry enthusiasm. 'I could get most horrendously jealous.'

'No need. I've never come across anyone like you, babe!' His voice went up an octave as her sharp little teeth gave him a warning nip.

He wanted to let her know that he wasn't just soft-soaping her because she was a ready and willing and oh-so-available lay. He loved being with her, every minute of it. Her candour and freshness delighted him, her vigour and spontaneity. With Minette, what you saw was what you got. And both were pretty fantastic. He ached to make her feel infinitely precious and fragile and wanted.

He gathered her up in his arms and laid her very gently on the bed, as though she were one of his father's treasured seventeenth-century canvases.

He leaned over her hungrily, levering off her shirt, peeling away her jeans, the scrap of nonsense that posed for her bra, the G-string panties. Oh, God, she was breathtakingly lovely stripped. Her skin so sleek and satiny and inviting.

Her eyes, in the dusk, were huge discs. 'Will I do?' she whispered, her lashes quivering against her cheeks.

'Christ, my little angel, you're perfect.'

He slid his hands all over her. He could feel her trembling with excitement. 'Lie still, babe. Let Greg do the work.' Very slowly he licked a nipple whilst at the same time his fingers slipped between her legs, making her gasp.

But she couldn't just lie still. She had to make love back. She wanted to love him and please him just as much as he was pleasing her.

Greg felt her tongue and her lips and her fingers exploring him in a number of very intimate places. And the sensation she was giving him was terrific.

He had told her the truth about his past love-life. There had been a number of women, and he was pretty experienced in the sexual field. But he had never made love to a woman who was so nakedly eager to please him, to give as much as she was taking.

She was nuzzling and sucking him now, making a huge fuss of his body as though he was some highly favoured deity. She was teasing him so beautifully he almost forgot that he had promised himself to give *her* the time of her life.

Arching himself over her, he pulled her back up the bed until her mouth was level with his again. Kissing her until she was helpless, he reached down and parted her legs wide, then glided softly inside her.

'Ahh,' she murmured, her breathing accelerating to fever-pitch. 'Heaven!'

'Paradise found,' he groaned, exploding deep inside her.

Greg showed her Venice: the great buildings and the sculptures and the paintings. He slipped her vital pieces of knowledge and information in a casual and quirkily dry way which she found irresistible – a complete contrast to her father's stern and headmasterly lecturing.

'This is all great,' she said, standing in St Mark's Square, throwing her arms wide and swivelling around to take in the whole stunning scene. A chronicle of centuries long past. 'But I'd like to see the living city as well as the dead one.'

She pulled him into the dark, narrow alleyways where thin threads of water glistened. Greg explained that these were *calli* – tributaries of the Grand Canal.

People in the crowded houses which seemed to grow straight out of the water leaned from the windows and chatted excitedly to each other across the shifting ripples. And everywhere she looked there were cats. Tiny, delicate wild-looking creatures, darting and squealing. They weaved in and out of doorways and along the narrow causeways like shadowy ghosts.

'Venice – city of culture and cats,' exclaimed Minette, trying to persuade a particularly appealing tortoiseshell to come a little closer. As she moved towards it the motionless she-cat gave a sharp hiss, springing away at the speed of light, ears back, eyes glittering.

They spent each day out and about in the city exploring, only stopping for wine or coffee in the breathtakingly expensive little cafés. Then, as the sun began its descent over the lagoon, they made their way back to the Palazzo Ambroni.

Minette would take a bath, wrap a towel around her and position herself by the window in the high bedroom to marvel at the orange luminescence of the sunset. Greg would steal up behind her, and sometimes she didn't manage to see the sun's grand finale, because they were locked together in each other's arms, oblivious to everything else.

After Antonio had served supper, and softly vanished to some far-flung part of the crumbling palace, they would drink wine and talk. And then they would go up to the bedroom and make love again, this time slowly and lingeringly, savouring each erotically charged moment.

On their third night, as they lay entangled together, sticky and drugged and satisfied, Minette said suddenly, 'Greg, I think I love you.' She spoke with faint apology. 'Do you mind?'

'No.'

'Aren't you going to say anything else? Just no?'

207

'I think I might feel the same,' he admitted. 'It's taking a bit of adjusting to. I've always been something of a fancy-free guy.'

'Pick up the babes and then put then down again?' she suggested.

'Yeah. And you?'

'A bit the same. But without the bed bit.'

'Yeah, well. Don't feel inadequate. I've had ten years longer to work on that than you.' He rolled over onto his stomach and looked down at her. 'Why did you run off with me? Was it to make a point?'

'With my parents, you mean? No.' She put her hand round the back of his neck, stroking the skin at his hairline. 'I simply wanted to. I really and truly wanted to. You might not believe this, Greg, but I haven't done much of what I really wanted before.'

'I believe it. And it's great to be so wanted.' He gave her a long, tender kiss. 'How long are you going to stay here with me?'

She sighed. 'I don't know. Maybe another day . . .'

'Oh, boy!'

'I'll have to go back to England, Greg. I'll have to square things with my parents. Running off to Venice with a guy they've never heard of will rock them even more than ploughing my A levels.'

'Yeah. I'll buy that!'

'And I'll have to get off my "sweet little ass", as you call it, and get some sort of job. I don't fancy being a kept woman. Not by my parents. Not even by you.'

'Sure.' He sighed.

She grasped at him fiercely, pulling his head down so that his lips crushed hers rather than just touching them. 'I've loved every single second of being with you, Greg. I don't have even the teeniest regret that I took off from Prague with you. You know that, don't you?'

'You've been a little angel.'

'And you've been a perfectly heavenly host.' She giggled, raising her knee and rubbing him tenderly in a number of sensitive places.

He sucked in his breath sharply and looked down at her with bemused affection.

'What is it?' she asked.

'I can feel some clichés coming on.'

'Such as?'

'Me saying things like, Don't go, babe.'

She grinned. 'I can match that. I could say: I hate to leave, but a girl's gotta do what a girl's gotta do.'

'Great stuff. You certainly know your classic cult films sweetheart.'

They gave up talking for a while and caught up on some more kissing.

'Listen,' he said seriously, 'I've got this frightening feeling coming on that I'm going to ask you not to sleep with any other guys, if you don't mind. Not for a while anyway.'

'I can't think of ever wanting to,' she said, kissing him very soundly, sliding her tongue into his mouth, then nipping his lips with her teeth to remind him that she was one sexy, hot kitten and that *he'd* better not be doing any tom-cat straying around either.

CHAPTER 16

Jocasta flew back to London from Paris with the sour taste of betrayal on her lips and in her heart.

In a fury of bewilderment she berated herself for having been such a fool as to be taken in by the charm of a deceiving man when she had hardly recovered from the experience of being taken in by the charming deceiver before him. By the end of the flight she had come to the conclusion that as far as men were concerned she must be the world's worst judge of character in history.

She fixed her mind on what to do next, refusing to allow herself to be ground down by the disasters of the past.

Three main strands of action presented themselves. Firstly she must go and see Miles and Ginny without delay. Secondly she must forge ahead as planned with her business promotion. Her proposed trip to liaise with entrepreneur Lars Sandstrom in Gothenburg needed to be confirmed as soon as possible. And thirdly – last but not least – there was Alexander to consider. On no account was he going to come out of this sordid little episode scot-free.

The next morning she telephoned his office at Westminster. She still had the private number which would link her to the personal secretaries in his private office. And she had no hesitation at all in using it.

After a short wait, she was put through to his office. She was instantly conscious of the wariness in the voice of the woman who took her call. Maybe the woman was like this with everyone, Jo thought as they spoke. In a job like hers there must be some pretty difficult calls to field. But somehow she felt that the prickliness was very personal. Something to do specifically with her, Jocasta Shand. She had the feeling that she was definitely *persona non grata*. A woman his staff had been instructed to beware of.

The unfairness of it made her simmer with renewed anger.

'I simply want to know if he's going to be in his office at any time in the next twenty-four hours,' she snapped eventually, irritated at being fobbed off with generalities and evasions.

'We don't expect to see him today,' the woman hedged. 'He's got two meetings in the City this morning, and then he's going on to do a TV programme.'

'Where? Which studios?' She bit her lip, knowing she was coming on too strong, sounding far too involved.

'I can't give out his precise whereabouts to just anyone, Miss Shand,' the voice at the other end told her stiffly. 'For security reasons. I'm sure you'll understand.'

'Yes. Yes, I understand perfectly. Thank you very much.' She snapped the phone's aerial down, and stood thinking.

She supposed she could phone around the TV studios. It wouldn't be hard to find out which one he was going to visit. If she kept her cool and asked the right sort of questions that was.

But she didn't feel cool. Thinking of Alexander and then of Max made her flare like a rocket.

She decided to go straight to Miles's and Ginny's place, and then with a sigh of frustration remembered that her car was still in Yorkshire.

As her brother had chosen to live in one of the most inaccessible spots of the English countryside anyone could think of, even though it was only forty miles from the centre of London, it was impossible to get there on public transport. She would have to take a taxi.

Damn, she muttered to herself, considering the prospect of having to make polite conversation for an hour or so with a total stranger.

Unthinkable, given the state she was in.

She rang a car-hire firm and an hour later picked up a roomy, gleaming Ford which purred its way through the morning traffic. She began to feel calmer. Driving in a teeming city demanded a special sort of concentration, a focusing of the mind which she found curiously soothing.

It was mid-morning by the time the car turned into the gates leading up to Miles's home: an elegant and perfectly proportioned Georgian house with three identical windows placed symmetrically on either side of the classical rectangular front door.

Ginny spotted her from one of the matching upstairs windows and came running down to welcome her. 'Jo! I thought you were still in Europe.'

The two women embraced politely. Touching Ginny's shoulders lightly as she kissed her cheeks, Jo had the impression of grasping a bunch of delicate and brittle twigs.

'I had to come back sooner than I'd expected. Urgent business.' Jocasta gave what she hoped was a positive and businesslike smile.

'Ah, yes. You're always working so hard.' Ginny smiled non-committally, standing aside and beckoning Jocasta into the house.

'Is Miles still in Oxford?' Jo asked.

'No. He came back late last night. He's just having a late breakfast before going along to the lab.'

'Ah.' Jocasta was disconcerted. She had been counting on having some time to discuss things with Ginny on her own, feeling sure that Miles would be taken up with work, as was usually the case.

As they were speaking he emerged from the kitchen, a tall and commanding figure with a pleasantly impassive expression on his well-proportioned features. 'Jo!' he said, leaning down to her and placing a dry kiss in the dead centre of her left cheek. Miles was not a person given to anything but fleeting embraces. He was gently and firmly aloof, neither touching very much nor inviting touch from others.

Jo sometimes wondered how he and Ginny had managed to produce a child as exuberant and spontaneous as Minette. To produce a child of any kind at all, come to think of it.

'Come and join me in some toast and coffee,' Miles said, leading the way back to the kitchen, a place of bleached oak cupboards and immaculately gleaming

213

steel surfaces which always reminded Jo of a laboratory. The room was clearly a reflection of Miles's taste and choice. Jo wondered if Ginny minded – what her own choice would have been.

They sat around the table and Jo was not surprised to find the atmosphere equally as tense as she had feared.

'Have you heard from Minette?' she asked cautiously, watching Miles pour coffee with the spare, precise movements and intense concentration he employed in everything he did.

'She telephoned us to say that she'd arrived safely in Venice,' Ginny said quickly. 'I was rather pleased about that.'

'Pleased!' Miles echoed with incredulity. 'Pleased that she'd got there without any further ridiculous escapades, or pleased that she'd bothered to spend a moment considering that we might have feelings?'

Ginny sighed. 'Both, Miles.'

Miles handed round the coffee. His hands were firm and steady, and the surface of the coffee within the cups was as still as a frozen lake. 'I'm sorry to say,' he said in clinical tones, 'that I am completely baffled by the behaviour of our daughter.'

'No, not baffled. Outraged,' Ginny responded quietly, taking her cup. Jo noticed that in Ginny's hands the coffee had become much more active, splashing over the rim of the cup and dribbling into the saucer. Ginny was obviously quivering with suppressed tension, but she still seemed determined to make a firm statement of her own point of view.

Jo was curious and intrigued. On previous occasions when there had been trouble with Minette, and intense

214

family discussions, Ginny had often had to retire to bed and take one of her various calming medications.

'I'm afraid that what she did was rather outrageous,' Jo admitted. 'And I simply can't say how sorry I am that it happened whilst she was with me and that I seemed unable to do anything to persuade her against it.'

'Jo, you mustn't feel responsible,' said Miles patiently, fixing her with his calm, dispassionate gaze.

Jo recalled that Max had repeatedly told her the same thing. But he had spoken with such warmth and feeling. And his gaze had been anything but dispassionate. Oh, Max, she thought, a spear of heat shooting up between her shoulderblades.

'But I did feel responsible,' she told Miles, with a hint of bitterness in her voice.

'Of course she did,' Ginny broke in swiftly, with surprising conviction. She looked up and faced her husband, fair and square. 'You see, Miles, that's how you make people feel.'

He gave a short, dismissive laugh.

Ginny leaned forward. 'Miles, listen to me, please. Why do you think I've spent the last few years in a daze of Diazepam and sleeping pills?'

'Because,' he said, still completely unmoved, 'our daughter was trying our patience beyond endurance.'

'Because,' Ginny went on, 'you made me feel personally responsible for it.'

'Look,' said Jo, getting up, 'these are private things between the two of you. I don't want to intrude.'

'No, Jo. You're not intruding,' said Ginny. 'You've been on the receiving end of Miles's shifting around his

215

guilt onto your shoulders just like I have. For even longer than I have.' This is to do with you as well as me.'

'Great heaven, you make me sound like a monster,' Miles exclaimed, his cool demeanour at last showing some sign of cracking.

'You're not a monster. You're just completely inadequate when it comes to basic human interaction,' Ginny said.

'Inadequate!' echoed Miles, stunned.

'Yes. It's a novel thought for you, isn't it?'

Once again Jo began to get up from the table.

'No, please stay. All of this concerns you too, Jo. I want you to hear it,' Ginny said quietly. 'I'd like you to know that I've at last realized how heavily we've relied on you to help us with Minette over the years. And that you've been absolutely wonderful. But now I think it's time we all stood back a little and let Minette learn to fly on her own.'

'Dear God. Have you gone completely mad?' Miles burst out.

'No. I think I've suddenly gone completely sane.'

'Our daughter is an utter academic failure. She's gone running off to Venice with a man we've never met, who could make her pregnant or give her some terrible disease. That's all perfectly acceptable to you, is it?' He was openly furious now, and extremely disconcerted – something Jo had never seen before.

'Minette won't come to any harm,' Ginny said calmly. 'She's got a strong sense of self-preservation. She'll take care of herself.'

Miles sighed in exasperation.

216

Ginny tapped on her saucer with her spoon, her face thoughtful. 'When I was Minette's age I did rather the same thing as she's doing.'

'What?' Miles could not have looked more shocked.

'I hiked around the south of France with a long-haired Parisian art student. We spent the days wandering through little villages and lived on bread and country wine. And at night we slept together in huge open fields under the stars.'

'Good God!'

Ginny smiled. The memory was clearly sweet. 'And you see, Miles, part of the reason I did that was because I had a father rather like you. Basically well-meaning, but cripplingly controlling and totally wrapped up in his own concerns and ambitions – a parent who viewed me through the end of a very narrow telescope. But my French artist wanted to see the whole of me. The real me without any pretence at trying to be something I wasn't.'

'Go on,' urged Jo, seeing that Miles was speechless.

'I suppose I went a little wild for a time. And then I came back home and I married Miles because he was the sort of man I felt secure with.' She turned slowly to look at Miles. 'Because he was like my father.'

Miles went very red in the face. 'What's your doctor put you on this time?' he enquired. 'Prozac, perhaps? They say it's a miracle-worker.'

Ginny shook her head. 'My doctor suggested I experimented with staying off all my pills for a time. So I have. I think she was right. Suddenly my head's cleared, and I've been able to think.'

Miles looked at her as though she might be dangerous, a bomb about to go off.

217

'And what *do* you think, Ginny?' Jo asked gently.

Ginny folded her hands and placed them in front of her on the table. 'Well, for a start I think it's time we stopped bothering you with our problems, Jo,' she said quietly.

'Ginny!' exclaimed Miles in a warning voice.

'No, let her go on,' Jo interposed quickly. 'Are you talking about Minette?'

Ginny considered. 'You've been wonderful to Minette, Jo. You've been like a second mother to her in many ways. But now, as I've tried to say before, I think we all have to back off from her. Give her a chance to find out what kind of person she is, how she wants to develop.'

'Good heavens,' Miles exclaimed angrily. 'What a lot of ridiculous psychobabble you're spouting, Ginny. Where on earth did you get hold of all this nonsense?'

'Maybe I'll tell you one day, Miles, when you're in a better mood to listen,' Ginny said calmly, although her fingers trembled and she clasped them tightly together. She swivelled round to look at Jo. 'You don't think I'm spouting rubbish, do you?'

Jo was suddenly beginning to understand a number of things she hadn't thought of before. 'No,' she said slowly, 'I don't think you are.'

'You see,' Ginny told Miles triumphantly. 'Jo agrees with me.'

'About what?'

'That we have to give Minette more freedom, of course. Talk to her about what *she* wants instead of what we want.'

Miles looked at his wife with hard, glacial eyes. 'Isn't that precisely what Minette has already engineered for herself?'

218

'And,' continued Ginny, quite ignoring him, 'I really do feel that we should stop calling so much on Jo to help us. We should let Jo get on with her own life. I'm sure she's plenty of things to worry about without having to think of our problems as well.'

Watching the intensity in Ginny's face as she spoke, the way in which she stared fixedly ahead, not daring to look anyone in the eye, Jo realized how difficult it had been for her to say these things. And how important they were.

She stood up. 'I think Ginny has a point,' she said quietly to Miles. 'And I think it's time I left. I really must get back to London.'

Smiling at them both affectionately, she quickly walked out of the kitchen and let herself out through the front door.

Miles came striding after her. 'Jo!'

She swung round to face him.

'Look, you mustn't take too much notice of Ginny,' he said briskly.

'Why not? Isn't it high time I did? That both of us did?'

'She's not herself at the moment – worry about Minette and so on. It's hardly surprising.'

'Miles,' Jo said patiently, 'I think Ginny is at long last very much herself.'

'Oh, for heaven's sake!' He sighed with frustration.

Jo could see that he was baffled and thwarted. Ginny was right. Although brilliant as a research scientist, Miles was little more than a self-willed child when it came to human understanding and simple give and take.

'I've learned something very important from Ginny this morning,' Jo told him evenly. 'She mentioned that I'd been like a second mother to Minette. And that was a generous and warm thing for her to say. It must have taken a lot of doing, because *Ginny* is Minette's mother, and it's just struck me how sickening it must have been to have me – your sister – encroaching on her territory for so long. She was probably sick to death of me and all my fussing over Minette ever since she was a baby.'

'Rubbish. Ginny never felt like that. She couldn't have managed on her own.'

'We don't know that, do we? Because we didn't give her a chance.' Jo stared hard at her brother. 'I heard Ginny's message, loud and clear. The silent message underneath the words. "Thanks Jo, but back off now," she was telling me. And quite right too – '

'This is all perfectly ridiculous,' Miles interrupted irritably.

'No, it's just something people like you can't be bothered to think through and get to grips with,' Jo said, as kindly as she was able. 'You like order and precision. Conflict and confused feelings are far too messy for you,' She opened the door of the car and turned back to him. 'There are no hard feelings, Miles,' she added.

'Will you be coming to see us again?' he asked, suddenly looking worried.

Jo smiled. 'Of course I will. But as a sister and a friend. Not as a guardian angel for Minette.'

She started the engine and looked up at Miles, seeing all his faults and yet still loving him because he was her brother and had for a short period in her life been almost like a father. 'Goodbye,' she said softly.

Looking in the rearview mirror as she drove away, she saw him standing in exactly the same spot he had stood when they had been speaking, still baffled. Behind him in the doorway, Ginny waved: Ginny, who was Minette's mother and needed to be left to get on with her job.

Jo had a fleeting sense of freedom. There was no longer Minette to feel responsible for. Now she only had herself to think about. But whether that was good or bad she couldn't quite decide.

Driving out of the gates, she suddenly felt terribly alone.

CHAPTER 17

Max took the earliest flight that he could get out of
Charles de Gaulle airport. He had left the hotel soon
after Jo, hoping that by some miracle he might get a
place on the same flight, gain another chance to explain
things to her before her feelings against him hardened
to set like concrete.

He had clung onto the desperate hope of making a last
attempt to stop her from walking out of his life, but her
aircraft was already moving down the runway, waiting
for its take-off slot, by the time he checked in. And the
next flight was not due to leave for several hours.

He paced the departure lounge like a caged lion,
going over and over the last excruciating hour and
cursing his past stupidity.

On the flight he found himself in a fever of impatience, desperate to get to London and start *doing* things
rather than thinking, thinking, thinking.

He thought about Jo. He saw in his inner eye the
grief, the disbelief and the anger on her beautiful face,
and was hardly able to bear the pain of the image. And
then he thought of Alexander Rivers and the way he had
so wickedly betrayed his former mistress, and used him,

222

Max Swift, as the means of doing it. The man must be a complete psychopath, he thought with grim rage. But then he reminded himself that it was only through his own gullibility that Alexander had managed to get his own way with such success.

Reaching London, he bought a copy of all the national daily newspapers, took a taxi to his flat in St John's Wood, dumped his luggage on the floor and then started combing through the political news.

It did not take him long to discover that Alexander Rivers was to give an important interview on one of the major TV networks later that morning. Telephoning round his contacts in the TV world, he found none of the reticence that Jo had encountered when enquiring about Alexander's whereabouts to the staff in his private office.

Max soon had details of both the location and the precise time of the interview. Pausing only long enough to take a quick shower and change into fresh clothes, he got a taxi to drive him straight to the studios.

Alexander Rivers had arrived at the central London studios around an hour before Max set out. Flanked by several political advisors, his favourite – and very decorative – personal secretary, Lucinda, and a clutch of security personnel, his entrance had all the glamour and awesome impact of a royal visit.

By the time Max finally made it through the doors – unaccompanied but instantly recognized by the excited reception staff – Alexander had already been through all the preliminary discussions, made a brief visit to the make-up room and was now in Studio One, chatting amiably to his interviewer, the formidable Crispian Patterson.

Crispian had been a member of parliament himself for several years, and was well known for aiming to make mincemeat of his former colleagues and quite often succeeding.

The reception staff fixed Max up with an identity badge which allowed him privileged access to those parts of the building barred from other less prestigious visitors. Technically this was giving him more licence than he was actually entitled to. His own series, which had made him a national hero, belonged to another network, and he was not a regular frequenter of these particular studios. But his general popularity was such that invariably he gained all kinds of favours and benefits without even asking – especially when those bestowing them were women.

The girl presenting him with the finished item blushed pink as she reached up to him, insisting on pinning it onto his jacket herself.

Smiling his thanks, he made his way to the studio's control room, where the production team for the programme sat at a desk which resembled a huge dashboard crammed with flashing lights. He slipped in unobtrusively and stood against the back wall, gazing up at the two rows of monitor screens above the control desk.

On four of the monitors he could see Alexander's handsome fleshy features and his thick dark hair, cut sternly short and brushed back in a way that suggested – quite falsely – that he was not a man over-concerned with his image. His fine brown eyes beneath his dark brows glowed with fire and apparent sincerity.

Slightly tanned, a little on the heavy side but radiating fitness and well-being, he fitted snugly into a dark blue suit whose expensive fabric glowed slightly under the lights. He sat back at ease in his chair, alert but not tense. A man altogether at ease with himself.

'You rotten, evil, deceiving bastard,' Max whispered to himself.

There was now one minute to go before the programme went on air. Exchanging anecdotes with Crispian, Alexander looked like someone about to settle down to a cosy drink with friends at the end of a satisfying day.

'You just wait,' murmured Max. 'Because if Crispian doesn't crucify you, I will.'

But even the wily Crispian, who knew all about what went on behind the scenes in the corridors of power, was struggling to get the best of Alexander. In fact Max had the impression that Crispian was struggling to hold his own. When Alexander put on his public face, he seemed to build invisible walls around himself and become impregnable.

Alexander was fortunate in having a memory that not only stored a multitude of facts with perfect accuracy but never let him down when it came to plucking any one of them out at random. He was able to match each of Crispian's statistics about the fluctuation in the numbers of unemployed, or the rise and fall in interest rates, with detailed figures of his own. His flow of rhetoric was as smooth as warmed oil – and he also had the ability to lie unhesitatingly with complete authority.

Inevitably the question of family values came up. Alexander leaned forward to Crispian, a look of grave concern on his face as he lamented the plight of children subjected to cruelty and neglect, the alarming increase in single-parent families, the soaring divorce rate. His voice became low and soft, almost caressing the microphone in its velvet intensity.

The projection of quiet sincerity was faultless as he explained to Crispian the urgent need for the country to return to the morals of the past, when the caring family unit had been regarded as something sacred and permanent. An issue, of course, which his government would place on their priority list when they came to power.

Max felt his fingers tighten as he listened, the nails digging deep into his palms. His breath was taken away by the stunning hypocrisy of the man on the screen. He realized that for most of the viewing population Alexander would be coming across as some kind of Christ-like figure. It would have been only too easy to believe it himself, if he hadn't happened to be in possession of some particularly incriminating inside knowledge about the real Alexander, behind the façade.

It was hard for Max to restrain himself from bursting onto the set, confronting Alexander and demanding that he tell the truth about the mistress he had discarded. About his cruel insistence that she should have the baby she was carrying – *his* baby – aborted. About the wicked schemes he had hatched to make sure she kept her mouth shut . . .

Holding himself in check, he waited silently for the interview to finish. At last it was all over. There was a

226

close-up of Alexander's face, serene and triumphant. Music sounded. The credits rolled up the screen.

A spontaneous clatter of applause broke out in the control room. 'You've got to hand it to him,' the programme's producer exclaimed, 'the guy's a complete professional, even if he's lying through his teeth.'

'Probably goes out every morning strangling joggers in the park,' sighed his female assistant. 'But he is rather splendid. I wonder why he's not married,' she added wistfully.

Max slipped unobtrusively out of the room and stood in the corridor, his eyes fixed on the doors to the studio. Eventually they opened and a laughing bunch emerged. Mutual congratulations were flying everywhere.

Max fixed his eyes on Alexander, and through the throng the other man must have felt the force of feeling behind that unwavering stare, for he suddenly looked up, trying to locate its source.

Max raised his eyebrows. His eyes widened just for a second. And Alexander realized that he was being summoned. He also understood with a politician's raw animal intuition that he would be taking some sort of risk if he made no response.

Disentangling himself from the sychophantic group around him, he walked up to Max, his hand outstretched in greeting. 'Max! Well, well. A surprise meeting.'

Max took the offered hand and clasped it briefly. He knew that it was imperative to avoid any demonstrations of feeling which would arouse suspicion amongst the loyal flock surrounding Alexander.

'I need to speak to you,' he told Alexander shortly.

Alexander opened his hands in a gesture of invitation. 'Max! Please, feel free! But as you see I'm under pressure of time . . .'

'Alone!' Max said softly.

The two men stared at each other, and the silence between them intensified. Max could sense the power of feeling that had built up inside him radiating out into the air, and he knew that Alexander sensed it too, that he understood that he was facing smouldering white-hot anger.

'There's an empty room just here,' said Max, indicating a tiny office whose partly opened door revealed bare walls, a table and a filing cabinet. 'Tell the entourage to wait.'

Alexander hesitated.

'Do it,' said Max.

Alexander turned to the waiting group, who had been laughing amongst themselves but were now becoming interested in the interchange between Alexander and the famous TV star. 'Give me five minutes,' he told them, smiling regally to reassure them that this unforeseen little interlude was nothing they need worry about.

Max shut the door behind them. The little room was stuffy and oppressive, with a stale odour of old newspapers and half-consumed snacks.

'Well?' Alexander's eyes were cold and assessing.

'You surely don't need me to explain what I'm doing here,' said Max. 'It must be obvious.'

Alexander looked away from him, straightened one of his already immaculate cuffs. 'In actual fact, Max, it isn't. Look, I really don't have much time . . .'

'Jocasta Shand,' Max cut in brutally. 'Her goodness and integrity. Your wickedness and treachery. That's what I've come about.'

'Very poetic,' said Alexander, pinning his cold gaze on Max and attempting to freeze him out. 'I take it you haven't been able to complete the little mission we agreed on?'

'Christ Almighty,' breathed Max, dizzy with rage, wondering how the hell he was going to stop himself smashing the complacent smile from Alexander's self-satisfied face.

'You've got things all wrong, Max,' said Alexander calmly. 'Jocasta may be beautiful and full of high morals. But what I said about her was true. She was a time-bomb. And probably still is, thanks to your ineptitude.'

Max realized he was dealing with a man whose emotions were not within the range of normality. He knew there was no point in reasoning or arguing with him. His aim must be simply to get answers to some basic questions and then put forward his own proposals.

'Did you arrange to have her stripped and assaulted in a lift in our Prague hotel?' he asked softly.

Alexander's face betrayed nothing. There was not a flicker of surprise, revulsion or remorse. 'I know nothing of that,' he replied.

'I believe you,' said Max. 'At least in so far as the details are concerned. I'm sure you wouldn't do anything so stupid as do your dirty work yourself. Dear God, Alexander, I thought you were a man of ideals. But you're just a sham – not much better than a common criminal.'

229

'You should know all about that, Max. Your record as a youngster was hardly whiter than white, was it? Brawling in the streets, disturbing the peace. Need I go on?' Alexander's active antennae were waving furiously, trying to find a lever with which to fight this man who had once seemed to be such a keen potential disciple and was now looking like a dangerous rival.

'Go on as long as you like. It's not a secret,' Max responded. 'I was fourteen when all that went down in the local police log-book. A bit of a tearaway. I was in care at the time, in a children's home in the East End. I went to a comprehensive school with two thousand kids on the roll. It was dog-eat-dog. You had to claw and fist and elbow your way to the top of the heap there, just to survive. You've never known anything like that, Alex.'

Scorn and distaste curled Alexander's lips. 'Maybe not. But you've gone down another road altogether since then. Look at you now. Give you a simple job that offends your delicate feelings and you squeal like a stuck pig, make a complete mess of it. You showbusiness boys are all jelly-soft sentiment when the going gets tough.'

His eyes locked into Max's, full of contempt. But Max simply stared back at him, declining to degrade himself by making a response, refusing to reflect any shred of emotion. His gaze was firm and unnervingly steady. Full of steel. Made rigid with that calm, unassailable authority that comes from the burning need to fight a cause you believe in with all your heart and soul. And just at that moment the only cause in Max's heart was Jocasta Shand.

A lesser man than Alexander would have slithered out of the room fast, mindful of the danger approaching. But Alexander was not used to being dominated, nor was he prepared to expose himself to that experience if he could help it. The desire to exert his supremacy was even greater than fear. Although, facing Maxwell Swift at this precise moment, he had to admit to a sharp spasm of that loathsome emotion.

'I may have gone down a different road. But I never forgot my past. I never went soft,' said Max. He smiled. His long, lazy, disarming smile. 'If I decided to take you apart with my bare hands, Alexander, I could do it with absolutely no problem whatever. Here – now.'

He saw Alexander's lips whiten.

'What do you want?' Alexander asked. 'How much?'

Max had not stopped smiling. 'I've all the money I need or want,' he said. 'That makes me a very fortunate man, doesn't it? And also one who can't be manipulated.'

'You were manipulated before.'

'For what I thought was a principle, God help me. Not for money.'

'Well, what, then? What *do* you want?'

'To make you sweat.'

Beads glistened on Alexander's top lip. 'Does that mean you intend to use the information she's given you to make things difficult for me?'

'Possibly.'

Alexander's eyes glittered.

'Of course, it would be very foolish of me to make that kind of threat to a man like you, Alexander. I might find myself at the bottom of the Thames with a bag around my head.'

Alexander showed no surprise at this suggestion, nor made any move to deny it.

'So,' Max continued calmly, 'I've taken the precaution of sending a letter to my lawyer with relevant details. Only to be opened – and passed to the press – in the event of my death or should I suffer a serious accident.'

'Such melodrama!' Alexander's lip curled again, but his eyes were wary and thoughtful.

'It gives me the freedom to be flexible in my plans,' Max said evenly, although the effort of acting a part and the strain of not being able to tear Alexander limb from limb was beginning to tell.

'So what are you going to do next?' Alexander enquired cautiously.

Max paused. He walked slowly to the door. 'I'm not sure,' he responded, grasping the handle. 'You'll just have to wait and see, Alexander.'

'Will you try to get her back?' Alexander asked, suddenly displaying a flicker of sharp interest.

Max turned, his face livid with feeling. He was unable to speak, his emotions were so strong.

'I presume she found you out and gave you your marching orders?'

'You could say that.'

'Did you sleep with her?' Alexander asked.

Heat flared in Max's face. He felt a thunderbolt of rage roll through his head. He held on desperately to his self-control.

'You did!' Alexander said with silky triumph. 'I have to hand it to you, Max. Getting Jo to open her legs within hours is no mean feat.'

'Drop dead,' said Max quietly, slipping through the door, his fury raging within, crushing the breath from his chest.

Alexander waited for a moment and then he, too, left the room, rejoining his group of supporters and spreading his hands again in that gesture announcing that all was well and going Alexander Rivers's way.

Walking down the corridor, deftly fielding the various comments and questions flung at him, his mind was active in other fields entirely.

It struck him that Max Swift was a formidable rival. Certainly on the sexual front. Competition stirred within him. He wondered about Max's performance in bed. How Jo had responded. And he wondered about Swift's obvious desperation to get back within her sheets.

He thought of Swift's likely determination in achieving that goal. And then he thought of the sweet triumph of winning her back himself instead.

CHAPTER 18

After leaving Miles and Ginny, Jocasta felt drained and exhausted. The traumatic events of the last few days were beginning to kick in to her system. She was finding it hard to untangle the jumble of thoughts crowding her mind. Attempting to form clear and rational plans was virtually impossible. And certainly there would be nothing to be gained by pursuing and tackling Alexander in this state.

She recognized the vital necessity of gathering up her energies again. And for that she needed to be on home territory, to have some time to herself.

Calling the car-hire firm from the in-car phone thoughtfully provided for their customers, she arranged to drop off the borrowed Ford at one of the firm's north country branches the next day. And then she headed for the motorway, took the north-bound exit and put her foot down hard on the accelerator.

Within three hours she was approaching the North Yorkshire moors, the broad and forbidding ridge that divided the vale of York from the windswept landscape of the east coast.

Her house was on the edge of a small market town, one of a handful of scattered dwellings converted from old barns or church halls belonging to the last century. Each house was hidden away in its own hollow at the base of the hill, which towered up behind them, giving protection from the raw east winds which blew in from the North Sea.

She parked the car beside the house and then ran up the wide, shallow steps leading to the arched doorway. Her house had originally been built for the storage and safekeeping of the horse-drawn carriages which had belonged to past owners of the Manor House, in the park opposite. The huge entry doors had been retained, but only a small section of them was now in use. It would have taken the strength of two men to push open the full expanse of the doors as they had originally been used.

She levered her luggage through the door, then flicked light switches to illuminate the lamps on either side of the free-standing wooden-slatted stairway. It was late afternoon now. A mist had formed over the hills and the light was gloomy under lowered grey clouds. The huge windows let into the high arched roof above struggled to admit any frail fragments of brightness at all.

Jocasta sighed. There seemed to be gloom everywhere. She threw her apricot jacket over the fat banister knob, carved to resemble a giant pine cone, and then walked through the rooms on the ground floor, checking that all was well.

Satisfied, she put on water to boil for coffee and stood at the huge window in her kitchen, looking out at the

235

small strip of cultivated garden which gently merged into the wild grassy base of the hill. On the flank of the hill a dozen or so sheep were grazing, silent and untroubled. It was a scene of utter peace. A complete contrast to the frenzy of Paris and London.

She heard the water beginning to boil. As she spooned coffee into a cup her eye was drawn to a small dish beside the kettle. It was plain white and in the centre was a cheeky face sketched out in red lines, with the word 'Smile!' written underneath. It was a gift Minette had bought for her years ago. A token of childish affection that had touched Jo so that she had always cherished it as something precious. And whenever she picked it up, she did indeed smile.

But now, today, there was something very strange about it, something that sent a shivery chill through her chest. The dish contained a cigarette end.

Jo had once smoked herself, but some years ago she had decided to stop. And since then she had developed a definite aversion to smoke. None of her friends smoked in her house, and Juliet, the teenage girl who came each week to whisk around the rooms with a vacuum and duster, and whose mother was a chain-smoker, thought the habit was vile.

A worm of fear crawled over Jo's scalp as she considered the possibility of someone's having been in the house whilst she was away. But why? And who?

The phone pealed and her body jerked with alarm. And then there was sudden anticipation. Max! It could be Max. Her heart leapt and then sank again. What use was there in thinking about talking again to Max? Ever.

'Yes,' she said curtly.

236

'Jocasta, my dear.' A rich bass voice throbbed over the line.

Her senses had been racing. Now they stilled. There was a sensation of intense disappointment. 'Lars,' she said, recognizing the seductive tones of Lars Sandstrom, the Swedish entrepreneur who had recently been dangling the prospect of some very lucrative new business connections before her faintly sceptical eyes.

'Yes, indeed. How are you, my dear?'

'Well. And you?'

'I shall be better when I've pinned you down to a firm undertaking to come and see me without delay.'

'I hope we're talking business, Lars,' she said crisply, hearing the unashamed flirtation in his voice.

A picture of Max flashed up behind her eyes. It was as though a piece of film had been dipped in the chemicals of her brain and had suddenly appeared as a photograph, razor-sharp.

She felt dizzy.

'But of course,' purred Lars. 'You know I would never presume to do otherwise, my lovely Jocasta. But, my dear beautiful Jo – one can always hope.'

Jocasta knew quite well that although Lars had both respect and affection for her, he was in no way seriously concerned with forming a relationship. Lars liked observing and playing games. Bed-games, most certainly, but nothing more serious.

'Well, I wouldn't like to be responsible for any poor man losing hope,' she returned drily, astonished at the ease with which she could slip behind this brittle and superficial façade, as though it were as simple as putting on a coat.

'Then I shall continue to do just that,' Lars said in his formal, correct English. 'You come to Gothenburg, my dear, and we will do a little business together – and then we will have a little fun.'

'That's rather provocative of you!' Jo said, unable to prevent herself smiling.

'My dear, sweet Jocasta. You English ladies are so cautious and correct. But when you come to Sweden again I shall show you how to live a little more dangerously.'

'I'm not sure I need any teaching,' Jo murmured, so softly that Lars failed to pick up the remark.

'Now listen to me,' he said, suddenly businesslike and purposeful. 'I want to talk about these drawings you've sent, and your proposals for a collection of quality wool and mohair fabrics. These are excellent ideas, Jo. They could be real winners. My shops are presently clamouring for something fresh and unique, just the kind of thing you're offering. Now all you need is someone in the know who can help you with the details of production and marketing, guide you through all the pitfalls so that you'll have a range ready for next autumn. You could make a fortune, Jo. These garments will sell by the boat-load. They could put you in the really big league.'

Jo was always cautious in the face of grandiose statements, although she was pretty sure that Lars Sandstrom's optimism was genuine and well-founded. He was a foxily shrewd entrepreneur. He didn't pick from the ranks and target people to promote unless he thought there was a ninety-nine per cent chance of their having success. Why should he? Their failure would only cost him money. 'And I suppose the "someone" to help me is you?' she commented.

'Of course. With the specialist advice of my excellent team also. We simply cannot lose.'

'So when shall we meet?' she asked.

'As soon as possible. My management team and the stock-controllers from all my stores are currently in Gothenburg. Would you be free to meet us say, tomorrow?'

So soon? she thought, startled. But why not? What was the point in delaying? What was there to stop her? Or, more to the point, who? Ginny and Miles were fielding Minette's problems. Her confrontation with Alexander could wait. And Max. Well, he was history.

'It really would be within your best interests to meet with us,' Lars insisted in his velvety growl. 'Jo, my dear, don't miss this opportunity.'

'No, you're right. I'll get the early-morning flight, but I might not be with you until the afternoon.' She would have to drive back to London to get a direct connection, or else take a local flight and have a stop in Copenhagen. Either way there would be delays.

'This is no problem,' Lars soothed, knowing all about the ins and outs of that particular journey. He paused, and she heard him take in a long, luxurious breath. 'We shall be delighted to see you however late you arrive.'

She laughed. His ripely seductive tone was truly outrageous. But somehow Lars always managed to get away with it.

'And after our business meeting is concluded,' he continued, 'you might like to relax a little and join me and my colleagues at my *sommarstuga* – my very beautiful house on the beach at the lakeside.'

'*Sommarstuga?* That means summer cottage, doesn't it?' she asked.

'Indeed it does. Your Swedish is coming along very nicely, Jo! I simply can't wait to teach you a little more. Now, what do you say to the idea of a little entertainment at the beach?'

'It sounds lovely. What sort of clothes shall I bring? Formal or informal?'

'As few as possible,' the deep voice purred. 'At my parties the really brave guests take a sauna and then roll naked in the snow to cool down.'

'In that case I shall have to pray that the temperature doesn't hit zero,' she responded, reflecting that the prospect of being naked under the eyes of Lars Sandstrom and his associates, however attractive they might be, didn't fill her with trembling anticipation. There was only one man whose eyes she longed to roam over her when she was naked. And he had been thrown out of her life. Finally. Completely.

She found that her mood had lightened a little after the stimulating discussion with Sandstrom. But glancing again at the cigarette end in the 'Smile' dish threw a fresh shadow of unease over her.

With elaborate caution she picked up the discarded butt between two fingers. Holding it as though it were diseased, she stared at it in the vague hope of making a discovery of some kind.

With a jolt of shock she registered the dark stain on the very end of the butt. Deep burgundy, so dark it was almost black. The traces of a thick, sticky lipstick which only a few women would choose to wear.

Her throat dried as she recalled the girls in the lift in Prague: their black clothes, their white make-up and kohl-ringed eyes, their plummy, almost black lipstick.

She dropped the cigarette end as though it were a poisonous insect.

'Oh, God,' she gasped. Ideas and theories began to buzz in her mind, sending her racing upstairs to her studio in the roof space. Wildly she looked around her. Her huge desk seemed just as she had left it, covered in sample knitted squares showing the different effects that could be produced with a variety of wools and stitches. Nothing had been disturbed. The walls with their portraits of different breeds of sheep seemed untouched also.

Her heart thundering, she glanced quickly across to the dark green filing cabinet where she kept her private papers.

There was a moment of pure shock as she registered the forced master lock which hung useless from the end of the cabinet, held only by a thin thread of metal. And then came the slow, sickening realization.

Her fingers shook as she pulled out the bottom drawer: the drawer not connected with her business documents. The drawer in which she kept Alexander's letters – every one of them, from the early days of their affair right to its bitter end.

They had all gone. The drawer was completely empty.

She sat on the floor, shivering with shock and a slow, creeping coldness.

Through the evening, as she emptied the luggage from her last journey and repacked her cases in

241

anticipation of a stay in Sweden, she was numb and robot-like.

In the night she lay awake, rigid and as cold as lead. And all the time she was listening out for noises in the house, tense with apprehension. What else might Alexander do? And was Max still collaborating with him? In her loneliness and isolation anything seemed possible.

The morning mercifully came eventually, and she was relieved to be able to get up and prepare for the new day. She dressed very formally in a sleeveless navy shift dress and a sleek matching jacket which was cut to curve in slightly at the waist. She wondered about wearing her hair loose and then changed her mind, twisting it up into a neat French pleat and pinning it carefully.

Looking in the mirror, she saw that the effect was decidedly cold and severe. She looked remote and untouchable. She didn't care. In fact she was pleased to project those qualities, for that was how she felt inside.

She glanced through the window to check on the weather. The Ford car she had hired gleamed silvery grey in the drive. 'Damn,' she swore softly, having forgotten all about it. She decided to use it to drive to the airport. If she got her own car out of the basement garage she would waste time swapping the two around in the drive.

As she was considering the options she noticed a dark blue saloon coming up the road. Her interest was caught as it slowed down on approaching her house. As it signalled to turn into her drive, her heart began to thump.

The blue car stopped just behind the Ford. There was a pause and then the driver got out.

It was Max.

Jocasta looked down at his gleaming fair head. And at that same moment he looked up at the house and she saw his face. She clenched her fingers, feeling out of breath, as though she had been running.

He might be a low betrayer and a deceiving bastard, but he was so striking, so wonderfully handsome. All male. His face was even finer-boned than she remembered, his shoulders broader, his hips leaner.

Jocasta swallowed hard, and her throat felt as though it were filled with hard objects. She moved back from the window so that she could still see him but he had no chance of seeing her.

She noted his expression. Fixed, hard, resolute.

Oh, God! she thought, suddenly shot through with fear.

Her pulses leapt like animals fleeing from a merciless predator. Her whole body shook. A confused medley of feelings roared through her consciousness.

She loved him, she desired him, she was besotted by him. She was afraid of him. She *hated* him.

He had moved out of sight now. He had reached the door. She heard the heavy banging on the wood and shuddered with fresh terror.

Think! she told herself. *Think*!

Picking up the phone on the desk, she punched out the number of the nearest local taxi firm. 'I want a taxi,' she breathed in quiet panic. 'To go to the airport. *Now*!'

She heard the patient voice on the other end asking for her address and a contact telephone number. Automatically she replied, but all the time her ears were registering the rhythmic assault on her front door.

Then she heard him calling out. 'Jo. Jo!'

Stealthily, as though she were a thief, she crept down the stairs and stacked her luggage behind the door, springing back in trembling fascination each time the hammering started again.

And then there was silence. Maybe he'd given up and was going away. Maybe he planned on coming back later. But then she would be gone.

She didn't know whether to be relieved or desolated.

There was a long, silent pause. She listened out for the sound of a car door slamming, an engine firing.

And then she saw the shadow of his tall figure approaching the huge sliding windows that opened from the main sitting room into the back garden.

The interior double doors dividing the spacious room from the hall were open, and she realized that he would be able to see her, standing hunched behind the door, her back pressed against the wood.

As his tall figure appeared outside the window she darted once again out of his line of vision, her heart drumming painfully. But she knew that he had had a glimpse of her, that he now knew exactly where she was.

She clasped her hands together, praying for the taxi to arrive.

Tension and uncertainty made her scalp tingle with sensation.

'Jo,' he called. And his voice was soft and reassuring and caressing.

Surely there was no need to be frightened, she thought. Max was not Alexander. He was not evil. She told herself all this and felt it in her heart. But at the same time the tiny contrary voice of fear and doubt refused to be silenced.

'Come on taxi. *Come on*,' she mouthed silently.

His shadow remained by the window for a few seconds and then disappeared. She heard the sound of a diesel engine, the alerting hoot of a horn.

She darted into the cloakroom beneath the stairs and pressed her nose against the reeded glass. She could just make out the newly arrived car, read the lit sign on its roof – 'Taxi'.

Guardedly she opened the front door a fraction and pushed her case through the gap. The taxi driver was getting out of the car now. He waved, signalled that he would carry the case for her. Slinging her hand luggage over her shoulder, she stepped through the door and closed it firmly behind her.

Instantly she was imprisoned in strong arms. 'Jo!' Max said, as if calling to her from a long way away.

She felt her teeth begin to chatter, although beneath her clothes there was a growing, suffocating heat.

'Don't, Max,' she murmured, sagging against him. 'Don't.'

She turned her head, her hair brushing against Max's chin. She saw the taxi driver hovering uncertainly, not venturing to come any nearer.

'Don't what?' Max said gently.

'Don't hold me like this!' she exclaimed in panic. 'You're so strong. You're frightening me.'

'Frightening you!' A ripple of shock shook his chest. Instantly he dropped his arms from her. When he spoke again, his voice was very soft. 'When I first saw you, Jo, the feeling I had was overpoweringly strong. The most physically and mentally strong sensation I've ever had.'

She looked up at him. Her heart lurched.

245

'But I'd never use strength to hurt you, darling. You know that, don't you?'

She looked up at him. She shook her head in a gesture of bewilderment.

'That first moment I saw you, I knew I'd found the person I'd been looking for all my life,' he said. 'I know it sounds trite, but there it is.' His eyes held hers for a second, quietly challenging her to say she didn't believe him.

Jocasta felt an uneasy hollow in her guts.

The taxi driver coughed. 'You're going to miss your plane, love,' he called out.

She turned, pulling herself out of her trance-like state. 'I'm coming – I'm coming.'

'Where are you going?' Max asked her sharply.

She stared at him, her suspicions aroused again, because Alexander's relentless treachery had unnerved her and killed her capacity to trust. Fear gripped her, twisting its cord tight.

'No, I can't tell you!' she exclaimed. She went swiftly down the steps and then sprinted to the taxi, wrenched open the door and got inside.

The driver followed with her case, levering it into the boot.

He swung himself into the driving seat and, sensing the urgency charging the atmosphere, instantly started the engine and reversed swiftly out into the road.

'Are you all right, love?' he asked kindly, eyeing her curiously through the rearview mirror.

'Yes.' She turned to look back at the house. She saw Max swinging himself into the blue car. Resolutely she swivelled to face forward again, and fixed her eyes firmly on the road ahead.

After a time the taxi driver said, 'He seems to be following us, love. Would you like me to contact my base and get them to alert the police?'

'What? Oh, good heavens, no,' she cried out in distress.

'Just a suggestion. Let me know if you change your mind. There are some real nutters around these days.'

The drive to the airport took thirty tense minutes. Max's car was still behind them as they drove up to the main building.

The driver heaved her case from the boot and found her a trolley on which to wheel it.

Meanwhile Max had parked his car on a double yellow line and was running across towards her.

'Blood and sand!' exclaimed the taxi driver. 'Isn't that Dr Snow from *The Long Road*?' He looked at Jocasta with fresh interest as she handed him her payment. She had the feeling he was baffled at finding any female with half a brain running away from this particular hero.

'Yes,' she gasped, grabbing the trolley and slipping nimbly through the gap just before the automatic doors slid together.

Running along to the rows of check-in desks, she registered Max standing behind the doors, grimly waiting for them to open again. And then two uniformed police came up to him. She saw him turn reluctantly, walk off between them.

She sighed with relief, thanking God for police vigilance on airport parking offences.

Having collected her tickets and boarding pass, she went straight to the departure lounge. Passing safely through the security checks, she breathed a sigh of relief.

CHAPTER 19

Minette thought that parting from Greg at Marco Polo Airport was one of the hardest things she had ever done.

'I never cry,' she sobbed, tears streaming down her face as she clutched him like a baby monkey clinging to its mother. 'I don't want to go. It feels like an amputation.'

'I'm kinda upset too,' he confessed. 'And I'm the one who's being ditched.'

'Promise to love me for ever and ever,' she wailed. 'At least until next week.'

'I promise,' he said gravely. 'At least until then.'

'You bastard,' she grimaced, thumping him.

Greg had seen to everything: booked her a flight, charged the fare to his credit card because she was cleaned out of cash and credit, organized the motor launch to get her to the airport, bought her a pack of little yellow scribbling pads because she'd said she would rather write her script for facing her father than read the latest blockbuster.

He held her against him and slipped his long, bony fingers into her hair, massaging the warm scalp beneath. 'Don't stay away too long,' he murmured.

She sniffed, squeezing herself against him even more tightly.

'We should be starting filming in Prague soon after Christmas, God willing,' he told her. 'I could get you a job on the set, sweetheart. No problem.'

'Yes. I might take you up on it. But I've got to sort things out at home first.' She stared up at him, her eyes shining with tears and appeal.

'I know,' he whispered, kissing the tip of her nose. 'You have to go and fight your dragons! You don't need to explain anything to me about making war and peace with the parents. God, what a bundle of problems those guys can hurl at you. And people say kids are difficult.'

Minette laughed. She eased a handkerchief from the pocket of his jeans, blew her nose on it and stuffed it into her own jeans. 'I'll keep it under my pillow and never ever wash it in a million years so it always smells of you.'

'You must be crazy.'

Her flight was being called for the final time. He bent and kissed her very firmly, then pushed her from him abruptly and gave her bottom a firm pat. 'Go away, little girl,' he said lightly.

Turning around, he started to separate himself from her, feeling a veil of moisture in his own eyes. Minette's fingers were still linked with his. He felt their arms extend and the fingers give a last fierce squeeze before they reluctantly slipped apart.

His hands and arms suddenly felt very empty.

Swiftly he walked through the main concourse, forcing himself not to look back.

★ ★ ★

It was a gloriously sunny afternoon when Minette finally arrived at her parents' house. 'Go away, sun,' she grumbled. 'I'm not in the mood for being as bright and beautiful as you.'

She dragged her cases through the front door. 'Hi, there! Hello, hello!' she called out, standing in the hall and swivelling herself around.

There was nothing but silence.

'Mummy – Mummy where are you?'

Her father's upright figure emerged silently from the door of his study. 'She's out,' he said.

The two stared at each other. It was very quiet in the house, and now, as they faced each other, it seemed to grow even quieter.

'Oh,' said Minette, instantly feeling helpless and stupid. Her father had always had that effect on her, even when she was a very small child. When he looked at her with his cool, clinical eyes she felt like the slides he stared at through his microscope rather than a living person.

'And how did you find Venice?' he asked, as if she had simply been on a weekend break.

'Interesting,' she responded crisply.

'Really? In what way exactly?'

'Oh, churches, museums, statues, paintings. All that kind of thing.'

'You found time to see some of those? Well, Minette, I'm delighted to hear it.'

His snuff-dry sarcasm grated painfully on her. After being with Greg, confronting her father was like moving out of a steamy sauna and diving into an icy lake. 'What did you think I'd be doing; lying in bed all day with some guy?' she burst out in exasperation, completely losing her cool and not caring a fig.

'If you're going to speak to me like that I shall go back to my work,' he said evenly. 'I've a great deal to get through this weekend.'

'Oh, Christ!' Minette screamed at him. 'Tell me something new.' She stamped off into the kitchen and thrust the kettle under the tap. In her fury and haste she had forgotten to take off the lid, and water shot up in a bouncing torrent, drenching her.

Wiping her face with a towel, she suddenly found herself laughing. And doing that reminded her of Greg – of his crazily acrobatic features which crinkled into a thousand merry lines when he laughed.

Thinking of Greg cooled her anger. She reminded herself of the resolutions she had made on the flight, not to be sucked back into the cold war she and her father had waged for so long.

She made coffee, strong and black, as her father liked it. She put the mugs on a tray and marched determinedly into his study.

He was sitting at his desk, as she had expected. In front of him were papers with carefully drawn diagrams and a pile of academic scientific journals. Thinking of having to plough through their contents made Minette feel slightly sick. But then she reflected that there was nothing her father liked more than being left on his own to do just that.

We human creatures are amazingly different, she thought. And that's brilliant, really.

She placed the mug on one of the few spaces on the desk-top. Perching on the arm of the chair at the side of the desk, she said, 'Talk to me, Daddy.'

251

He laid down his pen and turned to her. 'What is there to say, Minette?'

She was utterly flattened and humiliated. The last few days had been the most eventful of her life. Losing her virginity, losing her heart, finally becoming an adult. And all he could do was stare at her with cool and clinical detachment. 'You mean you're so disappointed in me there's nothing at all you can think of to say to me?'

His eyelids flickered. He did not speak.

Minette sighed. She could feel his acute unease at being challenged in this way. He preferred to keep himself behind walls of emotion-free politeness. And she guessed that underneath his unfathomable exterior his predominant sensation was embarrassment.

'One of my friends from school went off with the husband of one of her mother's friends,' Minette told him, clasping her mug against her chest like a shield. 'When she got back her parents were so angry they threw her out of the house. They'd burned all her clothes and sold her bed.'

Now it was her father's turn to sigh. 'I suppose there is a point you're trying to make with that sorry little story?'

'Yes. It's about parents getting angry.'

'Is that what you want me . . . us to do?'

'Maybe it would be better than pretending I'm invisible,' she said quietly. 'What do I have to do to stop being invisible, Daddy? Apart from signing on for another round of science A levels?'

'Are you trying to tell me that you went to Venice with a complete stranger in order to make me take notice of you?' he asked in a voice of ice. 'Is that it, Minette? I can hardly believe it, even of you. But if that *was* what you were trying to achieve, I'm sorry to tell you that it won't work.'

Bitter disillusionment surged in Minette. Would she ever be able to get through to him? She banged down her mug on the desk. Drops of coffee leapt out, making dark stains on her father's journals.

'I went because I was really keen on this "complete stranger",' she protested, becoming heated again. 'He's got a name, by the way. It's Greg. He's a really great person. I wanted to be with him because he made me feel like a really great person too. He made me feel – worthwhile.'

'Oh, these tired old platitudes,' Miles responded wearily.

From days gone by Minette knew that he hated any kind of sloppiness or imprecision in the way one expressed oneself. She jumped up, tears stinging her eyes. 'God, you're hopeless. There's absolutely no point trying to talk to you. You're like a block of wood.'

She saw him wince again, and for a moment she wondered if she had managed to touch him.

'Don't go,' he said sharply as she turned on her heel.

She spun back, a frail sparkle of hope bubbling up inside her.

'Do you know of someone called Maxwell Swift?' he enquired coolly.

Minette stared at him, trying to make connections. 'Yes. Just about everyone in the country does,' she added with deliberate provocation.

'Indeed. Is he some kind of pop star?'

'TV soap opera. He's a very fine actor and absolutely drop-dead gorgeous. Around half the women in Britain are in love with him.'

Miles looked as though she had waved something very foul-smelling at him.

'Why?' asked Minette, suspicious of her father's motives and automatically seeking to protect Jo by declining to give anything away until she knew what was going on.

'He telephoned the evening before last. He wanted to know if Jocasta was here.'

Minette frowned. 'Back in England, you mean?'

'I assume so. That is the location of this residence.' He looked at her and gave a dry little smile.

'And is she?'

'She was two days ago.'

'No! Really?'

'I see you're surprised.' He looked at his daughter with interested calculation, as though she held the key to an intriguing mystery. 'Am I right in thinking that Jocasta is in some way involved with this person Maxwell Swift?'

You bet, thought Minette, holding on hard to her inner thoughts in order to prevent them escaping and giving all sorts of games away. 'He was staying at the same hotel as us in Prague,' she said non-committally.

'I see,' Miles said thoughtfully.

I bloody well hope you don't, thought Minette. 'He threw a party in his suite and Jo went along as a guest,' she elaborated, making it all sound very casual and unimportant.

'Ah. He seemed rather anxious to trace her,' Miles said.

'So what did you tell him?'

'Very little. He already had her address and telephone number. What more did he need?'

Minette's brain began to buzz with speculation. 'Jo came here?' she asked curiously.

'Yes. She felt she had things to explain to us. About you.'

Minette could see that that made sense. But why would Jo be back in England and Max desperately trying to trace her? There must have been some sort of bust-up.

'Did she seem . . . OK?' Minette asked, frowning.

'"OK",' echoed Miles. 'What is "OK", Minette? Define it for me.'

Minette took a deep breath, wondering how long she would be able to hold out from hitting her parent over his nobly pondering head.

There was a clicking of footsteps in the hall and Ginny appeared in the doorway of Miles's study, frail and elegant in a swinging pink coat and black high heels.

'Minette!' she exclaimed. Hesitantly she held out her arms and Minette walked forward into them. They held each other for a few moments.

'Mummy,' Minette exclaimed, pressing her mother close. 'Oh, Mummy, you're just like a skeleton.'

'No, no, I'm absolutely fine.' Ginny held Minette away from her. 'But you. How are you?' She put her hands around Minette's face with such warm and unaffected tenderness that Minette caught her breath.

She had expected all kinds of emotional protestations from her mother:

We've been out of our minds with worry.

How could you put us through all this anxiety, darling?

Are you absolutely sure you're all right?

That kind of thing. Caring and understanding shot through with silently reproachful anxiety. Just the sort of thing to make you feel as guilty as hell.

But Ginny didn't seem particularly disturbed by her daughter's wayward behaviour. In fact Minette had the distinct feeling her mother was secretly almost approving of her recent escapades.

'I'm OK, Mummy. Truly. I'm fine,' Minette said, looking into her mother's delicate, fragile features and regretting the countless occasions she had given her a hard time.

Ginny slipped off her coat. She wore a matching pink dress underneath. She was as slim as a wand and her skin as smooth as cream. Minette was struck by how lovely she was.

'I'm sorry I wasn't here when you arrived,' Ginny told Minette apologetically.

'You've hardly been here at all for the past few weeks,' Miles commented.

Ginny glanced at him anxiously.

Minette sensed something in the atmosphere. 'Out all the time, Mummy? That's not like you.' Encouraged by a spark of wickedness that wouldn't be squashed, she said mischievously: 'Don't tell me you've secretly been meeting a lover.'

Ginny looked startled and hunted. And then she smiled. 'Secret meetings with a lover! Oh, no, Minette. My lover is here.' She touched Miles's shoulder lightly and he turned to meet her eyes very briefly.

256

He got up abruptly from his chair. 'I'm going along to the lab,' he announced, his voice gruff. 'There are some slides I need to look at.'

Minette stared at his departing back. 'Quitting the emotional fray as usual,' she commented with exasperation.

'He can't deal with emotional scenes,' Ginny said calmly, sitting down and crossing her slender legs. 'He never could, and I don't think he'll ever be any different. But he's a good, decent man. Don't think badly of him, Minette.'

Minette was astonished by this little speech. Her mother seemed like a changed person. 'Can you honestly say you're happy with him, Mummy?' she asked impulsively.

'Oh, yes. He's my life, really.' Ginny looked down at her beautifully manicured hands. Warm colour crept into her white neck.

'But he's so obstinate. So untouchable!'

'That's how you see him, Minette. And I'm really sorry about that.'

'So that's not how you see him?'

'We're man and wife,' Ginny said, looking up at her daughter with meaningful challenge. Two women facing each other as adults for the first time.

With a sharp jolt Minette suddenly understood that it must have been sex which had glued her parents' marriage together for all these years. Sex! All those secret and private things that went on in the bedroom. Her mother was telling her that her father was an ace lover! All his dammed-up human warmth must be channelled into a physical expression which he could share with only one person.

257

The idea of it came as a stinging shock to Minette. Not only the shock a child feels in stumbling across raw parental passion, but the strangeness of coming to terms with her father as a creature of flesh and blood. A human being of primitive spontaneity, whom she had always viewed as some remote, untouchable god.

My lover is here, her mother had said. And her eyes had been veiled with secrets.

Wow, thought Minette. You certainly live and learn. She suddenly felt forlorn and isolated: an only child, very properly loved and cared for, but basically one on her own. Her father and mother had each other, even though her mother was a nervy neurotic and her father obsessional about his work. But she, Minette, was alone, a little boat, adrift and bobbing. She ached for Greg.

'You know that I've been sleeping with this man I met?' she said to her mother brutally.

Ginny nodded.

'You're not angry?'

'As long as you were careful, I'm not angry at all.'

Minette was baffled. Didn't either of them give a toss about her?

Ginny leaned forward. 'Minette, I don't think your father and I have any right to be angry with you. I think we've failed you.'

'No!' Suddenly Minette was on their side.

'Your father was wrapped up in his work. I was wrapped up in him. I had no idea how to respond to you when you started clamouring for an identity of your own. In fact I felt rather frightened of you. And I let Jo take far too much of the strain. You two

258

seemed to get on so well. She was so much less feeble than me.'

'Oh, Mummy!' Minette knelt down by her mother's chair and took her hands. She stared at her, wanting so much to simply say, I love you, and not being able to. The long years of negative feelings towards her parents were like a gag in her throat.

Ginny squeezed her fingers. 'After you went off on your trip with Jo, I hit rock bottom. I was taking sleeping pills to get me through the nights and anti-depressants to get me through the days because I wanted to forget what an inadequate mother I'd been, and how I'd let Daddy bully you about your schooling. Oh, lots of things!' she exclaimed impatiently. 'I couldn't challenge him, you see. It felt like taking sides.'

'So you took sides with him?'

'Yes.' Tears stood in Ginny's eyes.

'What then?'

'A long story. But, in a nutshell, I took all my pills back to the pharmacy and then gradually I began to find courage to say things to Daddy that I'd never said before.'

'About me?'

'Yes.'

There was a silence.

'Why have you been out of the house so much?' Minette asked curiously.

Ginny gave a twisted little smile. 'You remember my friend Susanna Berwick?'

'Oh, sure. Rebecca's mother. Rebecca the model daughter with five A levels and an Oxford scholarship,' Minette said with bitter irony.

259

'Yes. Rebecca's thrown up her scholarship and gone to Romania to look after orphaned children.'

'Very worthy,' said Minette.

'Oh, yes. It's just that her own baby's due in six months and the father's vanished into thin air. In fact Rebecca has told Susanna she's not absolutely sure who *is* the father.'

'Gosh! Rebecca up the spout? Good for her!'

'I don't think Susanna sees it quite like that. She's in a terrible state. I've been going to see her every day, just sitting and listening whilst she talks and talks. Poor Susanna. But doing that has helped me tremendously, you see – being the person giving help, not seeking it.'

'Oh, Mummy!'

'And, of course, I've been pointing out to Daddy that beside Rebecca you're a positive angel!' Her smile was brittle, the skin around her lips quivering.

'And does he agree?' Minette wondered, her own lips tight.

Ginny sighed. 'I'm working on it,' she murmured.

'He'll never understand what I want!' Minette exclaimed, jumping to her feet and pacing up and down in agitation.

'What *do* you want?' Ginny asked.

'Oh, hell, I don't know. Time to think things through and find out, I suppose.'

'Well, then, have it.'

'How? What about money?'

'I've been talking to Daddy about that . . .'

'*No!* I won't let Daddy keep me. That's the very last thing I'll do!'

'All right,' said Ginny calmly. 'What, then?'

'I'll get a job,' said Minette. 'Anything.' Gloom seized her at the thought of some grinding and dreary manual work. And how would she get to any kind of job, living out here in the middle of nowhere without her own transport? She could hardly expect her parents to cough up a nice little car for her. 'Oh, bloody hell!' she burst out.

Ginny was looking thoughtful. 'Listen,' she said slowly, 'Susanna's husband is wanting to take her on a cruise. Susanna would really like to go – and obviously it would do her good – but she doesn't want to put her two little terriers in kennels. And then there are the cats.'

'Yes? So?'

'She's been looking out for a reliable pet- and house-sitter. But no luck so far. How about it, Minette? I'd guess they'd pay pretty generously. You'd have a few weeks to "think things through", as you call it.'

Minette considered for a moment or two. She thought of herself alone in the Berwicks' luxurious house, with just the animals for company. Just her and her thoughts. With time to do whatever she liked; no one breathing down her neck.

The vague aspirations that had been shifting in her mind for some time now suddenly arranged themselves into a definite goal. A bold and daring ambition that made her eyes gleam with speculation.

Could she do it? She didn't know. But at least she could try.

She turned to Ginny with an expression of true gratitude. 'Absolutely perfect,' she declared.

CHAPTER 20

Jocasta looked from the plane and saw the city of Gothenburg coming into view below her, spreading itself between the sea and a hundred inlet lakes, girdled round with a dark green forest. The plane sank down, dipping over the trees and heading towards the runway.

Unlike Minette, the very last thing Jocasta wanted was time to think. During the flight she had kept herself fully occupied – looking through her portfolio of sample yarns and designs, finalizing some new sketches and ensuring that her costing estimates for materials and labour in the proposed collection were accurate. She was keen that her products and presentation should match up to the interest Lars Sandstrom was showing in them.

Glancing through the window again, she saw the dark green tips of the massed conifers surrounding the airport rushing up to meet them. She packed all her materials into her leather display case, drew her seat belt a little tighter and leaned back in preparation for landing.

As her mind wanderered from the straight and narrow path of business, other thoughts came crowding in.

Max was there instantly; a portrait hanging in the gallery of her imagination, fixed and immovable. She recalled the precious moments when their bodies had connected, when their most intimate bodily juices and secretions had mingled. Even now, tender, secret places where he had caressed her still ached and tingled.

A hot flash of vicious rage ripped through her when she reminded herself of the way he had manipulated her, motivated by cold calculation. And then she remembered how he had held her so firm and close in his arms outside her house. The desperate fixed stare on his face as he'd pursued her in his car.

She sighed, weary and bewildered.

But when she stepped off the plane she had her professional businesswoman's armour firmly back in place. She was elegant, calm and in complete command of herself.

Lars Sandstrom was there to great her. He shook her hand and then swiftly hugged her to him, kissing both her cheeks. She felt the power of his strong will and his undeniably potent sexuality.

He guided her to a rather sinister-looking black Saab, and settled her into the black leather of the passenger seat.

'You look simply ravishing, my dear Jocasta,' he told her, starting the engine, which growled like a pride of lions. 'I hope you're looking forward to doing some very interesting business. Mmm?'

She gave a dry chuckle. The prospect of a healthy business deal was certainly pleasant – and, whilst it might not stop her heart aching, at least it would keep her mind steady.

'You're ready to go straight to work?' Lars asked. 'Not too tired from your journey?'

'I'm ready for anything,' she told him, smiling provocatively, having no intention of letting him call all the shots.

'Good, good. These are words which are always music to my Scandinavian ears!'

He drove swiftly into the city. Looking through the window, Jocasta glimpsed ribbons of silvery glittering water. The sea around Gothenburg was divided into countless inlets and lakes whose beaches were heavily used for pleasure and recreation. Immaculate wooden houses, some of them painted in clear pastel colours, dotted the shoreline. The white sails of sailing yachts ready to go out to sea stretched into the sky like the wings of giant birds.

Lars Sandstrom's offices were situated in the old part of the city, on the corner of a broad, tree-lined avenue. The outer façade of the nineteenth-century building was stern and dignified, but inside the decor and furnishings were very much twentieth century. This was an up-to-the-minute palace, furbished with stainless steel, exposed brick and starkly beautiful pale bleached furniture fashioned from a variety of Scandinavian woods.

In the open-plan reception area of Lars's suite, rows of visual display units winked and buzzed, their screens shimmering with iridescent characters. His personal assistant rose gracefully from her desk and came forward to greet them. She was a tall and beautiful blonde whose command of English was virtually perfect.

Jocasta responded courteously to her warm welcome, at the same time wondering if her employment contract with Lars involved sleeping with him.

Lars placed his hand beneath Jocasta's elbow and guided her through into his spacious office, where several of his sales directors were waiting for them. He brought forward his managing director, Gustav Jansen, and made introductions.

Lars then stood back, allowing his colleague to make the full impact his exceptional looks deserved.

Gustav Jansen was very tall, with white-blond hair, a gleaming golden tan and startlingly pale blue eyes which had the cold glitter of a Scandinavian lake under a winter sky. He was clearly in tip-top athletic shape – fit enough to run a marathon or tackle the most taxing black ski-runs.

His eyes slithered over Jocasta with a softly calculated and slinky seduction which she guessed was automatic when he was confronted with any woman between the ages of around sixteen to forty. He tilted his head back slightly as he gave her a concluding glance of approval.

Jocasta understood that she had the potential to charm him, the power to make him desire her. The thought made her body respond with a strange, chilling thrill.

She opened her display case and spread her sheaf of samples and sketches on the desk.

Gustav picked up each item, handling them in an almost caressing way. Jocasta knew that his eyes were as sharp as a hawk's that beneath the silky exterior he was making coolly appraising judgements which would have nothing at all to do with the sexual appreciation he had demonstrated a few moments before.

'These are good,' he said at last, his face smoothly impassive. He turned to look at Lars. The two men exchanged a long glance, which Jocasta guessed contained a number of messages previously discussed between them in some detail. Lars eventually gave a brief nod, indicating that he should go ahead with whatever decision he had made.

Gustav Jansen turned to her. Briskly he outlined the terms and the extent of a possible sales commission.

Jocasta gave a sharp gasp of surprise. She had never expected anything on this scale. He was mentioning figures running into hundreds of thousands. Truly big money.

Gustav's shrewd, chilling eyes connected with hers. 'We are talking here about a potentially very sizeable market, Miss Shand. You do understand that, don't you? I gather that you have not ventured into this league before?'

'You're quite correct. But I have considerable experience in processing orders. And I always meet my deadlines.'

Gustav's eyes glinted with approval. 'But will you be able to give firm reassurances on deadlines with an order of this magnitude?'

'No,' she told him evenly.

His eyes glittered. He lifted disdainfully quizzical eyebrows.

'This is entirely new territory for me, as you rightly observed. However, Lars gave me to understand that there would be advice and resources I could draw on here which would enable me to meet the targets you've indicated.' She turned and fixed Lars with a steady gaze. 'Isn't that correct?'

She realized that Lars Sandstrom had not shared all his speculative plans on her behalf with the icy Gustav

Jansen, and that there was most likely a covert struggle for power going on between the two of them. Her business ambitions – and very possibly her sexual favours – being at the top of the current agenda.

The thought was daunting, but also curiously exciting. Gustav turned to his boss. 'Well?' he said.

'I've already had preliminary discussions with the Gunters Group in Stockholm. They could give us production guarantees. There will be no problems about delivery dates.' Lars spoke with the quiet, casual conviction of an all-powerful entrepreneur. He turned to Jocasta, his smile easy and complacent. He had no difficulty in playing productive business games whilst at the same time engineering himself some intriguing entertainment.

Jocasta saw Gustav stiffen slightly. 'I see,' he said, his voice glacial.

The three of them joined the rest of the group, who were sitting around a large conference table talking earnestly amongst themselves. They broke off when Lars settled Jocasta beside him and then launched into a full but brief account of the purpose of her visit.

During the following three hours the group made their way through a series of hard-hitting discussions and negotiations regarding Jocasta's yarns and current range of knitwear, then moved on to her new fabrics and the proposals for a ready-to-wear collection of her designs.

She found herself swept along with them on a fast-flowing tide of expertise, marketing skills and awe-inspiring motivation. It was a frightening yet euphoric experience, like riding a rollercoaster with no grab rail or seat belt.

Finally a plan of action was worked out and specified, and a firm agreement reached on the sums of money at stake. Jocasta found herself stunned. She had never handled an account of this magnitude before. Her exhilaration soared up to a dizzy climax.

'Well!' exclaimed Lars. 'Excellent, my good friends. Excellent!'

The tension in the room eased. There were smiles all round and warm handshakes.

'Congratulations, Jocasta,' Lars said to her, smiling with foxy satisfaction. 'My colleague, Gustav Jansen, is not an easy man to please, as you will appreciate. But you seem to have convinced him with hardly any difficulty at all.'

Gustav was listening carefully. He glanced at Jocasta, his blue eyes glittering with the suggestion that maybe a time might come when she would like to please him in rather more intimate ways than a business deal.

Jocasta smiled back. Calm and unmoved.

Lars heaved his large body from his chair and threw out his arms in one of his characteristically expansive gestures. 'And now, my friends, I declare that everything to do with work is over for the day. We shall not think any more about targets and objectives. We shall think about having some fun. And so, naturally, you will all want to join me for a barbecue at my beach-house.'

It was a decree rather than an invitation. Jocasta saw sly and amused glances passing between the men around the table. It seemed, however, that they were not unwilling to be commanded, given the promise of good entertainment for free. Gustav Jansen, however, did not join in the general relaxed camaraderie. He slid an icy glance in the direction of his boss.

Jocasta could tell that he was annoyed to have been neatly outmanoeuvred. She guessed that it had been his intention to invite her out on her own – no doubt to enjoy an intimate dinner for two in an exclusive restaurant.

'If you will excuse me, I should like to go home first and change. I shall join you later,' said Gustav, rising to his feet, demonstrating to the company that he was not merely one of Lars Sandstrom's puppets. He turned to Jocasta and inclined his head courteously. 'I look forward to the pleasure of meeting you again, Miss Shand.'

Lars shepherded Jocasta back into his Saab and they set off for his beach-house on the outskirts of Gothenburg. 'You'll be wanting to know more about Gustav Jansen, I think,' he told her, with one of his deep bass chuckles.

'Will I?' Jocasta asked innocently.

'Oh, yes. I could see you were intrigued.'

'Strictly business!' She was forced to smile. Lars's boundless presumption was curiously entertaining.

'Gustav is one of the most shrewd and talented managing directors I've ever employed,' he continued. 'And I'm pretty sure that he's already making plans to branch out on his own.'

'I suppose that's a risk you have to face with talented employees.'

'Oh, yes. But it's no disaster. I shall find someone else. And I shall very much enjoy sparring with Gustav as a rival.' He glanced towards her, his eyes twinkling.

'He's not married, you know. He's what you British call
"fancy-free" – still looking out for the right woman.'

'Oh, really?'

'Come along, Jo, don't tell me that you're not just a
little bit interested?'

'I'm here on business, Lars,' Jocasta protested,
smiling. 'I've no intentions of raising any man's hopes
about a possible love affair.'

She stared out of the window, her face bleak. But why
not? she said to herself silently. I'm fancy-free too.
Instantly tears sprang into her eyes as she thought of
Max. Her heart contracted, but she she angrily pushed
the thought of him away.

Why shouldn't she simply think of herself, of her own
pleasure? Gustav Jansen was undeniably fascinating. He
was clever, ambitious, and very successful. She guessed
that he would make an excellent and entertaining escort.
She also had an intuitive suspicion that he was probably
highly accomplished in bed. And, whilst she had no
intention whatsoever of joining him in any sexual frolics,
the idea of his likely prowess was tantalizing.

'Such a long silence,' Lars commented, amused. 'It
seems to me that you could be more than a little
interested in my friend Gustav.'

She sighed. 'Does it? Well – maybe I could.' She
looked out of the window once more, but her eyes were
still misted over and she saw nothing but a blur.

Lars chuckled. 'All things are possible in this wonderful world of ours, my dear.'

The car came to a halt on reaching the tip of the islet on
which Lars's beach house was built. Stretching in front

270

of the house was a long expanse of sandy shore. There was a wooden boat-landing at its end. Several rowing dinghies were jostling for mooring space close by, and further along Jo could see a sizeable yacht, its sails furled, its stark bared mast stretching up into the sky.

It was early evening now, and the light was draining from the sky. The lake moved and glistened, a grey-blue mass of water, lit with points of silver light from the rising moon. Black shadows of trees stretched long tentacles across its smooth surface.

Inside, the house was very simple. It was built entirely in wood, with one vast room dominating the ground floor. There were a number of sofas and low tables and in the centre of the room a charcoal fire was burning in a cylindrical iron grate.

Flanking the main room was a large sauna cabin, a starkly bare kitchen and a cedar-clad bathroom.

There were candles burning everywhere – countless small fat candles in delicate glass holders scattered over the tables, and also several wooden candelabra, with ten or twelve tall slender candles in each.

The supper was set out on a long table running the length of one of the walls. There were pickled herrings and a variety of smoked fish to eat as appetizers, also countless different raw fishes and meats, sectioned and placed on skewers ready to be cooked over the fire as and when the guests felt inclined to eat them.

Lars surveyed the scene, rubbing his hands in pleased anticipation. 'In Sweden,' he told Jocasta, 'we love to have barbecues all the year round. When the weather gets colder, we simply bring the barbecue inside.'

271

Guests were arriving thick and fast. The room filled with talk and laughter. Everyone present spoke faultless English, and Jocasta had no difficulty in joining in the general chat.

She noted that the other guests were dressed very casually, in jeans and loose shirts. Some of them went off to relax in the sauna cabin for a while and came back clad only in a towel.

She looked down at the sleeves of her navy jacket and felt rather annoyed that Lars had whisked her straight from his offices to the beach-house without giving her time to change. She was both overdressed and uncomfortably warm. Slipping the jacket off, she draped it over a nearby chair. But even though her dress was sleeveless and moderately low-cut at the neckline she still felt inappropriately formal. She could imagine the other guests marking her down as a stiff and starchy Englishwoman.

She went to the bathroom and loosened the pins from her French pleat, allowing her hair to fall over her shoulders in a curving sweep. Instantly the severe effect softened. And with the addition of a some scarlet lipstick and a spray of spicy opium perfume she began to feel more in tune with the mood of a Swedish barbecue than a high-powered meeting around a board-room table.

Lars glided up. 'My dear Jocasta. You look sensational. But you have no drink! Please, help yourself to whatever you wish for. The refrigerator is full of champagne, and I have extra bottles cooling in the lake! You must drink as much as you like. Enjoy yourself!'

His companion stood behind him, a serene smile on her smooth and beautiful face. Jocasta recognized Lars's personal assistant, whom she had met earlier in his office suite. Clearly the personal aspect of her contract was exactly as Jocasta had speculated.

Lars had his arm around her hourglass waist. Being around a foot taller than him, she was able to demonstrate her affection by dropping kisses on the top of his bald head from time to time.

'Anita takes such very good care of me,' he told Jocasta. 'I cannot think how I ever managed without her.'

Anita smiled in amiable conspiracy at Jo, who instantly understood that whatever Lars's hidden intentions had been in asking her to his party, they did not include any plans for a seduction. At least not between himself and Jo. Lars looked as though he would have his hands well and truly full with Anita.

Anita slithered from Lars's grasp and after a brief absence returned with a goblet of champagne.

'Cheers!' She smiled, handing Jocasta the goblet.

Jocasta took a long drink. 'Cheers!'

At least there was the business deal to celebrate, even though her heart was giving a sudden lurch of new sadness. Whenever she forgot about Max for a few seconds, the return of his renewed memory was so sharp she sometimes feared she wouldn't be able to stop herself crying out with pain.

She felt a light touch on her arm. 'Good evening, Miss Shand.'

She turned to face Gustav Jansen. The look on his face was subtly yet unmistakably admiring. 'Do call me Jo.' She smiled.

'Well, Jo, I shall drink to the expansion of your business. I think you could be looking forward to the start of something very exciting indeed. I've always admired good, classical English design and cloth. But it is not always easy to find it – at the right price.'

They drifted automatically into a business discussion.

Jocasta found herself impressed by Gustav Jansen's lean blond looks, the intensity of his personality, his hawkish instinct for a sharp business deal. But when she looked up into his ice-blue eyes she found herself suddenly longing for vibrant, glowing deep blue ones – eyes that darkened and glowed in the heat of passion.

Her goblet seemed very soon to be empty. Gustav brought her more champagne. She began to relax.

'Have you tried the sauna yet?' he asked.

'No.'

'You should. It's a very pleasant way to ease the tensions of a busy working day.'

She looked at him over the top of her glass. She found his accent very attractive. The way he said 'plessant' and 'bissy' because the 'z' sound was difficult for a native of Sweden. 'I'll think about it.'

'It's communal, you know. I'm not making any improper suggestions.'

She looked down again, smiling to cover the complexities of her feelings.

'Or we could slip away and go to my place,' he suggested evenly. 'I have a lovely house on the edge of the forest. It will be a good deal quieter and more civilized than here. I have to warn you, the activities here will become rather – how shall I put it? – uninhibited later on.'

'So that means I'll either have to be uninhibited here, in public, or do the same sort of thing at your place in private? Is that it?' she suggested to him with a challenging smile. 'Is that the choice?'

'No.' His eyes held hers with clear, cold honesty. 'At my place you may do exactly as you like.'

He got up to refill his own glass. He smiled at her, cool and yet appreciative. 'Don't go away.'

Jo watched his tall, slender figure disappear in the direction of the kitchen. Around her the noise was becoming deafening. The room seemed to be pulsing with shouts and laughter. Wine had spilled on the tables, and the floor was littered with particles of discarded food. Everyone was packed together, thronging in and out of the doorways, laughing and jostling and embracing.

Her head swirled. Looking idly around the room, her eyes were irresistibly drawn to a man edging his way into the room from the doorway closest to the entrance. He was alone, he held no glass in his hand, and he was the only person present who was not smiling. As she watched him he raised one of his hands and pushed it forcefully through his thick fair hair.

Jocasta's heart thrashed against her breastbone; she found it difficult to breathe. The room and its multitude of guests blurred in front of her eyes, as though they had all been submerged under water.

She wondered if she was having hallucinations, if the long day's journey and the hard negotiations had totally zapped her brain. She thought she saw Max. But it couldn't be. How could it possibly be Max? How could he know where she was, for God's sake?

But she had to face facts. Because it was Max. And he had seen her and was making his way towards her with a look of grim purpose.

'No, oh, no!' she whispered, springing up and backing away as he came nearer.

CHAPTER 21

He reached out for her as she shrank away. She felt her wrist encircled by hard bone and drew in a sharp breath.

This was not the easy-going, laid-back Max she had seen on that first fateful meeting in Prague. This was a man with a mission, silently smouldering with some powerful emotion she could only guess at.

'How did you know where to find me?' she asked, trying to keep her voice steady.

'Not difficult.' His face was set and hard.

Oh, God! she thought as her brain began to click rapidly with speculations and theories. Did he know *everything* about her movements? How could that be? And why? Was it Max who had broken in and taken Alexander's letters? Had he been through all her papers, making a note of all her contacts? Was he still acting on Alexander's behalf? Surely not. She couldn't believe it, but instinctively she tried to pull violently away from him.

'Calm down,' Max said, tuning in to her panic. 'There's an easy explanation. I saw which flight you boarded this morning. I remembered seeing the name

Lars Sandstrom on the design sketches you had in Prague. I telephoned Sandstrom this morning and told him I needed to speak to you urgently. I told him I was your lover, that we'd had a terrible quarrel . . .'

She gave a little yelp of amazement and dismay.

Max looked down at her, his lips curving into a smile of gentle irony. 'Sandstrom was very friendly, very helpful. He suggested I come along to this party and make peace with you here.'

'Make peace!'

'His words, not mine.'

Damn Lars Sandstrom to hell, Jocasta thought. The scheming, devious bastard. He'd been playing amusing games with her, tossing her a red herring in the shape of Gustav Jansen to spice things up a bit.

'Jo, we have to talk to each other,' Max said urgently, squeezing her wrist so tightly she could feel the trapped pulse throbbing in her veins.

She looked around her helplessly, having no idea how to reply. She noticed that there were some interested eyes beginning to fasten on Max – female eyes, sizing him up and finding him fascinating and magnetic. And also familiar.

He was not a national figure in Sweden yet. But *The Long Road* was due to be screened in the Scandinavian countries in the near future and his picture would have appeared regularly in the newspaper previews. It would not be more than a few minutes before a name was put to his face – and after that no one would leave him alone.

'We need to go somewhere quiet,' he said tersely, glancing at the raucous champagne-drinking crowd and clearly having the same thought. 'Come on.' He released her wrist, slipped his arm around her and pulled her hard against him. His hand brushed against her breast, and despite herself she felt her body cry out with delinquent and forbidden longing.

'Very well,' she sighed. She could tell that he had no intention of being foiled this time, and she, in turn, had no desire to create a scene.

She went out of the house with him. There were a number of couples enjoying the open air, drinking, chatting, or simply embracing. Max directed her along the sandy shore of the lake and they walked along together, to all intents and purposes a loving couple – except that Max's arm around her was a fierce restraint, his way of letting her know there was no way he would give her the opportunity to escape from him.

They reached a deserted stretch of shore, well out of sight and earshot of Lars's beach-house. There were no sounds at all except the soft sucking of the waves at the sandy hem of the water. Max turned her to face him, still holding her firmly in the curve of his arms.

She made no attempt to resist him. She felt numb and cold. 'Max, it's no good,' she said wearily. 'What's happened between us seems to have killed something inside me.'

'No!' he exclaimed.

'Yes! And you must listen to me,' she warned him. 'At first, when I found out what had happened between you and Alexander – that you had chewed me over like dogs sharing a bone – I felt so angry I could hardly breathe. But there was something else. When I saw you at my house this morning I was afraid of you. Can you believe that, Max? I was truly afraid you might want to harm me.' She paused and drew in a long, sighing breath. 'But now, I just feel . . . nothing.'

He was silent for a long time, and she was grateful to him for that at least.

'I went to see Alexander,' he said eventually.

'Did you?' She felt her face grow hard. 'And is he still alive and kicking?'

'Jo, don't be like this!'

'Like what?'

'So brittle. So detached.'

'Psychologists call it ego-defence,' she said in a flat voice. 'It's something your mind does to protect you from getting hurt, from feeling pain. And even if you know perfectly well what your mind is doing you can't do anything about it. There's a deep, hidden part of it that keeps the barriers well and truly up, no matter how hard your conscious mind tries to tear them down. Don't you read any basic psychology, Max? I thought actors liked to get familiar with all that kind of thing as part of their work?'

She heard his breath coming in harsh, jerky spasms. He swore softly and she could tell that he was in a state of silent and desperate frustration.

She was glad. He deserved it, the bastard.

Then she looked up at him, at the fine lines of his sensitive face, at his gorgeous, kissable mouth. A bastard, yes: a wonderful, desirable, utterly lovable bastard! She felt her body sink against him, her arms move around him. There was a roaring in her ears. She told herself she must be drunk.

He bent his head down to hers, and instantly her feelings jack-knifed and she began to struggle against him. Her head felt light, her skull filled with air. Furred globules of iridescent pink light floated across her vision. He grasped both her hands in one of his and held them still. His leg hooked around hers and subdued their assault.

His closeness and the smell of his skin was making her dizzy. She recognized the drugged powerlessness of desire. She made a bitter attempt to resist him more ferociously than ever. She struggled wildly, desperate not to give in, her determination and strength awesome.

But he was too much for her. She saw his long, curved lips coming closer and tried to twist away, but his hand grasped her chin and forced her to join her lips with his.

Almost instantly she found her body drifting into a state of sweet submission. She felt herself held in a golden girdle of happiness. The grating, clashing conflict that had been raging inside her melted away to nothing in the warmth of Max's caress.

She felt her hands reach up in delight to stroke his hair and trace the shape of his skull. His kisses were arousing her so that her body came alight, tiny points of flame darting everywhere. But it was not just desire that she experienced, there was something even more profound, more wonderfully moving and mysterious beneath the sexual awakening. It was true human warmth and tenderness, the flow of feeling and compassion between two people who are in tune with each other.

As their lips and tongues moved together and she drank in the strong male sweetness of him she felt herself drowning in a sensation of peace and safety.

The night air sent shivery tingles over her skin as he unzipped her dress and pushed it down over her hips. The moist tang of the sea air mingled with the touch of his fingers moving softly over her throat. She wrenched off her bra, then took his hand and placed it against her breast.

He bent to take a nipple into his mouth and she threw her head back, wanting to howl like a she-wolf with the yearning she felt for him.

He pushed her down onto the sand. And now his hands were sliding up her thighs, moving between her legs, touching her in that wonderful, arousing way that she could imagine no other man being able to do. He seemed to know the needs of her flesh as though it were his own.

She heard herself panting, was aware of her hands tearing at his clothes, connecting with the satin hardness of his rigid stem. She heard her voice urging him to enter her, to thrust deep inside her and make her forget everything but the dizzy sensation of his lovemaking. He arched himself over her as she lay naked and spreadeagled on the sand.

'Ahh,' she breathed as he drove himself into her.

She imagined herself as a storm-battered ship at last coming into the harbour. He was her helmsman, her guiding star and the sheltering harbour walls all rolled into one. Covered by his warm, powerful body, feeling him possess the secrets of her flesh, she had a sense of being utterly safe.

And then she was singing out with pleasure, and he had to place his hand over her mouth to muffle the shrill animal cries that split the night quiet.

They lay together, their limbs locked, gently coming down from the heights they had scaled. Jocasta felt her pulses begin to steady. She gave a laboured sigh and Max eased his weight from her, realizing he was in danger of crushing her.

A sharp rush of cold air came between them. Jocasta looked up at him, her eyes wide and startled. It was as though she had been hypnotized, living through a beautiful trance-like dream, and now she was returning to the harshness of reality. The dream had been a warm cocoon of safety. But it had been no more than a dream, an eerie echo of her wish for something that could never be reality. Max did not offer safety. He was not a prince-like champion of shelter and trust and happiness. He was a master of deception and manipulation.

She squirmed out from beneath him and began to crawl around the sand, desperately trying to retrieve her clothes. And more importantly her self-possession and her independence.

He made a lunge towards her, trying to gather her into his arms again, but she screamed at him not to come near and he held himself back, squatting on his haunches, watching her, his face haggard and contorted.

'Jo,' he said softly.

She was sobbing now, her body shaking with agitation as she fumbled with fastenings and zips, her fingers clumsy and disobedient. 'Oh, my God, it's so obvious! How could I have been so stupid as not to see it? You're just here to keep me quiet again, aren't you? Alexander persuaded you to have just one more try. I can just hear him telling you to go and find me – Jocasta, that poor, dumb female animal to be tied up and kept chained and muzzled until he's ready for her to be set free.'

'That's absolute garbage. And you know it!' Max's eyes blazed through the darkness.

'Oh, no. Not garbage. The election's only two days away, isn't it? Alexander's big chance for the ultimate political prize. He'd stop at nothing.'

'Jo, why would he do this when there's nothing to fear from you?'

'Because he's paranoid, that's why. I told you before. There's a part of his personality that's crazy. Oh, he's very intelligent, and a brilliant manipulator, but he's not quite balanced.' She was struggling with a stocking, her wet foot refusing to work its way into the thin nylon. 'Oh, hell, hell, hell!' she yelled.

'Jo, I came because I wanted to be with you,' Max said quietly. 'It was nothing at all to do with Alexander.'

'I don't trust myself to believe you. No, that's wrong. I don't even want to believe you. I just want you to go away and let me pick up the pieces of this ghastly affair and get back to having a life again.' She gave up on her stocking and crammed her bare feet into her shoes.

'I love you,' he said, his voice very soft.

She felt as though he had slammed a fist into her face. To say that to her, so simply, with such feeling. 'That's cruel, Max. And wicked. How can you expect me to believe that after all you did to me?'

'Because it's true.' His head hung down in a movement of pure dejection, and she found her heart and all her feelings reaching out to him. Once again she was on the point of falling under the spell of his charm.

She jumped to her feet and began to walk away. Her high heels sank down into the sand and she bent to tear them off, speeding up into a run.

He was there instantly beside her, effortlessly matching her pace with his long athletic stride. She felt hounded and pursued. She stopped abruptly, swinging round to confront him.

'You and Alexander,' she said bitterly. 'If you'd both set out to torture me and then crucify me you could hardly have been more successful.'

'Jo!'

'Listen to me, Max, you've no idea what damage you've done. Do you know what I was trying to forget whilst I was with Minette on my European business trip?' she demanded, her eyes blazing. 'It wasn't my accident. It wasn't the grief of losing Alexander. They were nothing in comparison with losing my *baby*.'

He stared at her.

'I told you Alexander wanted me to have an abortion, and that I refused. Oh, that rattled him, I can tell you. But I never went ahead. I lost my baby quite naturally, through a miscarriage. The doctors were wonderful, they did all they could to save the baby, but it was no good. I think those few days were the worst of my life.'

'Dear God, why didn't you tell me this before?'

'I couldn't bear to talk about it.' Tears coursed over her cheeks and her body shook.

He held out his arms but she recoiled from him, shouting at him not to touch her. She began to walk away again. 'Tell me something, Max,' she burst out suddenly, stopping dead and almost tripping him up. 'Did you and Alexander chew over the ins and outs of my pregnancy when you were cooking up your dirty tricks campaign?'

'Yes,' he admitted with a sigh.

'He'd have been in a sweat, wouldn't he? He'd have been wondering whether I'd gone along with his wishes and had the abortion, and then he'd have been wondering whether I was going to go ahead and have the baby – and which of those would be worse if it got into the gutter press. He'd have told you that I needed to be especially carefully watched. Am I right?'

'Yes.'

Her fury was so great that she swung hard at him and caught him a sharp blow on his cheekbone. The impact cracked out like the report from a gun. 'The thought of you two talking about my baby makes me feel physically sick. It makes me hate you both more than anything or anyone in the world. Can you understand that?'

He stood, mute and stricken.

'I suppose when you saw me in Prague, very obviously not pregnant, you made the assumption I'd had the abortion?'

He was silent.

'Well? Isn't that what you thought?'

'Yes.' His face twisted with pain.

'Well, I'll tell you something, although whether you'll be able to understand it is another matter. When I conceived that baby I was very much in love with Alexander. Even after he'd started to push me away from him, I still remembered the love I'd felt. And I loved my baby for that reason. I could never have destroyed it. It was a part of what Alex and I had shared together.'

He flinched. 'Jo, please . . .'

'Go and burn in hell. Get out of my sight, Max. I can't bear to have you near me.'

This time when she walked away he made no attempt to follow her, but simply stood staring after her departing figure, a lonely dark shape on the wide expanse of sand.

When Jocasta eventually got back to the beach-house she had managed to stop sobbing. She felt drained and unreal. As she walked into the steamy heat of the main room she saw Gustav Jansen talking with a small group of people. He noticed her instantly and came across, frowning in concern when he took in her rumpled and distressed state.

'Jocasta,' he said in his attractive sing-song Swedish accent. 'Tell me what has happened to you.'

'I should have stayed in the house. Things have been getting a little wild out there, as you predicted.' She forced herself to give the impression of dry detachment and made her face mould itself into a smile. 'It was nothing important, Gustav. I'll go and tidy myself up a bit, and after that I shall be fine.'

'Would you like to take advantage of my earlier invitation?' he asked, polite and formal.

She hesitated. 'Yes, I think I should like that.' She looked swiftly around her towards the doorway, wondering where Max had got to. She could see very little beyond the pool of light thrown by the candles which burned in the house. Already she was bitterly regretting the cruel words she had flung at him, despite the vein of truth they'd carried.

Suddenly she saw his tall figure approaching the house. He was walking slowly, like a man who had suffered a bitter shock or was ill.

Compassion squeezed at her heart. She looked back at Gustav. 'Can we go straight away?' she asked him urgently. 'It's so stifling in here.'

'Very well.'

She pushed her way through the guests, making for the back door of the house, through which Lars had originally brought her. Gustav Jansen followed, taking her arm and leading her to a sleek silver BMW.

Strapping herself into the seat belt of the passenger seat, she watched Gustav slot the key into the ignition. The engine was so quiet she could hardly hear it. Dazzling light streamed from the headlights piercing the darkness and the dark silhouette of Max stood out in the beam.

Jo saw that he was anxiously scanning the line of parked cars, looking for her. She found herself shivering.

Gustav revved the engine hard and swung the car around in a U-turn. He was a forceful and skilled driver. As the car accelerated away from the house Max's figure faded and then melted into the darkness.

Gustav took her to his house in an exclusive part of Gothenburg some miles out of the city. It was as she had expected: stark and immaculate.

He switched on rows of brilliant spotlights which illuminated his collection of modern Scandinavian sculpture. He offered her brandy and sat down opposite her on one of a pair of huge granite-grey leather sofas. His cool blue eyes scrutinized her.

Jo was wondering what on earth she was going to talk about with him. And how was she going to let him know that there was to be no question of bedtime romps?

She need not have worried. Gustav was a skilled host. He launched into a smooth account of his interest in contemporary art, baroque music and rallying BMW cars, requiring her to make no effort at all besides the occasional polite question. He made no suggestive remarks, no attempts at seduction.

Looking around, Jo noticed a portrait of a dark-eyed woman on the wall. 'That's a marvellous painting – so life-like. Is she a member of your family?' she asked.

'No.' He gave a little smile.

She hesitated, unwilling to embarrass him with further probing.

'She's an artist's model,' he said, holding his goblet in cupped hands and swirling the liquid slowly. 'Very lovely, isn't she? And one might say that the skill of the artist is even more admirable.'

Jo looked back at the portrait. 'Yes, I agree. There's great warmth there, as well as superb technical skill.'

'The artist is someone very special to me,' he said quietly. 'But unfortunately she is married.' He took a drink of his brandy. 'Do you have anyone special in your life, Jocasta?'

Her heart swooped as she saw Max's face slide across her vision. Her pulses quickened and her eyelids prickled. She looked at Gustav, liking him but not wanting to give anything away. The wound that Max had opened was still gaping and raw. Far too fresh to be probed. 'There has been someone – but it's over now.'

'Ah.' Gustav pressed his pale lips together. 'It seems that we have something in common, Jocasta. Both of us unlucky in love . . .?' His eyes held hers.

She nodded her silent agreement. Earlier she had found the idea of Gustav Jansen's sexuality titillating. But not for a moment had she considered sleeping with him. The arousal he had sparked in her had simply been an echo of the roaring torrent of feelings Max had awakened.

'I think perhaps it would be best if I were to leave now,' she told Gustav with quiet authority. 'Would you drive me back to my hotel?'

'Of course.' Gustav appeared not at all put out by her polite rebuttal of his delicately unspoken invitation for her to spend the night with him.

Not only did he drive her to her hotel, he was adamant about escorting her safely to her room. The two of them walked down the corridor, talking companionably like old friends. Jocasta found herself warming to Gustav despite his cold and remote façade.

She slotted her card into the lock and then paused, smiling back at him.

'Am I permitted a goodnight kiss?' he wondered.

Jocasta straightened up and raised her head. 'Why not?'

His lips blended with hers with firm, steady pressure. It was a courteous and civilized embrace. Neither unpleasant nor dangerously stimulating. Jocasta had a sudden realization of how two people could sleep together and enjoy sexual coupling as an expression of human warmth even if they were not in love.

'No doubt we will meet again very soon as business colleagues,' Gustav said, drawing away from her. 'I hope we will become good friends too.'

Jocasta smiled. She touched his arm lightly. 'Goodnight, Gustav. And thank you.'

She watched him walk away. She raised her hand as he turned the corner of the long corridor.

A shadow laid itself across the wall as she prepared to open her door. Her sixth sense told her that there was only one person that shadow could belong to. Prickles rose on the back of her neck.

She did not turn round. 'No, Max,' she said. 'Enough is enough. It's over. Finished.'

CHAPTER 22

Jo flew back to England the next day and went straight to her house, locking and bolting all the doors and windows to try to give herself a sense of security.

She felt ill with misery, as though she had come down with a bad dose of flu. Time seemed to crawl. She found it impossible to slot back into the normal daily routine of her life at home.

It had been her habit to spend most of the day dealing with business correspondence and designing, after which the evening would be free for seeing friends either at her place or dining out. Now she could settle to nothing. She was jittery and tense. When the phone rang it sounded unnaturally loud, and she shrank from it as though it had an evil life of its own. She left the answering machine on continuously and only lifted the receiver when she knew that the caller was a genuine friend or business contact.

She was having difficulty in keeping her food down, and her guts seemed to have turned to liquid. She knew she must make an effort to pull herself out of this low place into which she had sunk.

She dug about in her big baskets of rolled knitting wools and selected a blended yarn of wool and silk that she hadn't tried working with before. Selecting needles and a pattern, she settled herself down to the gentle therapy of hand-knitting.

The quietness of the house disturbed her. She switched on the radio. The discussion programmes were all carrying items on the general election. Only one day to go. Excitement was mounting. There were recorded interviews with all the major party leaders. And then suddenly Alexander's rich, commanding voice was chiming in her ears. She laid down her work, staring at the radio in horrified fascination as though he might suddenly emerge from it.

The telephone on her desk gave out its ripe warble. Even whilst trying to ignore it she found her ears straining to hear the message through the sound of the radio. Longing to hear from Max. Dreading it.

With a shock she realized that the voice recording onto the tape was an exact match with the one speaking so eloquently from the radio. Leaning forward swiftly, she adjusted the volume knob on the radio. Now Alexander's pre-recorded radio voice filled the room. But at least his here-and-now voice on the telephone was drowned out.

Jocasta felt a sickening jolt of alarm. Why was Alexander phoning her? What on earth could he want? As the red light on the phone began to flash, indicating that the message was complete, she jumped up and stabbed her finger on the rewind button. She had no intention of listening to Alexander's message. She even went as far as considering going out to a nearby payphone and calling her own answering machine so as to erase his voice.

She told herself not to be stupid, and certainly not to be intimidated.

The day crept on, the hours slowly passing. Jocasta's knitting grew steadily and her mood became calmer.

She prepared a small supper and then settled down to watch the TV coverage of the pre-election news. She gritted her teeth, forcing herself to watch Alexander's smooth, handsome features as he made a final outline of his election promises. She listened to the soothing almost hypnotic tone of his voice, wondering if this calculated late-night lullaby to the nation would send them off into a calm sleep, ready to vote him Prime Minister when the polls opened in the morning.

She certainly felt in no mood to sleep. Nor did she relish the prospect of lying in bed for endless sleepless hours, fighting off thoughts of Max. She went upstairs to her bedroom, clutching a large whisky mixed with hot water. She read for a while, sipping from the glass until it was finished, and eventually sleep came.

When day broke she dressed in old jeans and a wool sweater and went out for a walk. She knew it was bad to stay in the house all the time, that she must pick up the scattered threads of her life and start to be a socially active person again.

She walked up onto the green flanks of the hill behind her house. The early autumn bracken was sodden underfoot, bare and trampled by the cleft hoofs of the sheep. Gorse bushes stripped of their foliage stretched out brown twiggy fingers. A frail golden-white sun gleamed behind the thin clouds, its brilliance occasionally breaking through and bathing the vegetation in a pearly luminous light.

It was a scene of heartbreaking beauty, and because her emotions were so raw she found herself on the point of weeping. The red heat of her anger against Max had cooled; she had gone past the point of wanting to shriek and hurl things about. There was just this continuous drone of sadness and wanting within her. She found it hard to imagine ever being happy again.

Returning home, she poached an egg and laid it on a piece of buttered toast. There was no special pleasure in eating it; it was simply fuel that her body needed to keep her going through the motions of living.

As she stirred her coffee she suddenly dropped her head into her hands. *This is serious*, she told herself. *I have to snap myself out of it.*

She took a bath and washed her hair. She put on some light make-up. She dressed in new black jeans and a bright red cowl-necked sweater she had knitted two or three years before and never worn because she had feared it clashed with her deep auburn hair. This morning she was in a mood to say, So what! – clash or no clash.

The rented Ford still stood in her drive. Damn, damn, damn! She'd forgotten all about it. It would be costing her a fortune. She used it to drive into the town, cursing herself for not being able to get herself together even to deal with the simplest things, that she would normally handle automatically with no bother at all.

The polling stations were open. She drove to the one allotted to her and collected a voting slip. Standing in the little wooden booth, she stood for a moment with her pencil poised over the names of the candidates. Squashing down an urge to run a thick black line through the whole paper, she eventually registered her vote for Alexander. She had always believed in and admired the principles he espoused, even though she doubted that *he* did.

Walking out into the street, she looked around, hoping she might see someone she knew. But although the faces she saw were friendly and smiling there were none that were familiar.

She went to the supermarket and bought some fruit and a chicken. She still had a curious feeling of unreality, as though she were another person standing outside her own skin, watching herself perform all these mundane tasks.

Back at home, she made calls to a few friends but was only able to leave messages on their answering machines. Like her, they were active in jobs or businesses.

She went back to her knitting, working an extra item into the pattern she was following so as to force her brain to focus and concentrate.

She noticed time beginning to crawl again. She dragged herself through the hours. When it got to midnight, and the first election results were expected, she slipped into her dressing gown and poured herself a hot whisky nightcap, using the same proportions which had helped her sleep the night before. Setting the glass on a low glass table, she switched on the TV.

The picture swam onto the screen. Voices droned. Her head began to feel heavy . . .

* * *

Through a haze of drowsiness she was aware of a drumming sound, growing louder and louder until her head felt as though it would split open. Snapping back into consciousness, she raised her head like a startled deer. Still fuddled and bewildered, she glanced at her watch. It was five-thirty a.m. And pitch-dark.

The drumming had stopped for a moment, but now it started again. Her heart gave a lurch of terror. Someone was at the door. Banging insistently, demanding to be heeded.

'Oh, God!' she whispered, raising a trembling hand to her forehead. She raised herself from the chair, her limbs stiff and heavy. Stealing softly into the hall, she approached the door as though it might explode. If only she had a dog, she thought. One of those vast, muscular beasts with a huge bark and teeth that would frighten the life out of anyone with an ounce of sense.

The drumming stopped. There was a moment of silence.

'Jo, are you there? Jo! Open the door.'

She sagged against the wall. She had had wild thoughts of a thief, a rapist, a murderer. Or Max.

Instead she was hearing the voice of the person she had least expected to seek her out. 'Alexander,' she said faintly.

'For God's sake, Jo. Let me in.'

She remembered the rhyme that had used to frighten her as a child:

Little pig, little pig, let me in.
Or I'll huff and I'll puff and I'll blow your house down.

She opened the door. Silently she beckoned him in.

She had not seen him in the flesh for months. As she looked into his handsome face her trembling nerves steadied.

With Max, a few days before, she had been wavering and unsure. One moment hating him, the next desiring him – loving him so much it made her ache. With Alexander now she felt nothing but a cold, resolute detachment.

'Drinking alone?' he commented, noting the half-empty whisky glass. 'And not answering the phone? Dear me.'

'What are you doing here?' she asked, bewildered. 'On election night – shouldn't you be at Westminster?'

'I'm in my constituency – the place where all candidates standing for parliament should be on election night,' he said smoothly. He arched his eyebrows and smiled at her. 'Surely you haven't forgotten that old ritual?'

'No, of course not.' She was unpleasantly reminded of Alexander's liking for making people feel small and stupid. Or maybe not so much liking it, but simply being unable to help doing it.

'So – how are things going?' she enquired.

He sank down into a chair. 'All over bar the shouting, as they say.'

'The result's been announced? Surely not yet!'

'Not officially. But there's no doubt about it. We haven't a chance in hell.'

'You've lost?' She could hardly believe it. His party was supposed to walk it.

He gave a dry laugh. 'The other lot have pulled all sorts of unexpected cats out of the bag. It's not a bloody massacre, but it means the enemy end up with a comfortable working majority.'

'I'm sorry,' she said stiffly.

'So – there we are! All my bright shining hopes down the drain for another five years.' He drummed his fingers impatiently on the arm of the chair and then looked up at her. 'How about getting me a consolation drink, Jo? A neat whisky'll do fine.'

She walked away to get a glass, wondering how she had ever managed to tolerate Alexander's automatic assumption of the right to issue commands.

'And make it a large one, will you, darling?' he added. 'I've got my driver waiting outside, so I've no need to worry about the demon breathalyzer.'

She poured him a half-tumbler from a bottle of the old malt whisky she had always kept in stock during their time together. His use of the word 'darling' echoed in her ears, awakening tingles of disquiet.

She handed him the glass and his fingers brushed meaningfully against hers as he took it. 'Cheers!' he said. 'Aren't you going to join me, Jo? Drink a toast to my bleak future?'

Jocasta sat down and reached for her unfinished drink. 'Your future won't be bleak, Alex,' she said, raising her glass briefly and taking a sip.

'No? Why do you say that?'

'Because you're one of the world's best examples of a survivor. And bleakness is something I'll guess you've never even experienced, let alone been prepared to endure.'

'Hard words, Jo.' His eyes sharpened and she could see that her willingness to challenge him had acted as a

stimulant, that his nerves were tingling with the anticipation of the cut and thrust of a spiky interchange of
words.

'What will you do?' she asked calmly. 'After the final
result is announced?'

He smiled, swirling the whisky in his glass into a
whirlpool. 'Ah! Well, first of all I shall make certain that
in public, at least, I'm seen to be a loser who can take it
on the chin with excellent good grace. I shall make some
very pretty speeches about my conviction that the ticket
my party fought on was the same one I'd fight on again,
that our hearts and minds and morals were in the right
place – '

'And *were* they?' she broke in.

His laugh was chilling in its lack of feeling. 'Who can
say? But our brave principles were obviously far too
much for the voters to swallow. All that stuff about the
rich making sacrifices for the benefit of the poor – more
money on education and less on weapons. Dear God, we
must have scared them *witless*.'

'You didn't think that at the time you were pushing
the manifesto,' she pointed out reasonably.

'No, of course I didn't. I thought it was what people
wanted – what they were ready for.'

'You made a calculated calculation,' she remarked
evenly, 'but you got it wrong.'

'Yes. That's it in a very neat nutshell.' He stared at
her with narrowed eyes. 'God, Jo, you're hellishly sexy
when you're being cool and analytical.'

'Really?' Her nerves screeched, but she made herself
keep calm. 'Am I "turning you on", to coin a vulgar
phrase?'

300

'Indeed you are.'

'Is that what you came for, Alexander? To get me back into bed?'

'You're brutally direct all of a sudden, Jo. What's got into you?'

She felt a dark, tell-tale flush crawling into her face when she recalled all that had happened in Prague, all that Alexander had done to manipulate and humiliate her. She remembered the four girls in the lift . . .

He leaned forward. She could smell his breath, sour with the whisky he had just drunk – maybe with several other tots before that.

'Oh, no, the question isn't what, but rather *who's* got into you isn't it?' he drawled, leaning back again and smiling with satisfaction. 'Of course! Maxwell Swift. That's it! So tell me, Jo? Was he a good performer? I've heard on my grapevine that these public property sex objects are invariably a bit of a let-down when it comes to delivering the goods.'

Jocasta had to hold on so tightly to her self-control that the joints of her fingers went white as they tightened around her glass. With elaborate care she put the glass on the table, fearing a messy breakage.

She knew that the last thing she must do was take issue with Alexander over his treachery in using her and Max as puppets in his power-games. Alexander would simply enjoy witnessing her outrage, and she, in turn, was not sure that she could hold off doing him some real physical injury. It astounded her to find herself thinking of the effect of a heavy glass vase on the side of his head, or his reaction to being threatened with one of her more lethal kitchen knives.

She lifted the glass carefully and took a drink of her whisky, gripping it firmly and instructing her hands on no account to tremble. 'You made a terrible mistake when you sent Maxwell Swift to me,' she said evenly. She paused, knowing that Alexander would be expecting a stream of bitterness against his own treachery and cruel manipulation. 'I was enchanted by him, you see, just as you'd planned . . .'

Alexander made a small grunt. It could have been satisfaction. It could have been distaste.

'But maybe more than you'd secretly hoped,' she continued, staring at him with deliberate calculation. 'I think it's been exceedingly difficult for you to discover that I fell rather hard for Maxwell Swift. You didn't truly consider that as an option in your plans, did you? You thought I might be temporarily dazzled, have a little fling, maybe. But you never thought about my becoming serious – falling in love with him. After all, Alex, it would be almost impossible for you to come to terms with the fact that I'd truly fallen for another man after being your mistress, wouldn't it?'

Alexander's face darkened, but Jocasta was way past being intimidated.

'It wasn't love at first sight,' she told him. 'Not for me, anyway. I'd go as far as saying I felt hostile to him – a TV idol who's public property, the lover millions of women keep in their imaginations. But then I began to see the real man under the glossy good looks. And later I discovered that the real-life lover more than lived up to the fantasy.' Again she paused, knowing that she was being cruel, knowing too that he more than deserved it. 'And in answer to your earlier question I have to tell you that Max was pretty hot stuff in bed, Alexander. In fact the two of us set each other alight. Something sparked off between us in a way you and I never managed.'

His smile faded. Jocasta realized how easy it was to deflate a man when you played dirty and started talking about the ins and outs of sexual performance. Even a man as pathologically thick-skinned and narcissistic as Alexander.

'You see, Alex,' she said with elaborate sweetness, 'if you were planning on getting me back into bed, or even getting me back full-stop, you've gone about it in exactly the wrong way. When you "introduced" me to Max Swift, you shot yourself in the foot. After him – '

'Swift's a lightweight,' Alexander cut in, 'and you're not impressing me with cheap jibes about sexual prowess. I know when someone's lying to me. It takes one to know one, as they say.'

Jocasta shrugged, declining to be drawn further.

'And what's more,' said Alexander, taking a large slug of his whisky, 'I've noticed that all your comments about Swift have been in the past tense. Which means that whatever bonfire was smouldering between the two of you is snuffed out. History.'

Jocasta stared at him. 'Does it?' she said coldly. 'Believe what you like, Alexander.'

He glanced at his watch. 'Christ – look at the time!'

'Time for you to be going?' she suggested, looking at him pointedly.

He got up, drained his glass and slammed it down on the table. He rebuttoned his jacket.

'No point flogging a dead horse, is there, Alex? You always knew how to cut your losses and clear off fast!' Jocasta commented, amazed at her calm. She accompanied him to the front entrance like a polite hostess with a departing dinner guest.

The moist night air curled around them as she opened the door. Beyond, in the darkness, there was the dim glow of the headlamps of a big saloon car, the dark shape of a driver quietly waiting.

'I hope your car has a good heating system. Your driver will be frozen,' she said.

Alexander made a dismissive noise in his throat.

'And before you go,' she said coolly. 'I'd like my house-key back.'

'What?'

'My house-key. The one I gave you in love and trust years ago. The one you loaned out to your hired thugs so they could come into my house and steal things that belonged to me.'

He gave a short laugh. 'You shouldn't make accusations you can't prove, Jo,' he said, with a smoothness that damned him.

'I'm not the slightest bit interested in proving anything. In fact I'm not interested in you at all full-stop any more, Alexander. An old lover is about as interesting as an old odd sock.'

Alexander was silent.

'Don't worry about the key,' she said sweetly. 'I'm going to get the locks changed. So, what next, Alex?' she asked.

He had been on the point of leaving. He turned. 'Oh, a dignified resignation as party leader in a few months.

Maybe a safe little job in Brussels with the European Parliament. Taking on a few corporate directorships, setting up a company of my own eventually. You mustn't worry on my account, Jocasta.'

He smiled. Ruthless and utterly self-centred, Alexander was not without the ability to see the irony of things. 'And after all that,' he added, with a twisted smile of farewell, 'we shall just have to see.'

Jocasta shut the door. *We shall just have to see.* We! He still thought he was in with a chance, she realized, walking slowly back to the sitting room and picking up the glasses from the table. He simply could not accept that she might prefer another man to him.

She had been telling the truth when she had told Alexander that he was a true survivor. People who didn't care about principles, didn't care about the nature of their career so long as there was plenty of money and power to be gained, didn't find it hard to survive. Nor did those who found it impossible to feel real love and sympathy for another person.

She washed the glasses, rinsing them carefully under the tap. She understood now that Alexander had never loved her, just as he had never felt a spark of true emotion about the child she had been carrying. His child. The baby had never been anything more than a possible threat to his driving ambition.

She remembered that in the course of their frank discussion tonight Alexander had never once mentioned the baby.

He had been running true to form, she thought with a wry smile – entirely himself, calm and detached. His realization of the way life events had been going against him seemed no more than a pinprick on a rhinoceros hide.

And yet, somehow, she had a sense of having gained the upper hand with him, just for a few moments. She had been true to what she felt; she had spoken out. And, despite Alexander's protestations to the contrary, honesty had briefly found a vulnerable target spot.

She began to turn lamps off in preparation for going to bed, giving up silent thanks for her lucky escape, for having been able to finally open her eyes to the true nature of her former lover.

She climbed the stairs, her legs heavy and lifeless. Having been bombarded with Alexander's invading egotism she now found the image of Max coming forward again, taking centre-stage in her mind. Her thoughts of him were suddenly infinitely tender, as they had been in their precious hours together, before ugly truths had emerged to split them apart. She remembered every word and phrase she had spoken to Alexander about Max. Words that had flowed out of her with the ease that truth always has over falsehood.

She stopped dead on the stairs, realizing with a sharp gasp of insight that it would not be impossible to understand and forgive. Her love for Max could have another chance. Surely.

Her heart leapt and then sank into stillness.

No, now it was too late.

CHAPTER 23

It was Minette's nineteenth birthday towards the end of the January of the next year.

Ginny decided to throw a party for her.

'Can't think why,' protested Minette, secretly pleased. 'I'm hardly an offspring to boast about. Jobless, penniless, and generally a bit of a mess all round.'

'You're simply finding your feet after a very difficult time,' Ginny reassured her. 'And you made an excellent job of house-sitting for Susanna. She said she hadn't seen the house looking so clean and shining for ages.' Ginny tilted her head, viewing her daughter with affectionate appraisal. 'I must say the idea of your dashing about with a Hoover and duster and a can of spray polish is a really novel one! I was absolutely amazed!'

You wait, thought Minette. You'll be even more amazed when you find out what I was up to in between pushing the Hoover around and polishing the windows.

Ginny consulted her neatly written birthday supper menu. A good deal of the food she would be serving was already prepared and carefully stacked in the freezer. Ginny was an excellent cook, and although she was not a natural party animal, being a basically shy person, she adored all the preliminary shopping, planning and preparations.

She frowned, wondering if there was anything she'd forgotten. 'I've asked Daddy to buy in some special wines,' she told Minette, nibbling reflectively at the tip of her pen.

'I hope you gave him plenty of notice,' said Minette. 'He'll need at least a month to research the market.' She wrinkled her forehead in a perfect imitation of her father's considered face and assumed a ripe, deep voice. 'Now then – do you think we should give the Tempranillo grape a try, or should we stick to a good Cabernet Sauvignon? On the other hand a Spanish Rioja might be a more acceptable accompaniment to the supper Ginny's planned. And there again we shouldn't forget the merits of a big Australian Shiraz.' She shook her head in mock despair. 'And then when he gets on to the champagnes . . . We might have to postpone things until I'm twenty.'

'No,' said Ginny. 'I gave him a deadline. And, as you know, Daddy always meets his deadlines.' She glanced up at Minette. 'And don't make fun of him. He's trying really hard at the moment.'

'To keep on the right side of us females?'

'Minette! Can't you ever be serious?'

'I am serious! Anyway, I'll say this for him, he's actually talked to me properly in the last few weeks. More than once. He deserves a medal!'

Whilst Ginny sighed and raised her eyes to the ceiling, Minette reflected that her father truly had made an attempt to forge some frail connection across the gulf that lay between them. She had noticed and she was grateful. But she hadn't yet found the secret of feeling at ease in his presence. There was still this need to prove herself to him. To achieve something significant that would make him respect her.

'Have you heard from Jo? Will she be coming?' Minette asked Ginny.

'No, I haven't heard from her recently,' Ginny said carefully. 'In fact I was wondering if you had?'

'Not a thing. I think she must have gone right off me since I ran out on her in Prague.'

Ginny hesitated. She hadn't told Minette about her forceful words to Jo on the morning she had called to talk to her and Miles about Minette's dash to Venice with a newly acquired lover. She hadn't planned to push Jo away, to warn her off Minette, so to speak. And yet she knew that was what she had effectively done – and maybe it was what she had truly wanted to do for a very long time in her heart of hearts. She had to admit that she had become increasingly jealous of Minette's longstanding affection for Jo.

And, curiously enough, since that time she and Minette had got along far better than they had for years – since Minette was a little girl in fact.

'I did send her an invitation,' Ginny said a little defensively. 'And I've telephoned once or twice, but she always has her answering machine on.'

'She was planning to fly over to Sweden for the New Year celebrations. My guess is she's still there,' Minette mused. 'She probably hasn't seen the invitation. It'll be with the mound of post lying on her mat.'

'I thought she was just going for a few days,' Ginny said.

'Ah, well. Maybe she decided to mix business with pleasure,' said Minette. She paused.

'That's the sort of thing you can't say without some explanation,' Ginny chided gently.

'Honestly, Mummy, I don't know much more than you do. Jo wasn't in the mood for spilling any beans when she was here at Christmas. Not to me anyway. Maybe Daddy knows something.' She frowned. 'No, I don't think he will either. I don't think she's telling anyone anything at the moment. She seems closed up in herself, afraid to trust anyone.'

'But you think there might be someone in Sweden she's become fond of?' Ginny wondered tentatively.

'I've no idea. That remark about business and pleasure was just one of my flip quips.'

'I always thought she confided in you,' Ginny insisted, unable to disguise a hint of reproach.

'She did once. Not any more.' Minette smiled at her mother, giving Ginny's shoulder an affectionate and reassuring squeeze.

She had no intention of running the risk of upsetting Ginny by telling her that she was, in fact, pretty worried about Jo. Despite the considerable energy Minette had expended thinking longingly about Greg and working on the secret project which was becoming more exciting by the day, she had still had time to think a good deal about Jo since their Prague adventure. She had puzzled over her sudden break with Max, and the quiet, withdrawn look that was constantly in Jo's eyes.

Jo had spent three days with Miles, Ginny and Minette over the Christmas holiday. She had talked with quiet enthusiasm about the new developments in her business, showing them the sketches of the range of garments that would be launched under her own label the following autumn. But on more personal subjects she had been cool and evasive. And on the issue of men she had been completely unapproachable. Minette had mentioned Max Swift's name only once during one of their private conversations. The response had been a long, silent stare, which had warned her not to make the same mistake again.

Minette had tuned in to the steely strength of feeling behind Jo's unspoken message, and, for the first time, she had been aware of a similarity between Jo and her father. Like Miles, Jo could be as walled up and secretive as hell.

Minette had been desperate with curiosity to know what had happened between Jo and Max. But, having gingerly skated around the subject once or twice, she had concluded that Jo would rather undergo having her fingernails pulled off than disclose anything.

Throughout her stay Jo had been pale and gentle and quiet. She had been very much as Minette remembered her following her dramatic fall from the bolting horse: keeping herself calm and still, as though she might injure herself afresh if she moved too sharply or spoke too loudly.

Minette had sketched out for her a brief verbal portrait of the time she'd spent with Greg in Venice. She had described the *palazzo* and the little alleyways bordering the tiny canals. She had told Jo about the various churches and galleries Greg had taken her to, and how he had teased her into a constant state of curiosity to find out more, see more.

Jo had listened attentively, smiling and showing a keen interest. She had asked all the right questions at the right time, and not just about the city but about Greg too. Yet still she was not prepared to say anything of her own experiences with Max.

When she had left to return to Yorkshire, she had given Minette a light kiss on her cheek. It had been perfectly amicable, but in great contrast to the usual warm hug she normally offered. As Minette had watched her car drive away she had sensed a terrible loneliness and uncertainty in its driver.

Minette pulled herself out of her reverie and looked at her watch. 'Mummy,' she called out from the the hall to Ginny, who was sitting at the kitchen table turning the pages of her new French cuisine cookery book, completely absorbed. 'I'm going out for a walk.'

'All right. See you soon.' Ginny looked up as Minette shrugged herself into a thick rust-coloured duffel coat and ran to the door. She wondered about her daughter's curious new interest in walking, a form of exercise she had always resisted before. It happpened once a week, always in the afternoon, soon after lunch. Ginny had been quite baffled at first, but now she was beginning to make connections and start guessing.

Minette ran down the drive, flinging her arms wide to embrace the damp, earthy-smelling air. She could tell she was in love. All the things she had read about connected with this state seemed to be happening.

At times she kept wanting to skip about and sing, and at others she wanted to bawl and howl because Greg wasn't there and she wanted him so badly. Her body felt weak when she thought about his piercing merry eyes and the way he had wrapped his long legs around her when they made love. Her heart revved up like a five-litre engine every time the phone rang – even though she had told him on pain of death never to ring her at home.

They had tried keeping in touch by writing. Minette had sent him countless letters packed with joky details and embroidered all over with inky kisses. But Greg was a mover and a talker. He had little patience with expressing himself on paper. His letters were curiously stilted, in no way a reflection of the funny, vibrant man she knew him to be.

Minette had been hurt. Sensing it, he had sent her a brief, terse note:

> *Send me the number of your nearest call-box. Air Mail. Priority. Be there the day after tomorrow at 2 p.m. English time!*

She had done as he'd asked, and two days later had raced along to the old-fashioned red telephone-box a mile down the road. It had rows of small red-framed windows and a door that took the strength of a giant to heave it open. She had been in position beside the phone a good half-hour before the appointed time, teeth chattering with cold whilst her nerves sang with anticipation.

When she'd heard his voice she had burst into wails of happiness. 'Oh, Greg, Greg, Greg!'

'Look, sweetheart. Don't waste energy bawling. Get on a plane and come and see me.'

'No!'

'Why?'

'No money.'

'Charge the fare to me.'

'No.'

'Why?'

'You know why. I need to have my own money before I come out to you. I need to have proved something to myself.'

'Christ, that might take for ever.'

'No! It won't. But I need just a tad more time. Please Greg . . .'

'OK, OK. Don't cry, sweetheart, it really gets to me – like I wish *you* would.'

She had felt his exasperation throbbing down the line. His eagerness too, and his intense desire for the two of them to be together again. Was it love – or just lust? Did it matter?

Over the past weeks there had been several more calls of a similar kind. She found herself living for those precious few moments when she was connected to him, fizzing with elation and feeling dizzily alive.

Running along the road on this moist grey afternoon, the phone-box in sight, she reflected on Greg's growing impatience at her reluctance to tell him what she was up to, the nature of this mysterious project of hers which kept needing more and more time – delaying their meeting again. She simply couldn't bring herself to tell anyone more about it until she was certain something good would come of it.

But now she was beginning to wonder how long he would wait.

Last week he'd been tender and joky.

'Are you being faithful to me, little pussycat?' he'd enquired.

'As a nun.'

'Good. I'm an old-fashioned guy at heart. I like my girl to be well and truly fixed on me.'

'And you?' she'd asked, eyes glinting as she gripped the receiver. 'Have you been keeping your jeans on?'

'Celibate as a monk.'

'Honestly?'

'Yeah. It's hell. And there's worse. I'm actually wanting to carry on with it – until I've got you again, babe. That's real bad news for a red-blooded guy – never happened to me before.'

'Oh.' Her heart had swooped, first with joy and then with humming anxiety. If she kept him waiting any longer, how could she possibly expect him to be faithful? They'd only been in each other's company for a few short days. There was no commitment on either side. Nothing to bind them together in the long term. Nothing at all, really, except a whole trunkload of lust and love.

She speeded up her run and then stopped dead in her tracks as she registered another person already stationed in the phone-box. This had never happened before, although obviously there was always the risk, even with an out-of-the-way rural call-box.

Damn, damn, damn!

She stood outside the box seething with impatience, making it clear to the woman inside that she needed to be in that box and on the other end of the receiver without delay. The woman simply smiled and waved. Minette made herself smile back.

After fifteen minutes had gone by she was no longer smiling. She knocked urgently on the door. The woman turned her back and ignored her. She was talking animatedly into the handset. On and on she went, until eventually Minette slid down onto the ground beside the box, hanging her head down between her knees, totally frustrated and in despair.

It was three-quarters of an hour before the woman emerged, letting the heavy door swing slowly back behind her. She was still smiling, offering casual apologies as though nothing was amiss.

'Bloody selfish bitch,' muttered Minette to herself, storming into the box and staring at the phone, willing it to ring.

It remained stubbornly silent and Minette glared at it, feeling murderous. She considered possible ways of getting in touch with Greg herself. She knew that he was working in Prague in preparation for the forth-coming film. There had been some delays in starting shooting because of casting difficulties, and it seemed that he was having a pretty hellish time all round. But she'd lost the envelope on which she'd scribbled his contact number in Prague, and, in any case, she didn't want to be the sort of girl who pestered her guy at work – or at play either.

She waited for an hour, pleading with the dumb phone to ring, but at last she had to accept that she would have to wait until the time for his call next week before she could speak to him. It seemed like years ahead.

Walking slowly back home in the darkness and drizzle, she had a horrible sinking feeling that because she had not heard his voice that day she had lost him for ever. Absolutely crazy and unreasonable. But that was how she felt.

She stumbled into the house, hoping to slink off to her bedroom and be mournful for a while in private. To her surprise both her mother and father were hovering in the hall, trying not to look as though they had been anxious and watching out for her.

'Good heavens!' said her father, seeing her tear-streaked forlorn face.

She looked at him. Some hidden urge drew her towards him. 'Daddy!' she exclaimed, throwing herself against him. He recoiled slightly, fingering her shoulders tentatively as though she were fashioned from egg shells.

Feeling that she had had enough rejection for one day, Minette grasped his arms and dragged them around her, forcing him to hold her firmly. There was just one pure moment of connection before he gently pushed her away.

Minette burst into sobs and flew up the stairs. 'I'm OK,' she heard herself shouting down to her baffled parents. 'I'm perfectly fine!'

In her room she stood beside her desk, her nerves twitching. She looked down at the pile of papers on the desk top: the yellow pads Greg had bought her at Marco Polo airport, which were now filled with endless scrawling lines of her long, loopy scribbling. And suddenly, from somewhere amongst the turbulence swirling inside, the resolution to the problem that had been bothering her for the past few days bubbled up.

Sitting at the desk, she began to write with frantic speed, the words almost falling over each other as they were formed by her pen. She wrote oblivious of time, her pen skidding crazily over the yellow leaves of the pad. When she heard her mother calling out, 'Supper,' she glanced at her watch and was astonished at how the hours had passed.

She flicked through the last few leaves she had written, reading hungrily and at speed. 'That's it!' she exclaimed, throwing down her pen. 'That's where to stop!'

A slow, warm wave of contentment washed over her. She got to her feet and stretched, then picked up her pen again and firmly wrote 'END' at the bottom of the final leaf.

The party was in full swing. A real family and friends party, with representatives from Minette's schooldays shoulder to shoulder with Miles's colleagues and genteel ladies from Ginny's charity committees. They were all with their various spouses and live-in-lovers, except for one lonely man who came with his golden retriever dog.

Minette circulated, playing the role of polite and dutiful daughter, chatting gaily to the guests, refilling their wine glasses and handing around the stuffed olives and skewered anchovies. She wore the slender gold chain her parents had given for her birthday, fingering it from time to time and guiltily wondering if she deserved it.

Her father had unexpectedly given her a substantial cheque too, pressing it silently into her hand a few days before and striding away quickly before she could say or do anything in response. When she had opened it out and looked at the amount she had rushed up to her room and burst into tears yet again. She cursed herself for becoming a real softy, spouting like a leaky tap at the drop of a hat.

The cheque had been instantly put to use, enabling Minette to employ the services of a local secretarial agency who were in the process of transferring the scribbles rambling over her yellow pads onto floppy disk. Minette marvelled that anyone could decipher anything at all from her hieroglyphics, but the woman at the agency had assured her that they were used to dealing with far worse scrawl than hers.

'Do you think I've remembered everything?' Ginny wondered anxiously, peering up from the open refrigerator as Minette went into the kitchen for a moment of respite from the well meaning questions of her parents' friends. She had been determindedly bombarded as she circulated:

'No career in mind yet, Minette, dear . . .?'

'Jobless! Why not go off travelling for a while, eh? See the world. They're all doing it these days, the young ones — lucky sods. When I was a kid . . .'

'Take up the law or accountancy, young lady. That's where all the money is . . .'

'You haven't forgotten a thing, Mummy. Everything's perfect!' exclaimed Minette, sighing heavily, then sitting down at the kitchen table and resting her forehead against the cool wood for a few moments. 'If anyone else asks me about my aspirations for the future I think I might freak out completely.'

'And exactly what might that process involve?' her father enquired with cool irony, coming in with a tray of empty glasses.

'I haven't decided yet.' She looked up at him. There was a split second of eye contact between them. Not much to go on, thought Minette, but things were definitely improving on the paternal front. The arctic freeze was showing clear signs of a thaw.

'Great party,' she told her parents, smiling her appreciation.

'I'm sorry Jo couldn't make it,' Ginny said, drawing out a magnificently complicated cream gâteau from the refrigerator and staring at it worriedly. Minette saw her glance up at the clock.

'So am I. But there's no point looking at the clock, Mummy. I don't suppose she'll make it now, even if she has managed to sneak out of her business meetings.' She smiled teasingly. 'It was only two hours ago that she phoned from Gothenburg.'

'Yes, of course,' said Ginny vaguely, poking at a rogue hazelnut that had eased its way from the immaculate precision of her decorative pattern.

Minette got up from her chair, taking a deep breath in preparation for going back to join the fray. There was no one at the party she truly wanted to spend time with. A quiet evening having supper with her parents, watching the news on TV and then snuggling up in bed with a book would have been far more attractive.

She didn't want to be ungrateful. In fact she hated the thought of it; her parents had been so bloody marvellous since she had landed back from Europe a fallen woman. Even so, she wished Jo were here. She wished like mad that Greg were here. *Oh, Greg.* Her body flared with warmth just at the thought of him.

She went back into the drawing room. Jenifer, an old schoolfriend who was looking distinctly tipsy, cornered her and started dishing the dirt about some of their old cronies. It was tacky stuff but totally irresistible. 'Remember that swot Rebecca, with the five A levels and the Oxford scholarship?' leered Jenifer. 'And all the men who fled in droves in case they were the one who'd got her pregnant?'

'Yes,' encouraged Minette, finding herself drooling for all the gritty details even whilst chiding herself for being an awful cow.

'Well, the latest is she's met this ancient guy of thirty-odd who's loaded and says he wants to take care of her and the baby when it comes. But Bec says she'd rather be her own woman and live in a one-bedroom flat on income support. Can you beat that? She must be out of her mind.'

As Minette considered her response to this information, imagining herself in Rebecca's place and rapidly reviewing all the options, the front doorbell rang several times – rather insistently.

Minette looked up, meeting her mother's eyes across the room. Ginny arched her eyebrows, mouthing to Minette that this was *her* party.

Minette got up. 'Duty calls,' she told her tipsy friend with a wry smile.

Expecting some late-arriving middle-aged couple of worthies, who would have fresh enquiries regarding her future destiny, she flung open the door, a falsely polite smile of greeting on her face.

The man outside was tall and beanstalky, dressed in crumpled jeans and sweatshirt and very much on his own. He was carrying an armful of red roses and a bottle of Krug.

'Hi, babe,' he said. 'Happy Birthday.'

CHAPTER 24

'Oh-my-God!' gabbled Minette, sagging against the doorframe, her legs suddenly as insubstantial as whipped egg whites.

'No, just me, sweetheart,' said Greg, dropping the roses in order to reach out and grab her before she sank into a heap on the carpet.

'How did you . . .? What have you . . .?' she mumbled as he pulled her against him and shut her up with a deep, fierce kiss that sent her feelings into a crazy spiral of dizzy delight and excitement.

After a while he reluctantly disentangled himself, unwinding her arms from his neck and peeling her away from him. Glancing into the house, he could see people moving around, curious eyes flickering towards him and then swiftly slanting away again.

'I think we should take a break from passion and go and be sociable, sweetheart,' he told her with a wry and tender grin. 'People may be wondering what you're doing, glueing yourself so tight to a perfect stranger.'

'Couldn't give a damn,' said Minette, making a swift grab to recapture him.

He sidestepped neatly. 'Hey, behave. Come on!' Taking her hand, he pulled her towards the sounds of talk and laughter.

Ginny, who had been hovering discreetly just out of sight, stepped forward now, her smile uncertain but unmistakably welcoming. 'Greg?' she murmured questioningly, extending her hand.

Minette watched Greg take her mother's hand in his, curving his long body in a gesture which courteously acknowledged her welcome. 'Hi there, Mrs Shand. Good to put a face to the voice,' she heard him say.

'Oh, please call me Ginny,' she heard her mother respond.

Minette stared open-mouthed at the two of them: her lover and her mother, seemingly involved in some kind of chummy conspiracy.

'Mummy – what's all this about?' she demanded. She looked at Greg but he was giving nothing away.

'You shouldn't be so careless, darling – leaving around little scraps of paper with intriguing phone numbers written on them,' said Ginny with a very straight face.

Minette gave a little yelp. 'Greg's number in Prague. The one I've been racking my brains about, trying to think where I put it!'

'I only found it a couple of days ago,' Ginny said apologetically. 'You'd put it under a coffee mug I discovered on one of the bookshelves in Daddy's study. The coffee looked to be growing mould.'

Minette was struck dumb. The notion of her mother calmly calling up an unknown number in Prague was so incredible she could hardly believe it had happened.

'Ginny had this wild idea I could come along to your party as some kind of birthday surprise,' Greg drawled, giving Minette a lop-sided grin.

'You devious bastard, plotting behind my back,' Minette shot at him, flushing pink with outrage and delight. 'And you too, Mummy! You're just as bad!'

Ginny smiled. It was a long time since she had acted so impulsively. And looking now at Greg and Minette, she had no regrets about it at all. But how Miles would react she couldn't imagine. 'Enjoy yourselves,' she told the two of them, smiling knowingly and gliding away into the throng.

'Calling you up in Prague. Getting you over here. I don't know what's come over her,' Minette exclaimed thunderstruck. 'She seems to be re-inventing herself. Maybe it's the menopause.'

'Maybe,' Greg agreed. 'But whatever, she's one hell of a lovely lady – and not one bit like I'd expected. Like mum, like daughter,' he murmured, looking at Minette and wanting to eat her. He wondered about the sleeping arrangements Ginny had planned, how free the household was. Whether her invitation was a 'come along but don't touch' kind of thing.

'And Daddy seems to be undergoing some kind of metamorphosis as well,' Minette mused, wondering how much Greg would remember of the grim tales she had told him about her parents during their first night in Prague. She surely couldn't blame him if he branded her the world's biggest liar.

Greg blew out a long breath. 'Metamorphosis? That's a big word, sweetheart. Have pity on me. My brain's jet-lagged!'

'You need feeding,' giggled Minette. 'You're always hungry. It must be because your legs are so long.'

'Yeah, and I know just the thing I'd most like to munch on. Take me somewhere dark and secluded, babe.'

Her eyes glinting with understanding, Minette grabbed his hand and pulled him into the the laundry room beyond the kitchen. They threw themselves into each other's arms.

When he kissed her, and his tongue probed and explored the inside of her mouth, Minette felt as though she might explode. His tongue seemed to know everything about her mouth. He might have been kissing her between her legs for the excitement he was generating. And then his fingers found that sensitive spot at the back of her neck, rubbing and massaging, squeezing her to the point of ecstasy.

'Oh, God,' she groaned. 'I'm going to be into multiple orgasms just kissing you.'

'Time to stop, then,' murmured Greg, pulling back from her with superhuman control.

'No,' she murmured, clinging to him.

He tickled her chin. 'I've got to get out there and play the perfect birthday guest – knock your parents flat with my wit and charm.'

'I suppose so,' she admitted. 'It'd be a bit ungracious of you to return their hospitality by knocking up their daughter in the back kitchen.'

'Christ! Don't scare the living daylights out of me with that kind of talk.'

Sneaking back to the kitchen like two guilty kids, they came face to face with Miles, who was standing at the table preparing to remove the cork from Greg's bottle of Krug.

Minette instantly had the feeling of being caught behind the bicycle sheds at school smoking cheap cigarettes.

'Ah,' said Miles, looking up and eyeing Greg from head to toe in his cool, measured way. 'You are the young man Minette's told us about, I presume?'

'Yes, indeed.' Greg just managed to stop himself from adding 'sir'. This guy had huge presence. He could well imagine how the growing-up Minette had found it impossible to resist his wishes and his compelling will.

'Not so much of the young, Daddy,' quipped Minette. 'Greg'll soon be on the wrong side of thirty.'

'My commiserations,' said Miles drily. He returned his attention to the bottle in front of him. 'And many thanks for this superb wine, Greg. I have to confess that I've never sampled Krug before. Very much a rich man's drink, wouldn't you say?' His steady gaze took Greg back to his childhood, when his father had used to bawl him out and make him feel as low as a worm. But Miles was not his father, and so his power to intimidate was negligible.

'Yep,' Greg responded crisply. 'I certainly would say.' His eyes connected with the older man's, letting him know that he was no push-over.

Miles dipped his head and focused his attention once again on the bottle. He grasped the curled end of the wire enclosing the cork and began to twist it. 'The wire around a champagne cork requires precisely six turns,' he commented evenly, beginning to count. As he reached six the wire obligingly detached itself from the cork.

Miles grasped the base of the bottle with the fingers of his left hand. 'One turns with the left hand and holds the cork firmly with the right,' he said with quiet deliberation. Almost instantly the cork sprang from the bottle-neck with a soft 'thlup'. There was not a drop spilled nor a speck of escaping froth to be seen as Miles deftly filled four glasses.

He handed Minette and Greg one each and raised a third. 'Happy birthday, Minette. I drink to your health and happiness,' he announced. Taking a quick sip from his glass, he picked up the remaining one and made a swift exit.

'Christ!' breathed Greg. 'Bloody impressive.'

'Told you so,' Minette grinned. 'He still scares the hell out of me.' Draining her glass at one gulp, she reached for the bottle and poured herself a refill, sloshing fizzy foam all over the floor. 'Come on, then. Time to face the great British public.'

Greg strolled into the wine-swigging, laughing crowd of strangers without turning a hair, and was an instant hit with everyone. Moving effortlessly from one group to another, he charmed them all with his easy one-liners and his whimsical rubbery grimaces. But it was his unswerving attention to whoever was speaking that really captured hearts. Who could resist a man who seemed to find even the most banal comments intriguing?

'The poor innocent things haven't a clue you're a fake,' Minette whispered to him. 'You're not interested in them at all, you rat. You're just a cold and ruthless

observer of the party animal in its natural habitat!'
She laughed up at him, bursting with pride and
adoration.

'Yep. These guys are no more than grist to my film
director's mill,' he agreed, looking around him, his
glance homing in on the ample Jenifer, who smirked
tipsily back at him.

'Eyes off!' Minette told him, giving his ribs a poke.
'You're mine. At least for tonight.'

'Talking of tonight . . .' His eyes gleamed down into
hers, making her knees buckle.

'You'll be confined to the guest room, most probably,' Minette said demurely.

'Jesus!'

'Come to my window at the witching hour,' she told
him, narrowing her eyes seductively. 'I'll let down my
long hair and you can climb up it, spurred on by the
prospect of a night of blazing passion.'

'Thanks, Rapunzel. Would it be OK if I just padded
across the landing on tiptoe?'

'Ahh!' she murmured much later, as he slipped into bed
beside her, stroking his hands in one long sweep over
her back and bottom and thighs, moulding her to him as
though she were a second skin.

'Shh,' he warned. 'I've got this phobia about being
caught bare-assed in bed with my hostess's lovely
daughter.'

His fingers were squeezing her nipples, then darting
downwards, parting her thighs.

Minette drew in her breath and let out a sharp
gasp.

He clasped his hand over her mouth. 'Cool it! This has got to be the quietest episode of lovemaking in the whole history of the world.'

Minette reached down and cupped him with her hand, tightening the pressure very slightly, until he too gasped.

'Now who needs to cool it?' she wondered, wriggling herself underneath him and letting out a long, silent sigh of pent-up bliss as he drove deep inside her.

The next morning they didn't wake until long after Miles and Ginny had set off to laboratory and committee work.

'How long can you stay?' Minette asked, stroking his face after they had made scrumptious pre-breakfast love.

'Got to fly back this evening.'

'Oh!' She forced her face not to crumple. 'Yes, of course.'

Greg slid out of bed. He walked over to the window and looked out on a brilliant winter morning. Gleaming white frost covered the lawn and slivers of thawing ice amongst the bushes caught the sun and sparkled like gems. 'Wow,' he said. 'And they say it's always raining and foggy in England.'

Minette sat up, feasting her eyes on his long, lean, naked body. With a huge effort of self-discipline she reminded herself that there were other things in life besides sex.

She stretched like a cat, her small round breasts tilting upwards. He crossed back to the bed and bent to kiss each one in turn, making her purr with pleasure.

There was the sound of a diesel engine in the drive, the clang of a van door closing. Then the doorbell.

Minette jerked as though a gun had been pointed at her. 'Oh, hell!' Her face flushed with colour as she flew out of bed and threw on a robe.

Greg listened bemused as she raced down the stairs two at a time. He heard the door open, a man's voice saying, 'Sorry to disturb you, love. Sign here.' And then there was dead silence.

He pulled on jeans and a shirt and walked barefoot onto the landing, looking down into the hall below.

Minette was standing statue-still in the middle of the carpet, clutching a fat packet.

He ran down the stairs. She stared at him, her eyes hunted, her arms still clasping the packet.

'Is there a live baby in there?' he enquired, amused. 'An explosive baby, maybe?'

Minette just kept staring at him, her eyes wide, her gaze fixed.

Greg put a kindly arm around her shoulder. 'Come on into the kitchen. I'll fix you some coffee.' He steered her onto a chair beside the breakfast table and gently prised the packet from the claw-like hold of her fingers.

'It might be fun to open it,' he suggested, switching on the kettle and rooting about to find coffee.

'Third jar along, next to the pepper mill,' Minette said. 'I don't think I dare.'

'Why?'

'Because – this is *it*!'

'What?'

'My project.'

331

'Really.' He turned and saw that her face had gone very pale. He looked again at the packet, his eyebrows raised.

'My book,' she explained.

His eyes sharpened, his interest escalating by the second. 'Your *book*? No kidding.'

'My novel,' she said softly.

'Wow! Well, come on, then, sweetheart. Open up. Let's have a look!'

'Oh, God, I don't think I've the nerve. Supposing it's a real turkey?' Her fingers shook violently as she made a futile attempt to pull off the sticky tape which sealed the packet.

Greg took it from her. 'Allow me.'

'Oh, no! Don't! Oh, please don't look at it, Greg. Please.'

Greg emptied the contents of the packet onto the table. 'One fat typescript circled with elastic bands. One floppy disk wrapped in protective foil,' he intoned, handing her the typescript.

Minette recoiled from her creation. There had been such a buzz to start it, such a magnetic pull to carry on, such a push to finish – flying on a wing of elation. But now she had lost all her confidence. She was terrified out of her wits that what she thought she had achieved was just a pipe-dream, a castle in the air built on sand.

'Listen, sweetheart,' said Greg with heartbreaking kindness, 'go off somewhere and hide yourself away and get to grips with this little baby of yours. But don't be too long. I've only got a few hours left to feast my eyes on your lovely face.' He bent and kissed her lips softly.

Minette suddenly realized that she would much rather have Greg there to hold her hand while she inspected her 'baby' than be on her own. 'Sit down,' she told him, placing herself on his knee and tearing the elastic bands from her script.

Greg peered over her shoulder. '*Losing It*,' he read out. 'Yeah, that's a nice title. I like it.'

Minette skimmed through the sheets. The words sprang out at her from the page. Seeing them processed and printed out so immaculately they seemed curiously important and serious. Not much to do with her at all. Was that good? she wondered.

'Tell me, does this story by any chance include a scene in a Prague park with some lewd activities on an empty plinth?' Greg asked.

'You'll have to read it to find out,' she smiled teasingly.

'I'd be glad to,' he said lightly.

She eased herself off his knee, picked up the script and put it into his hands. '*You* go away somewhere and have a look at it, Greg. I'm going to cook you a full English breakfast – the whole works. There'll be time for you to read a chapter and have a skim through.'

'OK,' he said slowly.

'That's how much I trust you,' she said in a low voice.

'Letting me hold your new baby. That's some trust.' He touched her arm lightly as he went away.

Minette opened the refrigerator and got out bacon, eggs, sausages, mushrooms and tomatoes. Thinking of Greg getting to grips with her story made her feel fantastically excited – and scared out of her wits. She arranged slices of bacon in Ginny's largest frying pan, then began to lay the table. Her fingers still shook. She dropped an egg on the floor and burned the first batch of sausages to the hardness of bone. Fumes filled the kitchen.

It was an hour before she had the food prepared and the kitchen once more a place in which one could exist without streaming eyes and paroxysms of coughing.

She shouted out for Greg and began to pour the coffee. She felt like a defendant in court, waiting for the decision of the jury and the sentencing of the judge. She knew that Greg was a formidable judge and jury. He was an avid reader of fiction, highly critical, and always on the look-out for a good story to put on film.

Greg laid the script on the edge of the table. He sat down and looked at the laden plate in front of him: a perfectly cooked English breakfast. 'Some achievement, babe!' he remarked drily, picking up his fork.

Minette swallowed, staring at him pleadingly.

'I'm talking about the novel,' he said. 'The food's pretty good too.'

'You like it? Honestly?'

'Yep.' He picked up his fork and began to devote his attention to her cooking.

'Well, say some more. Don't torture me!'

'It's got style, it's got wit, it's got heart. And it's a thumping good read. I think it could be pretty hot stuff. That enough for you?'

'Really?'

'Really and truly! It's only my opinion, of course.' He gave a crooked smile, tantalizing her. 'And I've only read three chapters and skimmed the rest.'

'I trust your opinion,' said Minette, leaning her chin on her hand. 'If you say it's OK, it must be OK.'

'Not necessarily,' he grinned, 'but I reckon I'm in touch with the kind of stories that are going well at the moment. And, incidentally, from what I've seen so far I'd lay bets it would make a terrific film script.'

'So what happens next?' Minette asked.

'You need a real sharp agent who's right on the ball. Do you know anyone?'

'You mean personally?'

He nodded.

She frowned, shaking her head.

'Pity.'

'Is that how it works? Knowing someone?'

'Yep, or knowing someone who knows someone.'

'Don't you have a chance otherwise? I can't believe that!' she exclaimed, full of indignation.

'Oh, sure, everyone has a chance, as long as they have talent – which you certainly have, sweetheart.' He laid down his fork and leaned towards her. 'But let's put it this way: imagine two people starting out, both with equal talent – one has friends in the business, guys who are in the know, the other hasn't. Who do you think gets the money and gets famous quickest – if at all?'

'Yes, I see what you mean.' She considered. 'Daddy has an agent,' she said thoughtfully. 'But Daddy publishes academic stuff.'

'Right, but his agent, or someone in the agency, probably deals with novels too. You need to get talking to your daddy and find out more.'

'Oh, God! I'd much rather you helped me.'

'Give your daddy a break, Minette.'

'What?'

'Listen, I haven't forgotten all you told me about when you were a kid. And that must have been pretty hellish. But that's over now. You and your parents seem to have made a new start. Build on that. Let him be involved.' He reached for toast and began to spread butter on it with thoughtful strokes.

Minette gaped at him. 'He'll think I've just been wasting my time writing fiction. He never reads novels.'

'OK, but that doesn't mean he despises good writers. Give the guy a chance, Minette. I made a real mess of things with my own father; I'd hate to see you do the same.'

Minette had never seen Greg this serious. It was impressive. 'All right, I will. Yes! I really will.' She jumped up, full of racing optimism. She put her arms around Greg's shoulders, covering his neck in buttery kisses.

'Your daddy?' she said. 'Did he know someone who knew someone, when you got started in films?'

'Oh, yeah. My daddy knows just about everyone. I let him get me off to a great start and then I hated him for not letting me do it myself. Great, huh?'

'Perhaps you should give *him* a break,' Minette teased. 'It's never too late.'

'You don't know my father!'

'You don't know mine!'

'OK. Truce.' He pulled her down onto his knee. 'What am I going to do without you? Tomorrow and the next tomorrow and the day after . . .?'

'I don't know,' she moaned. 'It's too awful to think about.'

336

They sat in silence for a while, just holding each other.

'If you got a really superb deal tied up for your book would you come to me in Prague?' he asked softly.

'Yes, of course I would. All the more reason for me to get things going quickly with Daddy's agent,' she said, her eyes lighting up with new courage.

'You do that. Right away after I've gone. No messing about.'

'It's a deal.' She stroked his face with tender exploring fingers. 'When do you start filming?'

'In a couple of weeks, God willing – and Max getting back from Australia.'

'Max is in Australia?'

'Having a well-earned break. He's been working so hard these past two years, I guess he's shattered. It can get to you, that kind of pressure. You know,' Greg added thoughtfully, 'there aren't many exceptions I can think of to the rule of getting a leg-up through contacts, but Max is one of them. He did it all on his own, the clever bastard! Superb looks helped, but the guy has real ability. I just hope he gets the chance to show it in this new film.'

Minette's stroking fingers paused. 'Have you seen him lately?'

'He came over to Venice at Christmas for a day or two.'

'By himself?'

'Yep.'

'Was he OK?' Minette asked curiously.

'Hard to say. Max is a damn good actor. He could really pull the wool over your eyes if he tried. I wonder

337

what happened with him and Jo? I really thought they were an item.'

'I wish I knew too.'

'He never mentioned her, not once. And I kind of got the feeling I shouldn't either. A real taboo topic.'

'She was just the same about him when she was with us. Talking about Max was a definite no-go area. And she was loking so pale and sad. Something must have have gone badly wrong – I had a really strong feeling about it.'

'Yeah.' He shrugged. 'Well, whatever went wrong between them, they were being pretty loyal to each other in not telling anyone else.'

'Yes. Oh, that's a really beautiful thought, isn't it?' said Minette, feeling suddenly disgracefully sentimental and tearful. She clung to Greg, choked up with the thought of the plight of lovers separated from each other by distance and horrible misunderstandings. Or both.

When her parents arrived back that evening Greg had already left for the airport and Minette had kept herself busy preparing supper and trying to hold her seething emotions in check.

She poured Ginny and Miles a drink.

'I'd like to say a big thank you for giving me such a lovely birthday,' she told them. 'And for being nice to Greg. And for just *being* there these past few months.' She stopped, then dared to add, 'And for not being there today, so Greg and I could have time together alone.'

338

Ginny smiled, biting her lips with pleasure. Miles gave a brief nod of acknowledgement, staring fixedly into his drink.

'And, Daddy,' she added briskly, so that he looked up, startled, 'there's something important I need to ask your advice on.'

CHAPTER 25

Max walked slowly along the south side of the great St Vitus cathedral, enclosed within the walls of Prague Castle. He reflected that the castle had been Prague's very beginning, its commanding position high above the Vitava river making it the centre of the surrounding lands.

Despite the deep and bitter cold of a mid-February afternoon, a small crowd had gathered. He felt their eyes on him, knowing that eventually he would most probably be mobbed, have to smile endlessly, sign numerous autograph books.

The cold struck into him. After a month in Australia, where the late summer had been sweltering with the sun blazing relentlessly down, his skin felt as though it had a blanket of ice wrapped around it.

There were sounds behind him, the shuffling of feet, people following him. Coming too close. Doggedly he walked on, refusing to be intimidated. He was making for the south door, the Great Golden Portal, which was used only on special occasions.

He quickened his pace slightly. The footsteps responded with a similar speeding up. Reaching the door, he saw that it was closed. He stopped, and those following him stopped also, taking a step back. He grasped the sturdy bronze ring fixed to the wall and banged it several times against the stone. Almost immediately the door opened. A monk was standing inside, beckoning him in, an expression of urgency and alarm on his face.

As Max moved forward one of his pursuers suddenly brandished a sword, its blade flashing in the light. There was a murmur of horror from the crowd as the man leapt forward, raising the blade high over his head with the clear intent of striking the man entering the door.

Still Max did not turn. A second man produced a sword from beneath his swirling outer clothing. The two armed men suddenly lunged at Max and began to beat him with the blades of their swords. He raised his arms, wrapping them around his head in a desperate gesture of self-protection. He could hear his heartbeat. So this was it; the moment had come.

It was all happening so quickly. The crowd were transfixed. They stood in silence, seeming unable to make any helpful response in the face of the bloodbath they were witnessing.

Max reached up and grasped the bronze ring, hanging onto it for support, determined not to fall to the ground under the onslaught he was being subjected to. But in doing so he left his chest exposed and vulnerable.

With gruesome roars of aggression both men stood poised before him. There was a breathless moment of stillness and then, in perfect synchronization, they leaned towards him, making a swift, clean plunge into the wall of his chest with their swords.

The faint but sickening sound of the crack of bones pierced the air. Blood oozed from Max's chest. His body jerked in a spasm of a mortal pain and he gave a terrible gurgling cry of despair before crumpling down onto the ground. A red pool formed beneath his chest, slowly expanding.

A low collective moan came from the crowd, but still no one moved.

One of the men bent down and put his hand on Max's neck. Raising himself, he smiled grimly at his accomplice and nodded in recognition of a task completed. The two looked around them, and then, with their swords still raised and their faces flaring with triumphant defiance, they charged off down the south wall of the cathedral, rounding the eastern corner and disappearing.

Still no one moved. The body on the ground lay solitary and abandoned, the focus of all shocked eyes.

A voice called out, 'Cut.'

Greg stepped forward from his observation position. As he walked towards Max he swivelled back and motioned to his assistant director. 'That was fantastic. Get it printed. That's the one we'll use.'

The shivering film crew let out a sigh of relief and began to move around, gathering up their gear, laughing and joking now this difficult sequence had been completed to the director's satisfaction. They began to think about a jug of continental beer and the rich stew and dumplings which the Prague restaurants were so good at and charged next to nothing for.

Greg bent down to Max, who still lay motionless on the ground. He touched his shoulder. 'That was really great. Just like for real. Hey, Max, are you OK?'

Max raised himself onto his elbow. He gave a dry smile. He looked like someone who had woken from a terrifying dream and was heartily glad to be back in the real world again.

A girl from wardrobe ran up, handing Max a heavy sheepskin-lined coat, helping him peel away the stained cloak and the tunic with its hidden bladder of cosmetic blood.

'This bloody cold,' he said, rubbing his arms vigorously with his hands.

'Yeah, it's getting to everyone,' Greg agreed. 'We'll call it a day.'

Max got to his feet. The crowd took tentative steps forward.

'I'm sorry,' said Greg. 'Looks like you're in for another session of signing. And being worshipped.' He chuckled. 'You and your adoring public.'

'Mustn't grumble. They're the ones who put the bread on the table.' Max wrapped his cloak around himself more tightly. Drops of very realistic fake blood dripped onto the ground. 'Poor Wenceslas,' he said. 'Hacked down like a dog outside his beloved cathedral.'

'True. Still, he did get to be a saint, which is more than most of us can hope for.'

The two actors who had played Wenceslas's assasins returned from their flight around the cathedral, swinging their swords in the air and grinning from ear to ear.

'Well done, guys,' Greg said with a wry smile. 'Got it right at last! Anyone for a drink?'

'I'll join you in a few minutes,' said Max, eyeing the eager crowd who were now closing in on him.

'We'll give you an armed escort if you'd prefer to make a quick exit.' Greg gestured to the grinning swordsmen.

'It's OK, I can handle it.'

'Fine,' said Greg, knowing that he probably wouldn't see Max until they got together to look at the rushes later in the evening. No one was seeing very much of Max at all off the set. It was not that he was failing to be a full member of the team – he was acting superbly, never fluffed his lines, never needed retakes, and he was always punctual at pre-shoot briefings and planning meetings. But when the work commitments were over he quietly vanished. Socializing was clearly not on his agenda.

Woman trouble, Greg had decided, feeling unreasonably hostile to Jocasta Shand, who he had marked down as the cause of all the trouble.

As Max was left on his own, so the crowd enveloped him. They were mostly eager women, wanting just to be near him. They made sure to touch him when they passed over their little books or scraps of paper for him to sign. He was in no danger of being mobbed, however. This Prague crowd was much more circumspect than some of those back home in the UK. There he had had hair pulled out, buttons torn from his shirt.

He signed and smiled, and signed again. Eventually the crowd began to drift away, the cold now delving deep into their bones.

A woman standing just out of sight behind one of the pillars of the Golden Portal watched him intently. The brim of her velvet hat fell across her forehead, shading her eyes. Her scarf was pulled up around her nose so that hardly any of her face was visible.

As Max turned to move away, towards the outer courtyards, she slipped around the pillar, hiding herself.

Once he had passed through the archway into the courtyard bordered by the president's palace she followed in his footsteps, keeping a safe distance between them.

Max turned up the collar of his coat, bowing his head in the face of the wind that whipped round the fortifications enclosing the buildings within the castle complex. Hoping not to be recognized, he dipped his chin down to his chest, speeding up now in anticipation of getting out of this freezing cold and into a hot bath.

The woman followed him as he turned sharp left and made his way to the long steps on which Minette had had her portrait sketched. Today there were no artists or novelty-sellers. The town was becoming deserted as the skies darkened and people sought the warmth of indoors.

She followed him down the steep, narrow streets, past the ornate baroque church and on down to the river at the point it was crossed by the Charles Bridge.

Max went straight to his hotel, an intimate, family-owned establishment with a superb restaurant and furnishings in sympathy with the culture and ambience of the old city.

Reaching the haven of his room, he switched on the bath taps to full and began to strip off his freezing clothes. He grimaced when he looked down at his chest, gruesomely stained with cosmetic blood.

Warmed and revived by a long soak, he dressed in jeans and a woollen jacket, poured himself a whisky and settled down to look through his lines for the next day.

The tap at the door did not register at first. He turned his head and called out for whichever member of staff it was to go ahead and come in. The tapping resumed. With a small sigh he got up and opened the door, his mind still on his lines.

Seeing Jocasta standing there came as such a shock that he wondered if he was having hallucinations. His mind had been filled with her for so long that it was hard to believe she was actually there – flesh and blood.

He could see that coming to see him like this was not easy for her. Her face was very pale, her eyes huge and watery, dark, questioning and troubled. Her chest rose and fell with deep, anxious breaths.

He swallowed. 'Come in,' he said, his voice hoarse and unsteady.

There was a moment of panic-stricken fear when he felt she might slip away as softly and mysteriously as she had come. But then she walked with grace and calm into his room and stood looking down at the script he had tossed onto the table.

He closed the door and walked to stand close to her. Close but not touching. He had a sense that she was not to be touched. She was wearing narrow black trousers and a coat in a soft shade of grey that was cut to swing from a deep curved yoke.

'Let me take your coat,' he said gently.

Slowly she slid it from her shoulders. He took it from her, lingeringly touching the places which retained the warmth from her body.

He saw now that she was wearing a sweater of soft turquoise-blue. There was a halo of soft downy fibres around it, waving rhythmically and glowing in the light.

'Please, sit down, Jo,' he said softly.

She moved very slowly. She seemed ghost-like and fragile, and he wanted to reach out a steadying hand to her in case she should fall.

She settled herself in a chair and looked up at him, gazing straight into his eyes and making his heart contract, stirring an instant desire in his guts. She gave a faint, distant smile, then, looking at the glass on the table, said, 'May I have one too?'

Battling with speculation, deep caution and a surging, roaring joy that refused to be smothered, he carefully poured whisky into a glass and added an equal measure of water. He set it on the table beside her and then sat down and faced her.

Why? he was asking himself. *Why now? Dare I hope?*

He told himself he must be calm and quiet. Matter-of-fact and reasonable. *Normal.* On no account must he frighten her away with protestations and an inquisition.

He smiled at her, allowing her to keep the initiative she had so miraculously taken in coming to him.

'I wanted to see you,' she said simply, staring into her glass.

The organs in his body seemed to be alive with electricity. He tilted his head, inviting her to say more.

'I . . .' She stopped.

'There was something you wanted to see me about?' he said encouragingly. He realized he was keeping his voice very soft, as though she were a precious glass and might shatter from mere vibrations in the air.

'No. Well, it's not quite like that. When I said "see you" I didn't mean that I wanted to see you *about* something. I simply wanted to . . . be in your presence.'

Max closed his eyes for a moment. 'That's a little like telling someone you truly care about them,' he said. 'You wouldn't say that without meaning it, would you, Jo? You wouldn't be so cruel?'

'No.' She smiled at him, and it was as if she were holding out her arms to him although in actual fact she was perfectly still.

A current of feeling flowed between them, waves of it lapping through the atmosphere.

'I've been in Australia,' he said.

'I know. Minette told me. She said you were very tired, that you needed a break.'

'Yes. I decided to pull out of *The Long Road*, so after that there was nothing to stop me wandering around the world, footloose.'

'You left the series? Oh, Max, wasn't that terribly risky?'

'A gamble, certainly. I was in the mood for it, Jo. When you lose something – or someone – very precious, all the rest seems less important.'

'Yes.' She looked at him wistfully. 'I know all about that.' She looked down at her hands. There was a tranquil, easy silence for a while.

Max found himself glancing at her, then looking away. Not believing she was really there, terrified that he might say or do something to chase her away.

'The filming is going well?' she said.

'Yes, I think so.' He looked hard at her, asking silent questions.

'I've been watching the outside location shooting,' she said. 'For the past few days.'

He was astonished. *Why didn't you let me know? Why didn't you come to me earlier?* Don't ask, he told himself, don't harass her.

'You were marvellous,' she said. Suddenly she smiled, her confidence returning. 'I suppose that sounds like the tired old phrase "You were wonderful, darling", doesn't it? But it was meant quite honestly. I really believed in the character you played Max. When the two actor assasins came to kill you this afternoon I nearly dashed forward to save you. Or rather Wenceslas.'

'Greg might have killed you instead,' he responded with irony, his feelings turbulent.

'And then you had to deal with all those adoring fans.' She smiled, shaking her head. 'You must have endless patience. I couldn't handle that kind of thing at all.' She gave him another slow, tender smile.

She seemed to him so serene and self-possessed, sitting there facing him without flinching, her forearms lightly folded in her lap. In contrast he found himself in a ferment of speculation and acutely conflicting feelings.

He recalled the searing anger and bitterness that had erupted between them during their turbulent hour together in Gothenburg. And the weary finality with which she had dismissed him on her arrival back at her hotel, after spending the evening with Gustav Jansen.

He reached for his drink. He had a crazy but powerful sense that her reason for seeking him out tonight was to tell him that she had forgiven him. Maybe even to say that she loved him. But how did he help her to get to the point where she dared tell him?

'I hear you've a collection of your own designs in production in Sweden, ready for the autumn season?' he said, keeping the conversation running on safe tracks.

She looked at him, puzzled. 'How did you know that?'

'Minette told me.'

She looked startled. 'Is Minette here in Prague?'

'Yes.' He was amazed she didn't know. 'In fact I assumed that Minette had invited you to join her, that she was the reason you were here.' He wondered if this carefully thought out remark might encourage her to tell him what he longed to hear.

'No!' she protested. 'It was my own decision. I came of my own accord. Nothing to do with Minette.'

He leaned towards her. 'Jo, tell me why you came. Please. I know it sounds hollow to ask you to trust me, but please try.'

'Can we –?' she began, then stopped abruptly as the phone warbled.

'Damn!' exclaimed Max, infuriated beyond belief. He pushed his hand impatiently through his hair. The phone continued to warble.

Jo looked at him and smiled, shrugging her shoulders. 'Go ahead,' she mouthed to him.

With a heavy sigh he picked up the receiver. Greg's voice came through. 'Max, we're waiting to go along and look through the rushes. Come on over.'

Max looked up as Jo rose to her feet, smoothing her sweater and pulling it over her hips. She gestured to him not to let her disturb his call. She bent to pick up her coat from the chair where he had carefully laid it.

'Hang on, Greg,' Max called down the receiver, flinging it on the table. But she was already at the door.

'Stay,' he pleaded.

'I'm tired now,' she said. 'I need to get some rest. I'll meet you tomorrow morning at the east gate of the Petřín Park.'

He put out an arm to restrain her and quickly withdrew it. There had been quite enough manipulation and persuasiveness in the past. He never wanted to treat her that way again. He had done a lot of damage and now he owed her the courtesy of allowing her to act on her own wishes and convictions. At the very least he should give her that.

'Nine o'clock.' She smiled. Her amber eyes held his for a second and then she turned away.

Max picked up the phone again.

'What's going on?' Greg asked.

'God knows.'

'Are you coming over?'

'Yes. Who's there?'

'Cast of thousands. No, seriously, there'll be just me, the AD and Minette.'

'Fine. Listen, there's something I have to tell you right now. I'm not going to be available for filming tomorrow morning. Sorry!'

There was a pause. 'OK. No problem. We'll do some of the shots where you're not needed.'

'I'll be there for the afternoon session. Prompt.'

Max let the phone clatter down onto the table where it fell upside down, emitting a moaning whine. It occurred to him that he had never before pulled out of a prearranged shoot.

CHAPTER 26

Minette sat at the desk in Greg's hotel room. She had pushed his chaotic heap of scripts and notes to one side and replaced them with her own script. She had been working on it for the past two days, armed with a dozen newly sharpened pencils and a very determined expression. 'Oh, bloody hell!' she exclaimed.

'Not again,' said Greg, who was moving restlessly around the room, unable to settle to anything. He was waiting for a call from his assistant director to tell him when the rushes were ready for viewing. It was a tense time, this period of expectation whilst raw film was being processed.

After the take at the cathedral this afternoon he had been elated, convinced the shots had been terrific, something really special. But then you never really knew until you saw the pictures up there on the screen. The roving naked eye and the camera's focused eye could tell very different stories. And on occasions the charge in the atmosphere at the shoot somehow didn't transmit itself onto film.

'Witch!' exclaimed Minette. 'That editor – I'd like to garrotte her with the aid of one of her blasted red pens.'

Greg walked over to the desk. Minette's typescript, having been adored by her agent – whom Minette had described as an elegant, articulate woman with terrifyingly penetrating eyes – and fought over by two publishers, had now been sent back to her. An editor at the publishers who had finally secured the novel had read through the manuscript, marking mistakes and offering suggestions for improvements. The polite accompanying letter had urged her to go through the whole thing very carefully, feeling free to make her own comments.

It was the suggestions for changes that were causing the trouble and frequent swearing. Minette simply couldn't see why a word of her precious story needed altering.

Greg looked over her shoulder. Her immaculately word-processed script was now peppered with little red dashes and omission marks. Question marks bristled in the margins.

'It looks like a bloody third-form essay that you wrote on the bus home with your brain out to lunch,' Minette fumed. 'And I should know.'

'What are you moaning for? These suggestions are perfectly in order,' he said, squinting down at the page.

'I don't mind having my punctuation altered – I know it's a bit wild – but she's got the nerve to change my words. Look – she's crossed out "saintly" and put "virtuous".'

'Yeah. That's because you already used "saintly" in the sentence before. A bit repetitive, huh?'

'Oh. Yes, I see,' she agreed reluctantly. 'But, see – she's crossed out a whole sentence here.'

Greg followed her indignantly jabbing finger. 'Yeah, that's because the sentence before said it all.'

'Huh?'

'It didn't need any more explaining. You got in all you wanted to say first shot.'

'Oh,' she said, crestfallen, realizing he was absolutely right – just like the editor.

'You mustn't get so edgy, babe. No script or novel is perfect when it comes hot off the author's sweaty brow.'

'No?'

'No. Not even from the top-flight people. I've seen some superb scripts that needed a hell of a lot of tidying up around the edges.'

'Hmm.'

'Look – with the money they're putting up front they must think it's pretty terrific. Six-figure advances don't just drop off trees.' He squeezed her shoulders affectionately.

'Yes.' She still sounded doubtful. The intense feeling of elation she had felt when her agent had phoned with the unbelievable offer for her book had slowly evaporated. It simply couldn't be true, they must have made a horrible mistake.

The seeds of doubt, once sown, had rapidly taken root. OK, maybe I did it once, she'd thought, but will I ever be able to do it again?

And then the agent had asked about her ideas for a second novel and she had suddenly found the sizzling store of her imagination as damp and soggy as a wet winter afternoon.

Sensing her uncertainty, Greg tried again. 'Look at it this way – an exotic plant that's a terrific eye-catcher might need one or two of its leaves trimming before you'd want to put it on display.'

'That's a neat way of putting it.' She smiled, beginning to be reassured.

'I could think of better ways if my brain wasn't in a state of exhaustion,' he said, stretching up and groaning. 'God, I'm bushed.' In a fervour of nervous anticipation, he crossed to the phone and called his AD, who confirmed that the rushes were just through. Ready for viewing.

'They're cooked!' he told Minette. 'I'm going to call Max. He mustn't miss these.'

Minette was only half listening, her attention back in her script once more.

'Damn!' Greg exclaimed suddenly, with a violence completely out of character.

Minette jumped with surprise. She looked up. 'What's the trouble?'

'Max.'

'What about Max?'

'He's copping out from the shooting session tomorrow morning, that's all. Hell!'

Minette jumped up and ran across to him, putting her arms around his waist and hugging him with ferocious energy. 'Oh, dear.' She knew that it was terribly important for the film to stay on schedule. The cost hour by hour was horrendous. And Greg had to account for every cent to his producer, who had put up the money. And was apparently no pussycat.

'What's going on?' Greg demanded through gritted teeth. It must be a woman!' Frustration seethed inside him. '*That* woman!'

'What are you talking about? What woman?'

'Jo. Your aunt, big sister – or whatever she is.'

Minette pulled away from him. She had never seen him this furious, and she was beginning to feel pretty cross herself. 'It can't be. Jo's in Sweden,' she said, making a huge attempt to be reasonable. She knew Greg was strung up like a newly tuned piano, with the responsibility for the making of the film resting almost entirely on his shoulders. His first big film, a make-or-break chance.

'You want to bet? I heard her talking in the background before he hung up. I'm sure it was her. You can't mistake those perfect English lady, cut-glass tones. She's here in Prague and she's after him. The bitch,' he added softly, to ease his resentment.

'Don't you *dare* call Jo a bitch,' Minette yelled at him, her eyes flaming. 'And she doesn't have "cut-glass tones". She comes from Yorkshire.'

'Sorry – means nothing to me, sweetheart. All I can see is that if she's a part of the action here and Max is already off-line, she's seriously bad news.'

'She'd never let him mess up his career. Or anyone else's, come to that,' Minette stormed.

'People who are crazy about each other do all kinds of things they normally wouldn't. Christ Almighty, I could do without this.'

He slumped down in a chair and rested his head in his hand. He knew that if the main actor on the set became unreliable it could totally throw everyone else's feelings about the film. Motivation could go out of the window. He'd seen it happen when he'd been an assistant director.

It was the director's job to set the morale for the whole crew and actors, to manufacture some kind of magic chemistry on the set and out on location. But one man could only do so much. You could create a fabulous feeling of team spirit, like a tough, wily games coach with a bunch of bolshie sophomores, but it only needed one of the main players to step out of line and all your careful preparations went down the toilet.

Minette saw the struggles going on inside him. She couldn't be cross with him for more than one minute together. She knelt by his chair and stroked his hands, which were taut with tension.

'I'm not a guy with starry Oscars in my eyes,' he said with a dry smile. 'I just want to bring this movie in on schedule and on budget.'

'You will,' she said. 'You will.' She wondered what on earth was going on with Max and Jo. She would have to find out if Jo really was in Prague, and if so where she was, so that she could go and talk to her.

'Sorry,' Greg said softly. 'I was right out of line back there.'

'Forgiven.'

'I thought we might have gotten into some real hostilities if I hadn't shut up fast,' he murmured ruefully, touching her face with gentle fingers.

'Hostilities! Me – with you? Wow, that sounds like it could be fun.' She pounced on him, nibbling at his lips with her sharp white teeth.

'Lay off!' he protested. 'You're a grown-up now.'

'A writer not a fighter!' she giggled.

'I loathe all kinds of warfare,' he said. 'I had enough of those for a lifetime at home.'

'Ahh, there, there,' she said. 'I'll kiss you better.'

He lifted her into his arms and gave her a long, hard kiss, then very gently pushed her away. 'Just an appetizer, sweetheart. Have to leave the rest until later. I've got to see those rushes.'

'Work is the curse of the lustful classes,' said Minette regretfully, getting up and dusting herself down.

CHAPTER 27

Max walked briskly towards the Petřín Park. It was a fabulous morning. After the dreary, chilling mist of the day before, suddenly the winter sun was brilliant, the sky a mixture of azure and gold, its clear crystal blue more intense than it ever was in the summer.

It was ten minutes before nine, the time Jo had suggested to meet, but he was determined to be early, on no account to risk missing her.

As he approached the entrance to the park he saw her standing beside the ornate iron gates – already there for him. She was wearing her grey coat again, and her head was bare. Her auburn hair fell loose over her shoulders, the rays from the sun shimmering and dancing over the gleaming strands. The whole of her person seemed to glow. The sight of her took his breath away, drove thoughts of anything but her clean out of his mind.

She put out her hand to him as he drew closer. 'Max,' she said, glancing briefly up at him with a wistful smile. She took his hand in hers, moving forward and indicating that they should walk together. She was wearing gloves, and he longed to peel them off so he could touch her skin.

They walked hand in hand along the broad pathways between the horse chestnut trees, whose stark, twiggy branches were traced out in sharp outline against the deep cobalt-blue of the sky.

He felt curiously at ease with her, even though a thousand questions were surging through his mind. She was serene and calm again, as she had been the evening before. It was as though she held some precious secret that had given her a new inner strength, even in the face of this strange encounter she had engineered. Surely one that had been supremely difficult for her?

'This is like getting to know a new friend,' she said reflectively. 'Walking together in the park and finding things out about each other.'

'Is that what you wanted?' he asked, not knowing whether to hope or despair.

'In a way.' She would not look at him, would not turn her head. She looked straight in front of her, swinging his hand in gentle rhythm. 'It was all so sudden for you and me, wasn't it, Max? We met and there was this overwhelming attraction we both felt. And then we were lovers. All in a few hours.'

He sighed. 'You mean we got it the wrong way round?'

She shook her head. 'Oh, no, that isn't what I mean at all. At that moment in my life you gave me exactly what I needed – a sense of being physically wanted and adored. It was probably the best thing that could have happened to me just at that time. I still felt tarnished from the accident – or maybe mutilated would be a better word. And I felt an even deeper inadequacy from losing my baby.'

He exerted firm pressure on her hand in sympathy.

'Losing a baby makes you feel like that. As though your body is somehow faulty, that as a woman you're a failure. And Alexander had already done a rather good destruction job on my self-confidence long before the baby went.'

'I think I'm lucky that you didn't kill me after what I made you go through on top of all that,' he said, his voice low with distress. 'When I realized just what I'd done to you I felt as though my heart had been cut out and there was nothing but a bleeding stump left.' He paused, cursing himself for overplaying things. 'You'll have to forgive me for the dramatics!'

She gave a small laugh. 'Maybe a drama is the way to think about it. Those days in Prague and the few hours in Paris seem curiously unreal when I remember them now – as though we were on a stage.'

'Oh, God, Jo. That's a turn-of-the-knife speech to deliver to an actor.'

'I didn't mean it like that at all. I'm just saying that for me those few days with you were magical. Like a wonderful fantasy.'

'I don't think I can bear this,' he said, keeping his voice steady by sheer will and the skill of his profession. 'You're telling me that what we took part in was no more than a wonderful fable. You're tying off loose ends, making your peace with me before you go away again to live your own life.'

She stopped, and at last turned to face him. 'No. It's not like that at all. I didn't come to do that.'

He waited.

'I came to make peace with the man I love,' she said.

His throat clogged so that he couldn't speak.

'It's been more than four months since our affair. And you see, Max, in those months I've thought about you nearly all the time. I've gone over and over all we said and did, and now I feel I truly *do* know you,' she said simply. 'And I want to make that feeling a reality.'

He could no longer keep apart from her. He needed to hold her. Placing his arm around her waist, he guided her to a wooden bench-seat where they sat down together, their bodies touching.

'That first night when I made love to you,' he said, 'that wonderful, terrible night. I knew that what I was doing was wrong, that in time it was inevitable you would have to suffer the most cruel wounding. But I couldn't stop myself. I wanted you so very much. Your body, your mind – all of you. And then, when I was such a coward, not courageous enough to face my mistakes and come clean with you, I thought of how you would hate and despise me.

'And I was right, wasn't I?' he finished, bowing his head. 'In fact your anger was more terrible than I could ever have dreamed. It was a pure, clean anger that I couldn't fight against. That's why I haven't dared try get near you again.'

'Yes. Yes, I know. I understand that now.' She sighed. 'Do you still see Alexander?'

'Good God! *No*!'

'He's landed a plum job in TV – did you know that?'

'I'd heard rumours. I can't stomach listening to anything about the man.'

'It's odd, but I can look at him quite dispassionately – neither slavishly admiring him nor wanting to tear him apart for what he did to me.'

'Then you're a saint.'

'No. I've just learned to see things for what they are. He was false – through and through. You were mistaken, but in your heart you were true.' She turned her face up to his, 'Alexander has hurt us both,' she murmured.

'Yes.' He looked down into her sad eyes, aching with regret.

'But he did do one good thing. Something wonderful, in fact. He brought us together,' she said slowly.

Finally abandoning his restraint, Max put his hands around her face and pressed his lips on hers. To his delight, her lips parted with a sigh, welcoming him. The firm, sweet warmth of her mouth made his abandoned heart sing out with joy and new life.

She took off her glove and placed her hand inside his coat, laying it tenderly on his chest. 'I've come to understand a lot of things in these last few months,' she told him. 'It's not possible to say them all at once. You made a bad error of judgement and I got hurt. And in turn I hit back and inflicted pain on you. But gradually I found that I was able to look into my heart and have the courage to recognize what was there. And it was love for you, Max.' Tears had gathered on her eyelashes and now they spilled over.

Max moved his lips over her cheeks, collecting the salty moistness, brushing her skin with a depth of love and tenderness that made her cry out.

His hands moved inside her coat; he needed to touch her body, trace its curves and hollows. Her breasts were even rounder and more voluptuous than he remembered, her waist curved and slender. As his hands moved over her belly they slowed and stilled. He felt suddenly hot and feverish, stabbed with a jolt of new knowledge which was both astounding and yet the most obvious thing in the world.

He drew back from her. She looked at him, her lovely amber eyes wide, her lips still slightly open.

'Why didn't you tell me?' he asked.

She smiled. Her eyes were filled with love. There was no trace of concern in them, no grit of anxiety to mar her serenity.

'You once told me that what had happened between us seemed to have killed something inside you,' he said slowly. 'I remembered that. Over and over, although God knows I wished I could have forgotten it.'

'Well, now there is something very much alive in me,' she said tenderly. 'Something you and I created together.'

He stared at her, shaking his head in disbelief.

'But why didn't you tell me? Did you think I'd react like Alexander? Surely not, Jo?'

'I didn't want you to feel under any obligation to me. That was all, Max. That was the only reason – quite simple.'

'You know I wouldn't have responded like that. Dear God – look at me, Jo. I'm crazy with delight. I'm over the moon!'

'Of course you are,' she smiled. 'I realize that now. But, as I've tried to explain, I've been rather slow in getting to know you. It's more difficult when the person's not there.'

'Well, I'm damn well going to be there from now on.'

'Good.' She smiled at him with that curious mischievous light in her eyes that was all the more startling because it was not something she often showed.

He looked at her with concern. 'Have you been well, Jo? Has everything been all right?'

'Yes. I've been fine. Of course I was simply terrified at first. I felt so alone – ' Her voice broke.

He held her very firmly in his arms. If only she had come to him sooner.

'I want this baby so much, Max. I want to feel your child growing inside me. And I want you and me to be together to love him or her when the time comes.'

They sat quietly for a while, hugging each other and kissing again. But although the sun was shining it was desperately cold, and they eventually felt the need to get up and go on walking.

'I would have come to you anyway,' Jo told him. 'Maybe a little later if it hadn't been for the baby.'

'I would have come to get you, darling. Baby or no baby. I'd decided to give you six months' grace, and that would be it.'

She laughed. 'Shouldn't you be working this morning?' she asked.

'Yes. But it's OK. I squared things with the team. There's no need for you to worry.'

'No, it's not OK. Your work is important, Max. You must go back now.'

'No. I'm not needed until one-thirty. Right now being with you, us being together, is more important.'

'We can meet up again this evening,' she said. And he could see that now the difficult task she had set herself was completed her old anxiety on behalf of others had returned. Once again she was the unselfish Jo, who worried about loyalty and commitment and other people.

'Are you trying to push me away when I've only just got you back?' he enquired mockingly.

'No, no. But I hate the idea of taking you away from your work. Last night – when I suggested this meeting – I hadn't thought things through . . .'

'It's all right. Everything's all right,' he soothed her. When he thought of all he would do to care for her during her pregnancy a glow of warmth stole through him.

'Is your new collection coming on well?' he asked her.

'Yes.' She fingered the grey fabric of her sleeve. 'This coat's a prototype. We've got a black one and a red one in production too.'

'It's beautiful. And what about that sweater you were wearing last night? Is that in the collection?'

'No – that's just a one-off I made myself. I started it after we'd split up. It was one of the things that kept me sane. My therapy sweater, I call it.'

They walked on, laughing together. Talking with ease, yet with that special care that people use when they've been apart from each other.

And then, without warning, she stopped dead, her hands pressed around her stomach. A sharp hiss of alarm escaped from her lips like steam escaping from a blocked valve.

Sweat prickled under Max's armpits. 'What is it?'

She stood quite still, her posture stooped and defensive. 'Ah!' she gasped, her eyelids clenching together. 'Oh, God! Jo!'

'I'll be fine in a moment.' She tried to straighten herself, but instantly she doubled up again, this time giving a little groan.

367

'It's the baby, isn't it?' he said, realizing. 'Is this what happened before?'

She nodded. Her lips were white. She looked up at him, her eyes staring blankly, full of bewilderment and fear.

'Darling, it's all right – it's all right,' he told her calmly, whilst panic leapt inside.

The whole of her face was white now, a thick, grotesque white that scared the hell out of him.

'Don't worry, I'll get you to a doctor.' Hell, but *how?* he thought. He noticed that they were almost on a level with one of the park's entry points.

Shepherding Jo to a nearby seat, he settled her down and said firmly, 'Don't try to move. I'm going to get help.'

He sprinted out into the road and waved violently at the passing traffic. Having no instant luck, he forced the issue by running out into the road in front of an approaching car. The woman driving was startled rather than outraged. She wound down the window and looked at him with a worried frown.

'*Nemocnice. Doktora!*' shouted Max, desperately re-calling some of the Czech words he had learnt just in case. He performed a mime of a person in pain needing help with such conviction that she understood imme-diately.

'*Blízko*. Just near here!' He gestured to the park. The woman registered a brief moment of doubt and then jumped out of the car, following him as he flew back into the park.

Jo was already on her feet. 'I can walk – I can walk,' she called out insistently, stumbling towards Max, clutching at her stomach as though to cradle the baby in her hands and stop it escaping from her. She looked at the woman behind him and then beyond, to the car abandoned in the road, its engine still running.

'Oh, thank you, thank you,' she gasped to the woman, clambering into the back seat of the car and sinking down, breathing heavily. Max sat beside her, white-lipped himself, not being able to believe this was happening.

The woman sprang back into the driving seat, now fully committed to playing a part in this unexpected drama.

'*Nemocnice!*' she declared, revving up the engine and letting out the clutch. 'Oss-pee-tarl.'

'No, not the hospital,' Jo exclaimed. 'I know a doctor here in Prague. I want to see him.' She looked at Max, appealing, pleading.

Oh, hell, more delay, he thought. 'All right, darling. Do you know where he'll be?'

'Dr Zanek,' she said. 'Off Wenceslas Square.'

'Ah! Doktora Zanek.' The woman raised her hand and jabbed her thumb in the air to register recognition. She accelerated with purpose, driving like the wind, swerving out and overtaking slow-moving vehicles.

Jo sat hunched, her arms clasped over her belly, her body rocking to and fro. *Come on, come on*! thought Max, willing the agonizing minutes to pass.

Caught in the crawl of traffic clogging the city centre, the woman slowed to a stop and gestured a little way down the street. '*Tam!*' she said. Cars behind her hooted impatiently.

'Here!' said Jo. Max found himself almost pulling Jo from the car whilst at the same time giving fervent thanks to the driver who had so valiantly helped them.

Still clasping her stomach, Jo directed him to the building which housed Dr Zanek's consulting rooms. He looked at the plates beside the door, written in Czech with English underneath. Sweat broke out on his forehead. The man was a cosmetic surgeon, for goodness' sake! Surely she needed an obstetrician? Well, he supposed any medically trained person would be better than nothing.

The cage lift ground its way upwards, seemingly taking for ever. Jo stood calmly, brave and quiet. But her eyes were wild with fear, like those of an animal in pain who had no comprehension of what was happening to it.

He pushed open the door of the reception office. The woman behind the desk looked up in surprise. 'I'm sorry,' he said. 'We need help. I don't speak much – '

'It is all right. We all speak English here.' She looked at Jo and then smiled. 'Miss Shand, I think?'

'Yes. Could Dr Zanek see me? Please, it's an emergency.'

Max held himself still. He imagined the likelihood of a consultant being available at the drop of a hat. He'd have a full diary of consultations; he'd be operating somewhere – or at a conference, in a meeting. Probably not even in the country at all.

'You are lucky,' the receptionist told them. 'He's had a cancellation.' She made a call through to his office, speaking rapidly.

The door from Dr Zanek's consulting room opened. His eyes travelled swiftly over Jo. 'Come in,' he said, beckoning to her. She stepped forward, leaving the

370

protection of Max's arm. As she moved into Anton Zanek's room and the door closed behind them Max had a feeling of bleak isolation and helplessness.

'Please sit down,' the receptionist said kindly. She went away and came back with coffee for both of them. She settled back to her work and said nothing else.

Max sat numb and miserable. A distant memory stabbed him: Jo screaming hate at him for the way he and Alexander had discussed her previous pregnancy.

Oh, Alexander had been so cunning, so clever and manipulative. Max could hear his compellingly authoritative voice speaking very softly, low and caressing as he'd spoken Jo's name. 'God knows, Jo's had a rough time, Max. There's no one in the world understands that better than me – or understands *her* better, for that matter.'

Alexander had turned to stare out of the window, his face deeply concerned and reflective. 'But a pregnant woman can do all kinds of strange things that are completely out of character. It's connected with hormones, I believe. Not their fault – nothing they can help themselves.'

And so on. Sweet hypnotic lies. Utterly convincing.

Max wanted to shake those elegant and treacherous pronouncements from his ears for ever. Poor, darling Jo. He had to make things go right for her this time. He stared at Dr Zanek's door, willing a miracle to take place behind it.

After minutes of torture, Anton Zanek emerged from his room. 'Please, Mr Swift, will you join us?'

Jo was sitting in a chair in front of Dr Zanek's extensive desk.

371

She looked up at Max, her smile uncertain. He could tell that she hardly dared move a muscle, that she was still holding herself rigid, willing the baby to stay attached to her.

'Well?' Max asked Dr Zanek, tense and tight.

Dr Zanek smiled reassuringly. 'I have examined Jo and I can tell you that there are no clinical signs of the onset of abortion. Her blood pressure is normal, there is no blood loss. The cervix does not seem to be dilated, although I didn't wish to probe too much, for obvious reasons. One should always leave well alone.'

Max listened. He was not reassured. 'Is there anything more that can be done?' he asked, pushing his hand through his hair with that impatient gesture Jo knew so well. She put out her hand to him and he felt a firm squeeze on his arm.

Dr Zanek shook his head.

'Shouldn't she be in hospital, under supervision?'

'I don't think so. As I said, there are no clinical signs – only symptoms. And Jo has told me she would feel very unhappy in hospital.'

Max stared at her. 'Is that true?'

'Yes.' She nodded.

'She tells me she wants to be with you,' Dr Zanek said simply, with a smile.

'You mentioned signs and symptoms,' Max said to Dr Zanek crisply. 'I take it a sign is something you can actually see or measure – like blood pressure or loss of blood – yes?'

'Yes, that is correct.'

'Whilst a symptom is something a person feels, like stomach cramp or chest pain?'

372

'Yes.'

Jo gave a sudden smile. 'Max is probably quite an expert, Anton. He's being playing the part of a doctor in a TV series for the past few years.'

'Ah, now I understand,' said Dr Zanek. 'So then I hardly need to explain more. You see, my friends,' he went on, 'I think that Jo's stomach cramps are probably no more than reflections of her anxiety about losing this baby. This can happen when a patient has had a previous bad experience or is ill – or under stress for some reason.'

This is all my fault, Max groaned internally. I've put her under worse stress than anyone could imagine and now she's desperately vulnerable.

Anton Zanek was speaking again. 'My theory is that the distress Jo is experiencing manifests itself as physical symptoms which mimic the actual experience she had when she lost the baby from her first pregnancy. You see, on that occasion she had actual signs of abortion – bleeding, severe pain, a dilated cervix. But today, as I have said, there are no clinical signs that give us cause for immediate alarm.'

'Mind over matter,' said Jo with a smile of irony. 'I feel better already.'

'OK, there's no instant danger,' Max responded with great reluctance. 'So what should we do now?'

'I suggest you take Jo for a cup of hot tea with two spoons of sugar and treat her to a beautiful cake or pastry. Some good simple sugar is what she needs: sugar increases serotonin levels in the central nervous system and serotonin is the good mood chemical; it dampens down anxiety.'

Jo laughed. 'A cup of sweet tea and a sticky bun! You make it all sound so easy.'

'Sometimes it's best to think of things that way. The Hotel Europa is just around the corner. Very Czech – very highly recommended.'

Max leaned forward urgently. 'You're smiling, Dr Zanek. But for me this is deadly serious. Please – tell us honestly – is it safe for Jo to be up and about?'

'Max, I don't want to be kept in a glass case,' Jo said firmly. 'Not even by you. Dr Zanek has already told you what I want to do. Be with you.'

'I'll cancel the shoot,' Max said.

'No. I'll go with you.' Her eyes were hard with determination, and he realized that there would be nothing to gain by overruling her – even if she would allow that.

'Jocasta will be more relaxed doing what she wants than lying in a hospital or a hotel bed supposedly resting but in fact fretting. That would probably only cause further trouble,' Dr Zanek commented, looking up from his desk where he was rapidly making notes on a small pad. He wrote his signature at the bottom of the sheet and drew a swift line underneath it.

'Now,' he continued, 'if you need a doctor, or to go to the hospital, give them this note.'

'What does it say?' Jo enquired, frowning at the alien words.

'I hope you need never find out,' Zanek said drily.

Max tackled Jo in the lift, his eyes harsh and stern. 'So what did he whisper in the wings before I was invited to the stage performance?'

She smiled at him tenderly. 'There were no secrets. I promise. And I'm going to be all right. Somehow I just know that.'

She felt the waves of pent-up feeling emanating from him, the electricity of hope and fear crackling in the air around him. And suddenly she felt strong again. Sure and confident. 'He said I had around an eighty-five per cent chance of keeping the baby. And that's not far short of the average for any healthy woman.'

'You simply have to be given the licence to do what you want, is that it?' he suggested drily.

'Yes. Who could resist a remedy like that?' She moved closer to him. 'You can touch me, Max. I'm not a porcelain figure in someone's display cabinet.'

He stared longingly at her, then bent to kiss her, his lips hard on hers, his tongue invading her sweet mouth.

'Ah, that's good medicine,' she said. 'The best. And when you've given me my sweet tea you're to go to work. Those are *my* orders.'

'Sweet heaven! Work! How will I manage that after all this? I'm a man who's been through all the dominions of hell in one hour. A broken reed.' Slowly his habitual lazy irony was coming back to him.

She reached for his hand as they left the lift. 'Anything's possible with the one you love at your side,' she said teasingly. But he knew she was serious.

CHAPTER 28

Greg looked at his watch. Twelve-thirty.

The film crew were setting up an exterior shot in a narrow Prague street. The street had been blocked off for the afternoon and the technical crew had moved in and were now completing the assembly of their equipment. The lighting crew, amidst a jungle of serpent-like cables, were calling out numbers to each other as they adjusted their lights.

Looking at all their complicated gleaming paraphernalia, Minette had the feeling that some major surgical operation was about to take place.

She had taken the day off from her typescript in order to be on the set with Greg. She had the feeling he might need some good loving support. 'A girl has to stand by her man,' she had told him with a wry grin, wrapping herself in one of his sweaters – which had the advantage of being long enough to keep her knees warm.

She knew that he hated to be followed around and so she'd kept a low profile, doing a little exploring around the make-up and wardrobe trailers, chatting to the girls and fingering the wigs and cloaks. A double-decker bus was parked at the end of the road. Inside it had been fitted up as a kind of mobile kitchen and café, where crew could get hot drinks and snacks. She had coffee and a toasted sandwich and when she went back outside again her breath curled up into the freezing air like smoke.

She saw Greg pacing up and down the street, his teeth gritted, desperately waiting for Max to materialize.

'Where the bloody hell is he?' he hissed to Minette as she approached him with a degree of caution.

'It's only one o'clock. Half an hour to go yet,' she said cheerily. Greg was the sort of man who only appreciated the soft "there, there" approach when it was being done tongue in cheek.

'He'll need at least forty-five minutes in make-up, minimum.'

'There'll still be plenty of time. Won't there?'

He gave an exasperated sigh. 'Maybe. It's not an easy scene for him. He's got a long soliloquy at the end. If he fluffs any of it we'll have to go over it God knows how many times.'

'He'll probably do it first take,' said Minette, who was rapidly learning all the film jargon.

'Yeah. Well, normally I'd believe that. But if he's not fully together and he's all screwed up . . .'

'He won't be,' said Minette, silently praying. 'And he'll know his lines from back to front. Is this the scene where Wenceslas goes to visit the poor and is stalked by his evil-intentioned brother?'

'Yeah. There's not much for the brother to do, thank God. Just skulk around a bit. It's really all down to Max.'

'Where does this scene fit in the film?'

'A couple of scenes before the murder scene we shot yesterday.'

'You shoot these films in such a broken-up kind of way it's hard to piece the whole story together,' Minette said thoughtfully, slipping her hand into his. 'It's like one of those drawings in kids' comics, where they show you parts of an object photographed in close-up and then invite you to guess what the whole object is.'

He smiled. 'That's a neat analogy.'

'I'm getting good at analogies. I'm practising,' she said.

'For the next book?'

'Fingers crossed.'

'You've got an idea?'

'Yes.' Her eyes shone with wicked anticipation at the thought of starting a new story.

He looked down at her. 'D'you know something? You're so lovable I could eat you. You're so funny and clever and sexy that I don't think I've a hope in hell of being able to live without you. Ever!'

'If you go on making impressive speeches like that, I don't think you'll have to!' She leapt up and smacked a huge, passionate kiss on his lips. 'Ahh!' they both murmured.

As she came back to earth again, from the corner of her eye she saw a tall figure levering himself out of a taxi at the end of the road.

'Your bacon is saved,' she told Greg gravely, with a huge sigh of relief. 'Look who's here.'

'Thank Christ,' he murmured. He followed her glance. 'Hey! Looks like our star man's brought important company with him.'

Minette stared as she saw Jo, fragile and beautiful in grey wool and black high heels, linked closely with Max, staring up at him adoringly.

'See!' Greg told her.

'You were right!'

'I often am. Now, peel her away from him, Minette baby, take a firm grip on her and don't let her out of your clutches and back into his until I've got this scene in the can. OK?'

'OK.'

'You've written a book!' Jo exclaimed, insisting on knowing everything about what Minette had been doing before she would say a word about herself.

'Yes. Amazing, isn't it?'

Jo shook her head in astonishment. 'It's simply wonderful. What did Miles say?' she asked curiously.

'Very little – but all of it highly complimentary. I was absolutely gobsmacked. And he was wonderful about pulling strings to get me a super agent. She scares the hell out of me. He probably arranged that too.'

Jo smiled, well able to imagine the scenario. 'But, tell me, isn't it unusual for people of your age to write a novel?' she asked in her thoughtful, balanced way.

'Yes. Aren't you proud of me?' Minette responded with a faintly challenging grin. It amused her to reflect that Jo's carefully phrased question was just the kind of thing to convince Greg that she *was* an uptight English lady, hopelessly genteel and reserved. She looked forward to watching him getting to know her a bit better – and changing his mind.

Jo smiled. 'In actual fact, I'm so proud I feel like shedding a few aunt-like tears.'

'Tears! That's not like you, Jo.'

'No, but I seem to be doing it quite a lot these days.'

'So do I,' Minette admitted.

They smiled at each other.

'Must be love,' Minette said, eyeing Jo with raised eyebrows. 'Come on, Jo. Spill some beans.'

'I'm not sure if I trust you.' Jo smiled. 'I might find my shocking revelations on the printed page, my dark secrets being read by millions.'

'Aha! People's dark secrets are all grist to my writer's mill!' She recalled Greg's use of that same phrase with regard to his own work and smiled to herself, foxy and roguish.

'Are some of my past secrets already there?' Jo wondered, her eyes narrowing.

'Spilled has-beens,' Minette chuckled. 'You'll have to wait and see.'

'Oh, dear,' Jo grimaced.

'It's all right,' Minette assured her airily. 'I'm not one of those kiss-and-tell authors. Any living characters appearing on my pages come in heavy disguise.' She leaned towards Jo and lowered her voice 'Now! I'm not going wait another minute. You and Max. Tell!'

Jo's face softened. She looked out of the window of the bus, where they were drinking their hot chocolate. 'I don't want to miss seeing him do this scene,' she said anxiously.

'It's OK. Make-up'll have him for another half-hour yet. Come on, Jo. I want to know all the juicy details. You're back with Max – that's obvious. And I can see from your face that it's heaven on earth for you. So when I can plan on being a bridesmaid?'

Jo opened her coat and smoothed her sweater over her stomach. She turned her head slowly and looked Minette directly in the eye. 'I don't suppose it's showing much yet,' she murmured, her face dreamy with love.

Minette was thunderstruck. 'Wow,' she said in awe. 'Oh, Jo, that's wonderful. I'm so pleased for you. So where was that little seed sown? Prague or Paris?'

'Hard to say.' Jo smiled. 'It could even have been Gothenburg.'

'What? You got it together with Max in three different countries in almost as many days?'

'Mmm.' Jo's lips twitched.

'Is there anything else totally astonishing I should know about my formerly staid old aunt?' Minette shook her head in disbelief.

'Isn't that enough for one day?'

'You know,' said Minette, taking Jo's hand and tickling her palm as she'd used to do when she was a little girl, 'underneath all that perfect-English-lady façade, you're a truly wicked woman.'

'He was brilliant, absolutely fantastic,' Greg enthused much later, when he and Minette arrived back at their hotel after a late dinner with Jo and Max. Before that they had all been to see the day's rushes. Jo and Minette had sat in silent admiration whilst a tense Greg and a calm Max frowned critically at the film, chewing the fat over whether this or that aspect of it was OK.

But all four of them, supported by the assistant director, had finally agreed that the day's filming had been a huge success.

'Yes, Max was brilliant,' Minette agreed. 'And so were you. After all, you were the one who set the whole thing up – and that little speech you made to set the scene before the cameras started rolling was simply terrific. Inspirational.'

'That was a very nice little speech of your own. I'm not used to such flattery. Have you been at the wine bottle? Are you tight?' he asked, making a grab for her.

'In what sense?' she enquired demurely, an all too willing captive. 'Drunk as a skunk, or so nice and snug in a certain place that you're going to have a really great time in just a few minutes?'

'You're not tight,' he decided, unfastening her shirt and dipping his head down to her breasts, taking a pink nipple between his teeth. 'Not as in drunk as a skunk, at any rate. I do so love a woman who likes to make love when she still has all her wits about her.'

Jo hung up her coat in the wardrobe in Max's hotel room. Just seeing it hanging there next to his shirts and jackets made her faint with longing for him.

She knew that he was still afraid for her and for the baby. When he touched her it was as though he were touching a precious work of art that might shatter at the merest hint of pressure.

She looked across at him. He was sitting at the desk in deep concentration, the film script open in front of him, studying his lines for the next day.

He looked up. 'You need to rest, darling. You should be in bed,' he said, his eyes dark with tenderness.

So I should, thought Jo. But not lying there like a nun in a coffin.

She went into the bathroom, slipped out of her clothes and soaked in a warm bath. After rubbing herself dry with a huge white towel, she arranged it around herself, tucking in one end lightly just above her breasts.

She went to stand beside Max's chair. She smoothed the hair from his forehead, her touch soft as silk. Taking a step forward, she pressed the length of her body against him, letting him feel the fullness of her breasts against his arms, the slight swell of her belly against his chest. A small twitch from her free hand loosened the towel and it slithered over her breasts and buttocks to land in a white mound by her feet.

Max made a small sound in his throat. He turned to her and she pushed his head down to rest against her breasts. 'I won't break,' she whispered.

He rose slowly and put his arms tightly around her. Their kiss seemed to go on for ever. Jo felt him loosen up and relax – and at the same time grow more tense, his mouth seeming to want to swallow hers, his hands grasping at her hair, fingers digging in to her scalp.

'I think maybe now it's time to go to bed,' she told him, breaking from him with difficulty, her breathing heavy, her hands stroking the nape of his neck, whilst her glance flickered longingly from his mouth to his eyes and then back again.

'Are you sure?' His eyes were dark with desire and tender anxiety.

'No doubt whatsover.' She took his hand. 'Come on.'

They lay together in the impersonal hotel bed and made love in the delicious way that came from being apart for so long and then understanding that they had not forgotten a thing about each other. And that there was still so much more to discover.

He was exquisitely gentle, entering her as though she were a temple. 'Let go, darling, let yourself go,' she whispered.

But he had an overpowering instinct to be tender, protecting this woman he so adored and the child growing inside her. *His* child. And so this time they made love with luxurious leisure, their passion quiet and restrained, yet no less ecstatic.

Afterwards, when they were exhausted and drained, they lay together cuddling and smiling, licking and nibbling at each other. 'I never thought this was going to happen again,' Max said huskily.

'But it has,' she responded, sliding a hand around the back of his head and kissing his lips. 'Just as it will again. And again and again . . .'

EPILOGUE

A year later Max and Jo, Greg and Minette were all four together again, for the London première of *Jewel of Bohemia*.

The previews had attracted a good deal of attention. This was Maxwell Swift's first big screen role, his first chance to show that he could really act outside the confines of TV soap. And Greg Shields, the young director making his debut, had surely taken a lot on himself, tackling a film of this scope. Some of the more hawkish critics would be only too pleased to report that the two of them had bitten off more than they could chew.

Greg was wound up like a coiled spring. When he had put on his black evening suit Minette had thought he looked so gorgeous she had wanted to tear it off him instantly and drag him to bed. He had flatly refused to wear a tie, declaring that a white silk polo-neck was good enough for anyone. And if British royalty were around, they'd just have to put up with it.

Max, in contrast, was totally relaxed, his bow-tie perfectly knotted, his fair hair gleaming like a lion's mane under the brilliant lights in the cinema foyer.

Jo, in a swathed gown of emerald silk, tried to keep herself out of the limelight, but Max brought her forward, refusing to let go of her.

Jo was gradually becoming used to living in the limelight which shone on the new wife of a screen idol. She had stopped jumping out of her skin when flashbulbs suddenly popped around her. She was no longer fazed when journalists telephoned to ask her opinion on what the well-dressed woman should wear underneath or seek her comments on the difficulties of juggling a demanding career and a new baby.

Max said she was the best PR agent he'd ever had. And she never sent him any bills.

Lars Sandstrom and Gustav Jansen were pleased with her also. Her 'Pure and Simple' collection which had been launched the previous autumn had been a great success. They had expected a good response, but nothing like the runaway sell-out situation which had developed once it became known that the elegant wool, silk and mohair clothes had been designed by Mrs Maxwell Swift.

'Oh, look!' said Minette, vivid in a red-sequinned tuxedo and jumping frantically up and down to see better. 'There's Princess Di. And who's that with her?'

'There's no one with her,' said Jo evenly, 'just security men.'

'She has to store up everything she spots,' Greg explained, 'just in case her mill runs short of grist.'

'I see your book is still on the bestseller lists, Minette,' Jo commented. 'How many weeks is that?'

'Can't remember,' said Minette. 'So that must be good.'

She waved violently, seeing her parents passing through the entry doors. 'Mummy! Daddy! Over here!'

There were hugs and kisses all round.

'Jake's fast asleep. He'll be fine,' Ginny reassured Max and Jo. 'The babysitter was cooing all over him. He's such a darling good baby. I've only ever heard him cry once.'

'Mmm, a most well-mannered child,' commented Miles in that enigmatic way of his which always left some doubt as to whether he was serious or mocking.

'Must take after his mama – perfect English gent,' Greg whispered to Minette, who gave him a warning dig in his ribs.

'I've read some very provocative reviews about this film, Greg,' Miles said thoughtfully. 'It's been suggested that your direction has a startlingly fresh and innovative quality.'

'That could lend itself to some interesting interpretations,' said Greg wryly. He warmed more to Minette's father every time he met him. A really genuine guy, even if he was stiff around the upper lip.

'It must be a very difficult task directing a film,' Miles continued reflectively.

'Don't you believe it,' Greg grinned. 'It's a simple question of endurance. Orson Welles once said that anybody could be a film director as long as they could stay awake.'

'Not true,' countered Max. 'And Greg's the last one to believe it.'

They took their seats in the auditorium. Minette saw the beads of sweat standing out like raindrops on Greg's forehead as the lights went down. She squeezed his hand.

'Marry me,' he said, leaning over. 'If this film is one half OK, I'm going to take your daddy on one side and ask him very properly for your hand.'

'You've already got it,' she said, linking her fingers around his.

'Oh, dear,' said Jo, clinging to Max's arm, her nerves tense on his behalf. 'You must be so full of apprehension, darling.'

'Not at all,' he said. 'I have a feeling this film's going to be a huge success. But if it isn't – so what? It's just a fantasy, a fable. And now I've got you, darling, and little Jake. Wonderful, perfect reality.'

'But . . .'

'Shut up,' he said tenderly, laying his fingers over her lips.

The credits rolled.

The audience, silent and transfixed after two hours lost in the fantasy world of celluloid, suddenly sprang to their feet, openly cheering.

'Sweet heaven; looks like I'm going to have to tackle your daddy,' murmured Greg to Minette.

Max stood up, acknowledging the congratulations which were falling around them like tossed flowers.

Jo slid her arm around him, her heart bursting with pride. 'A perfect fable and a perfect reality,' she said softly, for his ear only.

THE EXCITING NEW NAME
IN WOMEN'S FICTION!

PLEASE HELP ME TO HELP YOU!

Dear *Scarlet* Reader,

As Editor of *Scarlet* Books I want to make sure that the books I offer you every month are up to the high standards *Scarlet* readers expect. And to do that I need to know a little more about you and your reading likes and dislikes. So please spare a few minutes to fill in the short questionnaire on the following pages and send it to me.

Looking forward to hearing from you,

Sally Cooper

Editor-in-Chief, *Scarlet*

Note: further offers which might be of interest may be sent to you by other, carefully selected, companies. If you do not want to receive them, please write to Robinson Publishing Ltd, 7 Kensington Church Court, London W8 4SP, UK.

QUESTIONNAIRE

Please tick the appropriate boxes to indicate your answers

1 Where did you get this Scarlet title?
Bought in supermarket ☐
Bought at my local bookstore ☐ Bought at chain bookstore ☐
Bought at book exchange or used bookstore ☐
Borrowed from a friend ☐
Other (please indicate) _____

2 Did you enjoy reading it?
A lot ☐   A little ☐   Not at all ☐

3 What did you particularly like about this book?
Believable characters ☐   Easy to read ☐
Good value for money ☐   Enjoyable locations ☐
Interesting story ☐   Modern setting ☐
Other _____

4 What did you particularly dislike about this book?
_____

5 Would you buy another Scarlet book?
Yes ☐   No ☐

6 What other kinds of book do you enjoy reading?
Horror ☐   Puzzle books ☐   Historical fiction ☐
General fiction ☐   Crime/Detective ☐   Cookery ☐
Other (please indicate) _____

7 Which magazines do you enjoy reading?
1. _____
2. _____
3. _____

And now a little about you –
8 How old are you?
Under 25 ☐   25–34 ☐   35–44 ☐
45–54 ☐   55–64 ☐   over 65 ☐

cont.

9 What is your marital status?
Single ☐   Married/living with partner ☐
Widowed ☐   Separated/divorced ☐

10 What is your current occupation?
Employed full-time ☐   Employed part-time ☐
Student ☐   Housewife full-time ☐
Unemployed ☐   Retired ☐

11 Do you have children? If so, how many and how old are they?
_____
_____

12 What is your annual household income?

under $15,000	☐	or	£10,000	☐
$15–25,000	☐	or	£10–20,000	☐
$25–35,000	☐	or	£20–30,000	☐
$35–50,000	☐	or	£30–40,000	☐
over $50,000	☐	or	£40,000	☐

Miss/Mrs/Ms _____
Address _____
_____
_____

Thank you for completing this questionnaire. Now tear it out – put
it in an envelope and send it, before 31 January 1998, to:

Sally Cooper, Editor-in-Chief

USA/Can. address	*UK address/No stamp required*
SCARLET c/o London Bridge	SCARLET
85 River Rock Drive	FREEPOST LON 3335
Suite 202	LONDON W8 4BR
Buffalo	*Please use block capitals for*
NY 14207	*address*
USA	

BETRA/7/97

Scarlet titles coming next month:

THE MARRIAGE CONTRACT Alexandra Jones

Olivia's decided: she's not a person any more . . . she's a wife! She's a partner who's suddenly *not* a full partner because of a contract and a wedding ring. Well it's time her husband, Stuart, wised up, for Olivia's determined to be his equal . . . in *every* way from now on!

SECRET SINS Tina Leonard

When they were children, Kiran and Steve were best friends, but they drifted apart as they grew up. Now they meet again and Kiran realizes how much she's missed Steve . . . and how much she loves him. But before they can look to the future, she and Steve must unravel a mystery from the past . . .

A GAMBLING MAN Jean Saunders

Judy Hale has secured the job of a lifetime . . . working in glamorous Las Vegas! Trouble is, Judy disapproves of gambling *and* of Blake Adams, her new boss. Then Judy has to turn to Blake for help, and finds herself gambling on marriage!

THE ERRANT BRIDE Stacy Brown

What can be worse than being stranded on a dark road in the dead of night? Karina believes it's being rescued by a mysterious stranger, whom she ends up sharing a bed with! But better *or* worse is to come, when Karina finds herself married to Alex, her dark stranger.